'48

Books by James Herbert

JAMES HERBERT

'48

HarperPrism
A Division of HarperCollins Publisher

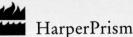

HarperPrism

A Division of HarperCollins*Publishers*
10 East 53rd Street, New York, N.Y. 10022-5299

A hardcover edition of this book was published in 1996 by HarperCollins*Publishers* in Great Britain.

ISBN: 0-06-105293-0

HarperCollins®, ®, and HarperPrism® are trademarks of HarperCollins*Publishers* Inc.

HarperPrism books may be purchased for educational, business, or sales promotional use. For information, please write: Special Markets Department, HarperCollins*Publishers,*
10 East 53rd Street, New York, N.Y. 10022-5299.

Printed in the United States of America

First HarperPrism printing: July 1997

Designed by Colleen Davie

Library of Congress Cataloging-in-Publication Data

Herbert, James, 1943-
   '48 / James Herbert.
     p.   cm.
   ISBN 0-06-105293-0 (hardcover)
   I. Title.
PR6058.E62A613   1997
823'.914—dc21   97-11097
                                    CIP

Visit HarperPrism on the World Wide Web at
http://www.harpercollins.com

97 98 99 00 ❖ 10 9 8 7 6 5 4 3 2 1

*For Kitty, who knew more than one Tyne Street.
Love and appreciation from us all . . .*

| 1 |

WHAT THE HELL WAS THAT?

My eyes snapped open and my head lifted an inch or so from the floor; a mess of thoughts stalled any sense.

I pushed the quilt I'd borrowed off my chest and an empty beer bottle rolled across the dusty carpet when my booted foot (I'd learned to sleep with my boots on) knocked it over. The glass made a dull *clunk* it struck a tiny center table. I raised my head another inch, my body tense, hearing now acute; I looked right, I looked left, I even looked up at the fancy ceiling. Early-morning sunlight flooded through the open half of the balcony doors, butting in on a gloom caused by boarded windows. A slight breeze tainted with the musk of decay drifted through with the light.

I listened.

Cagney, who'd found a dark corner to nest in—he liked the shadows; survival came with low profile—gave a mean growl, a soft rumbling that was warning rather than alarm. I brought up a hand to silence him and he obeyed; I could just make out the shine of his eyes as he watched me.

The quilt slid away when I leaned on an elbow and a sharp knife punctured the general ache inside my head, punishing me for the insobriety of the night before. There were plenty more brown bottles littering the floor around me, empty soulmates to the one I'd kicked over and counter-testimony to my long dislike of English beer. Skin scraped against jaw bristle as I wiped the back of my hand across dry lips.

Full consciousness arrived in a rush and then I was up, moving swiftly towards the light, crouched and quiet, ears and eyes alert for the slightest disturbance. I skirted the little round table and paused beside the open door to the balcony, keeping out of sight behind glass darkened by rotting blackout boards. Despite the early hour a dry summer heat maundered through the opening, its soft breeze carrying dust motes from the damaged city outside along with its sourness. I snatched a quick look into the sunlight, ducking back again straight away. Then I took another, extended look.

The last barrage balloons hovered over the battered landscape like bloated sentinels. Much closer, directly opposite, the grey and grimed trio on the memorial plinth bowed their heads as if in shame, the words Truth, Charity and Justice now irrelevant.

The Mall behind them was deserted.

What then? I'd chosen this billet because the balcony room offered a good view of anyone approaching the main entrance; it also gave me plenty of places to play hide 'n' seek in. The place was a warren of rooms, halls and corridors, a honeycomb of hiding places. It suited me fine.

But someone had discovered my sanctuary; the mutt wouldn't have growled for no reason. Maybe it was rats, skulking through the passageways, hardly afraid of humans anymore. Or another dog, a cat maybe. But I didn't think so. Instinct told me it was something else. Instinct and Cagney I'd learned to rely on.

I didn't waste any more time.

The motorcycle was where I'd left it last night, carpet rucked up around its wheels. That was another thing I could rely on: a single-cylinder Matchless G3L, this one painted buff for desert warfare, only never shipped out. A survivor. Like me and the dog.

I moved fast, scooping up my fly-jacket from the floor and shrugging it on as I went. The added weight in the lining provided a small comfort. Out the corner of my eye I saw that Cagney was on his feet, ready for action, but waiting for me. His stubby mongrel tail was erect, expectant. Within seconds I'd pushed the bike off its stand, mounted it and was switching on. I kicked down on the starter, hard but smooth, sensing the machine the way you can if you "know" them, if you love every working part, and the engine roared into life the first go (I'd given this baby a lot of care and attention).

The wheels left burn marks on the carpet as I took off, heading for the closed set of doors at the end of the room, doors that were just beginning to open.

I hit them hard and someone on the other side squawked blue hell as the heavy wood struck him. Paws grabbed at me as I shot through, but the Matchless was already too fast and all they found was empty air. Now I could smell 'em and believe me, it wasn't pleasant. One fool standing further back in the room jumped in front of me waving his arms like some demented traffic cop, so I swerved the bike and raised a boot. Groin or hip, I'm not sure which I made contact with, but he doubled up and swung round like a top, his whooshy grunt affording me some pleasure. Short-lived though, because the angle of the bike caused it to slide along the room's carpet, ruffling it up in thick waves. A few years' dust powdered the air as I fought to control the skid.

I lost it, though. The machine slicked away from me and I let it go, afraid of catching a leg underneath if we both went down together. I rolled with the fall, tucking in a shoulder and staying loose the way I'd been trained. I was up, crouched and ready before the bike had slithered into a fancy chest of drawers halfway down the chamber, ruining painted panels and gold carvings.

One of the intruders, his face ugly with dirt and aggression, came lurching toward me while his two pals behind the crashed doors tended their hurts. Cagney trotted into view and stood in the doorway, interested in how things were working out.

The Blackshirt, almost on me now, clutched an M1 carbine across his chest. Now either he was too crocked to aim the rifle, or he was under orders not to shoot me. I figured the second was most likely, because I knew by this time that his chief, Hubble, would prefer me alive—my blood would be better warm and runny. You see, he had a crazy use for me. Real crazy. But then I guess only the crazies were left. The crazies and me. And who said I was sane?

Well fuck you, Hubble, you and your goons. Satan's hot-house would be a long time cool before you took me alive.

Hubble's stormtrooper caught the glint in my eyes and changed his mind about following orders. He began to swing the weapon toward me.

His action was sluggish though, as if he had to think about the move rather than just react, and it occurred to me he wasn't only dazed by the slam he'd taken, but by the effects of the slow death itself: there was a darkness around his eyes and smudges beneath his skin, bruisings that were never going to fade; and the ends of his fingers were blackish, as if the blood had jellied at his body's extremities. That didn't make him any less dangerous though, just a little slower.

My own weapon, a Colt .45 automatic, standard U.S. issue, was in the holster I'd stitched into the lining of my leather jacket. Buck Jones might've made the draw, but I was no gunslinger. So I made the only move open to me.

I took a dive, rolling forward under the rifle barrel, head tucked in, legs curled up. As soon as my back hit the deck I kicked out with both feet, catching the goon in the lower belly and doubling him up. He almost fell on top of me, but I used my legs again to push him to one side. He gave a kind of honk and collapsed. I was on him before he had the chance to get his breath back, pushing the rifle towards him instead of pulling it away as he'd expected. The breech cracked against his jaw and his grip relaxed. In one swift action I wrenched the carbine from him and smacked the stock against the side of his face. His head snapped to the right and his body went limp.

I tossed the weapon aside and sprinted towards the Matchless. Cagney decided things were going pretty well and scampered from the doorway to join me, yapping his approval as he skirted the injured Blackshirts. I ignored his licks as I hauled the motorbike away from the wrecked cabinet, angry that my cover was blown, my regal refuge now useless. There'd be more of them around, searching for me, combing every room, every corridor, every damn nook and cranny, no matter how long it took.

I pulled the bike upright and swung a leg over. Voices came through from the balcony room I'd been using as a bivouac and I guessed Hubble's screwball army had been applying a pincer movement, working through the place from both sides. How the hell did they know I was here? I had the whole goddamn city—and there was plenty left still standing—to hole up in, yet he'd zeroed in on me. Shit luck. Someone must've followed me or caught me sneaking in. With anger as much as fear I hit the starter hard, but this time the engine didn't kick in first time. Those voices were getting louder and the men I'd already tangled with, 'cept the one I'd poleaxed with the rifle butt, were rising to their feet and regarding me with hate in their hearts. I tried again, adding a cuss for luck, and the engine caught, the machine roared into life. Music to my ears.

Running footsteps next door; they'd heard the music too. Cagney took off without me, heading into the blue as if he were the prey. Well maybe he had a point—they'd shoot him just for the pleasure.

The motorcycle's front wheel almost reared up as I took off; I had to lean low over the fuel tank, using my weight to hold the bike to the floor, as I fled the bad guys. There was a crack of gun-fire from behind and the cobwebbed face of a tall pedestal clock ahead of me imploded. Sculptured figures, all dusty gilt, clung for dear life as the old timepiece reverberated with tiny musical explosions. The marksman was either a shit shot or he wanted to unnerve me; maybe he was only warning others I was on my way.

I hurtled through the open doors at the end of the room and had to brake hard to avoid crashing through windows dead ahead; this was where the east face met the north wing. My left foot dragged floor as I brought the bike round in a skid that sent a small table and the ornate and no doubt priceless (but nowadays worthless) vase on its top flying. The vase shattered on the floor, but no one was going to complain.

Because of the blackout precautions, everywhere inside this place was gloomy, but enough light shone through chinks and cracks for me to find my way. I'd just entered the complex of pri-vate apartments and bedrooms so knew there was a stairway close by. Unfortunately it was too steep and narrow for the bike and I had no mind to try it on foot: speed was my ally and had been for some time now, y'see, and I had to stick to the escape route I'd already worked out. Besides, I'd be an easy target for anyone waiting to ambush me in the stairwell.

Another bullet whistled through the doors and thudded into the wall next to the windows; but I had the bike under control again and shot into the long corridor that would take me through the north wing. Fortunately the place had been cleared of corpses and evacuated as soon as the main tenants—God rest their poor

souls—had taken flight, so I didn't have to worry about rotting carcasses getting in my way. I opened up, burning rug, spewing up
dust, the engine's roar shaking the walls, filling the air. It didn't take
long to reach the west wing and that's where the real fun started.

I'd been making for the main staircase, which I knew the
Matchless could take easy enough, reducing speed along the way
to negotiate the trickier twists and turns, and I'd arrived at a long
picture gallery where I could change up a gear, make better headway. I'd zipped past Rembrandts, Vermeers, Canalettos (I'd spent
some time in this museum with its glazed arched ceiling and low
viewing couches set around the walls, enjoying the brilliance
before me but bitter, I guess, that these works of art now counted
for zilch), when a figure leapt out from one of the several openings, halfway down on my left.

He only clipped my shoulder as I went by, but that was
enough. I lost balance and slewed off at an angle, careering into
one of the gallery's small tables, knocking it aside before running
into a couch. I recovered enough to keep going, my fight leg
trapped between bike frame and seat, yelling as my pants ripped
and my skin burned. I pulled away, picking up speed again, the
gallery no more than a dirt track without dirt to me.

But again I had to brake as three men appeared in the little
lobby at the end of the hall, using the handbrake a split second
ahead of the footbrake pedal and leaning hard so that the bike
screeched to a clean sideways halt.

I sat there one or two moments, fists tight around the hand-
grips, holding the clutch lever, sweat soaking my forehead, running down my back. Vibrations from the machine's simmering
engine ran through my body. The three Blackshirts watched me
from the lobby, one of them grinning, knowing they had me
trapped. They all carried firearms, but none of them bothered to
take aim. Their hair was short, cut military-style, and their
shirts—black, naturally, although the effect spoilt by dust and
creases—tucked into loose black pants, the grimy uniform of
arrogance, the cloth of annihilation. These sick degenerates still
hadn't learned the lesson.

A shifting in the shadows behind them, and then another face,
a woman's face, appeared at their shoulders. She grinned too
when she sized up the situation.

I glanced to the left and saw the sap who'd tried to ambush me pulling himself up, disappointment souring his mug. Through the same entrance came another Blackshirt, this one thumping what looked like a pickaxe handle into the open palm of his hand, the dull *thwack* it made amplified by the long room's acoustics. The gleam in his eye and the twisted leer he beamed my way were anything but pleasant. Just to confirm the odds really were against me, the sound of running footsteps came from the far end of the picture gallery. The vermin who'd started the chase arrived at the opening down there and they also took time out to consider the state of play.

I turned back to the four who were creeping out of the lobby. They stopped, as if my look had caught them out, and now all of them grinned as I sat there revving up the engine. They had me, they were thinking.

And then I grinned too, and theirs faded away.

I took off, spinning the bike, swerving close to wall and seat, aiming straight at the luckless ambusher who'd only just picked himself up. His eyes widened, first in surprise, then in panic, as I hurtled towards him, the bike's roar deafening as it bounced off walls and curved ceiling. He managed to jump clear, throwing himself into the arms of his slack-jawed buddy, the axe handle trapped between their bodies. I was long gone before they'd had time to disentangle, veering left and disappearing through the opposite doorway to the one they'd used (luckily for me the gallery had more than its share of entrances and exits).

I was in a room whose main wall was one huge bowed window that, if it hadn't been for the blackout shades, would have over-looked acres of overgrown lawns and weed-filled gardens. Tall black pillars on either side of individual windows reached up to a vaulted and domed ceiling and over white marble fireplaces were big arched mirrors in plaster frames. (I'd taken all this in, you'll understand, on another day when my time was less occupied.) I kept the bike turning in a rough elongated semicircle from my starting point, tires screeching off a parquet flooring of rich woods, speeding up into the adjoining room, sure of the layout even in the dusky light. I straightened up, whipping past Corinthian columns, long velvet drapes, the breeze I was creating causing low-hanging crystal chandeliers smothered in cobwebs to sway; past blue and gold chairs, large paintings of ancient monarchs mounted on blue flock walls; past a marble and gilt bronze clock with three dials, a dark blue porcelain vase, a set of elaborate side tables, again all marble and gilt bronze; diverting round a circular single-pedestal table, before zooming through the open mirror doors into the next state room. (I knew exactly where I was headed because I'd had plenty of time to check out the whole set-up during my stay and, being naturally cautious, I had more than one escape route planned should the need arise, with certain doors deliberately left open to give me a clear run.)

What I needed was for those lunkheads to follow me rather than try to cut me off, because I was continuing the semicircle, the blue room itself parallel to the picture gallery they'd chased me from. I'd shuck a quick look to my left just before going through the doors into the grand dining room and observed that the small lobby which served both the gallery and the blue room was empty. Good. It meant they'd taken the bait—the Blackshirts were chasing instead of waiting.

Vases of withered flowers, an oval tureen and tarnished silver ewers with cobweb sails trailing to the huge lacklustre tabletop said it all: Grandeur given over to decay. The dusty red walls and carpet gave me the sickening feeling of passing through an open, festering wound, and the cold eyes of long-gone royals framed by dull gold followed me all the way. These crazy notions were brought on, I guess, by adrenaline overload; but what the hell, they kept my senses kicking.

I began to brake again for the sharp turn I was gonna have to make, and almost stopped completely inside the smaller ante-chamber filled with large tapestries I found myself in. Shoving one of those over-elaborate kneehole desks out the way with my front wheel, I went on through to a short passage room, then foot-wheeled a left into another gallery. A wide descending stairway was at the far end and that was my goal. I gritted my teeth and tightened my grip as I raced past the usual collection of master-pieces, aware I was travelling too fast to take the stairs but disin-clined to slow down—I knew my pursuers would second-guess me as soon as they heard the bike coming back their way. I braked hard at the last moment.

It was a bumpy ride, despite the fact that the Matchless G3L

was one of the first British motorcycles to be built with hydrauli-
cally damped telescopic forks, and the stairway itself was fitted
with a plush red carpet all the way down; my arms were rigid
fighting the acute angle, my butt barely touching the seat, every
bone in my body jolted as I kept the rear wheel almost locked.
Head juddering, bones rattling, I vented a staccato kind of wail
(I'd never taken the stairs at that speed before), and then the bike
was level for a piece and my wail pitched to a whoop of relief or
triumph, I'm not sure which.

On either side, two arms of the grand staircase swept up to a
balcony overlooking the next set of steps I was about to take, the
doorway at the top leading to the long picture gallery where they
thought they'd had me trapped; the Blackshirts had cut back and
were pouring through that doorway. The lead goon just had time
to raise his gun over the bronze balustrade and fire a wild shot
before I opened throttle and took off, sailing over the second set
of steps without touching one. My extended whoop came danger-
ously close to a scream as a bullet clanged off the bike's pannier
rack.

The shock of landing nearly threw me off, but I rode the
bounce, tires scorching carpet as I braked and fought to keep the
machine in a straight line. We screeched (yeah, bike and I) to a
stop inches from the opposite set of rising steps in the great
entrance chamber.

I grabbed a breath, then dug my heels into the deep pile, hauling the Matchless back to give me room to swing round. Shouts
and footsteps behind told me the mob was descending the curved
staircase. Someone released a burst of fire that could only have
come from a Sten gun and as I turned I saw holes puncturing
paintings around the walls. Maybe the shooter was trying to scare
me into surrender; or maybe he was just pissed off, as the British
say.

I'd cleared enough space when I heard a yap from close by. I
did a quick scan for Cagney, but he was nowhere in sight. Well
the mutt could take care of himself—hadn't he let me grab all the
attention while he'd sneaked down another way? I opened up
again, and the Matchless spun a smart turn, scuffing the bottom
step of the four leading to a marble hall beyond the entrance
chamber. That was where Cagney finally showed, loping along

the royal gathering place, avoiding the marble on either side of the red carpet which presumably was too cold or too smooth for his dainty pads. He lingered to wag his stumpy tail at me and I yelled at him to get the hell out. He took the hint and streaked past me towards the entrance doors.

My circle was taking me close to the staircase I'd just sailed over and the sight I caught was not an encouraging one: three of my pursuers were leaning over the stair rail aiming their weapons at me while still more scurried down behind them. The angle was too awkward for the marksmen and anyway, I didn't wait for them to get a bead on me. Their shots chewed carpet and chipped marble columns, but I was out of there, hunched over the handlebars, already passing through the entrance doors to the classy porch outside.

With my right foot scraping concrete I skidded around the double portico's stone columns and was soon out in the open; left again and a quadrangle surrounded by the four blocks of the ancient building itself spread out before me. Across the broad expanse of concrete and directly opposite the portico was a narrow archway, with even narrower pedestrian passageways on either side, leading through to the forecourt and open gates. In better times the ceremonial coach had used that archway, but now it was going to accommodate just one man and his dog. Cagney was already halfway across and I was catching up fast when I spotted the Bedford OYD tucked away in the far corner of the square. The army truck hadn't been there the night before, nor the night before that, so I figured the Blackshirts had arrived in it earlier that morning— a military vehicle suited their martial games just fine.

One of them, on his own and presumably the driver, straightened from the snub-nosed hood he'd been leaning against, his jaw dropping open, cigarette filling from it. His weapon must have been inside the cab of the truck, because he was soon pulling at the driver's door. He'd guessed my intention, and by now, I was too committed to change direction. He heaved himself up into the driver's seat.

Cagney had already disappeared into the shadows of the arch (which, incidentally, was beneath the balcony room I'd holed up in for the past few days—I'd run full circle, you see) and I accelerated, anxious to join him.

The Bedford quivered as the driver started her up, and then began to roll forward. Yeah, he'd guessed my game-plan all right and now I understood his: he was going to plug my escape point. Just to tighten things, an arm appeared through the open cab window and the black metal of a gun barrel pointed my way.

Maybe I could have tried for a different route at the last moment, through a courtyard behind me on my right and out into the street beyond (the two other archways directly ahead were sealed by sandbags), but like I say, I was committed. Besides, that would've meant slowing down, then offering my back as a target; even if he'd missed with the first bullet, he'd have taken me with the second. No, there really was only one choice and anyways, I was already two-thirds across and going a pretty fair lick.

A bright flash of gunfire came from the truck and even over the noise of the bike's 347cc engine I swear I heard the *thiddd* of displaced air as the bullet passed by.

I rocked a little to spoil his aim, mighty glad that driving and shooting at the same time wasn't this particular hero's speciality. That small pleasure lasted no more'n a heartbeat—it was plain the truck was going to reach the archway ahead of me. Another shot cracked out, just as wild as the first one, but it struck metal; the blackout shield over the front light whipped away. I tried a fancy swerve, but with every second our common objective was drawing us closer together and soon he'd have a target he couldn't miss. I hissed a curse—I mean, the beginning of one— when the Bedford's hood moved across the first passageway; that curse changed to a rage-roar as the truck stole some of the archway.

The rattle of gunshots from behind reminded me the truck driver was not the only contender. A hail of badly aimed bullets railed the wall ahead. The Blackshirts chasing me were too far away and maybe too excited to get off any decent shots as they came out of the double portico, but they sure as hell didn't help the situation any. Luckily they were keeping their fire to the right to avoid hitting the moving Bedford and from their angle truck and bike must've seemed pretty damn close. More puffs of plaster powdered from the wall beside the second passageway and at any moment—we're talking split seconds here—I expected to feel bullets thudding into my back.

Goddamn, the truck had covered the archway and the driver was slamming on his brakes to keep it that way. It slid onwards though, bellying across the passage. Another gunshot, the *crack* clear as a bell this time—hell, I was close enough to see the joy in the driver's eyes—and I felt leather rip at my shoulder. No numbness, no pain—no real damage.

I twitched the handlebars, no more'n a shrew's shrug, as the hood closed the gap, knowing I couldn't stop now even if I'd wanted to.

I kept up the roar, jaw straining, eyes narrowed, hands clenched tight around the grips, bullets spewing into the wall above and beside the passageway, truck still sliding, the hand with the gun waving at me, the gap closing down, tighter, tighter—

And then I was through, elbow skimming along the truck's hood bar, leather sleeve on the other side scuffing plaster. I was in the cool shade of the short passageway, my roar hollow-sounding, and then I was out again in bright, glorious sunshine, tearing over the wide forecourt for the open gates, their gilded ironwork rotting to rust, the tall railings on either side worthless protection against the death that had claimed almost all, bloodline having no privilege over blood type.

Through the gates I sped and around the old queen's memorial, past the statues of women and children I'd gazed at from the balcony room less than ten minutes ago, round to the other side where Victoria herself sat facing the long, elm- and lime-lined Mall. I swear I could feel her mournful eyes on my back as I fled Buckingham Palace, heading for another sanctuary in the dead city. Half a century ago she'd been proud mother to a fabulous empire and a great country; now there was nothing left of empire and precious little of country. Better then those eyes were only of stone.

Gunfire broke the thought that was fleeting anyway. I had a straight run ahead of me and I took full advantage: the Matchless approached seventy and I knew I could coax more out of her.

If I was gonna lose those bastards behind me I'd have to.

| 2 |

St. James's palace and Clarence House to my left, the overgrown park and lake on my right. Sally and me, we'd fed the swans in that park and laid together on the moist spring grass. But that was another lifetime, a different age, and this was now. Crazy that memories should override all other considerations, even at moments like this, choosing their own time, it seemed to me, with a mercilessness that suggested self-torture. But at least they were my link with the past, and the past was all I had left.

I avoided the few cars parked along the road, some of them askew, doors wide as if the drivers had skidded to a halt and attempted to flee before the Reaper finished his job. Probably there were bodies—rotted corpses or loose suits of bones—still inside some of them, but I wasn't looking, I had other things in mind.

The mutt, his sandy-brown coat glistening damp gold in the sunlight, looked over his shoulder as he heard me coming up. He didn't break pace any, but seemed pleased to see me.

"Lose yourself, stupid!" I yelled at him as I drew level. *"Get off the road!"*

I swerved into him to give him a fright and he veered away, making for a flight of stone steps leading off the main hike. I watched him go and returned my attention to the road just in time to avoid a Wolseley parked sideways across the Mall's center. Its passenger window suddenly shattered inwards and the metalwork of its doors punctured as bullets tore into it. The shots were wild, but that didn't mean they couldn't get lucky. I straightened up, keeping the Wolseley at my back, using it as a temporary

1 3

shield. Those Blackshirts were acting like good ol' boys from down South out on a nigger hunt, rednecks on a roust, the local sheriff one of 'em. Back home we'd pretended that kind of bigot didn't exist—theirs was another state anyways, a foreign country almost—and when the news informed us otherwise, we'd be pretty damn certain some black buck had raped another white girl so he, along with all his blackass cousins, was getting exactly what he deserved. You might say these days my opinion on such things has changed a little, 'specially now I'd kind of taken the place of that black boy.

Admiralty Arch loomed up, sandbags piled high in front of doorways and windows of buildings around it, red London buses and other vehicles clearly visible in the square on the other side. I kept the Matchless on a set course, building speed, putting distance between me and the truck behind. The roads through the arches had been narrowed some by barbed wire and guard boxes, but that was no problem for the bike—I was through in the blink of an eye and into the great square beyond.

With its loose jumble of immobile vehicles, Trafalgar Square looked like one of those frozen pictures you used to see sometimes on a movie screen, as if at any moment the action would start right up again and everything would get going, engines rumbling, car horns honking, people jerking into life. Last time Sally had brought me here—she was like an excited kid showing me the sights—the square and the sky above it had been full of grey pigeons; now even they were gone. The dry fountains with their silent sirens under Nelson's Column were surrounded by wooden barricades and where sections were broken or had fallen flat I could see brick shelters inside. I had it in mind to take refuge in one of them, or even hide behind a barricade, but as I dodged between cars, taxicabs, and buses, something moving caught my eye.

I'd never quite worked out how many survivors Hubble had recruited into his Fascist army—the Blackshirts had always appeared in small groups before now—but had figured their numbers to be maybe a hundred or so, and today they seemed to be out in force. Right then another vehicle was heading towards me and from its camouflage marking this one also had to be military. I paused long enough to establish it was a Humber heavy utility, a four-door station wagon that could carry at least seven passengers over heavy terrain. Like the Matchless I was riding, it was probably intended for the North Africa Campaign but never made it overseas. The estate was entering the square from the Strand and as I watched it nudged a black cab aside, then swung round a double-decker bus.

I took off in the opposite direction, weaving through the still traffic and catching a glimpse of the Bedford pushing its way past the barbed-wire barricades of Admiralty Arch as I did so. The Humber and the Bedford had to be in contact with one another by radio, maybe by one of those walkie-talkies, but I was confident I could outrun 'em both, the bike ideal for slipping through blocked roads and over debris. If it hadn't been for gasoline rationing during the war years, the roads would've been a lot more crowded, which would've suited me fine. No matter, I still had the advantage.

A bus poster wanted to know if I'd MacCleaned my teeth today, while a board at the base of Nelson's Column said that England expected me to enlist today. I went on my way, steering around a quaint little English taxi that resembled an upright piano, its headlights masked to narrow crosses, and past a Dodge van with a loudspeaker mounted on its roof, then squeezing by a platform truck carrying huge casks of God-knows-what, all of these vehicles abandoned by their drivers and passengers three years before, Blood Death victims who had not understood what was happening to their bodies, why their arterial veins were suddenly hardening and swelling, becoming rigid beneath their skins, why their hands were darkening, extremities filling, why smaller veins were becoming engorged, bulging then popping beneath the surface, blood beginning to trickle, then stream, from every orifice, their ears, their eyes, their nostrils, their mouth, from their genitals, their anus, from the very pores of their body, not realizing that their main arteries had begun to coagulate, their body's clotting factors all used up by their major organs, the brain, the heart, the kidneys, causing instantaneous hemorrhaging and necrotic bruising elsewhere, their chests and limbs cramping with agonizing pain until their skin split and everything vital stopped functioning, their curiosity, their awe, their fear and panic lasting mere minutes because the Blood

Death held no patience and no pity, each of them dying wherever they happened to fall.

Yeah, and they were the lucky ones—their horror was short-lived, literally, and their suffering only transient; although few in number, the *really* unfortunate victims took longer to die, some, even years. And then there were the rest of us, the minority, those left to grieve.

I kept pushing on, blocking thoughts, concentrating on escape. The idea was to get lost in the dead city, then hole up in some dark place and wait. That was the idea. The reality was something else.

A black Ford was heading towards me from the direction I'd intended to take, making me wonder if Hubble had every exit to the square covered. It seemed in no hurry, but was making good progress anyway, dodging in and out of frozen traffic as if the driver was enjoying the caper. It disappeared behind a bus marked EVACUATION SPECIAL, then its roof appeared among the jumble of other car roofs, threading its way through, coming closer all the time. Someone behind me blasted their horn hard and mean, a signal to the others maybe that I was outflanked. It was easy to picture their grinning faces.

But the game was a long ways from over. I had two choices: I could either evade the approaching Ford, using other vehicles as shields against the potshots they were bound to take at me; or I could cut across the square itself.

There were no breaks in the barrier closest to me, but those boards looked fragile enough—several winters of wind, rain and snow, with no one around to maintain them, must have left them rotted and feeble. It didn't take long to make the choice.

I stood loose-legged on the footrests, helping the bike hop the curb, then sat firm, shoulders hunched, head low, as bike and I flashed past the bronze lions guarding the giant column holding the old one-eyed sailor. I hit wood and it offered minimal resistance, splintering into mouldered pieces, my speed taking me through too fast so that I only just missed the waterless fountain on the other side. I zoomed around one of the redundant brick shelters behind the barrier and, hardly slowing down, I made for the broad set of steps that led up to the square's higher level, a road that ran past the great art museum, praying the Matchless would be able to take them, an insistent little voice inside my head telling me I was crazy, that those steps might not be steep, but they were *hard,* bone-breaking *hard,* with no carpet this time to soften the impact.

I stood on the "stirrups" again, pulling at the handlebars, trying, I guess, to coax the bike to fly. We hit the steps . . . too fast, too hard . . .

The Matchless rose up several of them, but the front wheel reared out of control, the handlebars bucking and twisting in my grip. We toppled backwards, the machine trying for a complete backflip with me doing my best to dissuade it. I had no real choice though, I had to let go. The engine whined as I slid down the seat and tumbled back, away from the steps and falling machine, arms raised over my head to protect myself as I fell.

The bike keeled over, falling at an angle and hitting stone with a crash of metal. I rolled clear as it bounced down after me and, with a moan of engine and a jingling of busted parts, the bike settled in the space I'd just occupied. I knew better than to try and start it up again—it was finished and I was in even more trouble.

I forced myself to a kind of crouch, groaning at fresh pains in my left leg and back, but wasting no time on them. I hauled myself up those steps, using hands as well as feet, then round and up the next, lesser flight, standing upright only when I was at the top.

More screeching of brakes told me what I really didn't want to know. The station wagon had turned up from the Strand, going the wrong way round the square, aiming to cut me off. Even as it rocked to a halt, doors were opening and black-garbed figures were piling out. One of them raised a rifle in my direction and I ducked back behind the parapet wall beside the steps, reaching inside my jacket as I did so.

I whipped back again, kneeling though, offering a smaller target, and sent off a shot towards them. They scattered, two of 'em taking cover behind a St. John Ambulance van, three more scuttling back to the other side of their own vehicle. I broke cover, running low, gun hand pointing in their direction just to give them something to think about. They knew well enough not to take chances, so they kept out of sight, a head bobbing up occasionally to check on me. I sent another bullet their way to let 'em know they were behaving sensibly.

I didn't have much of a plan 'cept to keep moving, using all the cover available to me. A bullet whanged off metal close to my head and I almost dropped to all fours. Another shot shattered the windshield of a nearby taxi. Traffic on this side of the square was thin and I knew I'd soon be running out of cover. Some of the Blackshirts were growing bolder, slinking through metal alleyways like beads of oil through conduits.

A wide expanse of emptiness opened up ahead of me, beyond it the steps to the National Gallery, a museum that at one time had contained some of the world's finest and most valued works of art. Most of the paintings and sculptures had been shipped out to less vulnerable places than a building in the heart of war-torn London, although some had been returned when the battle (or so it was thought) was almost over, and I'd been in and out of there plenty of times, so knew it was a maze of rooms and corridors, just like the palace. I'd thought that one day it might come in handy as a means of escape; it looked like that day had come.

So there was my plan: get inside, lose these neo-Nazi clowns, find a way out on the north side. No problem—as long as I could make it inside without having my legs shattered by enemy gunfire when I sprinted across open ground.

I waited until the Blackshirts had discharged another volley before setting off again, firing back at them just as wildly, but maybe a bit more effectively. They kept out of sight, aware that any kind of wound could prove serious without the right medical attention, and medical attention was just what the whole fucking world lacked.

I pounded road, running towards the flight of steps leading up to the gallery's entrance, which was behind a facade of high pillars (the English liked their pillars). A ragged line of bullets raked the wall ahead of me and I fell back, losing balance and going down on my butt. I swung the Colt round, holding it with both hands and returned rapid fire, sweeping the area from a sitting position, trying to at least scare the bastards if I couldn't kill 'em. Again, the ploy was effective—they hid, afraid to show an inch of flesh as glass exploded and metal punctured around them. Effective, that is, until the firing pin hit empty.

The clip was all used up and I couldn't reload sitting there in the middle of the road. I had to get into the shelter of the gallery before they realized I was theirs for the taking.

Ears deafened by gunfire, I scrambled to my feet and rushed the last few yards to the steps.

Stopping dead when I saw the figure watching me from the top.

Hubble had never been handsome, but I guess he had that arrogance of features that had some allure for the weak-minded. Pencil-thin moustache, beaky nose, he could have been a shorter version of his own hero, Sir Oswald Mosley, the leader of England's very own Fascist party, a degenerate who'd spent most of the war years locked away in Holloway Prison. No, Max Hubble— *Sir* Max Hubble—was never handsome, but on this warm sunny morning he looked a thousand times more unattractive, as though he were only a short distance from death. His stance, once stiff-backed, shoulders squared, chin jutting, was now bent, shoulders hunched, jaw-line sunken into a loose neck. The swagger-stick he had once used for Field-Marshal effect had been replaced by a stout walking stick, which he used like a third leg, and the uniform—black shirt and jodhpurs tucked into knee-length boots—seemed two sizes too big for him. The smudges beneath his eyes, the drained paleness of his skin emphasized by patch-work areas of broken veins, the swollen darkness at the ends of his fingers, confirmed what I'd already guessed. The disease in him had finally broken out.

We exchanged looks but nothing more. I understood the all-out effort to capture me that day.

I was Hubble's last-chance saloon. His final throw of the dice. His only hope. That is, my blood was his only hope.

One of his men stepped from behind a large poster advertising a Myra Hess piano concert (a regular event at the gallery during the grimmest days of the War), just outside the entrance, carrying with him a portable radio transmitter. I guessed that Hubble had used the gallery as his HQ that morning, directing operations from there, trying to drive me in this direction. Well, it couldn't have worked out better for him.

Others emerged from the entrance and from behind pillars, a ragbag army of the damned. Jew-baiters, niggerhaters, corrupt in their minds and now corrupt in their bodies. These days they had someone else to hate. Me. I was their Jew and their Black all rolled into one.

Okay, I was stunned seeing Hubble standing there, sick and
hunched up, but I hadn't lost all sense. I pointed the gun at them
and they all ducked, including their leader, who practically sank
to his knees. I hadn't forgotten the Colt was empty, but it seemed
they had—unless they hadn't even noticed. Waving it in the air
gave me the chance to start running again. I managed no more'n
three, maybe four, steps though.

Bullets from a Sten gun bit into the road before me, forcing
me to leap back, a hasty two-legged hop, arms in the air as if in
surrender. I just caught sight of a Blackshirt launching himself
from between two pillars of the entrance terrace above me,
swooping like a bat from rafters, expecting me to cushion his fall.
I sidestepped, but he caught my shoulders, bringing me down
with him. He must've winded himself, but even so, he managed
to get me in a neck-lock. He squeezed tight, attempting to choke
me into submission.

First I used an elbow, driving it hard into his stomach, then,
with the same arm, I clipped his face with the gun barrel, bringing it up like a smart salute. Spittle dampened my cheek and neck
as he blew a forced breath, and his grip relaxed just enough for
me to break free. I twisted, swiping him with the gun barrel once
more so that all opposition left him. He collapsed sideways and I
scrambled to my feet.

His friends were hurrying through the vehicle alleys and more
poured down the gallery's steps, all of 'em hollering banshee-like,
eager to get at me and teach me a lesson or two. So what if Hubble wouldn't let them kill me right off? I'd be dead sooner or
later, and all in all, I think I preferred sooner. It looked like I'd
have to force the issue.

I reached inside my jacket pocket for another clip, ejecting the
used one from the automatic in my other hand as I did so. I
noticed some were already pausing to lift their weapons and take
aim. This was it, then, I told myself. The moment had been a long
time coming, but I was more than ready. What was so good about
living anyway?

A goon had already reached me as my hand came out of my
pocket with the spare clip, screening me from the others. I
regret to say it was a woman, hair cut nastily short, face and
teeth smeared with grime, eyes red with shot blood vessels;

regret, because I whacked her hard, fist wrapped around the metal clip, and I didn't like hitting women, never have. Hell, I never *had*.

Her teeth broke under my knuckles and she crumpled without a murmur. Her place was immediately taken by another Blackshirt and I knew it would take more than a punch in the mouth to deal with this mean-looking bruiser. Yeah, we'd tangled more than once before and one time he'd even introduced himself. McGruder was his name and he was Hubble's first-lieutenant or captain of the guard, or whatever fancy and meaningless title Hubble had bestowed upon him. He was tall, six-three or more, built like an ox and, as far as I could tell, a long way off from the Blood Death. Big hands reached for me.

I moved back against the terrace wall, afraid to take my eyes off him, Colt and new clip of ammo still separated because of the previous distraction. By staring into his eyes I seemed to be delaying the final rush; taking my gaze away to reload would break whatever goddamn spell we were both under. He, and the others, drew closer.

The black Ford I'd seen earlier came out of nowhere, tires squealing, brakes screeching, one of its four doors open wide so that it hit the big man with a force that sent him sprawling. I caught sight of two faces peering out at me from the open car door and a female voice yelled:

"What are you waiting for? Get in, you daft bloody ape!"

The passenger, a man, had already slammed his door shut again but was indicating the rear door through the open window. The scattered Blackshirts were already moving in, some of them thumping on the Ford's triangular hood with their guns and fists.

"Get bloody well in!" came the woman's voice again and I guess it was her *language* that shocked me out of my stupor.

I yanked open the rear door and the Ford immediately took off, giving me a split second to hop onto the white-painted running board. I looped an arm through the door-frame and open front window, gun still held tight in that hand, the other quickly tucking the clip into my pants pocket before grasping the top of the open door. I hung on for dear life as the Ford's rush dispersed the Blackshirts again. A hand reached out from inside the car, grabbing my belt and trying to pull me in. That became more difficult as the Ford gathered momentum and the open door pressed against me, trapping me on the running board.

One of the goons had decided to stand his ground and I groaned when I saw him raising his Sten gun as we sped towards him. It was a stupid move on his part, taking his time to get a bead on me when he should have shot from the hip, because the car was on him before the gun was even chest-high. Self-preservation gave me the strength to push the door wide again and it caught the Blackshirt straight on, lifting the Sten gun and sending him spinning round, bullets spraying the air and busting the top windows of a nearby bus. The door's recoil crushed my chest, the sudden pain causing me to drop my right arm and lose hold of the Colt. It fell somewhere inside the car.

"*Will you get in here!*" came the woman's voice again, frustration more than anger giving it its pitch.

Instead I almost lost my grip and tumbled into the road as she steered onto a curb to avoid a truck blocking the way. I forgot my own manners, aiming a cuss at her that would've turned her cheeks red under any other circumstances. I hauled myself up and threw myself onto the back seat, the door slamming shut behind me of its own accord. Wheezing from the pain in my bruised chest, I sprawled across the lap of the other person sharing the back seat with me, the owner of the hand that had grabbed my belt moments earlier.

I noticed her sweet scent first, and then her gentleness as she tried to hold me steady. Breathing hard and shaking some, I looked up into her shadowed face. Her smile was as sweet as her perfume, and kind of, well, *demure* too. Leastways, that's how it struck me. A line of sunlight through the window on her side shot sparkles of gold through her light brown hair.

The car bumped again as it left the curb and I was jolted against her small breasts. Just as quickly I was pitched back into the other corner. The girl held on to the front seat, looking ahead over the driver's shoulder, her face anxious.

As I steadied myself I took note of my fellow travellers. Oddly, the man in front of me wore a brown trilby and a tweed jacket despite the heat of the day. His attention was on the road ahead too, so there was no chance to catch his features. I noticed, though, that his straggly hair (with no barber shops around any more we all had bad haircuts, although I kept mine reasonably short with sharp scissors and guesswork) did not quite manage to cover the burn scars that fingered their way up the back of his neck from beneath his shirt collar.

My angle was better to take in the woman—the girl—driver, and as I studied her she threw a quick glance my way.

"Who are you?" she said, her voice raised, but no longer shouting. Her accent was pure London, but not from the smarter end.

Before I could answer, something—debris of some kind, I guess—struck the windshield, cracking the glass. The girl wrenched the steering wheel round, hissing something tight and nasty as she did so, and the Ford executed a squealing curve into the broad, littered and mined street that was the Strand. Past taped shop windows we sped, avoiding small craters or fetal bundles that were carcasses in the roadway. Bullets *thunked* into metal behind us and I felt the girl beside me flinch. I took a peek out the rear window and saw the Bedford track was back in the game; the Blackshirts in the rear section had lifted the front flap of the canvas roof so that they could lean on the cab's top and take potshots at us. Luckily, the metal-encased spare tire fixed to the Ford's trunk was taking most of the strikes.

"And just who the hell are *those* people?"

The driver wasn't looking my way—she was too busy avoiding a Griff Fender removal van and a Shank's open-back track that had collided with one another years before and had remained locked together ever since, blocking most of the road's center— but there was no doubting who she wanted answers from. Before I could say anything a bullet shattered the rear window, whistling between the heads of me and the gift I shared the back seat with and finishing the job on the windshield in front. I pulled her down into my lap and crouched over her. The driver let loose some more curses as fresh air rushed through the car.

"We'd have pinched a convertible if we'd wanted the wind in our hair," I heard her shout over the noise.

"*Keep going!*" I advised, my own voice a little louder than hers.

She said something that I didn't catch.

"*I said, any idea where we should go?*" she yelled when I leaned closer and pressed her.

"Keep heading east. We'll lose 'em if you can pick up speed."

"Hey, you a Yank?" She risked a glance over her shoulder, and I got a better look at her face.

Her eyes were a hazel-brown and she was pretty enough, although the thinnest of scars cut diagonally across her cheeks, rising over the bump of her nose. Her lips were un-rouged, but still nicely shaped, and her jawline was firm, indicating some stubbornness in her nature. Her dark hair, curling over her forehead, was tucked neatly into a snood at the back of her head. Why I was noticing these things about the two women at this point of time, I had no idea; maybe I'd spent too long on my own and their effect on me was overriding more urgent considerations. I don't know; but that's how it was.

"Watch the road," I told her and she turned away, only just managing to pull round a two-toned Austin.

When she'd straightened up again, I said, "D'you have any weapons?"

At that time I had no idea of what had happened to my Colt.

Now the man with the trilby hat, its brim slouched low and shading his eyes, craned his neck to look at me. He shook his head, saying nothing, and his appraisal was cool.

"Why would we need weapons?" the girl driver called out. "The war ended three years ago."

I didn't answer her. We were passing the narrow street that served as forecourt to the Savoy and I was tempted to tell her to pull into it. We could have left the car and run through the hotel to its riverside entrance, easily picking up another vehicle parked on that side (I kept several there, keys in the ignitions). It might have been too risky though: our pursuers were close and probably would've caught up with us on foot. Besides, the Savoy was one of my "home bases"—I had my own grand apartment right up there on the third floor overlooking the Thames—so I was reluctant to bring the enemy so close to a sanctuary. Better to lose the Blackshirts before going to ground.

We passed blitzed buildings, some of them destroyed by the *Luftwaffe*'s bombs, others ruined later by gas explosions and electrical wires burning, still more by dropped cigarettes, lighted candles, or any manner of domestic accidents caused by victims of the Blood Death dropping dead in their tracks. The damage to the city was not yet over: gas mains still blew, water pipes continued to burst, and bomb-hit buildings still toppled long after they'd been struck. London was a dangerous place, even without this army of lunatics roaming the streets.

Strangely, no epidemics had spread after that black day of *Vergeltungswaffen*—vengeance—despite all the rotting corpses left lying around, but maybe that had something to do with the nature of the Blood Death itself and its effect on human and animal body systems. An attempt to clear up the place had been made by those who had the slow-death (and didn't realize it) until eventually even they were gone. Leaving just the crazies behind.

Oh, and there was one other danger, but that hadn't happened for a little while, so maybe it was over.

We entered the Aldwych, the gutted shell that had been St. Clement Danes just visible beyond the logjam of traffic ahead.

"Swing left!" I ordered, checking on our pursuers as I did so. The Humber station wagon was catching up with the Bedford truck, but both were having a tougher time than the smaller Ford finding their way through the tangles behind us. The girl did as she was told, sweeping round into Kingsway, tires bumping over tramlines. She had to reduce speed to work round a huge crater in the road.

I turned in surprise as the girl next to me spoke, her voice quiet but easily heard now that we were travelling more slowly.

"Are you the same as us?" she said.

I knew immediately what she meant. The man in front looked at me again, his eyes full of interest beneath the brim of his hat, and the driver stopped muttering curses for a moment to hear my reply.

"AB-negative? Yeah, I'm one of you," I said.

"Well, welcome to the club." The driver tossed me a quick grin. "And how about these loonies chasing us?"

I shook my head. "Slow-dying. They're finished, but they won't accept it."

"Is that why they're pissed off with you? Y'know—why them and not you?"

Once more I was a little taken aback by her language—girls in Wisconsin are not, *were* not, quite as loose-lipped—although it didn't seem to bother her companions. Probably they were used to it.

"They seem to think I can do them some good. At least, their leader does. When you come to the traffic lights up ahead, go right. Keep heading east."

"He wants you as a guinea pig, to do tests?" It was the girl next to me who spoke.

"No. He wants me as a refill."

"Blood transfusion?" It was the man in the hat and I thought I detected an accent. Polish? Not French. Maybe Czech.

"Yeah. He's a fool."

"But they tried, they proved it could not work. Blood types do not mix."

"He refuses to believe it."

The foreigner shook his head in pity, in disbelief, I don't know which. The car lurched and I wedged myself in, one arm against the back of his seat, the other against my own.

"Where you've come from," I said to the girl next to me, "were there many of you?"

She wore plain utility clothes. A pale blue dress with puffed shoulders, brought in by a belt at the waist, no stockings, brown shoes that were sensible rather than stylish. On her it all looked good.

"Not too many. AB-negative is rare."

Yeah, I know it, I thought. Too goddamn rare.

The driver, still carefully guiding the car around obstacles, cut in. "They took us away to a secret location after the plague struck and they discovered our type wasn't affected. It was down in Dorset, a sanatorium of some kind. They did tests, all kinds of things, trying to find an antidote for everyone else, but they failed. I suppose they were doing the same all over the country— all over the world."

I watched her profile. I guess I expected tears, but none appeared.

"Most AB-negs took off," she went on, "when what was left of the medical staff started dying." For a few moments she concentrated on squeezing through the middle of two tramcars stopped adjacent to each other on the broad street, then she said, "Hey, what's your name? As we seem to be saving your life it's only right we be introduced."

"Hoke," I told her.

"Hi, Hoke. Anything to go with that?"

"Eugene Nathaniel."

"Christ, you Yanks. Okay, I'm Cissie and the beauty sitting beside you is Muriel. Muriel Drake."

Despite her anxiety, Muriel managed another smile.

"And the chap in front of you is Willy," she said. "We picked him up when we found him hiking along a lane after we left the sanatorium. Only it's not really Willy, is it, Willy?"

He, too, managed a smile, but it was stiff, no warmth to it. He had a strong face, a prominent nose that I think must've been broken at some time, and eyes that looked beyond your own, eyes that kind of rummaged around *inside* a person's head, maybe seeking out its owninformation.

"No," he said. "My name is Wilhelm Stern."

The *w* sounded like a *v* and there was almost an *h* between the *s* and the *t*.

"German?" My voice was soft.

He nodded, and now his scrutiny of me had retreated, had drawn back swiftly, a flicker of alarm in his eyes.

I lunged forward, grabbing his neck with both hands, thumbs digging in, trying to join with the fingertips on the other side. He pulled away and I went with him, leaning over the back of his seat, jamming his head against the dashboard. His own hands tried to grab my wrists, but the angle was awkward, and I felt the girl called Muriel tugging at my shoulders, trying to haul me off him.

The driver, Cissie, struck out at me, battering my head with her open fist. *"Leave him be, you bloody fool! It's all over now, there's no point!"* she yelled.

It was no use though—in my hatred I was oblivious to either blows or entreaties.

Stern fought back, but I had the advantage. He pushed at me, but could get no leverage, while Cissie continued to beat my head and arms, now with the heel of her fist.

In her rage Cissie was paying more attention to me than the road ahead and the Ford hit something, something solid and immovable—maybe another tram—and we were spinning round, screeching a dry skid, engine whining while the tires burned off rubber. Then we struck something else and the girls screamed and I shot forward, losing my grip on the German, huffling through the broken windshield, taking whatever glass was left with me. I sprawled on my back on the Ford's long, triangular hood, the rest of the world spinning round me, too soon to know if I was hurt and too dazed to care. Then I slithered off the hood and down the white-painted fender, a slow-motion drift that ended on the road's hard surface. I was vaguely aware of doors opening and legs gathering around me. One of them kicked me, but it wasn't vicious enough to do any damage; more likely it was meant to rouse me. I blinked, more than once, and saw Cissie glaring down at me.

"You stupid bastard," she said, more in pity now than rage. "I told you, the war's over. We can't go on killing each other any more." Her eyes were softened by the beginning of tears.

The other girl, Muriel, knelt close to me. "Are you all right?" She touched a hand to my shoulder.

Stern, the goddamn *Kraut*, was pointing my own gun at me.

I struggled to get up, anger beginning to replace dizziness. I feebly attempted to reach for him, but Muriel shoved me back down against the crashed car. Her voice was quiet though.

"It isn't worth it, don't you see? Your kind of hatred brought us to this."

My hand was shaking as I stabbed a finger towards the German. "No, it was his kind of madness." My words seemed to be squeezed from my chest.

"My friend, if we do not get away from here right now, it will be *their* kind of madness that will kill us all." Stern waved the gun in the air, indicating the general. area behind us.

"Oh my God, they're almost here." Cissie bent down and started pulling at my arm. "We ought to leave you here, you big dope."

Muriel tugged at the other arm and I was up, looking over their shoulders at the advancing vehicles. The Humber was having difficulty squeezing through the gap left between the two trams further down the road, while the Bedford truck was closer, but having problems with a lamppost on the curb it had just mounted. The truck scraped by though, and began to gather speed again, the gunmen leaning on the cab roof pointing excitedly when they saw we were easy prey.

Parts of me were beginning to hurt like hell, my body by now having accumulated a fair share of cuts, bruises, and plain hard knocks; no bones broken though, nothing seriously torn—even where the bullet had ripped the shoulder of my leather jacket there was only grazed skin—so I knew I could function okay. I was still a little dazed, a bit numbed, but it wasn't a problem. I quickly scanned the immediate area, searching for another vehicle to get us away from there, and all I saw was a jumble of snarled wreckage. There'd been a mighty accident here at some time, no doubt caused by panic when the population of London had tried to flee the Blood Death. We might have made our way through, found a car on the other side, hopefully with the key still in the ignition, but the Bedford was almost on us, its occupants whooping with glee. We were shit out of luck.

And then I knew what we had to do. And I felt the blood drain from my face. And my hand was shaking a whole heap more than before when I raised my arm and pointed.

| 3 |

MURIEL WAS WATCHING ME AS THE OTHERS TURNED IN THE DIRECtion I was pointing. Our eyes locked and a faint line appeared in her otherwise smooth brow. There was a question in her gaze.

It was Cissie who put the question though. "The Underground? You want us to go down there?"

Stern was looking puzzled, too.

"They'll never follow us," I said, already moving towards the entrance.

"Of course they will," Cissie snapped back. "And then we'll be trapped."

I paused, taking in all three of them. "Believe me, they won't come after us."

A crash of metal against metal as the Bedford barged past a black Austin, tearing off the little car's white-painted fender in the process.

"If you want to stay alive, get moving!" I yelled, and I guess the urgency—and the fear—in my voice convinced them. A single gunshot from the approaching truck was the only other encouragement they needed. They ran, following me.

Although limping slightly, I was in no serious pain, and was soon inside the cool, twilight ticket hall of Holborn Underground Station. I let the others pass me and took a peek out into the street. The army truck was only twenty yards or so away, now pulling to a screeching halt.

I ducked back into the shadows and made my way towards the ticket office, stepping over dark shapes lying there in the half-light, ignoring them and hoping my new acquaintances were doing the same. The ticket office was a solitary booth erected in front of the opening to the escalators and as I reached for the door I called out: "Grab a mask each. You're gonna need 'em."

The two girls just gawked at me as I yanked open the door, but Stern had caught on; he'd already picked up a small cardboard box from the floor and was busy opening it. He pulled out a gas mask and handed it to Muriel. As I went into the booth he was looking around for more.

A suit of bones sat slumped on a high stool inside the ticket booth, the skull with its leathery skin and empty eye sockets resting sideways on the narrow counter in front of it, thin, mummified hands stretched towards the small pay-window as if reaching for fare money. Long strands of greyish hair hung loose from the tan-colored head and yellowed dentures lay on the shelf at the entrance of the open mouth, this itself guarded by the few remaining teeth, exposed and gumless, like crooked tombstones before a black vault. I was glad the light was poor, everything muted, hard to see.

I'd expected the stench to be worse, but I guess the corruption had run its course long before, the smells of that decay slowly fading, escaping through the ticket window and vents, until only a staleness remained, unpleasant, cloying, but no big deal. I'd say this ticket clerk had been one of the lucky ones: the Blood Death had hit him fast, killing him where he sat while others fled around him, so that the booth had become his personal mausoleum, his solitary, unviolated sepulchre. His mouldering had been his own private affair.

It didn't take long to find what I was looking for. I knew the clerk would have kept a flashlight or lamp close at hand for emergencies and, of course, the Blackout itself. It was a heavy chrome flashlight and I found it in a small corner cupboard just inside the door. I wasn't surprised when I flicked it on and nothing happened. Okay, new batteries. I started pulling out drawers, opening more cupboards, and soon found a whole box of unwrapped Evereadys. It took only seconds to eject the old ones from the flashlight and push in the new, and I held my breath as I switched on. A dim, round light appeared at the other end of the ticket office and I let my breath go in a quick sigh of relief: the batteries were weak, but they'd do. I was out of the booth and shoving the flashlight into the German's hand in an instant.

In the street outside I could see the Bedford truck, Blackshirts jumping down into the road from its back.

"*Gimme the gun,*" I barked at Stern and for a second he pulled away, holding the Colt out of reach, the flashlight in his other hand.

"It's not loaded, for Christ's sake!" I grabbed it from him.

By the time the first Blackshirt had reached the curb just yards from the entrance I'd inserted a new clip and fired off a warning shot. The Blackshirt, and the others following him, ducked instinctively and changed direction, spreading out to take cover behind the walls beside the entrance. Because the Underground station was on a corner there were two accesses, and I hoped they wouldn't have the sense to use the second, smaller one to our right. Two flanks I didn't think I could handle.

"*Take the girls down!*" I shouted, indicating the escalators behind the barriers. "*Get 'em in the subway and wait for me there.*" I gave the Blackshirts another blast to keep them occupied.

"Come with us," begged Cissie as Stern began pushing her and Muriel towards the escalators.

"*Soon as I can!*" I shouted back, then dodged behind the booth to fire off another couple of shots. The Blackshirts started to return fire, but they weren't taking time to aim, afraid of exposing themselves for more than a split second. Funny thing when you're living on borrowed time, as these goons outside were—life becomes even more precious. I knew they weren't going to rush me, that I could hold 'em there for some time; but sooner or later they'd figure a way to flush me out.

I took some well-spaced potshots, just enough to keep their heads down without wasting ammunition, giving the German and the girls time to get downstairs (hoping they'd have the nerve to carry on once they realized what they were descending into). After that I'd have my own problem: making a break for it with no one to cover me.

Well, that problem kind of solved itself.

It happened fast, and it happened without warning. One minute the Blackshirts were keeping out of sight, taking turns to spray bullets my way, filling the ticket hall with thunder, the next the black Humber Estate was roaring through the entrance, hurtling towards me, guns blazing from its side windows like in one of them gangster movies.

I backed away fast, firing from the hip, turning when the Humber crashed into the ticket office and limping towards the barriers, leaping over the nearest rail, using my left hand for support, barely breaking stride on the other side. The Humber had lurched sideways when it hit the solid booth, swinging round and throwing its passengers against one another. Its bodywork hid me from more Blackshirts pouring through the entrance after it, giving me time to reach the top of the frozen stairways.

I didn't need to look to know what lay on those stairs—I'd used another subway as a means of escape almost three years ago and had never wanted to repeat the experience. I also knew the Blackshirts wouldn't follow me down there—they didn't have the balls for it. But the human debris that littered the escalator—all those dead, rotted corpses of men, women, and children who'd tried to flee the Blood Death, thinking that the disease, the toxins, the chemicals, the goddamn *visitation,* whatever it was that Hitler had sent over in his revenge rockets, would never reach them in the tunnels beneath the city—I knew they'd be blocking the stairways, that they'd perished as they ran, and their skeletal limbs would now snag me as I went by, their heaped bodies would bar my way, forcing me to stumble through or to climb over them, giving the gunmen above time to find me in the darkness with a lucky bullet, or a hail of lucky bullets, and slow me down for good. So I forgot about taking the stairs.

I leapt up onto the center ramp between escalators and slid down on my butt, kicking aside any stiffs slumped over the rail as I went, gliding down like a kid on a sleigh, slowing myself by grabbing the middle lamp columns, controlling the descent just enough to keep me from taking a tumble.

Below I could see the dim light of the flashlight, the others waiting for me, the German having horse sense enough not to direct the beam at me. Glass from one of the dead lamps exploded as I swept by, showering me with fragments, and the light at the bottom of the stairs instantly vanished. I hoped Stern hadn't been hit (I had my own plans for him), but had taken the two girls into the safety of one of the platform entrances. I lost control then, plummeting faster than I could cope with, my trunk trying to overtake my legs so that I began to turn. More bullets split the air, keeping me company, but I must have been just about invisible as I slid further into the blackness. The automatic was back inside my jacket holster, where I'd shoved it before the ride, and I clamped a wrist against it as I began to spin off the ramp. The next thing I knew I was falling, toppling off the slide and onto the stairs, soft (but brittle) things there breaking my fall, cushioning the rest of my uncontrolled descent.

Probably I cried out—I don't recall—as I tumbled down, rolling onto things that seemed to collapse at my touch, until I arrived at the bottom in an avalanche of corpses.

I lay there, breathless and dizzy; and horrified. Something scratchy brushed against my cheek and I didn't like to guess what. The thought came to me anyway and I panicked, thrashing out at the darkness, pushing the dried husk away and kicking at anything within kicking distance. The smell whacked me then, and I choked, gagged, fought back the swelling nausea. Until I realized it was all in my mind.

Sure, the air down there in that huge mausoleum was foul, but it had more to do with staleness than rotting bodies. The corruption had run its course, you see, and the corpses had deteriorated as much as they ever would under these dry and stagnant conditions. When I'd first ventured into one of these places it had been in the early months after the holocaust and the dead were still decomposing, the stench unbearable; I should have understood by now that once the organs and internal body tissue have putrefied and finally disintegrated, there's little else that can happen—the body can only become a mummified shell. No, the stench had been in my mind, what I'd expected. And the horror was not in the atmosphere, but in the *presence* of so many cadavers gathered together in this black void.

"Hoke. Can you hear me? We are over here."

It sounded like the German's voice, but it was muffled, distorted by the gas mask the speaker was wearing. The light, dim and comfortless, was coming from a passage not far away.

"Are you hit?"

Ignoring him, I picked myself up and, still crouched, peeked over the curved stair rail at the light from the top of the escalators. Bright flashes and ear-deafening explosions sent me scrabbling towards the light, the sounds amplified by the tiled walls. Vague heaps on the floor did their damnedest to trip me as I went and other bundles I knocked into, carcasses locked tight in sitting or kneeling positions, toppled over to lay there in those same attitudes of rapid death. Bullets ricocheted off walls or found softer targets around me and, with only a few feet to go, I took a desperate dive into the passageway where the German and the two girls were hiding. I lay there sprawled and gasping bad air and would have stayed that way a lot longer if Cissie hadn't knelt beside me and pulled at my shoulder. She said something, but it was difficult to understand because of her mask. She tried again and I shook my head.

"No, they didn't hit me," I told her. I heaved myself up and the effort seemed to be getting harder each time I made it.

The light, weak though it was, hurt my eyes and I pushed the flashlight away. In its beam I could make out more bodies filling the passageway and I wondered if the girls would have the nerve to journey among them. Even though the stench was nowhere as bad as I thought it would be, I decided not to tell them they didn't need the masks. Their vision would be restricted through the lenses, especially in this poor light, and the gas masks might even make them feel insulated from what lay around them. I had no idea if my thinking was correct, but what the hell, it didn't matter.

"Let's get away from here, fast as we can," I said to Stern, taking the flashlight from him. Like before with the gun, there was some resistance, but it was minimal and quickly over.

"Are they following us?" he asked, his mask, with its stubby filter unit and big circular eye-pieces making him resemble a creature from another world.

"No, they won't come down here," I said, looking at the two girls.

"How can you be sure?" His voice was distant behind the mask, but his anxiety was plain enough.

"Maybe they're afraid of ghosts," I replied. Stupid. The girls clutched each other. "Come on," I added hastily, "let's get away from the noise."

In fact, the Blackshirts had already given up shooting, although we could hear their shouts, hollow and mocking, drifting down

and finding us where we hid. I moved on, the others in tow, nego-
tiating a passage through the tangled heaps and ignoring the
noises from behind us. We soon came to a steep stairway, more
bodies strewn over the steps.

"Where are we going?"

The question might have come from Muriel, but it was difficult to tell with the masks. Besides, I was ahead of them, concentrating on finding space for my feet on the steps. For the moment
I didn't want to answer her.

When I reached the bottom I shone the light back at the trio,
keeping it at their feet so they could find a way through. A
leathered head, shrunken and brown, seemed to follow their
passing through empty eye sockets; an arm, only remnants of
dried gristle clinging to its hand and wrist, slithered down a step
or two, disturbed by their progress, a single gray finger pointing
the way. I tried to keep these sights from them, but they needed
the low light so they wouldn't trip; wouldn't fall headlong into the
human garbage around them.

Cissie was in the lead, sensible flat-heeled, crêpe rubber-soled
shoes shifting through the debris, arms raised and fists clenched
for balance. For the first time I noticed she was wearing dark
slacks—blue, I think—and that while not as slim as the other girl,
her figure was trim enough, attractive even. Jesus, I *had* been too
long on my own—this was hardly the moment for that kind of
appreciation. I guess I must have lost concentration, because the
light wavered and Cissie lost her footing. With a tiny yelp she
came toppling towards me.

I caught her easily and held her there in my arms until her
panic subsided. She held on to me too and seemed reluctant to
let go.

She touched my face. "Why aren't you wearing a mask?" she
asked, voice muffled and eyes vague behind the misted glass of
her own mask.

I made a decision. It'd be tougher for them, but we'd all make
better headway if they could see more clearly. "You can take your
gas masks off," I said, pulling her aside so that I could direct the
beam back onto the stairs. I still held on to her with one arm.

"What did you say?" Muriel was frozen there in the light.

"I said you can take off the masks," I repeated more loudly.

"But the . . ." Cissie shook her head.

"It isn't so bad. These bodies decomposed a long time ago."

She pulled off her mask and stiffened when she breathed in the stale, tainted air. The snood at the back of her hair had come loose with the mask and she pulled it away entirely, shaking her head so that her locks swung free around her face. By the time Muriel joined us, Cissie had become more used to the atmosphere; or at least, had become less tense. Fortunately, beyond the circle of light from the flashlight It was too dark for her to take in very much. Muriel tugged off her mask as well and I watched her face wrinkle as she gasped in the air.

"Some light would be helpful." The German, his gas mask already removed and hanging by his side, was watching us from midway down the stairs. He came down swiftly when I swung the beam in his direction.

Close to me, he said: "What is your plan? Do we wait here until they are gone?"

His English was almost perfect, but again that v instead of a w, so aggravatingly consistent, had the muscles in my chest tightening, my anger boiling towards eruption. I barely held it in check.

But it wasn't only hatred for this German, this relic of the Master Race, that kept me silent. I didn't want to make decisions for these people. I was too used to being on my own, making choices for myself (Cagney was of an independent kind of nature). I didn't want anyone depending on me.

"Hoke, come on, tell us what we should do." Cissie was tugging at my jacket.

I mentally cursed them for coming into my life, even though they'd saved it. "We could wait them out," I said finally, "or we could go into the tunnels."

"*No!*" Muriel's reaction had a lick of hysteria to it. "We can't go any further. I won't. The platforms . . ."

We all knew what she meant.

"I'm with her," Cissie agreed. "God, this is bad enough, but what else could be in there?" She indicated the platform entrance.

Only plenty more of the same, I was about to say when something happened that took away any choice. From a distance, up the stairs and back along the passageway, there came the sound of

breaking glass instantly followed by a kind of muffled *whoomph.*
Then another: same sound, smashed glass followed by that
shushed explosion of air. As soon as a bright orange glow lit up
the top of the stairs I knew what those sounds were.

"They're using gasoline bombs," I said almost to myself.

The Blackshirts had tried to flush me out before with these
home-made bombs of bottles filled with fuel, a rag stuck into the
neck, then set alight, but I'd always been lucky—and too quick.
They'd either made them quickly, scavenging bottles from the
street or shops, syphoning off gasoline from fuel tanks of vehicles,
or they'd brought the cocktails ready-made with them. I thought
I heard their taunts, their voices carrying easily down the funnel
of the stairway, but the fire had already taken on its own life, passing from one dried husk-like body to the next, incinerating each
one as it went along, its muffled roar coming our way. Popping
sounds reached us, sharp, explosive retorts, as bones cracked and
gases ignited. The fire had an abundance of fuel to feed on, a trail
of kindling that led directly to us.

"Okay, there's your answer," I told them. "We can't stay here."

"But where can we go?" Cissie wasn't fooling anybody—we all
knew where.

"Like I said, into the tunnels."

I turned away, tired of the argument. It was their decision
now.

A huge billow of black smoke swept down the stairs towards us
and as I glanced up I saw the flames were not far behind. Reflections flickered on the walls and waves of heat washed over us.
Almost as an afterthought I checked the big enamel route map at
our backs, the flashlight hardly necessary now, and it told me
what I needed to know. The girls began coughing as more smoke
spilled down the stairway, rolling off the ceiling and curling down
the walls.

"Put your masks back on," I ordered, and they did as they
were told, following me as I backed out onto the platform. But
the German had dropped his mask on the stairs and instead of
finding another—there were plenty of masked corpses around
us—he went back to retrieve it. A few strides took him halfway up
the stairs, and as he grabbed it the first real flames appeared
above him. Bodies around him appeared to twitch and flinch in

the unstable light, as if the advancing firestorm was making them uneasy. An illusion, though; macabre, and scary, but no more than a trick of the light. Their clothes began to smoulder.

I gave Stern a warning shout, but it was already too late. As he straightened, pulling on the gas mask as he did so, there was an explosion of fire behind him, trapped gases and flammable material joining forces to give the inferno a special boost. I'm not sure if the German jumped instinctively, or the blast of scorching air threw him forward, but suddenly he was airborne, arms outstretched, back arched.

He was lucky—the flames never got the chance to engulf him completely. He landed on the floor, his jacket alight, and I rushed forward to roll him over, pinning him against the tiles and smothering the flames. Stern didn't struggle; he seemed to know exactly what I was doing. If he hadn't been a *Kraut*, I might have admired his nerve.

The heat from the stairs was unbearable as I dragged him over bodies out onto the platform, the flames above us spreading under the roof, rolling down like a raging river of fire, the ceiling its bed, its torrent of boiling yellows and reds and blacks fierce enough to scorch the eyeballs. It had a kind of terrifying beauty as it hit the wall at the bottom of the stairs and curled to the floor, devouring the dead things lying there before rearing up again in a huge fireball that ballooned outwards.

"Get back!" I yelled, and we all hit the deck together as the flames poured out at us.

I felt my hair crackle as I sprawled among the corpses filling the platform. Smoke created its own menace, blinding and choking, billowing from the opening as the flames retreated for the moment, falling back to consolidate, to feed before progressing. Now it was Stern helping me, pulling me up and away from the worst of the smoke, his mask giving him the advantage. I was retching, lungs filled with the black stuff, eyes streaming, and I felt other hands grab me.

A gas mask was tugged over my head and, although still coughing smoke dust, I caught the faint whiff of old disinfectant under the stink of rubber. I blinked my eyes rapidly and saw the blurred image of Cissie standing in front of me. She was pointing down the platform, her other hand on my arm, and I nodded in an exaggerated way, bowing my shoulders as well as my head. We moved off awkwardly, me still limping, going as fast as we could, like survivors of a subterranean battlefield, the conflict long over, only smoke and the dead left behind. We passed by cots pushed close to the curved platform wall, and bedding laid out on the concrete floor itself. Among those rumpled rags, filling every space, was all kinds of domestic stuff: kettles, fold-away chairs, suitcases, books, even a wind-up gramophone. A small wooden clotheshorse still stood, its hanging rags once a screen for some modest family and probably, like other carefully placed items along the platform, a marker for regular users of the shelter, a sign of territorial claim. A kid's doll, eyes wide as if still terrorized by the carnage around it. A crushed bowler hat, a single boot lying on its side, a pair of spectacles, lenses still intact. There were even one or two tiny portable gas or paraffin cookers, the kind used for "brew-ups" or warming babies' bottles, smuggled in by families who enjoyed their home comforts. An accordion propped up against a cot bed, a baby's gas mask—oversized and ugly, like a deep-sea diver's helmet—lying empty on a blanket next to it. Newspapers strewn across huddled bodies, faded headlines as irrelevant as the advertisements for gin or Brylcreem they shared the page with.

And the corpses. Avoiding them, stumbling over them, pulling them aside when they blocked our way. Thousands of them it seemed, there in the flickering light. Empty shells that had once been living beings, most of these people fleeing here when the rockets fell from the skies and others around them—in the streets, the cafés, the offices, the buses and trams and cars—started dropping dead before their eyes. A good many had probably neither seen nor heard the vengeance weapons fall, but the Blitz had conditioned them to seek shelter whenever the sirens sounded. Yet when they did, when they sought refuge in the street shelters, the park trenches, and even deep down in the subways, the Blood Death had followed, hunted them out, touching every one and poisoning their life's flow so that it hardened, congealed, became like concrete in their veins.

Only a special few escaping. Others living on, but for a limited time; dying, just taking longer to do so.

We hurried through all this, each of us holding on to our

emotions, following the dim white safety lines painted along the platforms, four feet and eight feet from the edge, all of us observing but cold to the horror, more than just panic overriding our compassion. Skull faces, eyes long since liquefied, the skin tight and dark like stretched parchment, torn in places—we saw it all, but quickly learned to focus on nothing.

I led the way, never allowing the weak flashlight beam to linger in one place too long, moving it away from the worst sights, finding a path through the slaughter, always aware that the fire was stealing up on us, progress helped by the body heaps. Its advance scout, foul, swilling smoke, threatened to overwhelm us despite our gas masks and I quickened the pace, aware that the train tunnel was not far. The smoke would follow us into the tunnel, but there would be fewer corpses to slow us down (and less material to burn). The flashlight showed more bodies lying on the tracks below and I quickly gave up the idea of using that level as an easier route.

Right about then a scream grabbed my attention.

I turned, swinging the flashlight around, and found Muriel on the floor, body stretched out but head and shoulders raised, supported by her elbows. She wrenched off her mask and began to scream even louder.

I was an idiot, but I guess it was a natural reaction: I shone the light on the cause of her hysterics.

The small body was lying beside a suitcase—I think the case must have concealed the child as I'd walked by, Muriel's outstretched arm knocking it over when she fell—and only tattered rags still clung to what was left of it. It was easy to tell that the little girl's eyes had been pulled out rather than dissolved, because hard ridges that were the remnants of tendrils trailed down her sunken cheeks; and where her belly should have been there was only a gaping, empty hole, all the organs gone, and although I didn't look too hard or too long, I couldn't help but notice that other parts of her were missing too, only stained bone left behind. I closed my eyes for a second or two, but the sight was replaced by a memory—*a terrible, sickening memory*—and I opened them again.

Oddly—*Jesus Christ, bizarrely*—Muriel reached forward to touch the long dull, hair that lay around the remains of the child's face, as if to stroke it, a gesture of pity and regret, I guess. But the hair came away in Muriel's hand and that was when her screams became wilder and her body began to shudder.

Taking her by the arm, I eased her away, lifting her so that Cissie could hold her, comfort her, and as the cries echoed around the Underground station I tore off my mask and quickly ran the light over the mounds of human remains nearby. I saw what I had dreaded.

Partially consumed corpses were nothing new to me, yet revulsion—and yeah, hatred, sheer bloody *hatred* for the scavengers who'd done this thing—filled my gut and set my own body shaking. I controlled it though, controlled my emotions and my shivering limbs, despite what lay around us, despite those torn and mutilated victims, their wounds—*their ruptured skins and absent parts*—not at first obvious in the altering light of the fire and swirling smoke, so easily missed among the shifting shadows.

Shifting shadows . . . At first I thought that's all they were. Little movements among the human remains and the litter. But they were too furtive, sometimes too brisk. And here and there tiny bright reflections shone back.

"Come on, we can't stay here!" I shouted at the others, jerking the light away, aiming its beam towards the end of the platform. *"D'you hear me? The fire's getting closer! Let move on!"*

I grabbed Muriel's wrist and pulled her away from Cissie, leading her onwards, not gentle at all, but let's say determined, channelling my horror into anger. I held the flashlight high, keeping its light off the floor, stumbling through the wreckage, but still catching those little, scurrying movements in the corners of my eyes. The girl was limp, so I had to drag her along until Cissie caught up with us and supported her, making the going easier. Soon the smoke was blurring my vision, its acrid smell scraping at the back of my throat. Behind me, Muriel was choking, her body bent over, but I wasn't gonna ease up, I wasn't gonna hunt around in that mess for more gas masks.

I threw a fast look over my shoulder, but there was too much smoke and my eyes were too teared-up for me to see any more than a blustering hellfire filling the station. By then we were nearly at the end of the platform and obstacles were fewer. Dense smoke cured against the facing wall, but I could see the black

hole of the tunnel next to it, a ramp leading down. Letting go of
Muriel I wiped my eyes with the grimy fingers of one hand, then
squinted into the dark. There were bodies blocking the ramp,
more of them lying between the tracks below.

"Help me with her," I shouted at Cissie as I stood at the platform's edge. I shone the weak light into her face for a moment,
and beyond the windows of the mask her eyes widened. I thought
hysteria might overwhelm her too, but she just nodded, steering
Muriel closer to the tracks, then holding her there. Hand on the
platform's lip, I hopped down, trying not to land on anything
mushy, wincing when I landed on my damaged leg. There was
less smoke at that level and, before reaching up for Muriel, I
aimed the beam into the tunnel. The light didn't stretch very far,
enough only to reveal more victims scattered there, dim heaps
that were more rags than human remains.

Cissie guided Muriel into my upstretched arms and I lowered
her onto the tracks. She leaned against me, her slim body racked
by coughing, as I turned back for Cissie, who followed without
hesitation, first sitting on the platform and swinging her legs over
before dropping down next to me. The German was crouched on
one knee, looking even more alien behind his mask, and he held
something towards me, something he'd found among the platform litter.

I took the oil lamp from him, a red thing with four windows
and a stiff hook at the top to hold it by. It must've belonged to a
station guard or someone who used the place as a regular shelter
during the war, and the question was, would it still function or
was it dry and useless? Although charred a dark brown, the wick
looked okay, and I gave the lamp a shake close to my ear, listening
for oil. Liquid slurped around inside.

Okay. No time to try it now, but it'd come in handy later. Stern
had joined us and as I returned the lamp to him the station
brightened and sharp, fresh heat washed over us. We all ducked,
but the flare-up was short, as if maybe one of those portable
cookers had exploded, adding to the conflagration. The smoke
went crazy for a while, billowing down the curved walls in murky
waves, swirling around us so that Muriel and I were left blinded
and reeling around in its choking thickness.

Something caught hold of me and started pushing, and it took a moment for me to realize it was either the German or Cissie, both of them protected from the worst of the smoke by their gas masks. Bent double and half-suffocated, I allowed myself to be led. We staggered into the tunnel, using the rails at our feet as guides, the hand at my elbow firm, supporting, keeping me upright when I stumbled, dragging me onwards when a coughing fit threatened collapse. From the strength of the grip I guessed it was the German holding on to me and would've shrugged him off if I hadn't been too busy retching.

Then the smoke thinned out and I could see again. I rubbed my eyes and realized it was darker, much darker here, and cooler, too. We were well inside the tunnel and up ahead it was so black we could have been on the slip road to Hades. It was damp, too, as if water was seeping through the old, neglected brickwork, the dank, musty smell strong enough to compete with the drifting smoke and fumes from the station.

I leaned on my knees and coughed up the dust I'd swallowed, blinking my eyes to get rid of the sting, wishing I had a gallon of beer to soothe my raw throat.

"Are you ready to walk on?" The German had removed his mask once more and was squinting anxiously at the tunnel's arched entrance and the advancing flames beyond.

"Sure, I'm okay," I said, running a sleeve across my mouth, no gratitude implied.

Cissie ceased tending her friend for a moment to say something. She, too, took off her mask when she realized we hadn't understood a word, and tried again.

"I said, where does this tunnel go to?"

"What the hell does it matter right now?" I replied. "You think we should wait for the fire?"

The light was shining right on her and I watched her lips tighten, her eyes blaze.

"Who the—" she began.

"Cissie, he's right. We must keep going." Muriel was still sagging slightly, one hand on Cissie's shoulder for support. She held a tiny handkerchief, not much bigger than a Wills cigarette card, to her mouth, and she was still shaking, little cough-spasms hunching her shoulders.

Cissie clamped her jaw tight, but the annoyance was still there

in her eyes. When she spoke again, she barely parted her teeth.
"All right. But, mister, you and me are filling out fast."

I couldn't help it, it wasn't the time, but I grinned back at
her. She looked good and mad, her face all sooted up, big hazel
eyes glaring, but I saw now she was young, maybe twenty,
twenty-one, and at that moment she had the angry-stern look of
a mother whose kid was gonna get one hell of a beating when
she got him home. I guess my grin got her more riled, because
she stomped off into the shadows ahead without waiting for any
of us.

Muriel threw me a reproving look and set off after her. The
German followed without comment, lamp in one hand, mask in
the other.

My shrug was for my own benefit—there was no one else
around—and I limped after them, shining the dismal light into
the darkness ahead to help them find their way. I was soon in the
lead again, warning the others of the "obstacles" laid between and
across the tracks whenever I came upon them. The atmosphere
this far along wasn't healthy, but it was breathable, and I assumed
much of the smoke was escaping through air shafts that we
couldn't see. The ground began to dip and it wasn't long before
we were treading through puddles, and then what felt like a shallow, stagnant pool, the water filthy black and oily in the light from
the flashlight. A lot of these tunnels had been flooded during last
year's awful winter and I guess we were lucky most of the water
had drained away from this one. In the distance behind us we
could hear the muted *rumple* of the fire, but when I looked back
I could only see a dull, reddish tinge to the darkness, a soft kind
of hue that pulsated almost benignly; somewhere along the way
we had rounded a slight curve in the tunnel.

Abruptly, the flashlight dimmed even more, revived, then settled at a weaker level than before. The batteries were fading fast.
I brought my little troop to a halt.

"Let's take a look at that lamp," I said to the German.

"By all means." Stern came forward and passed me the
square-shaped oil lamp. "And perhaps you will now tell us where
this tunnel leads to and how long our journey will be."

His English was almost perfect, but the *will* sounded like *vill*
and the *where* like *vare*—he spoke like Conrad Veidt as a Nazi

spy in one of those war propaganda movies—and it steamed me up plenty. I held tight though, biding my time.

Lifting one of the glass windows at the side of the lamp I shone the light directly at the wick inside. It looked okay, enough there to burn. As I passed the flashlight over to Stern and searched for my Zippo with my free hand, I told them about the tunnel and where it would take us.

"And how do you know these people who chased us will not be waiting there for us to emerge?"

Vaiting there. My jaw muscles clenched.

Cissie surprised me by speaking up. "They wouldn't know which tunnel we took. Plenty of Tube lines run through Holborn—we could come up anywhere."

"She's right." I found the lighter and flicked it on. "Besides, they probably think they got us with the fire." I held the small flame up to see their faces. Muriel looked about ready to fold.

"But how long is this tunnel?" she said in a quiet voice. "I don't know if . . ."

"You'll make it. It's the shortest route we could've taken."

"For a Yank you seem to know your way around." There was still some resentment in Cissie's voice, as well as some breathlessness.

"I had a good guide once. Someone who was proud of her city."

Silence then from the girls; I guess they'd caught something in my tone. But the German was becoming agitated.

"Then, as you say, we must keep moving. This place is not good."

I ignored him, tilting the lamp and touching the lighter flame to the wick. Before it had the chance to ignite, faint sounds came to us, too distant to make out what they were. The sounds were growing louder though.

We all looked in the direction of the fire.

I'd heard this kind of noise in the past, but couldn't remember where or when. The volume was turning up, as if the source was drawing closer. A hand closed around my arm and I found Muriel beside me, body tensed rigid, the whites of her eyes shining dully in the gloom. Then it came to me, where I'd heard such a racket before.

Although there were fewer animals kept in the London Zoo during the Blitz years of the war, the more dangerous kind even being put down in case they escaped while an air raid was in progress, Sally had taken me there more than once when I was on leave, enjoying the sight of some of those exotic creatures more than I did, I think. One time we'd wandered into an aviary and something had set the birds off—a low-flying aircraft, as I recall. The explosion of noise was incredible, all those different species of bird splitting the air with their gabble—a bedlam medley of panic, anger, fright, and maybe just plain comfort calls to their partners, who knows? We'd clamped our hands over our ears, but the hullabaloo had still come through, so we ran out of there laughing—we laughed at a lot of things in those days—leaving the birds to their riot. Even from a distance we could hear them, kicking up hell, screeching their tiny lungs out.

And that was the kind of sound I was hearing now. Not the same, because birds didn't live in underground passages, never did, never would. No, these sounds were similar, but different. Someone ran an ice cube up my spine.

Muriel pressed against me and I felt her draw in a sharp breath. Cissie moved closer to the both of us.

Squealing, that's what it was. Not birds' chittering. Squealing. Like high-pitched screams. Hundreds, maybe thousands, of them.

The light down the tunnel grew brighter. Fluttered, kind of. And then the first few appeared.

Small fireballs coming our way. Little units of run-amok blazes. Lighting the darkness as they came.

4

"WHAT ARE THEY?"

Muriel's hold on me was painful, but I ignored it.

"Move back!" I yelled, following my own advice and dragging the girl with me. It was hard to take our eyes off the fiery horde—there was something mesmerizing about these miniature infernos, some of them rising up the walls and falling back when they got so far, others spinning in the air to land on the tracks where they burned like tiny beacons, but most streaking towards us as if launched from some ancient war machine—and soon we were tripping over the human remains strewn around in the darkness. That's when we got wise and turned to run like hell along the tunnel, Cissie and the German a couple of yards ahead of Muriel and me. An anxious backward glance told me it was a race we could never win—the fireballs were nearly on us. I'd thought we could outrun 'em, that they'd be consumed by the fires that rode their backs long before they could catch up with us, but I was wrong, they kept coming and we kept running.

Dirty water splashed at our feet as high-pitched squeals filled the air. In the unsteady and almost useless light of the flashlight carried by the German I could see shadows here and there along the tunnel walls; it didn't take long for me to figure out they were safety recesses used by Underground workers to slip into whenever a train went by. Stern had noticed them too; he suddenly stopped and threw himself into one.

It would have left us almost blind if the other lights hadn't closed in on us. I reached forward for Cissie, caught hold, and pushed both her and Muriel into the nearest opening, crowding

48

in with them and pressing them against the back wall. I could feel them trembling, and Christ, I was shaking some myself.

The little burning creatures sped by, squealing their agony, the water they rushed through too shallow to douse the flames on their bodies. Some of them rolled over onto their backs so that steam and smoke hissed off them; they squirmed in front of us, shrieks echoing around the brick walls, until their roasted bodies gave up and lay still, the occasional twitch nothing more than their final death-throes. Muriel turned away and Cissie buffed her head into my shoulder when they both realized what the creatures were.

But I took pleasure in watching the rats burn. I may have even smiled there in the flickering shadows as their fire-ravaged bodies writhed in the black liquid between the track and their thin screams tore through the darkness, and their sharp, ugly snouts stretched and their jaws yawed, showing razor teeth, and their clawed limbs quivered until they crisped and flamed and became twisted, blackened stumps. Yeah, I'm sure I smiled, and I remembered too, remembered what these surviving scavengers had done, what they'd fed on all these years . . .

Some died in front of us, others scurried onwards, still aflame, dying as they ran, lighting the tunnel ahead as if showing us the way. I kicked out at one that came too close, sending it toppling backwards, flames turned to smoke by the water, but extinguished too late to save it. The rat spasmed, twitched, and I wanted to blast it with the Colt—I wanted to blast all of them—not out of mercy but out of revulsion, loathing, hating the creature in the way I hated the German, both of them species of the same kind, vermin who'd lost the fight to walk this earth.

But I held still, closed down my emotions as I'd learned to do over the years. It wasn't easy—it never was—but I coped.

Pretty soon the rats' death-wails became fainter, faded altogether, and their thrashing lessened, finally stopped. Their bodies lay scattered along the tracks, small funeral pyres that slowly dimmed, burning themselves out until only a few feeble blazes sputtered there in the dusk. We could still hear the distant sounds of those which had fled further into the tunnel, but eventually only the stink remained. Hell, the air down here was foul enough, all ventilation systems long since quit and no trains left to push out the staleness as they passed through; now, with drifting smoke and the stench of cooked meat, the atmosphere was almost unbreathable.

I felt Muriel sobbing behind me, the sounds suppressed but the body jerks uncontrolled, and the other one, Cissie, lifted her head from my shoulder and leaned back against the side of the alcove.

"It's all right, Mu," she said, rubbing her friend's back with a comforting hand. "We're safe now, it's all over."

There was no point in persuading her otherwise.

The German stepped back into view, the flashlight in his hand not much more than an orange orb, its beam barely penetrating the darkness. I heard him coughing and watched as the little ball of light danced in the air.

Joining him on the track I fumbled for the Zippo, found it and crouched, balancing the lamp on a rail as I did so. I lifted the lamp's glass side and flicked on the lighter.

"We cannot linger here," the German said between coughs. "We shall be overcome if we do not find a way out soon."

"There's only one way, and that's straight ahead," I answered, putting flame to the wick. It didn't catch at first, so I held the lighter there, concentrating hard, as if serious contemplation would encourage the waxed cord to kindle. Eventually the flame took and the light grew bright. I grunted, glad that *something* was going my way; it'd been an untidy day so far.

The sound of Muriel's weeping distracted me and I held the lamp towards the nook where the two women still sheltered. Cissie was holding her weeping friend in her arms, patting her back soothingly and murmuring comforts.

"Please tell them there is no time for this."

The German obviously believed they would take more notice of an ally than a foe. Probably—I wanted to think so—he was right.

"Listen," I said, calmly as I could, "we gotta go. The fire might not reach us here, but smoke's gonna draw through the tunnel like a chimney. It's not far to the next station—twenny minutes' walk at most, I figure, maybe less—so let's get going and save the bawling for later."

I hadn't meant that last remark to sound harsh—really—but I guess it came out that way. Cissie fixed me with a stony look.

"Can't you see she's had enough?" she said to me and I nodded in agreement.

"Lady, the whole fucking world's had enough, but still it goes on. Now you can decide for yourselves—stay here and choke to death, or follow me. 'S up to you."

I turned away and stepped over a smouldering rodent in the water at my feet, passing by the German, who stood there, stiff-faced and hard as rock. I soon heard his footsteps splashing after me.

"You bastards."

It was coldly said, no anger and scarcely a trace of resentment in Cissie's voice. Just a statement of fact, I suppose you'd say, and not far wrong at that.

I kept going, holding the lamp high, eyes fixed on the way ahead, or at least as far as I could see. There were still small flames moving away from us in the distance, some of those vermin refusing to lay down and die, and I couldn't help wondering how many of these creatures had survived the Blood Death, living on to enjoy the easy pickings of the aftermath. The medics and scientists had known the blood-groupings of animals were not the same as humans, yet still the death rate was comparable to that of mankind's; some research on our differences might have helped, but there'd been no time, no time at all.

I snapped back into the here and now when I heard the two women plodding through the water behind us. To my relief the sobs had stopped and Cissie was keeping her opinions of me and the *Kraut* to herself. The flashlight finally gave up the ghost, its light fading to nothing, and Stern tossed it away with a muttered curse in German. The clatter the metal flashlight made as it bounced off the wall made us all jump and although the thought of shooting him there and then was appealing, I kept the Colt tucked inside the jacket holster and waded onwards.

Pretty soon the water level had dropped away and only separate puddles spread before us, but the atmosphere itself had become even more foul. Smoke had been with us all the way but in the main had stayed close to the roof; now it was curling downwards, even coming back at us as if something was blocking the tunnel up ahead. It became harder to breathe and I told Stern to give his gas mask to Muriel, advising Cissie to put hers on, too.

"I lost it back there," she informed me stiffly as though really it was none of my business. "I don't think they help very much anyway," she added, just to let me know she felt no embarrassment.

Well, they were pretty handy when we were in the station, I thought, but I wasn't going to argue. I didn't have the energy.

Stern waited for Muriel to catch up, then handed her his mask. "If the smoke becomes too much . . ." he said, and she nodded gratefully.

I looked to the front again and had gone no more'n a couple of yards before I saw what was blocking the tunnel. Some of the smoke was rising over the top of the train, more seeping around its sides; but a lot of it was coming straight back at us.

Waving a hand in front of me in a vain attempt to clear the way a little, I told the others about the blockage. It took a few seconds to reach the train and I stood on tiptoe to peer up into its closet-sized cab, debating whether or not to climb inside and use the carriages themselves to travel through the next part of the tunnel. The others gathered behind me and I went round to the side, holding the lamp high enough for me to see into the windows.

Nothing should have shocked me by now—three years of living among sights that were the stuff of nightmares should have conditioned me—but the skull-head that returned my stare, with its black hollow eyes and gaping grin, made me jump back in fright. Stupidly, I'd expected the train to be empty. Of course passengers had been travelling on the Underground network all over the city when the disease had struck, the Blood Death drifting down into the tunnels, seeking out its victims like some predator roaming the burrows of the earth, and the Dead Man's Handle had jammed on as soon as the train driver had slumped over, cutting the circuit so that the carriages had come to a halt, staying there in the darkness while passengers died one by one. How many had escaped? I wondered. How many of the AB-negs—if there'd been any on board—had managed to crawl out into the tunnels and make their way back to the surface, only to wish they'd died with fellow travelers below?

The skull resting against the window still wore a guard's cap, its peak tilted by the glass to a rakish angle so that, with its unrestricted grin, the skeleton appeared to have kept its sense of humor. I didn't get the joke though, and was ready to unravel as I went back to the others. I was about to tell 'em to keep their eyes low when they passed by the carriages, but I never got the chance.

The flash that swept through the tunnel was like sheet lightning, its glare bleaching everything white before blinding us with its brilliance, the thunderclap that followed a split second later shaking the walls and deafening us all. Searing air blasted around us, but we were protected by the carriages we cowered behind, only our legs feeling a deflected part of the heat. The world around us may have become silent as we fell to our knees, but it continued to spasm and shake so that we sprawled between the tracks, bodies stretched, hands over our ears or eyes.

I'm not sure if I felt or sensed the train lurch, but an instinct sent me scrabbling forward onto the girls, using my weight to hold them still until the wheels shuddered to a stop. As I blinked some vision back into my dazzled eyes, I became aware that the air was suddenly cleansed, the smoke and filth pushed away by the blast; but even as I rubbed at my eyes and my hearing began to return, grime and dust, along with brickwork, started to fall from the ceiling and walls. Head still reeling, senses floating, I guessed what had caused the explosion further down the Tube line, but now was not the time to mull it over—although we'd been shielded from the worst of the blast, we were now in a worse predicament than before. And unfortunately it was getting worse still by the second.

I staggered to my feet, grabbing the lamp that was on its side but still burning as I rose, then swung round to peer into the flickering shadows behind us. The shadowy figure of the German was leaning against the train, his head turning from left to right as if he were trying to shake some sense back into it; and beyond him the train itself was burning, the flames further along the carriages contained by the walls and ceiling of the tunnel, but spreading fast towards us. Stern was abruptly lost from sight as great clouds of smoke swept between us.

The very air felt scorched, dried out, and suddenly it was hard to draw breath.

"*Back!*" I managed to squawk, but I doubt any of the others heard me.

I pushed the girls, herding them away from this new threat,

and Stern was not slow to figure it out for himself. He was soon alongside us as we staggered through the smoke and falling dirt. He held Muriel's arm while I hung on to Cissie, and as a tight group we stumbled back along the track, not thinking ahead, fear and heat driving us on, the thick, choking smoke swilling around us, increasing our panic, until it was exhaustion, not common sense, that slowed us down after a hundred yards or so. Muriel dropped to her knees first and Cissie followed her down.

Stern attempted to drag Muriel up again, but she was bent double, gagging on fumes, her body a dead weight.

I crouched close to Cissie. "Come on, we'll choke to death if we stay here." Even to me my voice sounded faint, kind of trapped inside my own head, but I think she heard me. She tried to tug herself free.

Her voice was distant, but at least I could hear her too; it seemed the explosion hadn't caused permanent damage to our eardrums. "Where can we go?" she asked. "We're between two fires, you bloody fool, and it's your fault. You made us come down here."

She had a point. But hell, what other choice had there been?

I scanned around, up the tunnel, down the tunnel, and wasn't encouraged. Out of the fire and into the inferno, I told myself. Some days were like that.

The German, his back against the wall, was coughing so violently I thought his gut might burst, and Muriel's arched figure was heaving, her throat rasping as she fought to draw in poisoned air. Back there the whole tunnel was alight, clouds of rolling smoke softening the blaze, and in the other direction, towards the station, even more smoke tumbled towards us, a thick, curling wall of it, so dense it looked solid.

I hauled myself up, but my legs barely supported me. My energy was sapped and my head was dizzy from lack of pure oxygen. A veil seemed to be drawing over my mind, and it wasn't unpleasant; no, it seemed like an escape, a retreat from the horror all around us in this black stormy hell. I fought it though, because fighting against things that were not right, legal, and fair was in my nature, always had been. That was why I'd gotten into the stinking rotten war before most of my compatriots in the first place. Sure, I was a fighter—life, and death, had made me that way—but this looked like the final battle.

I raged against it, even lifted a weary fist in defiance, but I knew I'd lost. There were no options. Like the girl said, I'd led them into a trap of my own making, and the price of that foolishness was death. We were gonna die alongside the vermin between the tracks.

And as the black smoke closed in and that flimsy veil floating across my mind thickened, something happened that sent a last reserve of adrenaline rushing through me.

| 5 |

EVEN THROUGH THE SMOKY MISTS, THIS NEW LIGHT WAS BRIGHT enough to dazzle. It seemed to come straight from the tunnel wall itself, only a few yards away, and it swept over us, taking us all in, its beam defined by the smoke. The speaker was invisible behind the glare, but his voice was clear enough.

"You're a sorry sight, the lot of yer." The voice was low, gruff, a little peppery, as if the guy wasn't excessively pleased to find us. "You'd better get yourselves inside," it went on in that growly way, "unless you want to choke to death. Come on, in 'ere, ladies first."

The German was on his feet, but the two gifts remained sprawled across the tracks, heads raised and looking towards the light. I figured we were being offered sound advice so I dragged Cissie up by her armpits, croaking out to Stern to help Muriel at the same time. Every muscle in my body ached and my shoulder stung from the nick it had taken earlier, but I managed to haul Cissie over to the light source, the lamp I'd been using left by the tracks. We must have looked quite a sight, covered in filth, clothes a mess, faces blackened and tear-stained, all of us coughing smoke so that we could hardly speak. Blasts of heat swept over us in waves and we could hear the sound of popping glass as the train's windows fractured. There were other noises too—the roof over the train falling in, old brickwork crumbling with the heat, and a deep rumbling, like an earthquake, was going on way below our feet. Between coughing fits, the girls were crying out, floating ash and smoke creating a storm around us, and I swallowed hard before lending my own voice to the racket by shouting at the man behind the light to quit blinding us.

When we didn't seem to be getting any closer I realized the light was pulling away, its spread becoming confined and outlining a doorway in the tunnel wall. I realized the door must have been in shadow when we passed it before and we'd been too busy running from those fireballs to notice. Possibly it'd been locked from the inside anyway, so useless even if we had spotted it. None of that mattered now though: the door was open and this surly guardian angel was inviting us in.

The light retreated along a bare-bricked corridor and we tumbled after it, collapsing inside the doorway in a tangle of bodies, too exhausted and overwhelmed by our escape to move another inch. As we lay there like decked flounders gasping air— dank and musty but oh so sweet air—I felt something, *someone* shuffling around us, back towards the door. I caught a glimpse of baggy, dark-coloured overalls before the iron door clanged shut behind us.

Although there was still a faint rumbling somewhere off in the distance and a weak vibration running through my hands and knees from the concrete floor, it suddenly became quiet, peaceful, as though the mayhem and madness had been left far behind. I could barely move, and thinking was too much effort; I just wanted to lay there and convalesce. The others were coughing up smoke, their breathing scratchy and difficult, and I wasn't much better off: my throat was raw and my thoughts were disassembled. It took a great effort of will to roll over from my knees and press my back against the wall so that I could look around.

The corridor was long and narrow, and at the end of it was a stone flight of stairs leading upwards. A softer light than the one carried by our guardian angel came from a paraffin lamp set on the second step, and when the flashlight switched off I turned my attention towards the door and the man standing before it.

I guessed him to be in his late fifties, maybe sixty even, a stocky little guy wearing dark blue overalls and a flat, white tin helmet with a large black *w* painted on it. It was the uniform of an Air Raid Precautions—ARP—warden, and I wondered why nobody had bothered to tell him the war had ended three years ago, back in '45. His face was kind of flabby and hard at the same time, a working-man's, used to fresh air and tough labor, a network of purple veins coloring his jowly cheeks; bushy eyebrows, stubby nose and small, gimlet eyes completed the picture. He looked us over and didn't appear happy with what he saw. He gave a disapproving shake of his head.

"All right, you lot," he said, "on yer feet. I don't know what you've gone and bloody well done, but even this place ain't safe any more."

As if to reinforce the message, a muffled explosion came from somewhere close by.

"Oh, good Gawd," he said, more to himself than us. He stepped over our legs, making his way towards the concrete stairs, but pausing when he reached me. He bent closer, squinting his eyes, then nodded as if confirming something he already knew.

"Always reckoned you'd be trouble one day," he murmured before moving on to the steps. He scooped up the lamp and turned in our direction again. "Listen, I can see you're all done in, but you can't stay 'ere. You're still in trouble, see? Somethin you set off in the tunnel has ruptured gas mains that feed into this bunker, an' that's caused fires that're spreadin right through the place. We're safe where we are for the minute, but that won't be for much longer. So unless we get movin right now, we'll be stuck. Understand? Get me? Stuck."

He was talking to us as if we were sapheads, but I guess we were all wearing dumb expressions, relief and exhaustion taking its toll. I was still wondering why I'd been given the double-take. The little guy was getting impatient. "When somethin blows under the streets, it can cause an upset somewheres else. Then that starts a nuisance in another place, a fire or explosion or somethin. Chain reaction, y'see. Build-up of gas, pipe gas or sewer gas, all bleedin lethal. It's a wonder the whole city's not in ruins by now."

"It was a gas pocket in the tunnel." The words hurt my throat.

"What's'at?" His beady eyes set on mine again.

"Burning rats ran past us in the tunnel. I think they reached some trapped gas further along the line."

He sniffed and brought out a grubby spotted red handkerchief from his overalls pocket to mop his face and plump neck. "Yeah, that was probably it, not that it bleedin matters right now." He nodded his head a couple of times, considering me. "So you are a Yank then? Thought you was, from the Yank flying jacket you always wear."

"You know me?" My brain was beginning to function again.

"I've seen you about, son. And this mornin I saw yer bein chased by them Blackshirts, you and these others 'ere. You didn't see me though, none of you did, I made sure of that. I watched you duck into the Tube station and reckoned on where you'd be headin if yer got the chance."

I struggled to my feet and gaped at him, one elbow resting against the wall, every muscle in my body stiff. The German and the two girls were beginning to stir themselves, but I wasn't sure if they'd been following the conversation.

"How did you know which tunnel to find us in?" I asked the warden, curiosity overriding the tiredness.

"Like I says, I thought I knew where you was headed. It was a chance, but you struck lucky, son. Now then, you got the strength to help your friends?"

I barely had the strength to stand upright, but I nodded anyway.

"Right, follow me." He began climbing the stairs, boots noisy on the concrete.

"Who is he?" Cissie asked in a hushed voice as she used my arm to drag herself up.

"No idea," I replied, giving her some help. "But I could kiss his fat head."

The German helped Muriel to her feet and she caught my anxious look.

"I'll be okay," she said quickly, her voice strained. "Once I get into better air I'll be fine."

"You lot comin?"

We could only see the glow of the lamp shining down the stairs, the corridor we were in now darkened, full of our own shadows, and without another word we set off after the warden, the girls behind me, Stern following at the rear. The old guy was waiting for us by another door at the top of the stairs, this one also made of iron.

"What is this place?" I asked when I reached him.

"Civil Defense shelter. There's a whole complex of plannin rooms on the other side of this door, all underground, too deep for any bombs to reach. They never counted on the poison though, never thought anythin could touch 'em down 'ere. All very hush-hush and all bloody useless."

"If it was so secret how did you find it?"

"It was on my beat, son. As a warden it was my job to make sure none of the street entrances was blocked."

He peered over my shoulder to make sure we were all together, then twisted the handle and pushed open the door. It was heavy, judging by the effort he put into it.

I touched his arm, moving closer. "You said you knew where I was making for. I'd like to know how."

My hand stayed on his arm and he looked down at it, then up at me. "I know where your base is, so it stood to reason you'd use the Tube line going back to the Aldwych, which is near the hotel you've been using. I've watched yer goin in and out of the place plenny a' times. Sometimes yer disappear for a while, but yer always come back to it. You like yer bit of luxury, don't yer?" He even gave a little chortle.

"You've watched me?"

Any humor vanished from his broad, ruddy face. "Yeah, I've watched yer, son. And I know what yer do." He turned away, but not before I'd caught the unease in his eyes.

"Hoke?" Cissie was pressing against me, her breathing shaky, coming in gasps. "What are you two—?"

"Forget it. Let's just concentrate on getting outta here." I took her hand and surprisingly—I thought she was still mad at me—she allowed me to guide her.

Once through the door we found ourselves inside another corridor, this one wider though, with openings along each side. Water covered its concrete floor and at the far end a carbide lamp burned, its white glare harsher than the warden's paraffin lamp but more effective. On the wall outside one of the open doorways was a yellowing poster, an upper corner drooping over, and as I passed by I saw there were two pictures of Adolf Hitler on it, front and profile, WANTED written large at the top, smaller headline type explaining why. FOR MURDER . . . it said. FOR KIDNAPPING . . . FOR THEFT AND ARSON. It should've added FOR WORLD GENOCIDE. Our breeze caused the opposite corner to curl over so that the paper folded and the mad *Führer* was out of sight. The floor shook beneath our feet and Cissie's grip tightened in mine.

I took a peek through a doorway and saw a plain square room inside, pipes running round the walls close to the ceiling. One of the smaller pipes was leaking in a couple of places, thin jets of water arcing onto the bare floor. The only furniture was an iron table with four straight-backed chairs around it; a black telephone sat on the table-top. It was a relief to see there were no human remains in there.

Other rooms were similar but with more furniture; two or three tables, green filing cabinets and cupboards. The pipes ran through every room, and there were more leaks, some pretty bad. There was another stairway at the end of the corridor, broader than the last and turning back on itself as it rose to the next levels. We used its iron handrail to drag ourselves upwards, the warden urging us on and getting mighty agitated with the ladies for holding us back. We'd just reached the next level when an explosion beyond a set of doors to our left shook the walls.

The warden clung to the stair rail until the world had settled down a little. "It's the gas cylinders!" he shouted at me accusingly, as if it were my fault, I'd arranged the whole thing. "They're kept 'ere for emergency power and now your bloody fire's got to them!"

My bloody fire? Yeah, sure. But you had to wonder what kind of genius built an underground bunker vulnerable to explosions *beneath* the city streets. We were both distracted by smoke curling through the gap beneath the heavy double doors.

"Which way do we go?" I asked as Cissie sank down next to me. Muriel stood with her back resting against the stair wall, the German supporting her, his impatience to get moving plain in his quick-shifting eyes.

"Upwards!" the warden shouted back at me. "There's sleepin quarters and plannin rooms on the next floor, and we can get out through there."

"Doesn't this stairway lead to the street?"

"It does, yeah, but the buildin over the exit collapsed and blocked it a long while ago. Thank Gawd there're others."

"No point in hanging 'round then, right?" I kept my voice calm—shouting would have only hurt my throat even more anyway.

"You're not wrong there, son." He'd calmed down a little himself, but he still looked scared. Letting go of the rail he bustled round to the next flight of stairs.

"Hey," I called after him, the stab to my throat making me wince. "What's your name?" I finished more quietly.

"Potter. Albert Potter, ARP warden for the Kingsway and Strand area." He seemed proud of the title and I almost expected a smart salute. He started climbing again, but I just caught his added remark. "Can't say I'm pleased t'meet you at last."

My limp was getting worse as I followed him, but I knew I'd only bruised the ankle—anything more severe and I wouldn't have been walking at all by this time. But tiredness was slowing us all down, I guess only our last reserves of adrenaline keeping us going. I'd learned a lot about that during the war, because flying a Hurricane at more than 300 miles an hour with a couple of superior Me 109s on your tail, it's the old energy-juice that takes over, overrides the fatigue that comes with too many sorties and not enough sleep, keeps your brain razor-sharp, until maybe a Spitfire can get to you and cover your back. Even if you got shot up, it was the adrenaline pumping that got you through the shock, helped you function until you'd baled out. Yeah, I'd learned a lot about what adrenaline could do for you in times of crisis, and I also knew that eventually it dried up, it could only take you so far . . .

The German surprised me by drawing level and taking me by the elbow. "Do you need help?" he asked. His face was black with dirt—hell, all our faces were black. 'Cept the warden's—his was just getting redder by the second.

I paused just long enough to pull my arm away. "Take care of the girl," I told him, my voice low and full of warning. I climbed on, leaving him there, but he was close to me again, this time with an arm around Muriel's waist, her own arm over his shoulder. I let them go on past and then it was Cissie who was by my side.

"You're slowing down, Yank."

"It's been a busy morning," I managed.

Her teeth flashed through the dirt, and I appreciated the smile.

"If you need a shoulder to lean on . . ."

"You're not sore at me any more?"

"Anyone can make a mistake. Besides, if those Blackshirts are as nasty as you say—"

"You had a taste of 'em."

"Trying to roast us alive wasn't very civilized. As for wanting our blood, well, we only have your word for that. I mean, for all we know you could be a criminal of some kind and they could be the only law and order left."

"You got a point. When you see 'em next, march right up and introduce yourself. Tell 'em about your blood type. They'll be pleased to get acquainted, wait and see."

She gave me a long look, then grinned again. "I'll take my chances with you—for the moment. Not that I have any other choice."

The banter might have continued—we were both dog-weary and this was a way of keeping each other going—but the next explosion that ripped through the underground bunker was the fiercest yet.

Although the blast was somewhere deep within the complex, the walls around us shuddered violently and debris began to fall through the stairwell from above. Brickwork caught the rail and shattered, throwing out pieces like shrapnel. Cissie yelped as she was struck on the forehead and she fell back against the wall. I grabbed her when she staggered down a step, and pinned her there while rubble and dust rained down.

"It's the ceiling at the top!" I heard Potter shout back at us. "The whole lot's gonna break loose in a minute!"

With Stern and Muriel just ahead of us, we clambered up to the next landing, spitting dust and blinking grit from our eyes.

"This way—quick!" The warden was holding one side of a double door open and we scooted through, the deluge behind us increasing, becoming a cascade of bricks, masonry, timber, and powder. Inside the door we could barely see, even though there was another carbide lamp on the floor—the warden must have placed these lamps in strategic places along our escape route—because it was like running into one of those famous London fogs the guidebooks told you about, "peasoupers" I think they called them in those days. The fog was smoke, and it swirled everywhere, thicker in some parts than others.

Potter hurried past us, his tin helmet knocked askew, and we followed after him like lost souls, afraid of losing sight of his broad back. Luckily, the smoke soon thinned out and we were able to see our way more clearly, although every so often we had to wipe our blurred eyes with sleeves or knuckles. We found ourselves in a huge open room filled with desks and large tables with street maps set on them, the maps marking out various divisions of the city and outlying areas. There were more maps around the walls, coloured pins indicating what could only have been other Civil Defense centers and contact points; metal lightshades, disturbed by the eruptions, swung low over the desks and map tables. As well as a phalanx of telephones, still in neat formation along the desktops, I glimpsed a whole battery of radio transmitters against a side wall. Only one thing was missing, but now wasn't the time to ask the warden.

We reached another set of doors on the far side of the room and beyond them was a broad hallway. But even as we staggered through, yet another blast rocked the floor, sending us stumbling forward. On my knees, I watched great cracks snake across the long expanse of concrete before us.

I had no idea what had gone up on the floor below this one—more ruptured gas pipes, drums of fuel stored there for emergencies, chemicals, who the hell could guess what was stored away in places like this?—but I realized this whole complex was now on self-destruct. Potter had been right about chain reactions. German bombs had inflicted the initial damage, but the demolition had continued long after the war had ended, a fault causing a fire in one building, which spread to the next, one explosion kicking off another, then another, a collapsing building bringing down its neighbor, that one in turn wrecking or weakening the building next to it. And so it went on, with no one left to contain the damage, or repair the faults. Like the man said, it was a wonder the whole city wasn't in ruins by now.

I had a nasty feeling about that floor ahead of us, and I guess that was what made me hesitate while the others picked themselves up and sped on. I saw a whole section shift, kind of tilt, and I knew what was going to happen next. So I moved, I moved so goddamn fast I could have been shot from a cannon. But it wasn't fast enough.

Even as I gained on the others, who by now were almost at the far door, I felt the ground beneath me start to give. For a second or two it was almost like racing downhill as the floor inclined, and I picked up speed, despite the limp. It was a curious sensation, the world falling away from me in slow motion, and I think I may have screamed or yelled or whined to showcase my terror as I began to slide. Then came a massive and sudden lurch and the section of floor I was on dropped away from me.

Instinct rather than calculation made me throw myself to one side, towards the nearest wall and the sturdy old iron radiator fixed to it. My hand caught the valve pipe at its base and my fingers wrapped around it. The pipe loosened in the wall, jerking out at least an inch, and for a moment I thought the whole thing was gonna dislodge itself; but it held and I hung there as the broad section of floor crashed down to the level below, sending up a huge cloud of smoke and dust and a sound like thunder.

Flames and sparks followed, licking at my heels as I dragged myself up, and someone far off was screaming. My hand curled over the top of the radiator, but I could feel my strength slipping away, the effort of holding myself there becoming too great. I groaned, too feeble to pull myself towards the jagged ledge where the others waited, their hands stretched towards me, their voices raised over the crackle and other rending noises.

I took a look down and didn't like what I saw: if the fall didn't kill me, the fire below would. Already I could feel the soles of my boots heating up and I guess the thought of a nasty death, one way or the other, encouraged a last burst of energy. I slid my left hand across the curved top of the radiator, taking the strain with my fight. But when I tried to grip with my left hand again, the sweat on my palm caused it to slip, slowly at first, until it fell away completely, leaving me hanging there by one hand, my body swinging round helplessly.

Then Stern was peering down at me, his face only a couple of feet away, smoke billowing around him so that for a moment his head seemed disembodied, floating in space. I realized he was leaning forward from the ledge, one hand on the end of the radiator, the other reaching out for me. It was a dangerous move on his part, but I saw no fear in those colorless eyes of his. For a split second though, a moment gone by so fast I may have imagined it, I thought there was a shift in those eyes, a kind of cold mocking that vanished as soon as I'd noticed it. His hand stayed just beyond my reach, then edged forward an inch or so as if he'd only been tormenting me. Maybe I'd got it wrong, maybe I'd misread his expression; that look might have been his own fear, because now he was risking his life even more by leaning closer. I just couldn't be sure.

"Take it," I heard him say over the roaring from below and the shouts from the others behind him. There were no hints in that gaze right then, only a blank—and equally as unnerving—coolness.

I hesitated. Would he let me go, pretend to the others I'd slipped from his grasp? There was no way of knowing and any- way, I didn't have time to consider. My hand slapped into his.

Then he was pulling me up, the movement strong and smooth, as though it was hardly any effort at all for him. I managed to hook a heel over the ledge, and then other hands were dragging me to safety. I rolled over onto what was left of the floor at that end of the hallway, my rescuers shuffling back to give me room, and I lay there on my back, drawing in great lungfuls of filthy, broiling air. They wouldn't let me rest though; I was pulled to my feet even as I choked on the smoke I'd sucked in, and the two girls stood on either side of me, steadying me until my head stopped reeling and some life returned to my arms and legs.

"Yank, you've got enough lives to keep a dozen cats happy." Cissie was thumping my back, helping me get rid of some of that smoke.

"Are you all right?" Muriel's touch was more gentle as she cleared soot from my eyes with her fingertips.

The warden had no patience for any of this. "You can make a fuss of him later, ladies. If we don't leave fight now all our gooses'll be cooked, and I ain't kiddin yer."

He ushered us towards the door and when I gave one last glance back at the pit they'd hauled me from, it was filled with fire, the flames touching the ceiling above. Potter hauled open the iron door and we piled through into a welcoming coolness. The door made a satisfying *clunk* when the old warden pulled it shut behind us, and because of its metal flanges everything sud- denly became hushed. The girls collapsed on the narrow concrete stairs that disappeared into the darkness above and the German went down on one knee, his shoulders heaving as he gasped in the cold dank air. It gave me some satisfaction to see he was as pooped as the rest of us, even if he'd disguised it a few moments ago. I watched those deadpan eyes, eyes that had seemed to be

looking inwards rather than out, and wondered why I felt no gratitude.

Leaning back against the rough brick wall, I slowly sank to a
crouch, wrists over my knees, eyes closed, taking deep breaths to
control the trembling that ran through me.

Potter interrupted the moment of peace. "Sorry to disturb you
folks, but we're not in the clear yet."

He sounded angry, as if he still blamed us for the destruction
of the Civil Defense shelter, and when I opened my eyes again I
saw his mouth was set in a grim line across his round reddened
face. Then I understood.

"You lived down here, didn't you?" I said.

"What?"

"I said, you lived in this shelter."

"Course I bloody lived 'ere. Safest place in London with you
and those Blackshirts runnin all over the place, shootin off guns at
each other. I just got on with me job and kept well away from
lunatics."

His job? I let it go for the moment. "Why did you rescue us
today, then?" I said, keeping my voice mild, just making conversation.

He gawked down at me in surprise, as if I'd asked something
dumb. "You had those two ladies with you, didn't you? I couldn't
see them come to any 'arm. What kind of bloke d'yer think I am?"

I liked that about the British. I'd learned a lot about old-style
manners and chivalry from the English pilots I'd flown with, and
I can't say it'd come as too much of a surprise—I'd spent most of
my life hearing stories about England and its people. Sure, much
of it was romanticized, I knew that, but the person who taught me
was someone you could believe in, someone who missed her
home country but allowed nostalgia to color her memories only a
little. She was one of the reasons I'd come over at the beginning
of the war, when England was crying out for trained pilots
because the *Krauts* were kicking at the door. The sting of it is, if
she'd still been alive, she'd never have allowed it. Not my ma.
She'd lost a husband, but she sure as hell wasn't gonna lose her
only son.

I didn't realize it, but I was smiling at the warden.

"Nothin funny about it, mister. Yer could've got these young ladies killed takin them down into the tunnels. The most precious things we've got left and you go riskin their lives."

He was still riled, but his eyes had softened, become tear-blurred. I didn't know what he was talking about and my expression must have shown it.

It was the German who put me in the picture. "Women are now the world's most precious commodity, my friend," he said.

"Vimmen" and "vorld." That just irritated me, and I noticed Potter giving him an odd, sideways look, but the "my friend" bit really got me hopping. If I'd had the strength I would've been at his throat.

But it was Cissie who was really stomping. "Oh, sure we are! Who else is going to give birth to more chumps like you two so they can grow up and start a whole new war just to finish off what's left of the human race." She'd been sitting upright on the stairs, stiff as a board, and now she pushed herself to her feet. "I don't want to stay here any longer. I want to see sunlight again."

The warden hurried over to her, his face big and anxious. "Don't you worry, miss, we'll get you out of here. Once we've climbed these stairs we'll be safe." He stooped to help Muriel rise, but held on to her when she turned to climb. His other hand gripped Cissie's wrist. "Look now, you ladies," he said almost apologetically. "You're not goin to like what we'll find up there, but try and close your minds to it. I had to put 'em somewhere, y'see, and I couldn't bury 'em all. 'Sides, there was others out there already, people who'd tried to get away from the poison. There's hardly any smell now, so that won't bother you, and you can keep your eyes closed if yer like . . ."

"What are you talking about?" Muriel was shaking her head, too tired to understand.

I picked myself up and walked over to them, explaining as I went. "He dumped the dead bodies from this place outside the back door. I wondered what was missing from inside the shelter."

"I had to, you can understand that," said Potter, appealing to me. "I had to make this place fit enough to live in."

"Listen, you did right," I reassured him. "And nothing could be worse than what we found inside the Underground station."

"At least there were no flies," he said as if it made a difference. "The bodies just rotted away, like. No maggots and not much stink after the first few weeks."

Yeah, no flies and no maggots. In fact, hardly any insects at all. I suppose we had to at least be grateful for that small mercy. God knows what kind of diseases could've wiped out the rest of us in the aftermath.

Distant rumbling from beyond the iron door and dust drifting down from the stairway's slanted ceiling got us moving again. Potter went first, lighting the way, and Cissie and Muriel followed close behind. I guess both were eager for that sunlight. The German, who'd remained on one knee, stood erect, the motion almost fluid, as if his steam had already been restored. I let him go on ahead of me—enemy at my back, and all that—then got going myself. Something heavy slammed against the door behind us, but none of us bothered to look back.

Christ, it hurt to climb those stairs—every muscle in my body was now stiffening up—and I favored my injured leg, using the rough wall to lean on. My shoulder didn't bother me that much but the rest of my arm felt like a lump of lead. Nothing was broken though, I was sure of that, so considering the punishment I'd taken that morning, I figured I'd gotten off lightly. If these strangers hadn't picked me up in the square when they did I'd've been not just dead, but *dried* meat, by now. And if the old guy, Albert Potter, hadn't rescued us from the burning tunnel, we'd all be cooked meat—yeah, choked, smoked, and goddamn coked.

Potter was dipping into his overalls pocket at the top of the stairs, the others squeezed behind him, so I waited further down, rubbing some life back into my arm. I heard a clink as he drew out a large metal ring, at least a dozen keys attached to it. The one he chose unlocked the door immediately and he pulled it inwards so that a gust of air rushed through. He disappeared outside and I wondered why it was still dark up there. I soon knew the answer.

The almost pitch-black place we stepped out into was bigger, much bigger, than the Tube tunnels further below, and huge, monolithic shapes loomed over us in the gloom. When the light from Potter's paraffin lamp fell on the nearest one, I realized those shapes were passenger vehicles, tramcars that ran on embedded iron tracks with electric cables overhead supplying the power, and the hangar-like place we'd escaped into was a large tunnel, a kind of under-passage beneath the city streets. It occurred to me as we stood there that those trams would be full of withered corpses.

There were hints of daylight coming from what must have been overhead airshafts along the tunnel's length and at the far end we could just make out a greyish hue that might have been the sloped entrance/exit. As our eyes grew accustomed to this new level of darkness we began to discern other forms lying in the roadway and across the sunken tracks, small black mounds, hundreds of them, and we were aware that they could only be the remnants of those who'd perished down here. Many, we assumed, were the remains of Civil Defense workers, laid there by Potter, himself.

Stern and the two girls lingered in the oasis of light, as if frozen there, afraid to move on. One of the girls—Muriel, I think, began to weep. What lay around us was no more horrific than anything we'd found inside the Underground station and tunnels—far less so, in fact—but the quietness of the place must have stirred something deep within them—sorrow, dread, an interweaving oppression of emotions—that held them there, shocked and grief-stricken. I guess the fact that they suddenly had time to reflect had a lot to do with their paralysis, but it was nothing new to me, nor to the old warden.

His gruff East End voice cut through the mood. "It's as good a tomb as any," he said, no pity, no remorse, in his tone, only a sepulchral hollowness caused by the high walls and ceiling lending any reverence to his words. "I've said a prayer over 'em," he went on, "which is more than most of the world's dead ever got, I expect."

"Let's just find our way out of here," said Muriel quietly, and the calmness in her voice surprised me. In the dim light I could see the glistening of tears on her cheeks.

Cissie, on the other hand, had channelled her sadness into anger. "Bloody well right! I can't breathe down here!" She looked towards the distant light and took a fierce step towards it, ready to march off in that direction. I caught her arm.

"No. It's too close to Holborn Station that way." I'd figured it out, finally got my bearings. The incline had to be the northern approach to the under-passage and I remembered how near that was to the station. "The Blackshirts could have left the entrance guarded, just in case we came out that way," I explained quickly as Cissie tried to pull herself free.

"He is right," Stern agreed. "They will be waiting."

Cissie ceased struggling and turned her head, looking in the other direction, towards a stifling blackness that seemed to go on forever. "Wait a minute," she said warily. "You're not suggesting . . ."

"There's no choice," I told her, not for the first time. And when I followed her gaze towards that eerie inkiness, I knew the day's nightmare wasn't over yet. Not by a long shot.

| 6 |

SO WE WALKED THROUGH THAT NIGHTMARE, KEEPING CLOSE together, a tight bunch, the lamplight defining the soft borders of our world, none of us caring to look beyond and none of us focusing on what lay within. The warden kept us to a narrow sidewalk and every now and again we had to step over rag bundles, clothes that had become shrouds. There were other doors set along the wall, but we weren't curious about them, not even a little bit—we'd got to the stage when all curiosity was numbed and we were only interested in getting to the end of that goddamn tram tunnel. If Potter knew what lay beyond those doors, he wasn't saying. As a matter of fact, he'd fallen into a sulky silence since we'd started off, his way of letting us know he wasn't happy about our continued association. To tell the truth, he'd wanted to leave us right there outside the bunker door, deciding he'd done enough for us already and that he would go in the opposite direction, towards the light, Blackshirts or no Blackshirts. He'd easily sneak past 'em, he assured us, but I wasn't willing to take that chance. As far as the goons were concerned, we were either dead or still trapped down there in the Underground, and I didn't want anybody persuading them otherwise. Potter might be gabby if he got caught and anyway, he was more useful leading us out of that place. The barrel of my Colt pressed against his plump belly won the day, and he figured it'd do no harm to stick with us a little longer.

We passed more trams with death cargoes and soon learned to avoid looking at the windows. It was weird though, because although we didn't look at them, each one of us felt those corpses behind the glass were watching *us*. We felt like intruders in some private purgatory, a kind of halfway stage where the dead passengers waited for the current to be switched back on so they could continue their journey towards oblivion. Okay, so maybe now and again our eyes strayed towards skeletal arms hanging over the sides of open-top trams or eyeless skulls leering out at us, but mostly we fixed our gaze on the warden's light, following the beacon like pilgrims following a cross.

We'd travelled some distance before we started to notice shadows moving along the opposite wall, a black shifting against black, and it was the German who brought us to a halt by raising his hand and pointing. Potter, in front, realized we had stopped and when he saw Stern indicating he raised the paraffin lamp, stretching his arm out. Tiny yellow lights shone back at us.

Muriel, close to me, whispered, "What are they?" The reflected lights were quite still now and I guess she thought if she spoke too loudly she'd set them moving again.

I'd already realized what was out there, but it was Stern who gave them identity. "Dogs," he said quietly. "I have witnessed"—*vitnessed*—"such packs roaming the ruins of Berlin, scavenging for any morsels they can find in the bomb debris. Often they would turn on their own weakest, then devour it. I have"—*haf*—"even seen them attack a lone child. If these animals are hungry we must be very careful."

I stared at him for a moment before turning back to those strange yellow globes that glowed like twin moons in a black velvet sky. Neither they, nor we, moved.

Without warning us, Potter produced the flashlight he'd used before from his overalls pocket and aimed its beam across the broad roadway, bleaching the mangy pack with its powerful light. They remained motionless under the glare, the sorriest bunch of skin 'n' bone curs you'd ever see outside a Bowery soup kitchen. They skulked, shoulders hunched, heads bowed, their coats dry and matted, and returned our gaze, those eyes now mean, jaws open just enough to show us their ochre teeth.

There might have been others hidden out of sight in the shadows or behind a couple of nearby trams, but I counted seven in the light. The closest one began swaying its shabby old head to and fro, near to the ground, and a low keening came from its throat. The dog wasn't pleased to see us and, considering what mankind had done to the planet, I couldn't blame it. One of its pals took up the note, only this one didn't wave its head around; no, it wrinkled its snout and showed us some more of its discolored teeth. Its keening descended to a growling and a thick stream of drool sank from its jaw onto the concrete floor. But it was the frothy liquid that bubbled between its teeth that bothered me more.

These animals were sick, and it wasn't from starvation. Sure, they were rangy, bones jutting like iron tools in canvas bags, but they'd been on a poor diet, eating the wrong things—and I didn't want my mind to linger on what. I could see the madness in each and every one of them, a catching thing that came from living in the new wilderness.

"Let's walk on," I suggested to the others, keeping my voice calm and the gun aimed at the pack. "Just slide away, smooth 'n' easy, no noise and no running. Let's not get 'em riled."

We started to file away, one by one, Potter leading, me taking up the rear, half-turned so that the Colt was still leveled at the animals, a veil that was shadow coming down on them as the light drew away. But that first mutt crept back into the light, following it along, crazy old faded eyes never leaving mine. Was it salivating because it was hungry? I wondered, or was that just madness drooling out? It gave a long growling moan and another dog joined it in the retreating light, this one all bristling fur and quivering ears. Then another came back into view, padding past the first two almost to the center of the road. It sat on its haunches for a moment or two, sized me up, then trotted even closer. It looked as unhealthy as its companions, but was bolder, hardly scared of me at all. Only a couple of yards away, it began stalking me.

I caught more disturbances among the shadows as others sneaked forward. Maybe they wanted a better look. Maybe they were working up the courage to charge. More padded footsteps, still quiet but swifter now, and when I looked to my left I saw a dog descending the winding stairway of a tram just three or four feet away.

I was walking backwards now, gun arm extended, and Potter and the others had made some distance on me, so that I was barely within the wide circle of light, the dogs on the soft fringes. Every time I took a step back, so the lead dogs took a step forward.

I'd come upon packs like this before in my travels across the city, starving creatures made wild by circumstances, and more than once it had been Cagney who'd frightened them off, standing his ground and ready to take on the leader if not all of them. By comparison, he was pretty fit, you see, and a lot stronger than his half-starved city cousins, so a few ferocious barks and a couple of threatening lunges were enough to see them off, no matter how many were in the pack. I can't say he was braver than those other curs, because some of those wild things had guts born out of desperation; but he was kind of arrogant, like he was superior, you know? Not because he was with me, he had a human and they didn't; no, my guess was that he'd always been that way.

First time we laid eyes on each other was a year and several months after the first V2s landed. I'd spent the morning working on my backyard allotments—these little suburban crop plots had always been popular in England, small pieces of land or gardens used for growing fruit and vegetables, becoming almost necessary during the war years when the authorities had even allowed a few public parks to be cultivated for food—and was boiling up some tinned sausages for my lunch on an open fire. Tinned food was my usual diet—easy to find, easy to cook—but I needed fresh vegetables if I was going to stay healthy. When I looked up from my digging to check on the sausages, I found the dog watching me from a bomb-site across the street.

Maybe I was feeling more lonely than usual on that particular day. I'd kept to myself after the Blood Death, you see, avoiding the crazies I met roaming the city, aware that the normals—those that were left—had abandoned the place for fear of epidemics breaking out, or just to get away from all those dead bodies, but there must have been something about that mutt that appealed to me. Sure, there were plenty of strays around, and not just dogs. Cats, chickens—unfortunately for the chickens, they didn't last long once I'd set eyes on them—pigs—yeah, same thing if I could catch 'em—horses, and I'd even observed a cow or two wandering along the roads. 'Cept for releasing horses from carts, putting any injured creature I came upon out of its misery, and slaughtering those mentioned for food, I'd ignored any surviving animals or birds, and mostly they'd ignored me. Oh, and there was one I'd hidden from. From a distance I'd watched a leopard loping along Regent Street—just once, I'd never seen it again—and I'd stayed out of sight in case it got hungry for warm flesh. Like I said earlier, the London Zoo had evacuated most of its dangerous animals, even put some down, at the beginning of the Blitz, so I had no idea where this cat had come from, and still don't.

Well, I *must* have been feeling pretty lonesome that day, because I called out to the dog. It was wary, though. Cocked one ear, angled its head, and kept well away. I guess it became a kind of game then, a challenge, me and the boiling meat against the canine's canniness. It looked interested enough, squatting there amid the debris of flattened houses, blackberry and eider poking through the dry earth and bindweed adding some color to the grayness of it all, but the interest was in the sweet smell of cooking rather than me. I'd noticed by then that all the animals who'd survived the holocaust had become "un-used" to humans, suspicious of us—or at least, of me—as if somehow they knew humans were responsible for the big foul-up. And who could blame 'em for that? But this run-down, red-haired mongrel's belly was ready to forgive all, because although it kept its distance, its nose was sniffing the air and one paw was raised as if to take that first step towards me of its own accord. And then an odd thing occurred.

It was a warm day, early in the year, May, I think. The winter of '46 had been real nasty (but nowhere near as bad and as scary as '47's), killing off most of the allotments and weaker wildlife, and it was obvious that this mutt had had a hard time of things. Ribs protruding, coat kind of threadbare, this old boy looked pretty beat up, and when I dipped into the can and pulled out a steaming sausage it became even more fascinated. And as I tossed the meat from hand to hand to cool it, then broke it in half, that timid paw touched the ground, taking the first nervous step towards me. I allowed a grin, but it froze on my face when something black and awful fell from the sky to land on the dog's back.

The heavens had been unblemished, not a cloud in sight, a gentle breeze the only interruption, but I'd neither seen nor heard the bird overhead and, so it seemed, neither had the dog. This was a huge bird, dark and ugly, with a wingspan of three feet or more. A goddamn great carrion crow, with claws like hooks, and a long powerful-looking black bill, sharp as a knife. Those claws dug into the poor mutt's flesh, while the beak stabbed at its head. The dog howled, but fought back, twisting and turning and snapping all at the same time. Blood was already beginning to flow from its wounded back, though, and it yelped between howls.

The Colt .45 wasn't always the only weapon I carried around with me; nearby, propped up against the curved roof of a half-buried Anderson shelter, was my other weapon, a Lee Enfield sniper rifle, picked up from a military barracks in another part of London. It was handy to have around for whenever I caught sight of one of those pigs or chickens—I'd even bagged the odd squir-rel in the parks—and I made towards it. Before I'd even picked up the rifle, three more crows had joined in the attack on the dog.

I was surprised and shocked: where the hell had they come from, and why were they picking on this poor old boy? Exhaling my breath, I took a bead on one of the newcomers through the telescopic sight, the original crow too mixed up with the victim itself for a clear shot. It was clinging to the dog's leg with its beak, yanking and twisting, trying to bring its prey down, while its friends swooped in when they got the chance, pecking at any exposed dog-flesh they could find. I squeezed the trigger nice and easy, aloof from all the excitement, and felt the rifle recoil against my shoulder.

The bird I'd targeted thudded to the rubble without a squawk and one of its companions fluttered away, screeching some kind of alarm. The other two were too absorbed in their work to take any notice.

By now the victim was rolling through the dirt in an effort to dislodge the crow on its back, biting and snarling, no longer howl-ing. it had guts, this skinny hound, but needed all the help it could get.

My next shot clipped a wing and scattered black feathers into the air, stunning the bird but not seriously wounding it. It hob-bled around for a few seconds, and that's when I got an idea of these birds' true size. They weren't carrion crows and they weren't rooks. These were the giants of the species: Ravens. I'd always thought these creatures lived on mountains and moors, or sea cliffs, but I guess I shouldn't really have been surprised: *nothing* was the same after the Blood Death. Maybe all the small mammals, frogs, lizards, or even dead sheep that these birds usually feed on had all been used up in their natural territory. Then I remembered I'd seen this kind once before in London, long before the Blood Death rockets had fallen, but I was too busy at that moment to remember where.

I aimed again and took off the injured raven's head with the next bullet.

That left one more to deal with, and this would be the trickiest shot of all. I moved closer, going to the road's edge.

The dog was putting up a brave fight, but not quite giving as much as it was taking. I knelt on the cobblestones, looped the sling around my upper left arm to take the rifle's weight, breathed out, and took steady aim, knowing it was gonna be tight, but what the hell, if I missed the bird and hit the victim, it would be doing the mutt a favor. Without hesitation, I squeezed the trigger with the pad of my index finger.

It was a true shot, square in the chest, and the bird, still clinging to the dog's back, flapped madly for a few moments before flopping to the ground, dead meat before it even landed. But the dog wasn't satisfied: it pounced on the carcass and broke the raven's neck with its jaws, then proceeded to drag it through the dirt, shaking it like a rag doll and tossing it into the air until exhaustion set in. The mutt wandered off a few yards and slumped to the ground, chin resting on its paws, weary eyes watching what was left of the bird.

Leaving the rifle on the cobblestones, I approached the panting dog to see if I could do anything about its wounds, but as soon as I drew near it rose and shied away, watching me all the time over its shoulder. It settled again immediately I retreated, this time keeping its eyes on me rather than the feathered carcass. I went back to my lunch and I guess the aroma of those boiled sausages was too much to resist, because the next time I looked up the dog was in the middle of the street, standing on all fours, bloodied but undefeated, nose twitching again. Tossing a whole hot sausage toward it, I went on with my meal, and when I glanced the mutt's way again, the scrap of meat was gone.

This went on for some time, one morsel following another,

each throw a little shorter than the last, until the scraggy-haired dog was sitting across the fire from me and we were finishing the meal together. Later I took it into the nearest house and bathed its wounds (there was plenty of water in this row of houses, although elsewhere pipes had been fractured by bombs during the war, or frozen and burst over the last winter). I found quite a few old scars on its body, proof, I guess, that survival hadn't been easy for it.

So that's how we met. Eventually I called the dog Cagney, because of the red hair (amazing what a scrub-down had produced) and a certain wise-guy attitude, and "it" became "he" because now the mutt had a personality. Cagney was a cross between a retriever and God knows what else, and he stayed independent, coming along with me only when he felt like it, disappearing for days, sometimes weeks, always finding me again at one of the several safe places I used all over the city once he knew where they were. I guess we were company for each other, and if he got offended whenever I got soused and ranted at him and the world in general, he never sulked for long. And if I got maudlin and shed a few self-pitying tears, he just let me get on with it, taking himself off to avoid mutual embarrassment. I didn't know his history, and he didn't know mine. We maintained a cool reserve between us most of the time, afraid, I guess, that tomorrow the other might be gone for good. Now I'd have welcomed his company in the tram tunnel as the mangy, slavering dog-pack crept up on me from out of the darkness.

"Hoke? Are you okay?" At least Cissie hadn't forgotten about me. Her voice echoed around the walls and the dogs hesitated.

"Keep walking," I advised her.

And in a short while I was following my own advice, catching up to the others as they held their hands to their ears, pained expressions on their faces.

The dogs? Oh yeah, the dogs. I'd taken out that first and meanest-looking one with two bullets to its head, the gunshots reverberating like thunder around the confines of the tunnel. Taking my old instructor's sound advice, I'd followed the first shot with a rapid second just to make sure. You didn't need to do that with a rifle, but a handgun is less powerful so you could never be sure if the first bullet had inflicted enough damage.

It'd leapt into the air, then dropped stone-dead, without a twitch, without a murmur and the rest of the pack had vanished into the void, running like hell from the thunderclap. I knew they'd return, and soon, because now they had a warm meal waiting for them, one of their own kind.

My own ears were ringing with the gun blasts and although I saw Cissie's mouth working I couldn't hear a word she was saying. Suddenly I was lit up by the full blaze of the warden's powerful flashlight, so not only was I unable to hear, but I was blind too.

Shielding my eyes with a raised hand I told him to get the light off me.

If he was deafened too he must have got the idea from my angry expression. The light blinked off and we were left in the softer glow of the paraffin lamp again. By the time I reached Muriel the ringing had toned down and I could hear voices once more.

"Surely those dogs wouldn't have attacked us," she said in her very correct manner.

"Things have changed," I told them all, not just her. "You can't trust the animals any more. Most of them are half-wild, the rest all-wild. And they're pretty hungry."

Cissie was pulling at her ear lobes. "You could've warned us you were going to shoot."

"Yeah. Sorry. I'll make a formal announcement next time."

I brushed past her and, taking the flashlight from the warden's hand, kept going, switching on the light again to play the beam along the road ahead. I didn't care if they followed or not, I just wanted to be out of that place and breathing fresh air.

The tunnel swept round in a long gentle curve and soon we came upon many other kinds of vehicles, cars and trucks, cabs, bicycles, even a wheelchair (we didn't examine the slumped bundle inside it too closely), their drivers and riders mistakenly thinking they'd be safe underground, just like the people who'd fled into the Tube stations. Well, they'd been wrong. We'd all been wrong. Every son-of-a-bitch who thought Good always conquers Evil and who'd gone to war to prove the point had been wrong. I couldn't help wonder—then and many times before—how that squared with a so-called "benevolent" God.

I trudged on, limping badly by now, exhaustion—mental and

physical—exaggerating the effects of my injuries and bruises; I remained oblivious to whether or not the others were keeping up with me, just set on reaching daylight before my legs gave out. And gradually I closed my mind down, shutting out all thoughts that had nothing to do with getting to the end of the tunnel.

Save one, that is. I couldn't stop thinking of when and how I'd kill the German.

| 7 |

WE CAME UP ON THE APPROACH ROAD TO WATERLOO BRIDGE, BAT-
tered, bruised, and shielding our startled eyes against the harsh
sunlight. We were all filthy, black from head to toe, even Potter,
and although the ramp leading out of the tunnel was gentle
enough, our lead-weight legs found the going tough. Our breathing was labored and old Potter was wheezing badly by the time
we reached the surface road.

The girls sank to the ground at the top of the incline, faces
turned up towards the sky, like sun-worshippers after a long, hard
winter, while the warden took off his helmet and mopped his
brow with his crumpled red spotted handkerchief. He muttered
something under his breath, complaining about "lumbago", I
think, and he rubbed the small of his back so's we'd get the message. Stern stood aloof from the others, taking in deep, purging
breaths, getting rid of the rank, sooty air he'd swallowed back
there in the tunnels. I left them to it, going over to the corner of
the ramp and peering round the railings back towards the big
intersection where the Strand met the Aldwych. The tram tunnel
had been built to avoid the traffic congestion at that point, beginning its descent in the middle of the broad bridge road and curv-
ing round below ground before straightening again to emerge in
Kingsway. Everything looked peaceful enough at the intersection,
with only the jumble of motor vehicles we'd weaved through earlier creating its own silent chaos. I sagged then, going down on
one knee, shoulder resting against the railing's end post, my face,
like the girls', turned up towards the clear sky.

My eyes closed for a second or two, and when I opened them

again I saw a solitary seagull sail across the blue, heading down-river, its haunted call as lonely as its image. With a weary grunt I pulled myself up again and crossed the road to the bridge's para-pet. Although small craft and floating debris littered the wide River Thames below, its waters sparkled in a way they never had during the war; the old river had cleansed itself and from where I stood I could see shoals of silver fish, swimming free of human effluent and, so it seemed, untouched by the great disease. The breeze was cool here, and somehow placating, soothing the dread that had traveled with me these past hours; only the sagging bar-rage balloons hanging lazily above reminded me that all really was not well with the world. I went back to the others.

"Listen up," I said to them. "We need to get off the streets for a while, at least 'til the Blackshirts have given up on us. The place I've been holing up in isn't far from here, so you're welcome to join me there for a while. When the heat dies down—say, in a day or two—you can do what you like." I meant that for the girls and Potter; Wilhelm Stern I wasn't gonna let out of my sight.

Muriel's face broke into a tired but almost radiant smile. "You mean the Savoy, don't you? That's the hotel you've been using, isn't it?" She brought her hands together as if delighted by the surprise, and even disheveled she looked a princess.

I frowned though, because even if I had decided to let the German go—which wasn't likely—mention of the hotel's name had sealed his fate. He and the Blackshirts were of the same mould, brothers-in-arms, comrades-in-creed, and if I allowed him to wander off, chances were he'd find his British allies and lead them back to me. My fingertips played along the teeth of my zipper, close to the shoulder-holster inside my jacket.

Almost as if he could read my mind, Stern said quickly: "I would be happy to go with you to this place. I think we all need to rest and perhaps make some plans."

His expression was serious, stiff even, the good volunteer. His eyes might have flicked towards the hand still lingering close to the gun butt just out of sight under my jacket, but if so it was too fast for me to catch. I knew he'd noticed though.

"It would be so lovely to return to the Savoy," Muriel was say-ing, unaware of the tension between myself and the German. "Even during the war it was a wonderfully exciting place to wine and dine. Do you remember the Lord Woolton Pie?" She had swung round towards Cissie, the brightness in her grey-blue eyes hinting at the sparkle that must have been there in better times. "You remember, Cissie—potatoes, carrots, mushrooms, leeks. The Savoy's chef created it specially for the Ministry of Food when rationing was so severe."

"Oh sure," her friend replied drily. "I used to hobnob there all the time. You know, with Clark Gable when he was in town, or Douglas Fairbanks Junior. Even good old Tyrone Power used to lie to his wife Annabella just so's he could spend an evening with me dancing to Carroll Gibbons and his band. Now let me see, what were they called. . . ? They were on the radio all the time."

"The Orpheans." Muriel hadn't caught the weary sarcasm. "Carroll Gibbons and the Savoy Orpheans." There was something edgy about her delight, as if it might break at any moment, leaving only bitterness to take its place.

"For God's sake, Muriel," Cissie snapped. "You know where I'm from. You know I would never have dared set foot in a swanky place like the Savoy, even if I could afford to!"

"I only meant . . . the recipe was used by housewives all over the country."

"Oh yes, what a wonderful example you toffs set for us common-folk. My-oh-my, if you lot could survive on spam and powdered eggs quaffed down with only the scummiest vintage wine, then the rest of us peasants could easily get by on good old Lord Woolton's bloody pie. God bless you, ma'am, if I had a cap, I'd doff it."

The shine in Muriel's eyes dimmed. She looked down at her knees, her weariness returned. In a softer voice she said, "My father used to take me to the River Room for lunch whenever he could find the time. We used to toast Mother's memory with a glass of champagne before we even looked at the menu . . ." Her words trailed off, but she remained in that position, head bowed, distracted, as if memories were continuing inside her head; and then Cissie was kneeling beside her, telling her quietly that she was sorry, hadn't meant to be a cow, her arm sliding around her friend's shoulder as she apologized.

I was impatient to get moving again. "The water's still running," I told them, and Cissie raised her head, scowling at me, wondering what the hell I was talking about. "The hotel," I said. "There's plenty of water. And the tubs are big enough for hippos."

The thought of a bath, cold or not, soon changed Cissie's mood. She examined her filthy hands and arms for a moment, took a token swipe at the dust on her slacks, then beamed a pure white grin from her sooty face.

"Now you're talking," she said, straightening up and bringing Muriel with her. "Come on, Mu, snap out of it. I'll let you scrub my back if you promise not to go all ritzy on me again." She hugged her companion, then looked at me expectantly. "Tell me there's tons of food, and not just Woolton Pie. I'm starving."

"If you don't mind tinned stuff."

"So what are we waiting for? My tummy's already screeching at me."

I glanced across at Potter, who was still pulling in short, gasping breaths and looking unreasonably hot in his dark blue overalls. "You coming with us?" I asked, and he returned my look with some sourness in those broad, sweaty features.

"You mean I don't have to? I can go on me own way if I want?"

"Sure. It's every man for himself."

"Oh, is it? That's good to know, son. I'll remind you of that next time yer stick a gun in me belly." He mopped the inside rim of his helmet with his red rag, then, with some dignity, placed it back on his head, tucking the strap under one of his plump chins. "Well, since my little hideaway has gorn up in smoke, I think I'll indulge in a bit of luxury meself. The hotel was on my watch durin the Blitz, so I know a bit about the place. I was quite pally with a few of the staff in there too, 'specially the volunteer ARPs and Red Cross nurses. Even had mugs a tea on the rooftop with the fire spotters. They were quite a bunch, I can tell yer. Heroes, the lot of 'em. Old William Lawes from the Works Department use'ta ponce about in a two-hundred guinea raccoon coat to keep out the chill when he was patrolling the roof. Left behind by an American guest in the Twenties who couldn't pay his bill, so I was told." He gave a short nostalgic chortle, then became serious again. "Course, we can duck down the basement to the Lincoln room when the mad bomber comes over next."

Before I could say anything more, Cissie cut in. "What are you talking about? What mad bomber?"

"Eh? You know who I mean." Potter looked at her, perplexed.

"They've been out of London for a while," I explained quickly, anxious to be on our way. Nostalgia and sunshine was okay at the right time, but this wasn't it: we were still in danger. But Potter had become rattled.

"D'yer think I'm in uniform for the fun of it?"

Both Cissie and I stared at him. Behind Potter I could see Stern was also taking an interest.

"I'll carry on me duty until it's all over," Potter went on. "Nobody's stood me down yet, and until they do I'll keep on with the job I was given. We old 'uns have got our uses, y'know. We can serve King and Country as well as anyone."

Maybe I shouldn't have been so surprised—this old boy had been living in an underground bunker for the past three years, getting rid of the dead bodies that filled the place to make room for himself, when he could have chosen to live anywhere in the city. He could even have followed other survivors and fled to the hills around London, or beyond, away from the worst of the holocaust and constant reminders of what we had done to ourselves. This guy had gone crazy all right, but only mildly so; he seemed harmless enough—so far—and anyway, I hadn't forgotten he'd saved our lives.

"Okay, let's get going," I said, unwilling to waste any more time.

Cissie was more than ready and Muriel seemed to have taken a hold on herself "You'll stay with us?" she asked Stern, who still stood apart from the rest of us.

His pale eyes took us all in. "Of course. That is, if no one objects."

Potter shuffled round to regard the German. "This feller's foreign, ain't he?" he said suspiciously.

"Forget it," I snapped. There was no time for a new debate. I did my best to sound neighborly. "Okay, Willy, you stick with us"—(like he had a choice)—"for now." Then to all of them: "There's a stairway opposite that'll take us down to the Embankment. The hotel's one block away."

Our footsteps sounded hollow inside the covered stairway and I think none of us liked being in the gloom again. But it wasn't for long and at the bottom I brought them to a halt.

"What is it?" whispered Cissie, her eyes wide and searching the road outside over my shoulder.

A finger to my lips quietened her. I stuck my head out and did a swift recce of the way ahead.

Warm air shimmered above the metal roofs of the scant traffic stuck there in the broad thoroughfare that ran alongside the Thames, but that was the only thing that moved. No noise, only our own breathing. Everything was abnormally normal. I stepped out, gesturing to the others to keep close.

We could see the modest riverside entrance to the Savoy a few hundred yards away, the narrow street it was located in rising gently, a small overgrown garden park opposite; a zigzag wall built during the Blitz to protect the hotel's rear access and river restaurant windows ran along the frontage. Several of the vehicles in the street had been parked there by me, their tanks full, keys in ignitions, batteries fully charged. The MG two-seater was for speed, the black Austin Taxi for maneuverability, the Bentley for comfort (never used so far), and the flatbed truck, a Foden diesel, which took up most of the street's width further down—well, that was for other purposes.

As far as I could tell, nothing had changed since my last visit three days ago—there were no new vehicles in sight and the single board I'd left leaning across the opening to the trench between the barricade and the hotel wall was still in place. But that didn't mean the enemy wouldn't be lurking inside the building itself, waiting for me to return. Until this morning the Blackshirts had never discovered any of my havens, so now I was extra wary. Hubble was stepping up his search, no doubt about that, and you didn't have to be an Einstein to figure out why: I've said it before—time was running out for him and his bunch of blood scavengers. Today, of course, he had even more reason to intensify the hunt: he'd discovered there were three more possible walking blood banks in town.

The sun's heat seemed raw after we'd spent so much time underground and soon the back of my shirt was sweat-soaked. I felt exposed and scared out there in the open, which may have added to the perspiration, but it didn't take long to reach the cover of the barricade. Lifting the plank of wood aside, I indicated to the others to go through, and with one last look around, I followed. The revolving door into the entrance hall was stiff with disuse and while Cissie struggled with it I let myself in by the glass side door.

The others crowded in behind me, nervously looking around the compact, low-ceilinged entrance hall, Muriel walking straight to the short flight of stairs leading to the floor above and peering up them. Cissie finally emerged from the revolving door, her glare telling me I should have advised her. From the relief on the faces of the others I guessed they were pleased to find there were no shrivelled corpses cluttering up the place, and I wasn't about to tell them otherwise, at least, not right there and then. Sure, there were plenty of guests still in residence, all of them dead, but I'd tucked them away out of sight along with members of staff as far as the rooms, stairways and corridors I used were concerned. Like the warden, I preferred them out of sight and out of mind. I had to give these people some warning though, because certain areas I'd left untouched.

"Stay with me and don't go poking your noses into any closed rooms," I said. "You wouldn't like what you'd find. And hey . . ." I paused, making sure I had their full attention. "There are some parts we have to go through that are gonna upset you. Unfortunately there's no other way . . ."

Muriel shuddered and turned from the stairs. Cissie held her own upper arms as if a chill breeze had followed her through from the street.

"I thought the hotel would be empty," murmured Muriel. "I didn't realize . . ." Her voice sharpened and there was enough daylight inside the entrance hall to see the astonished curiosity in her eyes. "Why would you choose to live in a . . . in a . . . *morgue* like this? There must be so many other places."

I brushed past her to reach the stairs. "This is just one of a few safe places, lady, and one I was already familiar with."

"I don't understand."

On the third step, I turned to look down at her. "Did you ever hear of the First American Eagle Squadron?"

She nodded slowly, but it was Potter who spoke up. "Yanks and Canadians who couldn't wait for their own countries to come off the fence."

"We joined in your war early, fought with the RAF when you

needed all the pilots you could get," I said, too weary to explain fully, but ready to satisfy this girl's curiosity if it would get her moving again. "We made our unofficial HQ in this hotel. Suite 618–619. We drank, we caroused, we played poker, we did anything to take our minds off killing and being killed for a coupla hours. The American Bar became our watering hole, though I don't remember any of us ever paying for a drink. Hell, we even got into Tich's Bar with the war correspondents." I didn't tell them about Sally, how I'd courted her here, my turn to impress her after she'd shown me all the good things in her town, bomb damage or not, how I'd loved her, and yeah, one year before the last V2s had landed, had married her here in the Savoy Chapel. 318–319 was our honeymoon suite, but the hotel had only charged us room rate and had thrown in champagne and flowers as a wedding gift. I didn't explain because there wasn't time and there was no point. Besides, these people meant nothing to me—I didn't owe them a thing. 'Cept maybe the German. Yeah, he had something coming, and that was why I wanted them *all* to stay with me for now. I wanted him to suffer just a little before he took his last breath, but I was too beat up to play it out right then. When I put the *Kraut* away, I wanted to enjoy the moment. Shit, I wanted to *celebrate* it.

"So why are we hanging around?" Cissie said, looking from me to the others, then back to me again. "You mentioned the water's still running, didn't you? And I bet the bar's open all hours, isn't it? So what are we waiting for?"

She joined me on the stairs and when I failed to budge because my thoughts were still otherwise engaged, she prompted me with: "Mine's a large gin and tonic, easy on the tonic, heavy on the gin. Hey, Mr. Fighter Pilot, did you hear me? A girl could die a thirst aroun' here." Her attempt at Mae West was pretty cruddy—maybe it was the hint of hysteria that spoilt it—but it changed my mood. For a short while, anyway.

I took them up to the next level, through an art deco foyer with dusty chandelier and fountain-etched mirror, then up more stairs into twilight corridors, past doors with fancy names— Iolanthe, Mikado, Sorcerer, Gondoliers—and over thick carpets that smelled of mildew. The further we ventured, the darker it became, until after a sharp turn the way ahead radiated a palish grey again. Soon we'd entered that grey.

"Oh dear God." Muriel's fingertips covered her lips.

"How could. . . ?" Slowly Cissie had turned her eyes on me, away from the spectacle that spread out before us, away from the vast front foyer where the rich and the gracious and the businessmen on expenses had taken late-morning or afternoon tea, or evening cocktails, in elegant easy chairs or sofas set between brown marble columns and exotic potted palms, surrounded by tasteful murals and high mirrors, ormolu clocks and knee-high tables laid with finest chinaware and tiered cake-stands, served by waiters in tails, with reception clerks in morning dress bustling through it all with courteous calm, the war outside an inconvenience but never a hindrance to the Savoy, service as normal even if the building itself had become a little battered and the menus reduced to basic (if stylish) fare; where now rotted figures slumped in those same elegant easy chairs, or sprawled across those knee-high tables amid broken crockery, or lay on carpets thick with dust, the foyer nothing more than a vast emporium of horribly macabre tableaux, each one solidified in death, the plants merely dried stems, the chandeliers grey with dust, and the humans only desiccated husks. And beyond this, through the open doors to the grand restaurant overlooking the park and river, opened only for lunchtime custom in the dark days, the scene was repeated, but rendered even more grotesque by the sun's brightness through the high, broad, taped windows. Cissie had diverted her eyes from this to look at me with . . . with what? Not with Muriel's astonished curiosity when we'd first entered the building. Horror, then? Yeah, horror and something more. Dismay would come closest. Her sentence might have finished with, "How could you live in a charnel house like this and remain sane?"

Well, lady, I hadn't claimed to have all my marbles.

I didn't say that, though. I just couldn't be bothered any more. I ignored those bewildered hazel eyes and her unfinished question.

"The stairway's along here," I said instead, moving off to the right towards the Savoy's stately vestibule and entrance hall, sensing their eyes on my back, their disgust. I kept walking and knew they'd follow me anyway, like frightened stray sheep in need of a leader.

Up a broad set of steps I took them, past a balcony overlooking the vestibule, then down a high-ceilinged hallway towards the stairs next to the defunct elevator. On the way, but without changing pace, I took a quick peek into a half-open doorway, checking on the Velocette Mk II motorbike I'd hidden away in there. It nestled in the shadows like some great black and fabulous insect, tank full, parts greased and free from rust, spark plugs clean, all primed and ready for a swift start, and just a glimpse of it stirred something deep down in my gut. It was the sudden urge to get away, I guess, to climb aboard that machine and roar out of the hotel and free myself from these people and the liability that went with knowing them. Involvement was something I neither wanted nor needed, because that kind of burden only brought grief.

My own exhaustion smothered the impulse no sooner than it was roused (besides, I hadn't forgotten Stern and why I wanted him here) and I kept going, heading towards the staircase beside the elevator.

It was a sluggish climb and by the time we reached the third floor our line was strung out. Without waiting for the others I left the stairway to walk down a long gloomy corridor, coming to a halt and waiting for the others to catch up only when I reached the sharp left turn at its end.

The German was the last one to reach me and briefly I wondered why. He was much stronger than the others, so had he taken time out to explore possible escape routes while trailing behind, investigating rooms close to the stairway on the landings we passed, looking for doors to the fire escape? What the hell— he had a fight. None of it would help him, though, not when the moment came.

I turned my back on them and unlocked the door to Suite 318–319.

8

To them it must have looked like an Aladdin's Cave—an Aladdin's Cave of junk, canned food, cardboard boxes, and weapons, all kinds of stuff that came in handy when you lived in a city where shopping was free but nobody produced anymore; and where blood-bandits roamed the empty streets, so that shopping was sometimes a risky business.

My suite in the Savoy had lost some of its elegance because of the clutter, no doubt about that, and there was a whole lot less room than when I'd first moved in. We were crowded inside a tiny vestibule between the bedroom and sitting room, the jumble spilling into both, and to our right was a marble bathroom with a stirrup pump that fed from the half-filled tub standing in the doorway in case of sudden fire (what good the pump would do in a real emergency was debatable, but it might at least buy me time to escape into the hallway). The pastel-colored walls of both rooms were easily overwhelmed by the flashy labels of canned foods and mixed jars, and only the king-size bed was free of clutter in the maze that was my refuge; the mess was everywhere, things piled high on easy chairs and mirrored dressing table, a selection of handguns and cartons of ammo on the lounger, a shotgun leaning against the writing desk. Boxes full of items I couldn't even remember poked out of the half-open closet. A radio that would never broadcast again stood on a small occasional table by an armchair heaped with magazines and books, and on the fancy Louis-Seize escritoire was my wind-up gramophone, a stack of dusty records next to it, Bing Crosby still on the turntable.

The two girls had already wandered into the sitting room and were gawking about—ration-book kids in an overstocked candy store. I didn't know what they'd been living on the past three years, but from the wonder in their eyes I guessed their cuisine had been pretty dull. Muriel glanced back at me, gave me a smile, then went to a cabinet set against the near wall where a mountain of canned stuff was piled high. She picked one out and the mountain threatened to topple; it steadied itself, though, and she read the can's label.

"Creamolo Custard Pudding," she said in awe.

Cissie giggled and put a finger against another label. "Fancy Quality Fish Roll," she read aloud, and her interest instantly moved on. "Mrs. Peek's Puddings. Batchelor's Peas. Oh wow, peaches . . ."

"Ostermilk for Babies?" Muriel said questioningly from another stack.

"Look." Cissie again. "He's got coffee. Three whole bottles of Camp Coffee."

"Handy eggs." Muriel. "Ugh, dried whole egg."

"All I can get hold of," I put in, beginning to enjoy their enjoyment.

"Spam. Oh dear, lots of Spam." Muriel sounded disappointed, but I could tell she was joshing.

"And Weetabix," said Cissie, a grin spread all over her face as she scanned the rest of the room. "Bovril, Ovaltine, Peak Frean biscuits, marmalade. My oh my, you're determined not to go hungry, Yank." She drew in a sharp breath. "Are those fresh vegetables over there?" she asked, pointing.

"A week or so old," I assured her. "Grew 'em myself on one of my allotments. It wasn't easy after last winter."

She was already picking up potatoes and examining each one individually. "After everyone had gone or died at the sanatorium we tried to grow our own, but somehow it never worked out. I suppose we'd both have been useless as land girls, but that's the problem when one of you has been brought up in a London pub and the other's the daughter of a lord." She indicated her friend, and it was easy to figure which one was the lord's daughter.

"Didn't you get supplies from the nearest town?" I asked, surprised.

"We were too scared to go far," replied Muriel, her interest still on the gold mine of food around her. "The nearest houses were as far as we strayed. Mostly we ate from the center's own stores. We were afraid we'd catch some disease off the dead, or even be infected with the Blood Death itself. Nobody knew anything, you see, not even the scientists in charge of research. Are those cabbages I see?"

She hurried to another box on the floor. "Oh, and Brussels sprouts, and onions. You must have worked hard to have achieved all this, Mr. Hoke."

"Just Hoke," I told her, then shook my head. "All I've done is kept a few things going. It isn't much, considering."

"May I?" Stern had followed us through to the sitting room and had lifted a single pack of Camels from a carton on a straight-backed chair.

I nodded and he quickly broke open the pack. He put the cigarette between his lips, then searched around for matches.

"Over there," I pointed to the mantelpiece over an extinct electric fire.

As he took a box of Swan Vestas from my stockpile of matches, he studied himself in the dust-dulled mirror above the mantelpiece and frowned. He was filthy, but it must have come as a slight shock. Maybe he'd always thought his kind didn't pick up the dirt like the rest of us.

"I need to wash," he said, more to his own reflection then me. "You say there is plenty of water in this hotel?" Now he was looking at me, but only through the mirror.

"The Savoy has its own artesian wells, but the pumps are out of action. The tanks are still pretty full, though."

"Me first," Cissie insisted quickly. "I can't go another minute stinking like this."

I guessed stinking wasn't a word Muriel used a lot, especially when it applied to her own body, but she was nodding in agreement. "Yes, I'd like to get cleaned up too. Then perhaps we can enjoy some of this lovely food; I'm beginning to feel quite faint and it's not just from fatigue."

I addressed them all: "You're in a building full of bathrooms, so you won't have to take turns. But stick to this floor, don't go wandering off."

I noticed the German, now puffing away at his cigarette, had strolled over to the M1 carbine leaning against the writing desk and my hand went inside my jacket when I thought he was going to pick it up. Instead he passed by the rifle and went to the tall window overlooking the park and River Thames below. The drapes were open, but a lace curtain covered the glass.

When he raised a hand to draw the lace aside, I said, "Leave it alone. I close the curtains at night if I'm using light—" I indicated the candles and lamps set around the room "—and in the daytime the netting is always kept in place."

"In case someone looks up and wonders?" he mused, and although I couldn't see his face, I knew there was a half-smile there. "Quite unlikely, wouldn't you say?"

"Unlikely or not, I don't take chances."

"I could do with a stiffener." Potter had sat himself down on the edge of the sofa and was eyeing the array of bottles crowding the low coffee table in front of him. Gin, vodka, and several brands of whisky—Famous Grouse, Haig, Johnnie Walker, and even good ol' Jack Daniel's, as well as bourbon and rye—all of them severely rationed during the war, but not nowadays. Hell, there was even the Savoy's own special blend to drink, a Scotch as fine as any I'd tasted, and I'd tasted a lot during my lonely nights in this city. Then there were the wines—hocks, moselles (yeah, German, old stock, I guess), clarets and burgundies, even some vintage stuff—sharing space on the edge and underneath the table with cartons of cigarettes—Lucky Strike, Camel, Wills Capstan, Churchmans No. 1, and some I hadn't even taken note of. Genocide had turned me into a heavy smoker as well as an inebriate.

"Help yourself," I said to Potter as his roving gaze took in all that was on offer. "I'll get you a clean glass."

"No need, son, no need." He gave a satisfied grunt and reached for the Grouse. "Plannin to drink an' smoke yerself to death, was yer?"

He didn't wait for a reply, nor did I bother with one. His plump fist closed over the neck of the bottle and he gave the top a twist.

"Yer know, I was always scared to come inta the Savoy after those last V2s dropped." He paused to hold the bottle up and examined the golden liquid before he drank, the loose cap in the palm of his other hand. "Even though I'd seen you comin and goin a few times, I was still frightened of what I might find in 'ere. I coulda raided the American Bar easy enough if I'd had the spunk to come inside, but nah, somehow it wasn't in me."

He took his first swallow, the whisky glugging into his throat.

"You weren't afraid of entering the Civil Defense shelter," I reminded him.

"That was different. I knew most of them people. I wasn't as funny about it. But this lot in here—toffs, rich people, even some of our own leaders, members of the War Office an' that—well, I didn't feel it was my place to intrude." He took another, longer, swig from the bottle, wiped his mouth with the back of his hand and eyed me again. "If yer know what I mean."

I didn't think I did, but I was in no mood to think about it. I faced the others. "You can have your own separate rooms along this hallway, but don't go any further. All the suites on this side of the third floor interconnect, though the doors are locked right now."

"You are a cautious man, Hoke." Stern had remained by the window and the light shining through the nets revealed how spoilt his tweed jacket and pants, so neat and clean when we'd first met, had become. A sleeve and a pocket were torn, his shirt collar crumpled; yet as he drew on the cigarette, his arm across his chest, hand holding his other raised elbow, he still had that air of superiority about him, that icy arrogance we'd come to expect from the "master race." Movies and propaganda had told us this was how they were, how it was part of their Aryan nature, and I'd never doubted it for one moment.

"A cautious man . . ." he went on, and I wondered if it was mockery I saw again in those colorless eyes ". . . yet today you were almost caught by those Blackshirts, as you call them."

"Sometimes it happens," I said by way of explanation. Going to the coffee table, I picked up a Johnnie Walker, one-quarter full, its cap missing. "But it won't happen again," I added before taking a long, long drink.

✠ ✠ ✠

That evening, using two of my three portable gas cookers, I made them all a meal. It was only Spam, tinned peas, and boiled potatoes, followed by peaches and custard, but they made ecstatic sounds as they wolfed it down.

Earlier I'd shown them other rooms they could use as their own sleeping quarters, the two girls moving in to a suite next door to mine, Potter and Stern in separate rooms further down the corridor, the old warden at the end of the line. I kept all the interconnecting doors locked. They were surprised to find that these rooms were used as store rooms as well, although none of them was as cluttered as my own suite, but there were no complaints. Not that I cared one way or the other. I left them to settle in and went back to my rooms where I threw off my filthy, ripped clothes and showered—the reduced water pressure still allowed a Niagara Falls soaking under those big Savoy shower heads. Although goosebump-cold, the water freshened me up a whole lot. A fast shave was followed by some attention to my injuries. The wound where the bullet had passed through the shoulder of my leather jacket was only skin deep and iodine (Christ, that *hurt*) with padding held in place by sticky plaster took care of it. My ankle was puffy and soft, but I knew no bones were broken, so the swelling would go down within a day or so if I bandaged it tight. The bruising on the same leg was just beginning to show through and was already looking ugly; it stretched from calf to mid-thigh and the muscles underneath were stiff and painful. For a while walking would be a problem, but no big deal. Cuts and grazes were soon dealt with and the rest of the bruises could take care of themselves. My hair was singed—the front looked like scorched corn—and the skin on my face and the backs of my hand was puckered and flaky; likewise, though, no serious damage. Oh yeah, and the knuckles of my right hand were scraped raw. All things considered, I'd been lucky that day—more lucky than I deserved—and I'd also been taught a lesson. Lately I'd become complacent, figured myself too smart to be nailed by the crazies. Well, I'd been wrong. Stupid and wrong. And the booze was taking over. Like I'd told the German, it wouldn't happen again.

Before I pulled on chinos and T-type shirt (Lord knows why, but I'd stuck with military underwear, and this undershirt with

short sleeves had been washed a hundred or more times) I
checked all the guns in the room, making sure they were oiled
and loaded, even though they were always kept that way. Still
shaky after nearly being caught out that morning, I guess.

Taking the .45 from its jacket holster and tucking it into my
waistband, I left the suite and limped barefoot through the third-
floor corridors and hallways, checking stairwells and windows all
round the building. Because the Savoy was really in two parts, I
couldn't look over the main drag outside, the Strand, without
going down and up again, but that didn't bother me. I was certain
the hotel was secure, otherwise there'd have been a reception
committee waiting for us when we returned. I scouted the place
pretty well though, and didn't go back to my rooms until I was satisfied there was no hostile incursion. Ankle throbbing like hell
along with other parts of me—the bruise over my chest felt like a
thick sheet of lead had been bolted there—I poured myself a
whisky, using a glass this time, but still taking it raw. It did me fine.

Still tired, but feeling a little better, I washed some glasses and
the accumulation of plates and dishes I'd collected over time in
the bathroom sink, then began to prepare chow for myself and
my unwelcome guests. I think I would have slept twenty-four
hours solid if I'd closed my eyes, so I didn't allow it. I kept going
because that was the only thing to do, and besides, I was so hungry a horse would've only made first course.

The German showed up first, politely rapping on the door and
waiting for me to open it. He'd found fresh duds from somewhere—white shirt, dark slacks, but same brogues he'd been wearing that morning—and if they looked a little snug on him, it didn't
matter, he still wore them well. He'd shaved too, and his hair was
slicked back with water so that it looked shiny, kind of sleek.
Although he looked nothing like the German actor Conrad Veidt,
the image kept coming back to me; maybe it was his manner, stiff,
watchful, arrogant, and yeah, even charming in a snake-like way. I
wasn't gonna admit it to myself then, but all those propaganda
movies had worked on me as they had on most people on our side
of the conflict, and I didn't want to be persuaded otherwise.
Hatred has its own fodder, and I was a pig for it.

Inviting him in, I told him to help himself to a drink. He
opened a bottle of wine.

We hardly spoke a word to each other, but I felt his eyes on me as I got on with cooking and he sipped the wine. Albert Potter appeared next, shuffling in without announcement, still in his blue overalls, helmet tucked under his arm. Making straight for the coffee table, he poured himself the same brand of hooch as before. The conversation didn't exactly flow even then, mainly because of the tension between myself and the German.

The girls arrived ten minutes later, both of them looking a whole lot prettier than when they'd emerged from the tunnels. The wife of whoever had once occupied the suite next door had great taste in fashion, and it looked like the husband hadn't been mean with her dress allowance. The girls' outfits were simple but classy.

Muriel wore a light green knee-length skirt, cream square-shouldered blouse tucked into the waist, the ensemble a little looser than Cissie's who was, well, a little more upholstered. Don't get me wrong—both girls were slim, but Cissie had been given more curves. Her pleated skirt fell just below the knees and she wore a matching jacket, despite the heat of the day (I think she wanted to make the most of what she'd found in the closets), with a white blouse underneath. Neither one wore stockings, though I was willing to bet the previous tenant had plenty—that was their one concession to the weather, I assumed—and both had on high heels that did a lot for the shape of their legs. I had to admit it was swell to see the female form looking so goddamn good again, although it went no further than that for me. Not at that time, anyway.

Their hair gleamed from fresh grooming, Muriel's light-brown locks curling round one cheek, Cissie's darkly vibrant curls resting over her shoulders. The thin scar line across her face was barely noticeable as she smiled at us three men.

The German, who'd cleared an easy chair for himself when he'd entered the room, stood to attention. "It is wonderful to know that such beauty still exists," he said to them with oily sincerity.

Cissie ignored him, following the warden's example by heading straight for the cocktail bar—the booze-laden coffee table where Potter was holding fort. He tipped his glass at her in greeting.

"Give me something strong, long and life-preserving," she begged. "Something I can regret tomorrow."

"Well there's gin, but I can't see no tonic," said Potter, lifting bottles and scouring the collection in front of him.

She looked at me accusingly and I said lamely, "There's no call for it."

"All right," she said. "Open a tin of peaches and use the juice. I'm a girl who's used to roughing it."

For the first time that day I grinned. I quickly found the right can and punched a hole in its top with the opener, then handed it to Potter, who'd already worked on the gin.

"Ice would have been perfect," Cissie complained jokingly, "but I suppose the Savoy isn't what it used to be. Mu, I expect it's champagne for you?"

It was as if a shadow had darkened her friend's face. "A glass of wine will do," she responded quietly, and I remembered she and her father had toasted her mother's memory with champagne in this very hotel.

"Vino it is," piped Potter, picking up the bottle already opened by Stern. "And a very sensible choice, if I may say so. Leave the hard stuff to reprobates like me."

"And me," piped Cissie.

They drank and watched me cooking over the small stoves on the floor, no one saying anything for a while. I think that initial coolness between us all was due to something more than just unfamiliarity: I think it was because there was no trust between us yet, despite what we'd been through together that morning. Even though we were the survivors of a scourged world, we weren't sure of each other, we weren't comfortable in each other's presence. It was different between the two girls—they were already friends—but the rest of us were strangers. Heck, one was even an alien, a *Kraut* at that. Just sharing the same blood type wasn't enough, not by a long chalk. Part of the problem, for the girls I mean, was that in a depleted society, our gender roles took on a whole new significance, and they weren't quite ready for that just yet. None of us were. And to add to the girls' discomfort, they couldn't be sure if any of the men they were with were quite sane.

The ice only began to break when I started serving up the food.

9

THE INFORMATION DIDN'T COME OUT LIKE THIS; IT WAS IN NO SENSE as concise and dispassionate. The evening developed in its own easy way, you see, after a while people just gabbing when they felt like it, their bellies a little fuller, their heads a little mellowed by the booze; a person could be maudlin one minute, cold-blooded the next, emotional after that, a real mixture of sentiment and hard fact. Regret figured a lot, nostalgia for the good things now gone even more; but grief, having had three years to settle, was pretty much subdued. Here's what most of that evening's parley amounted to.

First Cissie, her whole name Cicely Rebecca Briley. Like me, she was of mixed parentage, her father English, mother Jewish. Her folks had run a public house in Islington and she had helped out behind the bar (illegally, of course) until old enough to find herself proper employment, one that might help the war effort. That was back in '41 and she was sixteen at the time. With most of the able menfolk off fighting the war, the country was crying out for women to fill the men's jobs, so Cissie began her working life on a lathe in an engineering company.

On the same day the factory was bombed and a flying piece of metal scythed across her face, her parents' pub was demolished by another pilotless plane—these were the doodlebugs, the flying bombs, the first German V1s to be used on England and Belgium in June '44. Henry Briley was dead when the Heavy Rescue squad dug him out of the rubble, but his wife, Rachel, Cissie's mother, survived almost another three days with both legs and pelvis crushed, and one arm missing. Cissie's stay in hospital was only overnight—beds were needed for the seriously ill or injured—and when she left there was no home to go to. It took her two days to locate the hospital they'd taken her mother to, and by that time Rachel was dead. Home gone, parents gone, job gone, there wasn't much left for Cissie. She moved in with relatives and joined the ambulance service, channeling all her anger and grief into the work and quickly realizing hers was not the only tragedy of this devastating war. Within a year and with Hitler losing, the V2s replaced the V1s; and then everything changed.

Naturally she couldn't figure out why everybody around her was dropping dead even though the rocket bombs were falling in other parts of the city; but then, nobody could, not even the military and the government itself at first. All hell had broken loose, but the panic was short-lived, as short-lived as the people themselves. It was horrific, a hideous nightmare, the deaths so sudden and so gruesome to watch; and not knowing if they were going to be next added to everyone's terror. Soon, because Cissie remained healthy while everyone else was dead or dying, she was taken into hospital and blood-tested. Before she knew what was happening she was in the back of a truck with a bunch of other AB-neg blood-types being driven down to the special sanatorium in Dorset, and it was in the truck that she made friends with Muriel Drake, a fellow passenger and blood kind.

All manner of tests were carried out on the AB-negs at the sanatorium, but still no scientist or medical officer could figure out why they were immune from whatever it was that had been released by the V2 rockets. To make progress towards a solution even more difficult, those very same investigators were falling dead themselves, and it was only when a couple of medics with the immune blood type were found that any sustained research was achieved. Another problem was that it was only in the last decade that truly extensive research was being carried out on blood groupings, so very little was already known. Now they were learning fast, but it was too late.

It seemed the disease, gas, poison, virus—the military still didn't know what had been inside those last V2s—worked on the blood system, stimulating the chemical reaction that caused coagulation so that within minutes in most cases, the blood hardened inside the large veins of the bigger muscles, this leading to—and it was Muriel who remembered the term—thromboembolism. The veins in the heart, lungs, brain, as well as other less life-threatening areas, were completely blocked, while minor veins became engorged. It meant that because of the blockages, the excessive free-flowing blood had nowhere to go and nowhere to return to—"venous occlusions," Muriel called that effect—so massive swellings and leakages occurred all over the body. The cramping pains victims suffered because of this effect were excruciating, rendering many unconscious before death itself claimed them.

So, they realized anti-coagulant therapy would be ineffective, because it would only promote further hemorrhaging, and clotting drugs would only intensify the thrombosis. And they still hadn't discovered why AB-negative blood refused to react to the Blood Death, why they themselves, and their human guinea pigs were immune. You have to remember that all the advanced nations of the world were desperately working on a solution, an antidote, any kind of cure, the allied countries keeping in close contact with one another, but none so far had come up with an answer. Time had run out swiftly, and eventually the remaining doctors in the sanatorium ran out too. One day they just walked, leaving no note, no explanations, no excuses. They'd realized it was hopeless.

For the guinea pigs left behind it was almost a relief. No more tests, no more blood drained from their bodies to be taken away in glass tubes, no more tissue samples cut out, no more needle jabs—and no more vanishing into the sanatorium's special, restricted wing where, it was believed but never confirmed, because no patient ever came back, operations were performed on the AB-negs (the rest suspected that experimental blood transfusions were being carried out). When those principal doctors fled, all order went with them. First the soldiers guarding the "inmates"—no AB-negs had stayed on voluntarily after the first week—had absconded, soon followed by all the remaining staff and researchers. These people knew by then that death was hanging over every one of them, and they could think of better places to be when it happened.

Soon after, the guinea pigs, about a hundred in all, went their separate ways. Cissie and Muriel decided to stick together.

Muriel Drake was from a higher branch of society than Cissie, although even as a daughter of a lord she had been treated no differently from anybody else at the sanatorium (panic is classless, I guess). For whatever reasons, the two girls got along and did a lot to keep up each other's morale in those dark days. Like everybody else, they'd lost family and friends, and at the sanatorium they never knew when an amiable nurse or guard was going to cash in their chips right in front of them. Now that the place was emptying fast, they made their plans together.

Muriel's mother, Lady Daphne Drake, had been struck down in the first year of the war, but not by anything the mad *Führer* had sent over. A No. 14 bus had knocked down Lady Daphne as she'd tried to cross Piccadilly Circus during the Blackout, after she'd enjoyed Jack Hulbert singing for the conga and outwitting Nazi spies in *Under Your Hat,* the bus killing her instantly and leaving Muriel pretty much alone with her father, Lord Montague Drake—Muriel's two older brothers, who had joined the Forces as soon as war was declared and much against their father's wishes, were in other parts fighting the Germans, one with the Navy, the other with an RAF squadron based on Malta. Muriel had not heard from either of her brothers since the Blood Death outbreak and, not knowing if they shared the same blood type as her, assumed they were both dead. Although the family home was in Hampshire, most of the time she had lived in their Kensington apartment; at seventeen she had joined the ATS, the Auxiliary Territorial Service, and was soon serving as a subaltern. Nothing heroic in that, she'd assured us: it was a natural role for any patriot. And hadn't Princess Elizabeth herself joined the ATS just before her nineteenth birthday?

On the day the first Blood Death V2s had rained down, Muriel had been having lunch with her father at Simpson's-in-the-Strand when the waiter, who had just served them with mulligatawny soup, which was to be followed by cold roast gosling and salad— strange, she had told us, how she had never forgotten that day's menu despite the horror that had accompanied the lunch—had keeled over onto their table, his skin turning blue, the veins in his hands and temples protruding as if about to burst. His eyes had started to bleed.

Muriel, not unreasonably, had proceeded to scream the place

down, while her father, who was attempting to help the distraught waiter by opening his shirt collar so that he could breathe
more easily, suddenly clutched at his own heart. Her attention
now solely on her father, Muriel hadn't noticed that virtually
everyone else in the restaurant was going through the same
paroxysms, and when Lord Drake's skin began turning blue, his
hands and cheeks ulcerating at an unbelievable rate, his veins
swelling like the waiter's, she fainted. When she had eventually
come round again, every person who had not fled the restaurant,
including her father, was dead. She had run out into the street,
out into a dying city, and only later did it occur to her that she
hadn't even heard the bombs drop.

Like Cissie, she was rounded up within days, blood-tested,
then taken down to the Dorset sanatorium.

Even while this secret medical establishment was slowly being
abandoned, she, Cissie and a few others had been reluctant to
leave the security it offered, afraid of what they might find in the
strange new world outside. But three years was a long time to be
cooped up anywhere; also, rations were finally running low. Neither desperation nor bravery took them back to the capital
though: it was homesickness that had done that.

And as they'd driven one of the few vehicles left behind at the
sanatorium through the country lanes they had come upon Wilhelm Stern.

As we listened to the German tell his story, the sun sinking low
over the Thames outside, flushing the walls of the suite a soft red
and deepening the shadows, it seemed to me he was a little light
on detail. Sure, he told it convincingly, but there was something
about the guy that made me unwilling to trust him. The fact that I
still regarded him as the enemy had a lot to do with it, right?
Yeah, no doubt about that. But he'd said something back there in
the tunnel that firmed up my suspicions.

That evening Stern said he was a navigator on one of the *Luftwaffe*'s medium-sized bombers, a Heinkel He 111, which had been
dropping mines along the east coast of England in April 1940,
when the plane had been hit by ack-ack. With his clothes on fire
he'd parachuted from the blazing bomber, and the rush of air had
extinguished the flames, although not before his back and neck had
been severely burned. The He 111 had crashed at Clacton, a few

miles away, killing (he'd learned later) two civilians and injuring a hundred and fifty others, and he and the rest of the crew were captured and shipped off to Island Farm POW Camp down in Wales. That, he told us with an almost apologetic smile, was the extent of his personal war on Britain, although in March '45, a week or so before the fatal V2s were launched, he and sixty-five other German POWs had escaped from the camp (I vaguely remembered reading something about the escape in the British newspapers at the time). It was while Stern, who had become separated from his *Kameraden*, was trying to make it to the Welsh coastline where he hoped to steal a boat that would take him across to neutral Ireland, that the world about him changed.

The dead were everywhere and he couldn't comprehend why. Deciding to keep away from the towns—now for two reasons: as far as he knew his country was still at war with Britain and America, and he was still a prisoner on the run; and he thought the plague that had killed everyone, including most animals he'd come upon, must be contagious—he scavenged from farmhouses and empty cottages. He survived almost a year that way until the harsh winter of '46 forced him to venture into a town.

He told us he must have gone into shock because of what he found there, since he'd lost all memory of those first weeks. When reason eventually returned he left the town, heading east, travelling in cars and abandoning each one when it ran out of gas, finding another to continue the journey in, determined to make it to the opposite coast, there to find a boat and cross the English Channel to mainland Europe. From there he would return to his homeland, perhaps to die, for at that time he did not know how widespread the plague was, whether the Continent itself had been devastated. On his journey he had come upon an army base and had steeled himself to enter it. With nothing more than a scarf coveting his mouth and nose, Stern had located a battery-operated radio transmitter and, using fresh batteries, had tried to contact his own base in Germany. There had been no response. All night he sent messages, praying for some reply, from anyone, from anywhere, but still there was no contact.

Giving up all hope, he'd sunk into deep despair, unable to understand what had caused the disease and why he had survived it. The whole of the next day he had contemplated ending his own life—not only did there seem nothing to live for, but his personal guilt at having lived while everyone else appeared to have perished was crushing. That thought evaporated with the next dawn when he realized it was his duty to live on, he owed it to his people and to his *Führer*. He made no mention of the Master Race, but it was in my mind. I figured Stern thought the fittest had survived, so affirming Hitler's attitudes on breeding and the natural order. Stern was living proof of his leader's theories and to die now, especially by his own hand, would refute all that.

So, he wandered on, looting grocery stores for food and sleeping in empty houses. And then he had chanced upon other survivors, a kind of community living in a tiny village. They'd treated him with suspicion and, on hearing his accent and learning he was German, they'd driven him off, almost killing him in the process. It seemed they blamed him in full and personally for what they called the Blood Death, and he was lucky to get away with his life. For a long time after that he had lived on a remote farm near the New Forest, first clearing it of its corpses, then cultivating a few crops as best he could. The winter of '47, even worse than the previous year's, had put an end to that.

His food had to come from village stores and shops, and so he lived on the fringes of these places, alone and, he admitted to us, "somewhat insane in the head." With the summer of '48 the desire to return to the "Fatherland" returned and his journey began again.

The vehicle he was travelling in soon broke down—lack of maintenance rather than shortage of gasoline—and it was while trudging down a country lane looking for another means of transport that the two girls came upon him in their Ford.

Their greeting was different from the kind he'd received two years before, and he was grateful for that. As far as Cissie and Muriel were concerned, well, they were just overjoyed to find another live and healthy human being. His nationality meant nothing to them, not after all this time, and he certainly felt no enmity towards British civilians. He agreed to accompany them to the capital, although he told them that from there he would continue eastwards, possibly using the River Thames to reach the estuary and the English Channel. Stopping only once to refill the Ford's tank from a garage handpump along the way, they soon reached London. And hit trouble. Namely, me.

I put the question to the two girls, not the German. "For all you knew, I could've been the bad guy, and the Blackshirts the only law and order left. So why help me?"

"It was Cissie's decision," Muriel replied, indicating her friend. I stared at the dark-haired girl.

She shrugged. "I didn't like their uniform. I had bad memories of Mosley's Blackshirts before the war and that lot this morning didn't look any different." Another sip of gin and peach juice. "I told you my mother was Jewish. Besides, you looked desperate and I like desperate types." She grinned at me.

It wasn't enough, but I didn't push it. Oswald Mosley, founder of the British Union of Fascists and Jew-hater, had been interned at the beginning of the war, his vicious party of bigots broken up. Before that, he'd led marches into the very heart of Jewish ghettos in London's East End just to provoke the people into dots. He was one bad man and later, as the Allies were taking back Europe, grim stories of the Nazis' attempted extermination of the Jewish race reached the rest of the world and the British public finally understood the full horror of the ideals Mosley had aligned himself with. Those ragbag black outfits had meant only one thing to Cissie and, as she'd been driving the car at the time, her companions could only go along with her. She was a gutsy lady.

A little juiced by now, they had begun to ask questions about me, but I ducked them. We still hadn't heard the warden's story.

Albert Potter, his nose a deeper shade of red by this time, was only too pleased to gab, three years of loneliness and a good few measures of Grouse loosening his tongue some. Too old to join the British army, he'd volunteered as an ARP on the very day Neville Chamberlain had mournfully declared war on Germany, and he had dutifully served through both Blitzes on London, twice being buried beneath rubble himself. His home was in an LCC block of flats in the Covent Garden area and when this, itself, was eventually demolished by the *Luftwaffe*, he and his family had moved into the basement of a school that was being used as a civil defense HQ. (It was here that he first learned of the secret Civil Defense bunker beneath Kingsway, where he later became "door watcher.")

He had won three commendations for heroic action during the war years, we were proudly told, once for single-handedly clearing an entire building of office workers when a DA (delayed action bomb) was discovered on the rooftop, the second time for reviving an unconscious woman who had choked on a stale (she later claimed) piece of Battenberg cake in the Lyon's Corner House on the Strand, and thirdly for preventing a bus carrying several passengers from toppling into a bomb crater during the Blackout by dashing in front of it waving his flashlight at great risk to life and limb. He'd served King and Country as well as any man could, despite the taunts and jibes from the public, who tended to regard all ARPs as jumped-up little Hitlers, mad with the tiny powers given them. Well, that had never bothered him. Like Stern, Potter knew his duty, knew it then, knew it now. And when his wife died of the blood disease, "Gawd bless 'er," and his daughter, Katie, thirty years of age, still single, and serving as a gun site operator near Cheltenham, had never got in touch so was presumed dead too, he had only one purpose left, and that was to continue with the job he'd been given. Only when the war was finally over would he hang up his helmet, collect his medals, and retire to the countryside.

We'd looked at each other uncomfortably, but none of us felt like breaking the news. At least believing the war was still raging had given Potter a reason for carrying on, misguided though it was. Besides, the war never had been officially declared over. Sure, it had ended when those last V2s fell, but there had been no one in high office left to say, "Okay, enough is enough, let's call it a day." Or if there were, they were off somewhere, either living away from the cities or deep down in some secret Blood Death-free bunker. That got us onto other topics, like what had happened to the governments of the world, why hadn't the scientists or medical profession been able to contain the disease, and what the hell was in Adolf Hitler's mind when he released such destruction (assuming he still had some kind of rational mind left after his dreams for world domination were shattered)? Had the *Vergeltungswaffen* been one cataclysmic mistake? All big questions, to which we had no answers.

Perhaps the biggest question though, because all the others meant nothing as far as the future was concerned, was this: How many of us were left? Just how many AB-negs were there in the world? Muriel said someone at the sanatorium had told her that

AB-negative blood types amounted to only approximately three percent of the global population, and it might be that their Rhesus Factor (whatever that was) was hostile or non-submissive to the virus or gas released from the rockets. The problem, this person had gone on to say, was that not enough was known about different blood types and time itself was running out fast for new research to be mounted, intensive though that research might be. The truth was, doctors and scientists were a swift-dying breed, along with the rest of mankind, and no matter how concentrated their minds, oncoming death brought about certain disabilities.

There was a silence for a while after that, all of us lost in our own thoughts. Cissie collected the dirty plates and dumped them in the bathroom sink; then she was back in the doorway, yet another question in her eyes. She voiced it: "Does anybody know what happened to the Royal Family?"

Potter made a sound, a kind of heavy rumbling sigh, as he poured the last of the Grouse into his glass. His rheumy eyes watched the liquid, but I don't think he saw it; his mind was on other things. We waited for him to speak, aware he was preparing to tell us something that we wouldn't like. Well to me one tragedy was as bad as another, and they were all part of the grand catastrophe; all except my own, that is. The German was of the same mind, because there was only interest in his cold expression and none of the fearful apprehension revealed in the eyes of Cissie and Muriel.

It was Muriel who prompted the warden. "Did they die of the disease, Mr. Potter?" she said.

"I suppose so," he replied, "but not in the way yer might think." He took a long swallow of whisky and wiped his shiny lips with the back of his hand. "Yer know, Queen Elizabeth, Gawd bless her poor soul, was never more pleased than when the bombs fell on Buckingham Palace durin the Blitz. She could look them poor people who lived down by the docks in the eye and say, 'We're takin it too, we know what it's like.'"

He let the empty whisky bottle slip to the floor as he drained the glass. Shaking his head as if in both admiration and regret, he continued, "Do y'know, them little girls, them little princesses, used to knit socks for the Red Cross in the evenings. Princess Elizabeth—Lillibet she was called by the family—she joined the

ATS, like this lady said." He gave a nod towards Muriel. "Worked as an engineer, got her hands dirty on engines and suchlike. And King George, he spent evenings makin parts for RAF aeroplanes, just like a common man. The King and Queen never left us, not even when the Blitz was at its worst, never even thought of sendin their youngest, Margaret Rose, out of the country to some safe place. They stayed together and stuck it out, an example to us all."

I studied the faces around me, curious to see their reactions. Muriel's expression was rapt, a mixture of emotions like the warden's; both pride and sorrow shone in those gray-blue eyes as she waited to hear the tragedy that was about to unfold. Cissie's eyes were a little unfocused, as if tears were about to roll.

"The public didn't know for sure," Potter went on, "but the rumors spread almost as fast as the plague itself. Some said the Royal Family was dead within the first hour of those rockets landin. Others said the whole lot of 'em, includin old Queen Mary, was given cyanide pills by the King's Physician when reports came in of how horrible the Blood Death was and how fast it was spreadin. But I'd got into the Kingsway shelter when I found out what was happenin out there, and I heard the true story first-hand, because even though the Civil Defense personnel were droppin like flies all round us, reports were still comin through on the wires."

"You really know?" Muriel was leaning forward, hands clasped over her knees.

"Yes, miss, I think I do. On that terrible day the Royals was rushed down to Windsor and as soon as the authorities knew what was goin on, a single-engine aeroplane was sent to take 'em out of harm's way. There's a wide and very long road that runs through the park up to Windsor Castle itself; the public was never aware, but it was there as an emergency runway in case the country was ever invaded.

"They got on the plane all right and so we heard, they even took the Crown Jewels wrapped up in newspaper with 'em. But the plane had barely took off when it came crashin down again, explodin into houses outside the town."

There was a tiny, shocked gasp from Muriel and I saw that Cissie had closed her eyes.

"Radio contact broke off just as the pilot was reportin a safe take-off, and the authorities reckoned he'd been struck down by the disease right at that moment. No other explanation, y'see. "Course they were all killed, bodies burnt in the wreckage, but there was no public announcement. Hell's bells, there was enough occurrin without demoralizin the people completely."

I could've smiled, I could've wept, at the absurdity of his last remark. But it was Stern who broke the silence that followed.

"Do you know what happened to your Winston Churchill?" he said, and I could see the "Vinston" annoyed Potter as much as it did me. He glowered at the German.

Then he raised his empty glass in salute and said, "Old Winnie." He shook his head, looking down at the floor. "They say he topped hisself, shot hisself dead. All too much for him in the end, y'see. He'd put everything into winnin the war for us, and he'd finally done it, it was almost finished. Then Hitler sent his secret weapon over and had hisself the last laugh. It would've been too much for any man."

And that quietened us a whole lot more. Tears were running down Cissie's cheeks and Muriel had her head bowed. Potter rummaged among the bottles on the coffee table for fresh whisky and Stern sat stiff-backed, his face a mask. Me, I just poured another Jack Daniel's.

Grief is only finite, you know? Sure, over the past years I'd thought a lot about death and those I'd lost, about the major players, the little guys too, friends, acquaintances, kids I'd gone to High School with, good pilots I'd fought battles with. You don't forget, but you hold down the memory; or at least, the emotion that goes with the memory. After a while it fades, the emotion, because the soul can only take so much. The numbness eventually sets in, although, if you're really lucky, that can happen right away. Generally though, it'll take months, maybe years, before you begin—and only *begin*—to pull through and start to think straight again. In my case I only had two people to really grieve over, because my folks were dead before the war even started, Ma in '38 of cancer, Dad soon after in '39, of heart disease. I had no brothers or sisters, and other relations were too distant to cause much concern. Those two people closest to me, wiped out by the Blood Death, took up most, if not all, of my mourning.

As I looked at the strained faces around me, I realized my new and unwanted companions were still in a state of shock. The girls had been cloistered from the worst excesses of the disease for some time, and the warden had taken his own mental route for dealing with the situation. Now Cissie and Muriel had ventured beyond the confines of the sanatorium and local villages to witness the full horror of the V2s' legacy for themselves, and Albert Potter had finally come into contact with other survivors, and *their* sanity, such as it was, had to be nagging at his own delusions. As for the German, well, even he had to have had family, people to weep for, so he had to be suffering too. Maybe guilt—it was his countrymen who had unleashed the final holocaust—figured in his emotional state also; race responsibility for such annihilation would have to lay heavy on any man. Unless, of course, the only person he really mourned over was his *Führer*, whose actions he considered to be both appropriate and heroic.

I watched Stern and tried to guess what was going on behind that mask; he remained inscrutable though, despite hitting the juice and chain-smoking along with the rest of us. Funny thing is, he never got soused, nor maudlin, no matter how much he drank. But then, neither did I that evening.

|10|

DIVING, DIVING, DIVING . . .

The two Fw 190s had chased me to thirty-eight thousand feet, and the air was thin up there. I'd had no choice, there was only one way to get away from them, because they were like angry hornets on my tail, relentless, dogged, and out for revenge. They'd watched me shoot down one of their buddies at twelve thousand feet, and that'd made them pretty sore, because their buddy, in his superior plane, should've finished me. I'd been in his sights, sure enough, but had flipped over just before he'd fired and gotten behind him, winging him with my own guns. I'd followed him down, giving him another burst, and the Fw 190 had gone into a spiral, an entrail of white smoke marking his descent. He didn't bail out and I'd hoped he was already dead.

His two friends came steaming in, angry—hell, they were insulted—because I was on my own, one against three, and they'd thought they'd have some fun with me.

They'd assumed they had me when I leveled out. A Spitfire might have gotten away from the Focke-Wulfs, but my Hurricane, with its eight Browning machine-guns in its wings, was a clumsier animal and I knew I'd have to take desperate measures. There was only one way to outfly the Germans, but they'd have to follow me. I headed upwards, into the blue, taking the Hurricane to the limits. And the Focke-Wulfs came after me.

Thirty-eight thousand, cockpit rattling around me, and I leveled, took her into a dive. Thirty-seven thousand feet, thirty-six, -five, and my belly's pressing against my spine. Picking up speed, though, control column vibrating in my hand. Can't hear them, but I feel the bullets tearing into my left wing. Diving faster. No more gunfire—the Krauts are beginning to have problems controlling their aircraft as all three of us pick up speed.

Thirty thousand feet and my speed's up to four hundred miles an hour, considerably more than the Hurricane's limit. Diving, faster, faster, everything shaking around me, engine's screaming, my goggles are fogging up, sweat's beginning to blind me.

Twenty-five thousand.

Twenty.

I manage to twist my head, look behind me. Can only see one pursuer, and he's pulling out of the dive, giving up the chase. Where's his pal? Can't see the other Focke-Wulf. Have to assume it's still on my tail.

Nineteen, then eighteen.

Too fast now. Christ, much too fast. I tear off the goggles. Can't believe it when I look at the instrument panel. Everything's quivering, but still I can see the speedo's needle. Not possible. I'm approaching six hundred miles per hour. Nobody's gonna believe this. If I ever live to tell the tale.

And now it happens, the thing I'd dreaded. They call it compressibility. It's when everything gets dampened, nothing works as it should. The plane is out of control, the stick's all over the place.

Jesus H, I'm down to twelve thousand.

I grip the control column, try to pull the Hurricane out of its dive, but it won't listen, it won't obey. Pulling harder, both hands clamped around the stick. The plane won't haul up. Oh dear Lord . . .

Eight thousand feet.

Seven.

Six.

That's it. I'm done. I'm locked into that seat by pressure, no way can I get out of the cockpit. Not giving up though. Too much to live for. I pull harder.

Five.

I begin to pray.

But forget the prayer and start to scream.

Everything becomes white, like the center of an explosion . . .

And I woke up. Thank God, I woke up. And as I sat there, bolt upright in the bed, body wringing wet, limbs trembling, I realized it wasn't the imminent dream-death that had awakened me. The light knocking on the door came again.

Moonlight flooded the room so that the walls, the furniture, the rumpled bedsheet, were bathed ghostly white. I stayed where I was, still in shock, my mind completing the dream that was, in fact, a memory: Coming out of the dive at the last moment, skimming over the treetops, the Fw 190 which had remained in pursuit not so lucky; it'd hit those same trees and exploded into one huge fireball. The German pilot's screaming face, imagined by me as I sat there in the moonlight, resembled Wilhelm Stern's. Fortunately for me on that day almost seven years ago, the rest of my squadron hadn't been far away, and the wing commander himself had hurtled towards me along with two other Hurricanes and chased off the surviving Focke-Wulf, giving me hell over the radio for wandering away from the main battle as he did so. It wasn't the first time I'd had that dream, but it was no worse than any of the others that disturbed my sleep almost every night, drunk or sober.

The rapping on the door came again, still light, but more urgent this time, as though the person outside were becoming impatient. Or desperate. The doorhandle turned, but with no effect—I always kept the door locked at night.

Tossing back the sheet, I snatched my pants from the foot of the bed and pulled them on. Before going to the door, I picked up the .45 from the bedside cabinet and cocked it. Index finger outside the trigger guard, barrel pointed at the ceiling, I padded barefoot over the bedroom door.

As if sensing me on the other side, a muffled female voice called softly: "Hoke, please let me in."

Quickly turning the key, I opened the door a few inches. I could see only a shadow outside in the hall.

"Please," she repeated, and I could tell she was close to tears.

I stood aside, pulling the door open a little wider, and Muriel slipped through the gap. The moment the door was shut tight again and I'd turned to face her, she was in my arms, her slender body shivering despite the night's warmth.

I resisted at first, remained stiff, unyielding, gun hand still raised towards the ceiling, the palm of my other hand wavering inches from her back. Then I smelled her sweet perfume and I remembered what a woman's embrace was like. My hand closed against her back, pulling her towards me, and I lowered the gun to my side. I breathed in the aroma of her freshly washed hair, then the scent she'd used on her skin, on her neck, her breasts. I even enjoyed the faint taint of wine still on her lips. A pressure inside me was released, the tightness in my chest loosened. I held on to her for a moment, maybe a few moments, and closed my eyes. My mind reeled in her presence.

It had been so long, so very long . . .

But the numbness within me returned, the rejection of true feelings that was my only defense against the terrible thing that had happened to the world and to me overrode those stirring emotions: I stepped away from her. In the silvery light from the window, I saw the glistening of tears on her cheeks and I saw the confusion in her eyes.

"Hold me," she asked in a hushed voice.

I couldn't. I didn't want to. I knew if I took her back into my arms I'd lose something that had kept me together these past three years, the detachment I'd come to wear like a suit of armor. I did not want to become vulnerable again.

Her bare shoulders were trembling still and the moonlight shimmered off the silk slip she wore. She watched, her tears catching that same light so that crystals shone from within their trails, then slowly lowered her head.

"I'm so afraid," she said.

And I gave in, so easily, so goddamn willingly.

Her weeping dampened my naked chest and I felt tiny spasms jerk her whole body with each sob she uttered.

"Take it easy," I said to her quietly, at a loss for any other words of comfort. "We're safe here."

Her hair was sensuous against my skin. "I saw them, Hoke," I heard her say. "There were so many."

"Who? Who did you see?"

She lifted her head to gaze up at me. "I saw their spirits. The people who died in this hotel—I saw their spirits wandering the hallways and corridors. I saw them on the stairways, lost souls, just drifting, with nowhere to go. It was so sad, Hoke, so pitiful—and so frightening."

"I told you all not to leave your rooms tonight." My anger was false, a diversion from what she was telling me, because I didn't want to hear such things. Memories were enough to cope with.

"I had to get out. I needed to see more of this place, perhaps only to revisit better days. Can't you understand that?"

I shook my head. "It was a stupid thing to do."

She wasn't listening. "I went as far as the main stairway, the one by the lift. They were just shadows at first, a shifting in the dark, until they began to emerge, slowly at first, as if my own concentration was helping them take form. Then they were all around me, drifting, floating, and oblivious to each other. Even for those who were together, elegant women in long, flowing dresses on the arms of men in dinner jackets and winged collars, there appeared to be no contact between them. But the anguish in their eyes, the misery in their features . . ." Her head rested against my chest once more. "Was it only my imagination, Hoke? Or were they real. . . ?"

"A dream, that's all," I told her as I held her tight, my arms pressed against her back, the gun now awkward in my hand.

"But I wasn't sleeping," I heard her murmur.

"Illusions, then. Don't you get it? The shock of seeing all those corpses earlier today is still messing with your head. Believe me, I know about it, Muriel, I've been there myself. You, me, Cissie, old Albert Potter, and the German—we're the only living, breathing things in this hotel."

"I didn't say they were living—"

"There are no ghosts." She jumped at the anger in my voice. "The dead are dead. Anything else is fantasy. You understand, Muriel, you understand?"

My free hand was gripping her upper arm and she flinched at its sudden pressure. She tried to pull away.

"Okay, okay, I'm sorry," I soothed, annoyed at myself for letting her wild talk get to me. "Just relax now and try to put those thoughts out of your mind. They'll fade away eventually, I promise you. They'll fade away for good."

Her body seemed to sag and she leaned back into me, her hands down by her sides, her weight against my chest. I let her weep, my hand stroking her hair, and soon I became aware of the hardened tips of her small breasts through the thin silky slip, nudging my skin, arousing feelings I'd long since subdued. I fought against it, against yearnings that had been denied for so many years, aware that it was wrong, the wrong time, the wrong circumstances. And afraid she would be repulsed.

Her weeping had stopped and she suddenly became taut once more, as though aware of what was happening. But instead of pulling away, she relaxed into me and the contact between us took on a new intensity. The very air around us seemed charged, as though an electric storm was gathering inside that cluttered bedroom. Impossible, but it seemed so real, and I soon realized that energy was building inside our own bodies and not in the atmosphere outside them. For me it became a kind of agony, an ecstatic craving that battled against other emotions, feelings and memories that would not be cast aside, not just for this, not just for—*the image appeared stark and horrifying in my mind, her body lying there on stone steps, her belly torn open . . .* I tried to block the thought, but still the horror of it lingered.

"Hoke?"

Now I was the one who trembled, the one who fought back tears and turned my head away.

Muriel held my arms and shook me gently. "What is it? What's wrong?" she said.

"It's okay," I lied, suppressing the dread within me. "It's nothing."

"For a moment I thought you'd seen the ghosts too."

"I told you, there are no ghosts."

"Then why were you afraid just now?"

"It wasn't fear."

"No?"

"No."

"So why are you shivering?"

There was only one way to stop her questions. I kissed her. Hard. Angrily.

And she responded, pressing her lips just as hard against mine, as if there was a fury in her longings also, a fierce aching that had been there for a long time. We fought against each other in a battle that was for fulfilment, not conquest, each of us clinging so that flesh touched flesh and desire met with desire. It was a struggle that required an outcome and we both knew it.

She drew her head away and whispered something. I became still and looked at her questioningly.

"I need more," she said, her voice barely audible over our gasps for breath. "I need to lie next to you."

I hardly hesitated, because any resistance was gone, lost in those first few moments. After wiping away the rivulets of tears from her cheeks with the thumb of one hand I led her to the bed and lowered her onto the wrinkled sheet. She kept her arms around my neck as I left the gun on the bedside cabinet and I took in her scent, not the perfume she'd found in her suite, nor the soap she'd used on her hair, but the aroma of her womanhood, of her arousal. The sheet beneath us was an unblemished white in the moonlight and her skin was of that same whiteness; the slip she wore was a shade darker, its reflections soft and silvery. Only by closing my mind to the past could I release myself to the present, and the vision of Muriel lying there, her arms outstretched to receive me, her legs slightly parted, one knee bent, helped me banish that other time. We needed each other badly and any reservation was swiftly put aside.

I sank down onto her, taking most of my own weight on my elbow so that I could gaze into her moon-bleached face and into those eyes that sought more than just passion. There was an urgency there, but also—or so I told myself at the time—a need for some kind of security, maybe a commitment.

My fingers, still trembling, slipped beneath the strap on her pale shoulder to ease it aside. Resting my hand there, curled around her shoulder, I lowered my face so that our lips brushed against each other. The touch was deliberately delicate, unlike the bruising kiss of moments before, and it excited us both; still we kept the encounter tentative, moistening each other's mouths with tiny stabs of our tongues, resisting the impulse to crush, to give ourselves completely, the restraint soon becoming unbearable, the years of abstinence heightening the tension, increasing the pleasure.

It could only last a matter of seconds and when finally we pressed into each other, teeth clashing, our lips hurting, I felt a roaring inside my head, a rush of charges surging through each limb, each part of my body. My hand left her shoulder to find her small, firm breast, and my fingers tightened on its solid core. I heard her gasp at the sudden pain, but the sound became a moan, and this was of pleasure.

Her hands slid round my neck, kneading its flesh and the hard ridge of my spine, her fingertips retreating so that they could come between us to work themselves against my chest, digging into the muscles there, smoothing over the ridges. It was my turn to gasp when her fingers probed the bruising. She quickly took her hand away, afraid she'd hurt me too much, and I felt those fingers flatten against my stomach, causing the muscles there to shudder involuntarily.

Our kisses were equally wild, our breaths equally as desperate, and when her tongue entered my mouth and pressed against my own tongue, I became even more aroused. One of my hands tugged at the slip, pulling it down, away from her breasts, and I took time to drink them in with my eyes, because they were so naked, so bare, so sensual, like delicate spheres carved in marble; and then I drank them in with my mouth, taking each nipple in turn between my lips and drawing them in so that they stood wet and proud as Muriel squirmed beneath me. I heard the quiet rustle of the sheet as her legs parted and when I rose from her again, I saw that the smooth material of her slip had ruffled up over her thighs, leaving a deep, alluring shadow between them. It was another flawless sight, an image that set my mind reeling as all control, all reason slipped away from me.

Muriel's chest was rising and falling with her own breathlessness and her hair framed her sweet face on the pillow. Her hands suddenly busied themselves with the waistband of my pants, and then I was free, her fingers closing around me and drawing me towards her so that I cried out with the wonderful shock of it. Her thighs opened wider as she guided me down between them and her cry was louder than mine as I entered her body, the resistance only slight, the hesitation only minimal. Again her cry turned to a moan of pleasure as I travelled further, the journey now smooth and easy, like gliding through warm butter, and her narrow hips rose up to meet me, her hands, her arms, pulling at me fiercely, urging me on, never, it seemed, wanting that journey to end. But quickly I reached the furthest point, and we clung to each other, her tears dampening my chest and shoulders once again.

Only then did we pause, and my own tears fell into her hair. She felt the wetness and held me tightly, but now with a tenderness that had nothing to do with passion. It couldn't last though, that moment of caring and compassion—our physical demands were too great, our sexual needs too critical. We began to move against each other again, each thrust becoming wilder, our senses rushing towards that point in our bodies where our juices could fuse and our energies meld. When my flow finally streamed from me I buried my face against her shoulder and groaned, and I stayed that way until the fluttering spasms grew less in intensity, ebbed away, left me exhausted.

Slowly my body and my mind relaxed. And for the first time in three years I found a temporary peace.

I lit another cigarette with the one I'd just finished and settled back against the bed's cushioned headboard. The shadows in the room had altered as the moon beyond the high windows had drifted upriver, and it was hard to make out Muriel's form as she lay beside me beneath the single sheet, her hand resting lightly on my thigh. The scent of spent passion lingered between us, a sweet-sour musk that was both calming and sensual at the same time, and I remembered how Sally had called it "love-fragrance," believing it was some kind of invisible shroud that enveloped lovers after the act, bonding them for a little longer. Yeah, I'd laughed at the time, laughed like a hyena, making her mad at first, until she'd joined in the laughter, but punching my arm all the same. I'd liked the idea though, despite my teasing. At least, I'd liked it with Sally in the picture. Now the thought only stoked up my guilt.

"Hoke?" There was a quiet huskiness to her voice. "Are you all right?"

I could just see the outline of her hair and her arm in the darkness, the vague glint of her eyes. As I drew on the cigarette she was briefly bathed in its warm glow.

"Sure, I'm okay," I replied.

"You were telling me about your parents."

Lighting the fresh cigarette had interrupted the flow; the aroma of our love-making had rekindled a memory.

"Like I said," I went on, "Ma was English, with a touch of Irish thrown in. Peggy. 'Peg o' my Heart' Dad liked to call her, naturally enough. They first met when he was over from Wisconsin for an agricultural fair—he dealt in farm equipment, bought 'n' sold anything from machinery to fertilizers. Had a fair little business going just after the Great War and he was kind of anxious to get a head start with all the new technology for farming."

"That's where you're from—Wisconsin?"

I nodded in the dark, and added a 'yes' for Muriel's benefit.

"Peg was a maid in one of your small, country hotels Dad was staying in, and when I was growed up enough to be interested he told me it was her 'sparklin eyes' he first fell in love with, the rest of her 'bout two days later."

"And your mother—did she fall for him so quickly?"

"Guess she must have, because when he left eight days later she went with him. Just took off, the pair of 'em, bill paid, notice given, but no explanation to anyone. Back to Winona, Wisconsin, USA. They got hitched right away and a year later I arrived."

"Wasn't she afraid? A new country thousands of miles away from her own family?"

"Ma had none to speak of. Her old man had been an Irish immigrant, who hadn't treated Grandma too well. Peggy was his only daughter. When his wife died, he returned to Ireland where he probably killed himself with booze, according to Ma. Oh, he'd found his kid a job in a washhouse before he'd left, so I guess he figured he'd done his duty. And that was fine by Ma—at fourteen years of age she figured she was better off without him. When she married Dad, she didn't know if her old man was dead or alive, and she told me years later she hadn't cared."

Muriel's fingers moved to my arm and she stroked it, elbow to wrist.

"She was never bitter about it though. Hell no, she was too thankful for her new life with Joseph, my dad. But y'know, although she never had a family to miss, she had something else to hanker after. Ma never got tired of telling me about her home country and I never got tired of listening."

Muriel couldn't see me, but I was smiling at the memory. It felt good to talk about my folks after all this time and, for a while at least, it was holding down thoughts of Sally.

"She regretted leaving England?"

"No, I didn't say that. She'd found her happiness in Wisconsin, but that didn't mean she didn't get homesick now and again. She read me books by English authors all the time, and when I was old enough, got me to read 'em myself. Got me interested in the country's history, too. Maybe the only regret she had was that I wasn't getting an English education and I wasn't being brought up the British way. She took a lot of pride in the traditions and manners of this country of yours, even though she was only from working stock, and sometimes I wondered if those funny wire-framed spectacles she wore later on in life weren't just a little rose-tinted. Her dream was to bring me over here for a short while, show me all those things she'd told me about, but the cancer put a hold on that."

My smile was gone and I took time to inhale smoke. Muriel's hand was still on my arm.

"She passed away in '38, and Dad followed her eight months later. His ticker, the doc said, disease had worn it out. I always believed it was heartbreak that did it, though; or at least, hurried it along. I think he just didn't want to go on without his Peg any more."

My smile had come back. It gave me some comfort, the thought of Dad going after his Peg, darned if he was gonna let her explore the great unknown on her own. "Your Ma's got no sense of direction," he'd always joked with me. "Lose herself in the parlor if she didn't have me around to call her." Well, wherever she'd gone, I hoped he'd caught up with her. And I was kind of glad they'd both missed the horror that was to come.

"You were left alone?" Muriel's hand tightened around my arm.

"Alone ain't so bad," I lied. Alone was hell on wheels. Alone was a slow trip to insanity. Alone was the worst thing any man, woman or child could live with. My smile was gone again, wilted away in the shadows.

"By that time I was living away from home anyway," I went on before self-pity set me blubbing again. "I was in Madison, attending the University of Wisconsin, studying engineering. Dad's company was in bad shape by the time he died, and his brother, a wiseacre even Dad didn't like, offered to take it off my hands, lock, stock, and barrel, for no money at all. Well, that suited me just fine—what did I want with a pile of debts and a head full of problems when I was barely scraping eighteen? My uncle was welcome to 'em. Besides, I was supporting myself well enough by bike racing and some barnstorming at weekends."

"What's barnstorming? I've never heard of that one before."

"Air acrobatics, I guess you'd call it."

"You were flying at eighteen?"

"Sure. When I was ten years old, Dad took me over to a barnstorming show in a field just outside town. Gave me a dollar to spend while he looked over a couple of crates he had in mind for crop-dusting, something that was becoming pretty popular about that time. I wandered off towards an old airplane I'd spied soon as we drove in, a beat-up Fairchild, as I recall, and when I handed its pilot the dollar and asked for a ride, well, he sized me up, bit the dollar, and lifted me aboard. 'Course, I told him Dad said it was okay, and that was good enough for this flyer, whether he believed me or not. And once I was up there in the clear blue air, high over the whole goddamn world, everything below shrunk into insignificance, well, I never wanted to come down again. I knew flying was the thing I wanted to do with the rest of my life.

"But Ma—'specially Ma—and Dad didn't agree with my ambition, though when I kept ducking school so's I could wander around our local airfield we came to an arrangement. They'd pay for me to take flying lessons if I promised to stay in school and study hard. Anyway, I think Dad had an idea floating around in the back of his mind even then, because by the time I was sixteen I was crop-dusting for his farmer friends and acquaintances in our own second-hand plane."

I leaned forward in the bed, wrists resting over my raised knees, cigarette butt warm between my fingers. I kept perfectly still, ears keen, eyes straining at the reflected moon-light on the opposite wall.

"What's wrong?" Muriel sat up next to me, the sheet falling around her waist.

I shushed her, listening still. I felt her body go tense beside me.

"Thought I heard something," I said eventually. "Must've been wrong."

Relaxing against the headboard again, I reached for the

cigarette pack on the bedside cabinet. This time I remembered to offer one to Muriel, but she shook her head, a movement I barely caught in the darkness. Lighting one for myself, I stubbed out the old cigarette in the full ashtray by the bed, and dropped the pack into my lap. Smoke drifted across the room, thin specters that caught the light by the windows. Muriel rested her head on my shoulder, her hair tickling my flesh.

"Tell me more," she urged, as if my story reminded her of a different reality, a better time than the present.

"There's not much more to it." A second lie, but there was only so much I was willing to tell. "When war broke out in Europe, I knew immediately what I wanted to do. All those tales Ma told me, about her life in England, the places she'd worked and lived in, about the kings and queens, dukes and duchesses, all those books she'd read to me and the ones I'd read myself when I was older—hell, I even knew the rules of cricket. Dad had always kidded me I was more British than American, and I kind of liked that, made me feel different, something special. I guess that was because I thought Ma was so special. Huh, sometimes when I was little I even copied her accent." I gave a shake of my head. "Y'know, she never did lose that accent in all those years she was married to Dad."

I exhaled smoke, enjoying its taste, its smell. It'd been a long time since I'd felt so relaxed and I figured it was due to the talking as much as the lovemaking. The booze at dinner had loosened me too and I was almost—only almost—beginning to feel glad of the company. I should have known it was dangerous to let others into my life again.

"You've stopped talking again." There was no impatience in Muriel's voice, only amusement.

"Yeah. Just thinking."

"You said when war broke out you knew what you wanted to do."

I blew smoke away from her face. "I wanted to help the Brits fight their war with Germany any way I could. So I began flying aircraft, bombers mainly, up to the Canadian border. Because of the Neutrality Act, America couldn't export planes direct to the UK, not even over to Canada, so we used to fly 'em as close to the Canadian border as possible, then tow 'em across the line by rope and truck. It was a crazy way of getting planes to you, but it worked. No rules broken."

She laughed, a soft fluttery sound that did us both some good.

"It wasn't long before I got another bright idea. I hitched a ride on a bomber out of RCAF Training Station Trenton to the 1st American Eagle Squadron over here and they let me sign up as a pilot officer. I had the flying hours and they needed the men, it was as simple as that. So I became part of your war, long before my own country decided to get involved."

I closed my eyes, feeling some relief. But that was it, I was done, I didn't want to tell her any more. Anything else would dredge up memories I'd fought too long to keep down. Fortunately, Muriel didn't press me further. She must have sensed my change in mood, realized that more questions might arouse too much pain in me, release the bitterness I was holding in check. I liked her for that. Yeah, at that moment I almost loved her for it.

Opening my eyes, I leaned over and dogged the cigarette, then turned towards her. Her hand moved across my chest, her touch as sensuous as before, though less demanding, both of us at ease with one another. She shifted her body, offering her lips to me in the dark, and I accepted, my own mouth brushing against hers, the kiss tentative at first, but soon becoming firmer as fresh desire began to climb. Our tongues probed, we tasted each other's juices. Her hand slid down my chest, over my stomach, dipping beneath the rumpled sheet, finding my hardness and causing me to gasp as her fingers encircled and gripped me tight. I pulled her to me, one hand cradling her hip, and she turned her face towards the ceiling as my lips pressed against the softness of her neck.

Now she was gasping, and she squirmed her body so that she was beneath me, her legs parting once again as she murmured words I couldn't hear. Her breasts rose into me as her breathing became more uneven and her grip went to my waist, her hands pulling at me, her murmuring taking on a new urgency, her passion revived, her hunger just as desperate as before. I felt the familiar rush inside me, the incredible surging of senses, blood pounding in my chest so that I could hear its sound . . . could hear . . .

She cried out as I abruptly turned away from her, wheeling round in the bed to stare at the big windows. The pounding . . .

somewhere in the distance out there. Lighting up the night sky. And drawing closer by the second.

"Oh my God," said Muriel, panic rising in her voice. "What is it, Hoke?"

"Bombs," I told her flatly.

"But—"

"We'll be okay. Don't worry about it."

My back was to her and she slid closer, her hands reaching for my shoulders. I winced as her fingers touched the graze the bullet had left along my right shoulder earlier that day.

"Who is it, Hoke?" she pleaded. "Who would be bombing London now? Is it those people who chased us?"

"Listen," I said, my eyes still watching the windows.

The deep drone of engines came to us between the sounds of bombs exploding.

"An aeroplane?" she asked incredulously.

"You got it."

The windows suddenly lit up and rattled in their frames as a bomb fell somewhere across the river.

"I don't understand. Why would any—"

I cut her off curtly. "They're German. Possibly just one man, still fighting his own personal war. He's insane, d'you understand that?" I didn't know why I was angry at her; maybe it was because suddenly I had to explain things that I'd gotten used to.

She flinched as another bomb hit the other riverbank, the blast shaking the hotel's windows, this time with even more force.

"He comes over every once in a while, usually when you think things have quietened down again and he's given up. Given up or dead."

"It's madness."

"Like I said."

Another explosion, this one on our side of the Thames and fierce enough to make the whole building tremble. Muriel pulled me round so that she could squeeze between my arms, and I was about to suggest we take cover on the other side or beneath the bed when another noise came to us, a harsh, demented rattling from the corridor outside our room. She tried to burrow into me and I wasn't sure which was scaring her most. The rattling grew louder, a terrible cacophony that resembled a stick running along iron railings, only a thousand times more piercing.

Then we heard the old warden's voice. *"Air raid warning, everyone under cover, please go to your nearest shelter!"*

The door burst open and Potter's bright flashlight lit us up on the bed. We shielded our eyes and the light dropped. I blinked away the dazzle and when I looked back at the doorway I saw there were two figures standing there.

Another blast outside—this one mercifully further off, the German bomber moving onwards—diverted my attention for a moment or two, and when I turned towards the doorway again, only Albert Potter was standing there flashlight in one hand, his air raid warning rattle in the other. The second figure, Cissie, had gone.

| 11 |

I BROUGHT THE FLATBED TRUCK ROUND, A HARD LEFT FROM THE Embankment into the gentle rise that ran between the park and the Savoy's rear entrance, and was surprised to see Cissie sitting on the curbside opposite the hotel. I grinned when I saw who was keeping her company and I wondered at it too.

They both looked up when they heard the chug of the truck's diesel engine and the girl's concerned frown switched to a guarded smile of welcome when she realized I was the driver. Cagney quickly rose from his haunches and gave a pleased yap, then chased after me when I drove on by. I headed towards the end of the narrow street where there was room to turn the long vehicle round so it faced the right direction, easy to get away in a hurry should the need arise. Another road ran beneath the buildings at the end of the street, but it was blocked by other vehicles, its first few clear yards only good for maneuvering. A few hundred yards away, one of the buildings of London's law courts was still smoldering from last night's bomb damage, but I couldn't see any other wreckage. The crazy German bomber pilot was unpredictable, but I hoped he'd had his fill of laying waste for a while: sometimes he came over several nights in a row, sometimes he wouldn't appear for a few months; I guess it all depended on his disposition. I hoped some day a bomb would jam in its bay and blow him and his Dornier to smithereens. After completing the laborious parking procedure, the truck's left wheels cracking pavement stones, I jumped down from the cab and made a fuss of Cagney, who'd been waiting for me.

I ruffled his ears, something he didn't like, never had, and he growled low and menacing, so I did it some more. Before he got too riled I hugged him to me and got a face full of tongue for my kindness. The taste of dust didn't seem to bother him and he would have slobbered me to death if I hadn't stood and pushed him down when he reared up with me. Taking the hint at the second shove, Cagney trotted off back along the street, making, to my surprise, straight for Cissie, who was still sitting on the curb observing us.

Cissie averted her gaze before I reached her, studying some point in the distance, her neck and shoulders kind of stiff-like. I sat next to her, laying my leather jacket with its added weight of Colt .45 on the ground between us.

"Hyah," I ventured.

"Hello," she responded without much interest.

Cagney settled in the middle of the road, facing us, head resting on his paws. He yawned as he watched us.

"Hot day again," I said, making conversation.

The back of Cissie's head bobbed in agreement. Today she was wearing a dark-brown dress that matched her hair, puffed at the shoulders, slim at the waist. No stockings and, when she finally turned my way, I saw she wore no make-up. She eyed the dust in my hair, on my hands, on my face, but ignored it for the moment.

"Is that *your* dog?"

"He's nobody's dog."

"He was waiting outside when I came down for a breath of fresh air. I thought he was a stray."

"He didn't run away?"

"He was wary at first, so I just sat there and talked to him and after a while he came over and sort of slouched down next to me. Wouldn't let me pat him though, moved away every time I tried."

"Cagney doesn't like people very much. Seems to think they're to blame for everything that's happened."

"Did you say Cagney? His name's Cagney?" At last her face cracked into a smile. "After James Cagney?"

"Well his real name's probably Rex or Red, but he wasn't saying when we met up. I decided on Cagney and the mutt didn't seem to mind."

"Has he been with you for long?"

"Coupla years, maybe."

The sun beat down on the dusty roadway and pretty soon Cagney's eyes drooped shut. I took a rumpled rag from my pants pocket and wiped sweat from the back of my neck and underneath my chin.

"D'you have any idea what time it is?" Cissie asked, a coolness still there in her tone.

I looked over my shoulder and squinted up at the sun. "'Bout four, I'd guess. Busted my watch way back, had no use for it anyhow. Hell, I got no appointments to keep."

"So where have you been all day?" She was looking directly at me now and I wondered at the suspicion in her eyes. "You left before any of us were awake. Even before Muriel was awake, apparently," she added meaningfully.

This time I looked away, staring up at the hotel's taped windows. The thought that so much death lay beyond them was depressing. "I had things to do," I replied eventually.

She must've understood that was all I had to say on the subject, because she didn't push it any further. I liked her for that.

"How've you survived, Hoke? How have you lived on your own like this for three years?" Curiosity, and maybe some concern, was edging aside her coolness.

"It's easier to get by when you've only got yourself to take care of. You can move faster and make your own decisions. It's a lot easier this way."

"You sound bitter."

I gave a small, dry chuckle. "Really? Well now." I left it at that.

"The aeroplane that came over last night . . ."

"A Dornier Do 217. German medium bomber, the Flying Pencil they used to call it. Whoever's flying it doesn't realize the war's over, or doesn't care. And there's no way we can communicate." I tucked the rag back into my pocket. "Maybe one night I'll be waiting for him in a Spitfire or Hurricane and finish it once and for all."

"No. No more killing, Hoke. Hasn't there been enough?"

"Try telling it to that guy." I indicated the sky with my thumb and I could have meant the mad German pilot or the Creator Himself. It didn't matter which.

"What's the point of continuing the hatred? Look what it's already done to us." She lowered her head and I could see the beginnings of tears glittering in her eyelashes.

I could stand my own self-pity, but not somebody else's. I pushed myself to my feet and reached down for my battered and torn leather jacket. "I'm gonna clean up, then get a bite t'eat," I said.

She joined me, brushing dust from her seat, and suddenly I was the one who was curious.

"How d'you get out of the hotel? Past all those dead people, I mean. Weren't you afraid?"

"Of what? Empty shells? You think I'm scared of ghosts too?" From the glint behind those unshed tears in her eyes I guessed Muriel had offered some kind of explanation, maybe even some excuse, for last night. "No, I'm more afraid of maniacs still dropping bombs or lunatics trying to steal my blood."

"I can ease your mind as far as one of those threats is concerned. Let me show you the safest place to be in the hotel when the bomber comes over again."

I led her across the street and through the brick, zigzag barrier protecting the Savoy's River Room windows and back entrance, Cagney immediately out of his doze to follow us. Inside the gloomy entrance hall I picked up the flashlight I always left in a corner by the stairway in case of emergencies or my own late-night arrivals, then took her downstairs to the hotel's vast basement area. We entered a long room on the left of the hallway and I played the flashlight over pink-curtained bunk-beds, all of them numbered.

"Sleeping quarters for the rich and famous," I explained. "At the first sound of an air-raid siren, Savoy guests were ushered down here for their own safety."

I moved the light on, showing Cissie the discreet alcoves, heavy drapes across them turning their interiors into small but private chambers. "For your royalty, dukes and duchesses, even princes and princesses. If they were gonna shelter from the bombs, they were gonna do it in comfort."

I picked out a bust standing on a pedestal at the far end of the room. "Abe Lincoln," I told her. "This place is dedicated to him. The Yanks who came here looked on it as another tiny state of the Union wedged between the Strand and the Thames. A lot of work for the U.S. was carried out down here, and a lot of bridges built between your country and mine." I shone the light up at the ceiling and around the pillars. "It's reinforced with thousands of feet of steel tubing and timber beams, all strengthened by concrete. The place is bomb-proof, Cissie, so if you get scared next time that damn crazy starts blitzing us again, just get yourself down here. Safest place in town."

Despite what she'd said about ghosts up there in the daylight, I felt her shiver beside me.

"Thanks for the tour," she said, "but can we leave now? There's something horrible about this room."

I turned the flashlight on her and saw her eyes were wide and constantly moving, as if she expected something to jump out at her from the dark at any moment.

"I thought you weren't afraid of ghosts."

She was already backing away. "I'm not, but it's like the Underground station down here, it feels like a mausoleum. Hoke, have you looked behind those curtains?"

She had a point. It was one thing to be surrounded by the dead, but another to be enclosed with them, especially in the dark. I began to feel uneasy myself.

I followed her from the Abraham Lincoln Room and we climbed back to ground level. She became calmer standing in the light from the entrance doors, but I could tell she was still agitated. Could be I'd made a mistake below ground, because it had only underlined the fact that we were holed up in one huge tomb, and whether Cissie believed in spirits or not, the idea had to be a mite unnerving. Y'see, I'd forgotten how accustomed I'd become to living with the dead all around me. These people, save for Potter, weren't used to the new cities yet.

"How long have we got to stay here?" Cissie demanded to know.

I'd been trying to make things easier for her, so I guess I got a little irritated by her tone. "Lady, you can leave whenever you like."

"But . . ." she started to say, "But surely . . ."

I was stone-faced.

"Surely we'll stay together." Her hands were held towards me, palms facing, more in exasperation than pleading. "We need each other, Hoke, can't you understand that? Could you really go on living by yourself, with only . . . only a dog for company?"

Cagney, who'd stayed in a sunny spot by the entrance, cocked his head. He looked from Cissie to me, as if waiting for the reply.

"Cagney's been enough so far," I shot back. "He doesn't gripe and he doesn't need nurse-maiding. Yeah, I'll stick with the mutt."

She left me then, stomping up the stairs, head and shoulders stiff with suppressed—outrage, resentment, good old-fashioned pique? I didn't know which—and I had to resist the urge to call her back. Cagney made a noise deep in his throat, a kind of drawn-out groan, and rolled his eyes at me.

"Quit it," I snapped, and went back out into the sunshine.

Muriel was waiting for me when I eventually got back to the suite. She was standing by the window, a hand parting the net curtain so she could watch feeble strands of smoke rising from somewhere across the river, another piece of real estate damaged in last night's explosions. She dropped the curtain and hurried towards me as I closed the door.

"I've been so anxious," she said and stopped a few steps away when she saw the dust in my hair and clothes. "My goodness, what have you been up to? You look so . . . dirty."

I'd left Cagney outside where he could guard the corridor, a position he was well used to by now, so I didn't have to contend with his growling suspicion of this stranger in the room. Again I wondered at his swift acceptance of Cissie, particularly as I hadn't been there to make the introductions in the first place. I remembered I was still rankled with the girl, so any credit I gave her was limited. Tossing my jacket onto the bed and ignoring Muriel's question I headed straight for the bathroom. She followed me in.

Muriel started the shower for me as I tugged off my undershirt and I heard her gasp when she saw the massive bruising on my chest and the inflamed edges of the gunshot nick showing around the dressing. She took in some of the other cuts and bruises on my arms and body, shaking her head in sympathy as she did so.

"Does it hurt badly?" It was a dumb question and she knew it. "Do you have any pain-killers that I can get for you?" she added quickly.

I shook my head and took her by the elbow. "I'm gonna take my shower alone," I told her.

"Let me help. You must be sore all over."

Yeah, I was sore, and I ached too, some of that from the day's work I'd just done, but I didn't need anybody's help to wash myself. "I'd like some privacy, Muriel."

Disappointment, hurt—I guess both were in those grey-blue eyes of hers. "Can't I stay and talk to you? Last night—"

I cut her off. "Last night was last night. You needed me, and I wanted you—last night. Today's another day, kid." Bogart wouldn't have put it better.

Now she looked stunned. "I don't understand," was all she could think of to say.

"Look, you came to me for one thing last night, and you got it." I'd never spoken to a girl like that before and I think I was almost as shocked as Muriel, although my anger covered it. Not only had the world changed, but I had too. I didn't back off though, and the English Rose before me wilted under the blast. "You think you fooled me with all that stuff about seeing ghosts? Christ, I knew what you wanted soon as I opened the door. You and your friend, you just want a man around to look out for you, keep you out of danger, keep you fed. Well you picked the wrong guy, y'hear me? Maybe you better start cosying up to your friend Vilhelm. Sure, he'll take care of you. Didn't you know he's the new Master Race?"

"Why are you so angry?" she pleaded. "What have I done?"

Why? The heck of it was that I didn't know myself. Maybe I was scared of getting involved with other people after I'd spent so long looking out for myself. Was I angry at their intrusion, the sudden burden of having all these people around me? Or in truth, was I plain ashamed of myself for taking this girl to the same bed Sally and I had first made love in? I felt my face redden and it wasn't through rage. Yeah, that was it, or at least a big part of it. Maybe it was foolish, but I felt I'd betrayed the one love of my life, someone I'd sworn eternal love for, no matter what. Stupid kid's stuff? No, not really. Despite the war going on, and both of us knowing that we could die the next day or even that night, we'd made promises to each other that we vowed to keep. Not only had I broken my part of the deal, but I'd done it in the very bedroom Sally and I had honeymooned in. Although I'd had pangs of guilt at the time—all of them easily overwhelmed by the moment itself—the real sense of what I'd done had hit me with its full force when I'd opened the door to Suite 318–319 and found Muriel standing there. Sure I was mad, madder than hell, but not at Muriel, not at Cissie, not at any of them ('cept Stern, but that was different). I was mad at myself. And I was ashamed. The combination was bad.

But I couldn't say all this to Muriel. No, instead I spun away from her and smashed the heel of my hand into the mirror over the washbasin, cracking the glass and fragmenting my image. I heard her give out a small scream and when I glared at her over my raised arm, my palm still pressed against the splintered glass, blood beginning to drip into the sink below it, she seemed about ready to run. I felt stupid, but I must have appeared insane.

I was ready to make some comment—it could've been an apology or a cuss—when Cagney started barking up a storm outside in the corridor. We heard shouting, more barking; something thumped against the bedroom door.

I moved fast, pushing Muriel aside and taking time to snatch the Colt from its holster inside my jacket. Then I was at the door, yanking it open. I stopped dead; gun-hand extended.

Cagney was upset. He was damn-near rabid. Crouched low, snout wrinkled over yellow teeth, haunches quivering, the dog was getting ready to launch itself at something or someone standing beside the door I'd just thrown open.

"It is wild." Shit—vild.

I took a step forward into the corridor so that I could see him. The German had his back pressed against the wall and there was real fear in those pallid eyes of his. Like mine, one of his arms was outstretched, at the end of it the muzzle of a small automatic. He was pointing it at Cagney.

My reaction was almost instinctive, the thought and the movement instantaneous: I smashed my own weapon down hard on Stern's exposed wrist. Spittle shot from the German's open mouth with the shock and his gun clattered to the floor. He bent forward, clutching at his arm, and I brought my gun hand up again, catching him on the forehead so that he straightened and his head slammed against the wall behind. He slid to the floor and I went with him, grabbing the lapel of his jacket and jabbing the Colt's muzzle into his scarred neck.

"Please stop."

His jaw must've been numbed, because the two words weren't that coherent. I understood them though.

"The animal . . ." he managed to blurt. "It was . . . it was going to attack me . . . when I tried to enter your room." That's what he tried to say, but it didn't come out quite that well. I couldn't have cared less anyway—I was ready to blow his brains out.

"Hoke."

Female's voice, but I wasn't taking enough notice to decide whose. It was time to settle the score with the German and I was just mad enough to do it right then and there. Blood oozing from my cut hand made the gun's grip slippery, but still I pressed it into the flesh of his neck. A scream then and I glanced round to see Muriel standing in the doorway. It was Cissie who attacked me though.

Her knee connected with the side of my head, knocking me aside. Then her fingers tangled themselves in my hair and she pulled me backwards, so that I sprawled onto my back. She followed through by kneeling on my chest and grabbing at my gun hand, while Cagney leapt around us, yapping and too excited to figure out which one of us to attack. With a quick swipe of my other hand, I knocked Cissie away and raised my shoulders off the carpeted floor, the Colt finding its target once more.

"Don't shoot him!"

Now it was Muriel who was getting in the way. She positioned herself between me and the stunned German and screamed down at me.

"Stop it, stop it now! We can't go on killing one another, don't you understand?"

To complete the picture, Albert Potter came lumbering along the corridor from his suite. For some reason he still had the warning rattle he'd used last night in his hand and for one bad moment I thought he was gonna blast our ears with it again. Instead he shouted: "What the bleedin 'ell's goin on? Can't a fellah get a decent kip around 'ere?" Mercifully, he tucked the rattle back into one of the large pockets in his overalls.

Cissie, a leg still across my chest, finally got both hands around my wrist and pulled the gun away from its mark.

"Please, Hoke, give it up," she pleaded and there was a sob at the end of her words.

I glanced at her, saw the tears beginning to roll, and I guess it was that that took the wind out of me. I was still full of rage, but some of its energy had left me. I let my head slump back onto the carpet, and as I lay there, staring up at the ceiling, I relaxed my grip on the gun, let my arm go limp. Still Cissie clung to my wrist, not trusting me.

"Okay. I'm done," I assured her. "Just get him outta my sight for a while." They knew I meant Stern and not the dog who, now that the commotion was over, was trying to lick my face.

I heard someone helping the German to his feet, and then he was standing over me, looking down. There was no wariness in his eyes, no fear, only a simmering anger.

"You are a fool," he hissed. "There was no need for this. I am not your enemy."

I ignored him, then suddenly remembered the gun he'd been aiming at Cagney. I sat up, fast, Cissie's grip instantly tightening on my wrist. With relief I saw that Potter had picked up the German's weapon.

"What's this then?" the warden mused, as if he'd never seen a gun before.

"It's a U.S. military issue Colt 380," I informed him, and he nodded his head like he knew all along. "Don't let Stern have it," I warned.

"Do you really think I would shoot you?" Stern sounded almost regretful. "After all that has happened . . ." He waved his hands around as if indicating the world outside. "I found this weapon in my room and kept it for my own protection. I believe I was wise to do so. But do you honestly believe I have the desire to kill again? If you do, then you really are insane, Hoke. The Blood Death has made you so."

With that he walked away from us, one hand held to his injured forehead. He disappeared inside his room and we heard the door close quietly behind him.

✱ ✱ ✱

Supper that evening was a miserable affair. No one felt much like talking and Stern didn't even join us. Let him sulk, I thought, it didn't bother me none. Potter did his best to get things going by reminiscing, relating stories of the Blitz, some of them funny, some of them not so. He told us how one night when he was on his rounds, he'd found Ed Murrow, the famous American war correspondent, lying in the gutter outside the Savoy, not rolling drunk, as Potter had first assumed, but picking up the sounds of wailing sirens and enemy bombs hitting their targets with his microphone, these authentic noises of war to be broadcast across the Atlantic. He told us about the authorities' grand idea of turning gas masks into Mickey Mouse faces so the kids wouldn't be afraid to wear them; how once he'd chased a couple of looters through Covent Garden only to see them both blown to pieces before his eyes by a land mine, one of the looter's legs landing on his shoulder as he'd stood there surprised; how on a cold, frosty dawn he'd come upon an elderly, white-haired lady sitting up in bed, totally bewildered as to why she was in the open, one floor up, two walls of her house completely demolished. He told us about the fireman he'd witnessed breaking down a warehouse door across the street, the poor man sucked inside by the firestorm when the door collapsed, to be burnt to nothing, not even his bones left in the ashes; the warning whistle Potter always carried but which got stuck in his throat when a nearby explosion caused him to suck instead of blow, only a hefty blow on the back by a Heavy Rescue worker who wondered why Potter was turning blue saving his life when the whistle popped back into his mouth; the effigy of Adolf Hitler, wearing baggy gray bloomers, hanging by the neck from a crooked bus stop sign in Whitehall; the milk-can horse painted with white stripes so that it wouldn't get knocked down on dark winter mornings.

Potter rambled on, amused and saddened in turn by his own stories, while across the room Muriel gave me an occasional long meaningful look, which I ignored, and Cissie, who'd taken over the cooking, shot me an angry glance from time to time, which I also ignored. We ate mostly in silence, Potter finally giving up the chatter, and both girls left the suite as soon as pans and plates were washed. Muriel's "good night" was kind of stiff, and Cissie didn't bother. So the warden and me, we cracked open another Jack Daniel's and finished it between us.

He was a mite unsteady when he left me that night, and he said a funny thing. He swayed in the doorway and laid a stubby finger against that beetroot nose of his, giving me a wink at the same time.

"I know what yer business is, son. And it's okay by me. Bloke's got to do what he thinks is best, even if it is 'opeless.

I won't tell another bleedin soul, seein as 'ow yer keepin it secret yerself."

He shook his head, his eyes bleary with the booze.

"But it can't be done, boy. It can't bloody well be done. There's too . . ."

He just shook his head again and walked away.

"Too bloody many . . ." I heard him say as he tottered down the corridor.

| 12 |

I'D CLEARED THE STREET. THIS WAS THE LAST CARCASS. ANY OTHERS were out of sight, inside the buildings. Like they say—*said:* Out of sight, out of mind. Only they weren't; I could still see them in my mind's eye, slumped in chairs, sprawled across tables, curled up on floors—dried-out, feather-light husks, dusty, brittle refuse. My mind could always see them inside shops, restaurants, offices, dwellings, factories, stations, vehicles . . . Christ, the list went on forever. But I couldn't take them all. As Potter had remarked: "There were too bloody many . . ."

I lifted the bag of bones onto the back of the truck, oblivious to its shriveled eyes, like black raisins above its yawning, meatless mouth, and it slithered down at me from the pile, a reluctant evacuee. Its bony fingers snagged against my sweatshirt as I pushed it back and I was too tired and too seasoned to feel any revulsion. When the desiccated corpse was settled, I picked up my jacket lying on the curbside and the rifle leaning against the truck's rear wheel, then climbed into the cab.

Once this had been an ordinary city street, its houses untouched by Hitler's worst, the corner pub still open for business; but weeds now grew between the cracks in the pavements and vehicles rusted away in the road. But it was the silence that got to me. After three long and lonely years, I still hadn't become used to that eerie hush, not in undamaged streets like this where everything seemed so normal. It was as if the place was . . . well, haunted. I thought of Muriel's ghosts back at the Savoy and got angry with myself.

Slamming the truck's door after me, I tossed my jacket onto

the passenger seat and settled the rifle in the footwell on that side, its muzzle leaning against the open window opposite, pointed away from me but within easy reach. The girl had been wrong, she was haunted by memories, not by specters. Even I'd imagined the sound of voices, laughter—music, too—drifting up to me as I'd lain awake nights in that grand rotting mausoleum. Couple of times I'd even gone to the door and listened, opening it when I was sure there really was something going on downstairs, the noises always vanishing the moment I stepped out into the corridor. Just night-notions, that's all they were. Dreams when I hadn't even realized I'd been asleep. Muriel would soon get to realize that imagination had a way of playing tricks on you when you were in a low frame of mind. They weren't just dreams either, they were *wishful* dreams, dreams you hoped would be true, cravings for life to return to normal, to the way it had once been. Daybreak always put things right again; as right as they were ever gonna be.

I turned on the engine, took one last look at the deserted street out the side window, and drove off. Although weary from my labors and a little hungover from the night before, I kept alert, constantly on the lookout for the unexpected. One time about a year and some months ago, a crazy had jumped out at the truck I was using, an Austin 5 ton, as I recall, its flap sides and back easy for loading. He was waving a butcher's meat axe over his head and hollering gibberish at me. Maybe I should have stopped, but it was the middle of winter and this guy was stark naked. And oh yeah, around his neck under a long greasy beard he wore a ragged necklace of severed, blackened hands. When he realized I wasn't gonna stop, he threw the axe at me. Luckily, his aim was poor and it broke through the windshield on the passenger side, so I kept going, heading straight for him, figuring he wasn't in the mood to discuss his complaint. Well, he didn't even try to dodge me, just kept coming forward, screaming and shaking his fists; and I didn't try to avoid him either. I ran right over him, and when I stopped further down the road and looked back, I saw his naked body was still twitching. By the time I'd climbed out and walked back to him, he was trying to crawl along the gutter, his back broken, both legs crushed. It wasn't out of mercy that I put the gun to his head and fired, nor was it out of spite:

those feelings didn't come into it. No, I was just carrying on as usual; I was just tidying up.

When his body finally lay at rest, I added his corpse to the rest of my cargo and took him with me.

There were other creatures I had to keep a lookout for, mainly cats and wild dogs who'd lost any road sense, but mostly I kept my eyes open for Blackshirts, who had a nasty habit of appearing when I least expected it. Although it was a big city, it was inevitable that our paths should cross from time to time. Our battles were usually short and sharp, and I always had the advantage that their sickness had slowed them down considerably.

Today was a good day though, the summer making up for winter's severity, when there were twelve-foot-high snow-drifts along the streets. The sky was clear again, but a slight breeze coming in from the east was keeping things a little cooler. With my full load, I avoided craters, debris and any other wreckage along the route, heading north, the way well known to me by now. Within twenty minutes I'd reached my destination.

I drove straight up the ramp into the stadium whose stands had once held over a hundred thousand people at a time. I passed through the tunnel and emerged inside the vast arena itself. Driving past stacked gasoline cans and boxes of explosives, I headed into the center aisle whose banks were formed by piled-high rotted corpses, turning at its center into a narrower lane, the stink hardly bothering me these days. Occasionally I spotted movement among the heaps, the vermin disturbed but not intimidated by my presence. I used to waste time taking potshots at them, at the scavenging dogs too, but nowadays I didn't bother: when the time came, they'd burn along with the corrupted things they feasted on.

Soon I reached a clearing, the grass there long and unhealthy looking, and I brought the diesel flatbed to a halt. I stood on the running board for a while, just listening, checking around me. As I gazed over those great mounds of human debris I wondered how much more I could accomplish. Almost three long years I'd been filling this huge arena with the dead, always aware it could be no more than a token gesture. Lime pits and thousands of cardboard coffins had been made ready in the early days of the war in case they were needed, but nobody had predicted the Blood Death. Most of the population had remained where they'd dropped. 'Cept for these people. At least they were gonna receive some kind of burial.

It didn't take long to unload this, my last haul of the day, and soon I was on my way back across London, leaving the grimy walls of Wembley Stadium behind, a place where once crowds had gathered to roar their excitement, but which was now just one huge and silent burial vault.

One day, when I was satisfied I'd done all I could, it would be their crematorium.

|13|

I'D CLEANED MYSELF UP AND WAS SPRAWLED HALF-NAKED ON THE bed, a glass of Scotch held on my bruised chest, cigarette in my other hand, when there was a knock on the door.

"Hoke? It's me, Muriel. Can I come in?"

I inhaled, exhaled, lifted my head and took another sip of the Scotch.

"Hoke."

She sounded impatient. The doorhandle rattled.

With a groan, I rolled off the bed, placed the glass on the cabinet, and grabbed my pants. Cigarette drooping from the corner of my mouth, I unlocked the door and opened it a few inches. Smoke curled out into the corridor.

Muriel was wearing a different outfit, a cream blouse and loose, brown slacks, her hair drawn back on one side with a slide. She looked good—even *grubby* she'd looked good—but I didn't let that affect me.

"You've been gone most of the day again," she said, and there seemed little sense in replying to the obvious. After a pause: "Can I come in for a minute?"

Leaving the door open so that the option was hers, I picked up a shirt lying across the back of an easy chair and shrugged it on. I didn't bother with the buttons, hoping her stay would be short; I sat on the edge of the bed, close to the Scotch. Muriel closed the door behind her and stood in front of me.

"No point in asking where you went to, I suppose?" Her neat, pencilled eyebrows were raised.

"Had things to do," was my response.

"Why so surly, Hoke? The other night . . ." She left it there, waving a hand in exasperation.

What could I tell her? That guilt was busting my head, making me feel Sally's presence all around me in that room? It was stupid; I knew it then, I know it now. Three years dead and I was still grieving for her, mourning for the life together we'd been denied. The whole fucking world gone to damnation and I was still focused on my own loss. And now I not only suffered the guilt of survival, but of betrayal also. It was morbid and it was irrational; but when I closed my eyes I still saw my young bride in this room with me, breathed in her perfume, heard her whispers. And I had closed my eyes.

I opened them quickly.

"We . . . I . . . made a mistake," was all I could think of to say, and in truth, I wasn't sure if I was addressing Muriel, or someone long since dead.

"A mistake? My God, man, don't you realize we're living in a whole new world with a different morality? I wasn't asking for love, just comfort, compassion. I was frightened, don't you understand?"

Or staking a claim? I wondered, then hated myself for the cynicism. I dragged on the cigarette, confused, maybe even disgusted with myself. Anger was burning me.

"All right," she said in a resigned, kind of stiff-backed voice. She was tired of reasoning with me and I couldn't blame her for that. "I only wanted to let you know that Cissie and I have arranged a dinner party for us all downstairs in the Pinafore Room."

I stared up at her as if she were the unbalanced party here.

"Hoke, we've got to put the past behind us. It's unreasonable of you to carry on despising Wilhelm Stern just because he's a German. Gracious, not only did he not personally start the war against us, but he actually played very little part in it. He was shot down and captured in 1940, for God's sake!" Her tone changed and she looked at me appealingly. "We've got to forgive and forget, don't you see? How else can we build a new life for ourselves? Some order has to come out of all this and that can only be if we put past grudges aside."

She strode to the writing desk and leaned back against it, arms folded, eyes intense. "It's time for those of us who are left to come to our senses, to introduce some kind of order to our lives. What else is there otherwise? Lawlessness? Chaos?"

Calmer now, I swung my legs up onto the bed and rested my back against the headboard so that I could watch her across the room. She was *serious*. The planet had gone to blazes and she was talking law and order. Resting my cigarette hand on my raised knee, I cocked my head at her.

"You don't see it's all finished?" I was genuinely surprised. "You don't see that our so-called civilization has gone AWOL? Jesus Christ, Muriel, there's nothing left for any of us."

"We're alive, blast you, and there are many more like us, waiting to make a fresh start, waiting for the survivors to come together again, perhaps even hoping for a new leader. It can be better than before, we can avoid the same age-old mistakes."

Maybe she was right. That's what I thought as I smoked the cigarette, my gaze never leaving hers. Someone had to start things rolling again and probably—*no doubt*—it was already happening in other parts of the globe. So why not here, in what used to be one of the world's greatest cities? I studied Muriel in a way I hadn't before. She was a slight, almost fragile, kind of girl, but I could see the resolve in her, a steeliness that I guess came with her breeding. Lord knows, as a kid my head had been filled with literature portraying England's upper classes as people of fine character and great purpose (although Ma had warned me it wasn't all true), and at that moment I was beginning to glimpse those qualities in Muriel. I'd witnessed the good old British stiff-upper-lip style in plenty of the RAF types I'd flown with, so I shouldn't have been surprised to see the same trait in a Lord's daughter. Okay, a romantic view of the English—at least, of their gentry—but I'd had plenty of evidence to back it up since coming to these shores, and looking at Muriel across the room, that intensity still in her eyes, her jaw delicate but determined, I suddenly thought she might just have the backbone to see it through. Another thing I realized, though, was that my kind of cynicism could play no part in her vision of a bright new future. But that didn't mean I'd discourage her. Truth was, I didn't care one way or the other.

"*Will* you join us, Hoke?" Her tone softened, her arms had

unfolded. "Stern and Potter cleared some of the rooms down-stairs and even raided the hotel's foodstores. We've set up a makeshift kitchen in the private dining room next door to the Pinafore, and Wilhelm even went out and found us two portable oil cookers bigger and a touch more sophisticated than the ones you've been using.

"He left the Savoy?" I didn't like the idea.

"We've all been out today. What did you expect us to do—remain cooped up all day in this place waiting for your return? For myself, I traveled across town to Daddy's Kensington apartment."

"By yourself? Christ, woman, why?"

"Are you really that dense, Hoke? I wanted to visit our old home, is that so unreasonable? After all, it was why we returned to London anyway. I have certain things of sentimental value there, photographs, diaries and, yes, even jewelry. Things I want to keep to remind me of better times. And clothes, my own clothes. Yes, I know I could choose from any fashionable Knights-bridge shop, but I wanted certain items I already possessed, is that so difficult to understand? Cissie would have done exactly the same if she'd still had a home to go to. Instead she stayed behind and helped get everything ready."

"But—" I started again, then let it go. "Okay. How did you get there?"

For the first time since she'd entered the suite she smiled. "I was going to use any motorcar I could find still working. Instead I found a bicycle that wasn't rusted completely—it was inside a shop—so I used that. It squeaked a lot and the tires need pumping up, but it got me through all the parked traffic in the streets."

"D'you have any idea where Stern went to?"

"I told you, he found us some better cookers, so obviously he got those from one of those big camping stores nearby. Potter went off on his own too, probably patrolling the streets looking for UXBs and incendiaries. He's quite dotty, you know." She moved from the writing desk and stood at the end of the bed. "Why so pensive, Hoke? What's troubling you now?"

Dogging the cigarette, I replied, "The city's a dangerous place."

"The Blackshirts, you mean? I didn't catch a glimpse of one.

But then, it *is* a huge city. Anyway, I'm sure they assumed they'd killed us all when they set fire to the Underground station."

I wondered. Would Hubble and his Looney-Tunes army think we were dead by now? The notion that he'd lost four valuable blood donors would have sent Hubble into a frenzy and I pitied the fool who'd broken the news to him that they'd fire-bombed the station. If only that were the case, if only Hubble believed we were gone for good . . . On my own travels that day I'd seen neither hide nor hair of any Blackshirts, although that wasn't unusual; as Muriel said, it was a big city. Besides, I always kept off the beaten track, taking sidestreets rather than main thoroughfares. But heck, it was a pleasant enough thought on an otherwise grim day. Muriel took advantage of my sudden smile.

"You'll come this evening, then?"

I blinked.

"Our little celebratory dinner," she persisted. "You'll join us downstairs?"

"What're you celebrating?"

"Just being alive. Isn't that enough?"

Sometimes I thought it was too much, but I didn't say that. "Okay, I'll be there. But don't get the idea I'll be making any new friends."

"All I ask is that you be civil to Wilhelm." She left it at that.

They'd found hundreds more candles from somewhere and had filled every nook and cranny with them so that the Pinafore Room resembled some holy shrine. They were supplemented by two or three oil lamps in strategic positions around the room, and the heat and waxy smell took some getting used to at first. Behind the thick, rich drapes daylight was fading and, despite the candle-glow, there were dark shadows in the room, especially in its corners. Warm scintillas of light reflected off tall glasses and cutlery set around the long table, and cedar panelling, studded with silver buttons, on the walls and central square column lent a soft ambience to the proceedings. It was a ritzy setting for a dinner party, an evocation of more pleasant times.

I paused in the open doorway, Cagney at my side, his nose in the air, sniffing out food.

Muriel was chatting to Wilhelm Stern before a tall mirror over an empty fireplace at the far end of the room, and an elegant couple they made, she in a slim floor-length gown that shimmered silver, cut high from shoulder-to-shoulder, with long tight sleeves, her hair once again held to one side but this time by a decorative comb, while he wore a dark evening suit, white handkerchief, probably silk, peeping from his breast pocket, his tie a deep gray worn against a white shirt. They'd made an effort for this evening's *soirée* (clinging to the wreckage?) and I was relieved to see that Potter, who'd suddenly appeared at a double door on my left, hadn't bothered to fancy himself up at all: he still wore his warden's all-in-one outfit, although he'd brushed it down and his helmet was nowhere in evidence.

Spotting me, he called, "Grub's up soon, son," and pointed a stubby thumb over his shoulder at the room behind. He gave me a broad, yellow-toothed grin. "There's time for a pair o' teeth first, though. What can I get yer?"

I frowned.

Muriel wised me up. "Albert means an *aperitif*. As I'm sure he knows," she added, looking meaningfully at the warden and smiling. She turned her smile on me, but it had an uneasy edge to it, as though she was a little nervous.

As I walked the length of the table towards them Cagney trotted before me, his excuse for a tail wagging in anticipation of the food he could smell. He disappeared through the opening behind Potter and I heard Cissie's muted cry of welcome. The mutt was getting used to people again too fast and that concerned me: I didn't want him to lose his usual caution in case eventually it proved dangerous for both of us.

"We're using the Princess Ida Room as a makeshift kitchen," Muriel told me, and I remembered that all the names of the private dining rooms along this floor had something to do with Gilbert and Sullivan operas. "Cissie's in there playing chef and I must get back to help before she starts getting cross." She eyed me up and down as she sipped her drink. "Thank you at least for putting on a fresh shirt."

I checked her eyes for sarcasm, but she quickly looked away. My pants were a little wrinkled, my boots none-too-clean, and my torn leather jacket was thrown over one arm, pistol tucked inside.

The shirt *was* fresh though, one of a bunch I'd picked out of a Regent Street menswear shop's smashed window, none of which I'd gotten round to wearing until now. I guess it would've looked better with a tie, but ties never had been one of my things, even in peacetime. Muriel moved closer to me, away from the German.

"What would you like to drink?" she asked, but again she averted her gaze when I looked directly into her eyes. "Gin and tonic, a Martini, sherry. . . ? We're well stocked, as you can see."

"Scotch'll do."

"Good boy," approved Potter. "Think I'll join yer." He bustled over to a small, round dining table that was loaded with the hard stuff. Rubbing his fleshy hands together he cast his eye over the wide selection. He spied the Scotch, another bottle of his favorite Grouse. "Lovely," we heard him mutter.

"Hoke . . ."

It was the German and there was a wariness in his approach. I laid my jacket over the back of a chair at the head of the long table, folded so that the concealed holster would be easy to reach, before facing him.

"It is extremely foolish for us to regard each other as enemies," Stern said, his manner relaxed, but still that apprehensive cautiousness in his eyes. "In the war I was merely a navigator doing my job, as were you as a fighter pilot. I mean you no harm now and would"—*vould*—"hope you no longer wish me any harm. We were airmen loyal to our own countries, but all that is in the past. We can no longer live that way. We should endeavor to live in peace and, as the British themselves say, let bygones be bygones." Speech finished, he offered me a hand to shake.

Unfortunately, I didn't take to the idea of shaking the hand of someone I would eventually kill, so I ignored the offer. His pale eyes momentarily hardened, and then he smiled as he let his hand fall away.

"So be it," he said coldly. "I have made an effort to be civil—or indeed, civilized—and I shall continue to do so. You will make up your own mind about how you regard me, but I must warn you, I shall always defend myself."

"Please, Wilhelm." Muriel looked anxiously from me to Stern. "This isn't necessary."

"Have I not just tried to make that very point?" He never took his eyes off me. "I will behave honorably, but Mr. Hoke must decide for himself. I have offered the hand of friendship and he has rejected it, but still I will not be the one to make trouble."

Potter arrived between us with two tumblers of Scotch in his hands, one of them held out to me. "Bottoms up," he said cheerfully, as if he hadn't noticed the exchange between myself and the German.

"Yeah," I responded, taking the tumbler and tipping it against my lips, my gaze still not breaking from Stern's. We all turned when another voice called from the far end of the room.

"Dinner's coming along nicely." Cissie was in the doorway to the Princess Ira Room, wiping her hands with a cloth. "So I'm going to socialize for a bit. I think a large g-and-t would go down very nicely right now." She tossed the cloth onto something behind her and headed our way.

"You've earned it." Muriel quickly busied herself at the drinks table, glad to turn her back on the tension between Stern and me, I guess. "I think I'll have another one, myself."

Fumes from the portable oil cookers kept drifting through from next door to mix with the smell of melting wax, but they didn't spoil our feast any. We kicked off with oatmeal soup and dumplings, followed by "brisket of beef," as Cissie announced, and while tinned beans and peas may have been a poor substitute for turnips and parsnips, they didn't spoil the taste of this particular meat pie. Together with potatoes and carrots (fresh, from my own home-grown stock), it made one of the finest meals—no, *the* finest meal—I'd had in three years, and by the time we'd finished pudding—semolina and Prince Roly—we were all fit to bust.

I was at the head of the table for no other reason than I'd left my jacket over the chair there, and on my right was Cissie, who wore a coffee-colored, below knee-length evening dress, which was a mite too tight for her. Muriel was on my left and our conversation throughout the meal had been minimal—she was still edgy, probably afraid trouble might flare up between myself and Stern at any moment. Stern sat next to her, old Potter opposite him. Cagney was under the table by my feet, well fed and snoozing, content to be among friendly people again (although he'd given a small warning growl every time the German got too close), and at the far end of the table, facing me, was a strange, almost exotic creature, silent, unmoving, and black, with a pink napkin tied around its neck. Muriel had introduced me to it when we'd first sat down to eat.

"Meet Kaspar," she'd said. "He's our guest this evening because for many years the Pinafore Room was used by members of what was known as The Other Club, a collection of, well, rather eminent people, and politicians—Winston Churchill was one such person. The politicians dined here whenever parliament was in session, industrialists and other powerful men joining them. You'll see there's seating for fourteen around this table, but whenever there was an empty seat and the number of people present was an unlucky thirteen, they brought out Kaspar the cat. They tied a napkin around his neck and served him every course."

There was something I didn't like about the three-foot-high black animal. Maybe it was its down-turned head and pointed ears, or its sinuous, snake-like tail that looped round in an almost full circle, or its arched spine etched with scrawls that looked like esoteric writings. I couldn't figure out why, but as the evening wore on, I realized it was just the creature's dark, brooding presence that made me feel uncomfortable; there was something ominous about it, as if it were a portent of doom rather than a good-luck charm. Now, over coffee and brandy, and some fine cigars Potter had scrounged from somewhere, the seal of the box they came in unbroken, the conversation returned to Kaspar.

"We found it on a shelf at the back of the room," Cissie was explaining. "We thought it would add some dignity to the proceedings." She giggled at Muriel, hand to her mouth like a schoolkid. She'd joined the menfolk in the brandies. "D'you think it'll bring us luck?"

I reserved judgment and it was Stern who answered.

"I have never understood if the black cat means good or bad fortune to the English. Are you saying it is good?"

Potter piped up. "Always said meself if a black mog crosses yer path, yer was in for a spot of bad luck."

"No, no, that's wrong," argued Cissie. My grandad always told me a black cat was good luck."

"Wasn't that only on one's wedding day?" put in Muriel.

"No!" Cissie and Potter cried together.

"There are only five of us around this table anyway," I pointed out, stabbing the air with my cigar. Blue smoke drifted towards the ceiling.

"Well spotted."

I shrugged at Cissie's sarcasm.

"We were just making up the numbers." Muriel gave her friend a worried glance. "I mean to say, we're hardly a crowd, are we? What kind of discussions do you suppose they had in this room? With all those important club members—ambassadors, dignitaries, newspaper owners and editors, as well as the politicians themselves—some very momentous decisions must have been made. No church people were allowed in, by the way. But the Prime Minister himself—"

"Don't matter, neither way." It was out of character for Potter to interrupt Muriel; it'd been plain throughout the evening that he regarded her upper-class credentials with some respect, if not awe. It seemed too much whisky, wine, and brandy had blurred the class division for him, and I, for one, was glad to see it. "Don't matter how grand they was, how much power was in their hands, they come down with the plague jus like everybody else. 'Cept us. We didn't. Money couldn't buy it off, an nor could fame. Neville Chamberlain—the gerk, I mean berk—to Jessie Matthews, Ivor Novello to Herbert Morrison, Martin bloody Bormann—'scuse me, my dears—to Groucho Marx, all dead, see? Unless . . ." He waved his finger around the table. "Unless they was like us, our blood thingy. We're special, see? All the others . . . werl, all the others . . ." He seemed at a loss. "Werl, they're gone. Finished."

"Then why do you still patrol the streets, Mr. Potter?" The German was leaning forward, a cigar between his fingers. "If almost everybody else is gone, why do you continue with your work?"

The logic didn't please the old boy. "I should give up me duty jus 'cos things've changed? Without orders to stand down? With the *Luftwaffe* still knockin ten bells out of London? You Germans never did understand us English, did yer?"

"And you English never quite understood we did not want war with your country. The *Führer* had a great . . ." he considered the right word ". . . affinity with many of your people."

"Oh no, not very many." Cissie looked about ready to toss her wine at Stern. "What you really mean is he had an affinity with a certain type of Englishman. Some of our so-called ruling class didn't think Adolf Hitler was such a bad chap."

"That is not quite correct," Stern replied, as smooth as Conrad Veidt. "A good number of the English common people understood the Jewish problem, for instance. And I think all classes accepted our fight to play a major role in the governance of Europe."

"Only other Fascists believed that."

"Please let's not argue among ourselves." Muriel obviously didn't like this turn in conversation.

The German was quick to respond to her plea. "I did not mean to cause disagreement between us, but you must understand that I, too, loved my country, and I have suffered as much as anybody in this room."

I placed my empty brandy glass on the table and dropped the butt of my cigar into it. My hands remained on the tabletop, about a foot apart, fingers clenched. "Oh yeah, we understand, Vilhelm. After all, you were a good German, weren't you? A good, fighting Nazi."

He regarded me warily, trusting me not one little bit. "All Germans are—were—not Nazis."

"Hoke . . ." Muriel warned.

"Of course not." I leaned forward. "And you, personally, never really had the chance to fight us, did you? You got yourself shot down right at the beginning of the war, so we can't hate you, can we? You hardly had time to cause much damage, and besides, you were only a navigator anyway, so didn't *personally* pull any triggers or push any buttons."

"That is certainly the case. I told you—"

"Yeah, you told us you were captured and interned in April 1940, isn't that right? So why should we bear you any grudge? Hell, you practically played no part at all in the war."

I felt Cagney stirring under the table, his weight shifting against my foot. I thought he must have sensed the rising tension in the room.

"But you were lying, weren't you, Vilhelm? You didn't want us to think bad of you, not while you could use us. At least, while you could use the girls here."

The color—what scant color she had—was draining from

Muriel's face. She was beginning to realize the party wasn't going to turn out the way she'd planned.

"What"—*vot*—"are you suggesting, Hoke?" Stern had placed his own brandy glass before him, although his cigar remained between his fingers. Was there a sneer on those thin, humorless lips; was there hatred behind those passionless eyes of his?

Keeping my hands on the table, I rested back in my chair. My tight grin lacked any pleasure.

"I'm suggesting you're a lying son-of-a-bitch," I informed him quietly.

"Stop this now!" Muriel was on her feet. "It's time you grew up, Hoke. This bitterness against Wilhelm—and yes, against us—is utterly pointless. Even though we saved your life you still resent us, you still look on us as some kind of burden, a nuisance you could well do without. Do you honestly think—"

"Let him have his say, Mu." Cissie's anger was suppressed, her interest centered on me. A low, rumbling growl came from beneath the table.

Stern's smile was like my own: no warmth to it. "Why do you bait me like this, Hoke? Is it because you are a rather absurd and intolerant man who will not accept the idea that Germany did not lose the war after all? That in the jaws of defeat the German Reich snatched victory with a weapon so brilliantly lethal it irrevocably altered mankind's destiny? That the Americans, with all their sophisticated weaponry and manpower, and the British who, if we are to be honest, were merely a spent force hanging on the coattails of their overseas masters, could suddenly lose to an army they thought defeated? Is that why you hate me so and imply that I am a liar? And isn't this what you expect me to say, Hoke? Isn't this the kind of Fascist language you want to hear from me? Isn't this just your own idea of how a German thinks, talks?"

Muriel and Cissie were staring at Wilhelm Stern, shocked by his words. Potter, bleary-eyed and heavy-lidded, opened his mouth to speak, but nothing came out.

My smile had frosted and my thumbs were twitching against my fingers. "No, Stern," I said finally, "that isn't why I'm calling you a liar. Y'see, you made a slip while we were down there in the tram tunnel. You told us you'd witnessed starving dogs roaming the bomb-blitzed ruins of Berlin."

158 / JAMES HERBERT

His expression changed when he understood his mistake—his very stupid mistake.

"Because, Vilhelm," I went on, enjoying his discomfort, "the RAF didn't begin their raids on Berlin until August 1940, four months *after* you told us you were captured and interned over here."

I leaned forward on the table again, a fury inside me that was intense but as cold as his pale eyes stiffening every muscle. "What *did* you do in the war, Vilhelm? I'm betting it was something pretty nasty if you had to keep it from us three years after the event. Yeah, there were plenty of your kind over here in England, pretending to be Polish, Dutch, Czech, Belgian, all kinds of run-aways and asylum seekers, but in reality spies and saboteurs. Which were you, Vilhelm? Did you get to blow up any munitions factories? Maybe that's how you got those scars on your neck, not escaping fast enough once you'd set the explosives. How about that, Vilhelm? Saboteur or spy—which was it?"

I don't know where it came from, but the gun was in his hand in the blink of an eye, and it was pointed at me. I realized he'd deliberately kept one hand—the one holding the cigar—in view on the table while I'd been talking, the other one sneaking into a pocket for the weapon he must have picked up—from a police station, from the corpse of a serviceman, or even from some-where in the hotel itself—during his hunt around earlier in the day, because I hadn't returned the one I'd taken from him yester-day. There was more movement by my feet, Cagney rousing him-self. We all heard his bad-tempered growl.

"The gun is merely for self-protection," Stern informed me. "I have no wish to fight with you, Hoke, but neither do I intend to be harmed by you."

More commotion under the table, the mutt pushing his way through legs and chairs. Cagney suddenly appeared about halfway down, his teeth bared, a deep snarling-growl coming from his throat. He wasn't watching the German though; he was facing the door at the end of the room.

While Stern was distracted, I leapt from my chair, twisting so that I was at the back of it, and reached into my jacket pocket. My fingers were curling around the pistol butt as the door Cagney was facing burst open.

14

MY FIRST THOUGHT WAS TO SHOOT THE GERMAN; MY SECOND— and it was only a split second after the first—was to duck the gunfire that came my way.

Fortunately, the Blackshirts weren't aiming to kill, only to frighten us all into immobility, but it didn't work that way with me, because I took a dive as the mirror behind me shattered and the room erupted with the sounds of machine-gun fire and the girls' screams. I kept rolling 'til I was behind the thick central column as candles split in two, a lamp in one corner exploded as if hit by a cannon, and splinters from the wood panelling spat across the table. I came up on one knee in time to see Cagney scooting into the room next door. Good move, I thought as I peeked around the column, hoping to get a clear shot at the Blackshirt who was causing most of the damage. But he was waiting for me to show myself again and he peppered the column and the space next to it with a hail of bullets so that I had to fall back to avoid a faceful of lead. The drapes over the windows were shredded, the glass behind them smashed, as I cowered out of sight, biding my time. The gunfire abruptly ceased—out of ammo, I assumed— and then so did the shouts and screams. I acted fast, whipping round the square-shaped pillar, gun-hand extended, searching out my target.

Smoke wafted across the room, with it the smell of cordite and candlewax. And something more. The familiar stink of the intruders themselves, a kind of cankerous odor that they carried with them like some unclean aura.

Cissie was huddled over the dining table, Potter on his knees beside her, while Muriel had backed up against the wall, shocked rigid. Stern held his hands high in surrender, his pistol lying on the tabletop. Blackshirts crowded the doorway, their ragged midnight garb and the array of weapons aimed around the room a dispiriting sight. The only person still moving was the goon who'd done the most damage—he was clumsily trying to fit a new magazine into a Sterling submachine gun. Again I acted fast, realizing there was no point in trying to take them all on with one small sidearm; there was one chance for us and a slim one at that. I was over the table, scattering glasses and coffee cups, before they could make their next move, their disease-induced slowness my only advantage. I came up behind Stern and locked an arm around his neck, my .45 pressed hard against his temple.

"Hold it right there!" I yelled at them, trying to keep the shakes from my voice as well as my gun hand. I pulled the German against me, using him as a human shield.

Five or six Blackshirts had managed to squeeze through that doorway and now every one of their guns was focused on me. The goon with the Sterling finished reloading and lifted the weapon chest-high, his hands as unsteady as mine.

"The German's dead if any one of you so much as scratches an itch," I warned.

Stern could hardly breathe, let alone speak, but damned if he wasn't gonna make the effort.

"*Shut up, Kraut!*" I hissed into his ear. "I guess it didn't take much searching to find your Fascist pals today when you left the hotel."

He tried to squirm free, but I held him firm, digging the gun barrel even harder against his head just to cause him more discomfort. The temptation to shoot him right there and then was almost overwhelming, but I needed him—*we* needed him—as a hostage.

"*Back off!*" I shouted as more Blackshirts pushed their way further forward. I was the one who backed away, bringing my protection with me. I didn't like the craziness in their dark-smudged eyes, but then maybe they didn't like the craziness they saw in mine, because they became still sure enough. We had a stand-off—or so I thought—and that was a slight improvement in the situation.

"One bad move," I warned them, "and your *Kraut* friend's brains'll be dripping from the ceiling."

I'd made up my mind to drop the one with the submachine gun first, then the two mugs on either side of him, each of them packing two pistols. When the rest scattered for cover I'd deal with Stern. All else was in the lap of the gods, but I was damn sure I'd never let them take me alive, I got ready to change my aim and the German stiffened even more, as though aware of my intentions.

"By all means, Mr. Hoke, shoot our alleged *Kraut* friend if it makes you happy."

The voice drifted through the hallway outside the Pinafore Room and I knew whose it was, although I'd never heard the man speak before 'cept once on a BBC radio broadcast early on in the war. I hadn't realized he knew my name either and then it dawned on me that he'd obviously learned it just that day, and the informant was right here in my arms.

The Blackshirts at the door stirred again, stepping aside to let their leader through. Sir Max Hubble appeared, propped up by McGruder on one side and his thick walking stick on the other. What was left of the candlelight did nothing to soften his appearance and I heard one of the girls—Cissie, I think—utter a small, fearful cry. Hubble came to a shambling halt a few feet inside the room.

"Well, Mr. Hoke, aren't you going to shoot this man?" His sharp, wheezy voice was mocking as if he were taking pleasure from the situation. Maybe he enjoyed bluffing.

Well I had nothing to lose, so was prepared to call it. "Unless you all move out so we can leave, I'll do that."

Stern tried to tear my arm away, squawking something into my shirtsleeve that I couldn't catch. I held him fast, half-choking him with my grip.

"I'll tell you what," Hubble said, his bluish lips beneath the thin moustache managing to form a smile. "We'll do it for you." He nodded at one of his men, who raised his pistol and pointed it at Stern's head.

Yeah, sure, go ahead, I thought, and then I saw the man's finger tightening on the trigger. "Jesus," I breathed.

"*No!*"

It was Muriel who cried out and ran forward to stand between us and the Blackshirts. "You said nobody would be harmed. You promised me."

She was staring straight at Hubble.

I couldn't believe my ears or my eyes. The gun wavered in my hand as I gaped at her back. I caught movement in the corner of my eye and saw that Cissie was pushing herself from the table, watching her friend open-mouthed.

"It's up to the American," I heard Hubble say. "He has the choice of either laying down his weapon and surrendering to us, or forcing us to shoot the person he's holding, and after that, him. We have other blood now."

Cissie's fist crashed down on the tabletop, nearly causing more than one gun to go off. "You brought them here!" she shouted at Muriel. "You betrayed us. My God, how could you?"

Even in the flickering light I could see Muriel's face whiten as she faced her accuser.

"Miss Drake's father and I were great friends," said Hubble as, like Muriel, he turned towards Cissie, using his whole upper body to do so, as if his neck had lost that small function. "Our principles, our ideals, were the same, so is it surprising that Lord Drake's daughter should share those same values?"

I have to admit I'd never gone much on small-talk and after three years of none at all, save for the last couple of days, I wasn't surprised to learn I still didn't. And anyway, why gab? I knew all I needed to know.

Shoving Stern aside, I shot a hole through pistol-man's throat—he'd had to be first because his trigger finger was already halfway to squeezing. I would've taken Hubble next, but Muriel was in the way and, as much as I despised her, good old-fashioned propriety wouldn't allow me to shoot her in the back; so I settled for the goon with the Sterling, who was about to open fire again. I only winged him, but it was still enough to make him screech like a barn owl and collapse into three Blackshirts behind him, spoiling their aim and creating enough disorder for me to slide back across the table towards Cissie. I nudged her aside so I could get off a few clear shots at the enemy.

She screamed a warning as more Blackshirts came pouring through the double doors of the Princess Ida Room, and that was when I realized we didn't have a hope in hell. The only thing in my favor was the gun in my hand and my speed, but I couldn't shoot them all and I had nowhere to run.

Something—Lord knows what—struck me hard on the forehead and I went down, poleaxed. The next thing I knew, boots were stomping me and rifle butts were jabbing at arms and ribs. The Colt was wrenched from my grasp, bright flares were bursting inside my head, and somewheres a long way off someone was screaming.

All I could do—and there was no choice to it—was retreat into my own private sanctum, those lights fading fast, giving way to total darkness. I liked that darkness, I liked it a lot.

|15|

A DULL BUT SUDDEN PAIN SEMI-ROUSED ME; THE STING OF THE second—it might really have been the third or fourth—had my eyes opening. I wasn't happy at what they saw, so I closed them again and another slap, this one on the other side of my face, convinced me to keep them open. I had to blink them several times though, partly because the light hurt and partly because they couldn't believe what they saw.

The light was everywhere, shining from the massive chandeliers in the ceiling and the low lamps set around the great lounge area. Yet more brightness flooded through the glass doors and windows of the riverside restaurant at the end of the lounge, as well as from the direction of the foyer and main entrance. For a moment I thought I must be dreaming, that the grand old hotel had returned to its former glory only in my unconscious mind; and then I took in the rotted corpses, many of them still seated or slumped in elegant but dusty chairs, while others lay on the carpeted floor, pushed aside with the furniture so that there was a clear space near the vast room's center. Blackshirts were still busy creating more space, pushing back low tables and easy chairs, upsetting chinaware and cake stands, throwing more corpses into heaps near the mirrored walls, shifting those already on the floor with their boots, not caring if skulls crumbled and skeletal hands broke loose.

I looked up at the person who'd struck me and groaned when I saw his staring death's eyes, the dried blood around their darkened lids, caked like biscuit crumbs in the lashes, the ulcerations and cyanotic discoloration of the man's cheeks and jaw. He grinned down at me, exposing bleeding gums, and when I tried to strike out at him I found my wrists were tied to the cushioned arms of a high-backed seat, the kind of formally comfortable arm-chair in which patrons of the Savoy had once taken afternoon tea or pre-dinner drinks.

My senses started to come together more rapidly and when I saw that my shirt had been ripped away to expose my left arm and shoulder, I began to suspect what I was in for. Panic hit me and I struggled to break free, the goon just leering over me, tickled by my efforts. I stopped when I noticed Stern, Cissie, and Potter on their knees not far away, a bunch of Blackshirts covering them with an array of dissuaders—clubs and knives, as well as guns. And there came Hubble, just arriving, being helped down the carpeted stairway from the foyer by McGruder and another man, his decrepit body about ready to fail him. His smile when he saw me was no more than a tight grimace.

"Aren't the lights wonderful?" he remarked as he approached, his red-flecked eyes gazing up at the ceiling. "It's been so long since we've witnessed such splendor, so very long." He paused briefly to regard the kneeling prisoners, and he nodded as if counting their heads one by one before continuing his shambling journey towards me. Behind him, descending the stairs, was Muriel and there was a phoney kind of proudness to her, as though it took some effort to hold her head high and avoid the accusing eyes of her friend, Cissie. She passed by the kneeling prisoners without giving them a glance, even though Cissie called out to her.

Hubble came to a stop before me, both hands resting on his cane, fingers like blackened claws wrapped around its grip, the two aides standing close by in case he should falter. He had an old man's tremble—and an old cadaver's stench.

Still he peered around him, his bent torso twisting with each turn of his head, admiring the chandeliers before gazing across the huge lounge itself, his eyes half-closed as if to shut out the more gruesome elements.

"If one didn't look too closely it would seem the grand old days had returned to the Savoy," he mused. His speech had a high-pitched sibilance to it that was as thin and frail as his bones, and standing there in his loose black uniform, bent over his stick, flesh hanging from his scrawny neck like an empty sack, and with "carrion" strewn all around him, he reminded me of an ancient buzzard. He went on, delighting himself rather than me: "The hotel's own oil-fuelled generator was so easy to get running again—it took my men, the ones who know about these things, less than twenty minutes, even after all these years of disuse. I'm surprised you didn't attempt to start it yourself, Mr. Hoke; but then, I suppose the last thing you wanted to do was draw attention to yourself."

Some of his words were hard to catch; it was almost as if he were speaking from another room. He deserved a reply and I gave him one.

"You crazy bastard—"

He raised a shaky hand to shush me and, I have to admit, it did. What the hell could I tell him that deep down he didn't already know?

Now he turned to me, his head leaning close, the odor making me want to gag. "It's odd, isn't it?" he said between labored breaths. "All this time chasing you and never once a moment for conversation between us."

"I didn't think we had much to talk about," I replied, trying to avoid the foul air he was exhaling.

Muriel had joined us by now.

"You happy, Muriel?" I inquired, looking past Hubble. "Betraying your friends to these third-rate Nazis give you some kind of thrill? Like father, like daughter, I guess."

"My father would have gladly sacrificed his life for his country," she snapped back, her remoteness giving over to anger. "But he recognized the poison that was slowly crippling our land."

"Ah yeah, the Jewish poison, right?" My head was beginning to clear, but that only made me more conscious of the throbbing pain in various parts of my body, results of the beating I'd received. Shit, I'd hardly got over the lumps and bruises from my last run-in with these people.

Hubble hadn't liked my sneering tone. "Even England's abdicated king was aware of the Jewish threat, as were many others of influence. If our own government had not been in the pocket of Jew creditors and extortionists, and so fearful of the proletariat itself, which was forever whining, forever demanding, malcontents who despised the natural social order, then perhaps the world would have had a very different and glorious future."

"Oh Christ . . ." I began to say.

"The Jews murdered Christ, Mr. Hoke."

Some life had returned to those dead eyes of Hubble's: they shone with a zealot's passion.

"The Duke of Windsor and others of nobility would gladly have aligned themselves with Adolf Hitler's wondrous vision for mankind," he went on, warming to the sermon, his voice even notching up half a gear. "And they would not have been alone. Many leaders and eminent people—academics, industrialists, militarists, too—would have joined the crusade to purge our civilization of its insidious corruption and regenerative breeding, you know, discreet negotiations between ourselves and Hitler's emissaries that would have benefited both Germany and the United Kingdom were well underway before that fool Chamberlain was tricked into declaring war on a nation that should have been our greatest ally."

Something had occurred to me while he was ranting and once more I stared past him at Muriel.

"Didn't you tell us your own brothers fought against Fascism, one in the navy, the other in the airforce?" I said to her.

"It was their duty to defend their country." Some color had returned to her pallid skin, brought there by her own anger. "It didn't mean they agreed with our government's misguided hostility towards Germany."

There was probably some kind of screwed-up logic to her argument, but I wasn't in the mood to figure it out. "Just tell me why you turned us in to this bunch of madmen? I thought they, at least"—I nodded towards the kneeling group—"were your friends."

"Isn't it obvious?" she replied, her rage controlled again, her coolness back. "Sir Max has to be saved. The irony is that I recognized him on the steps of the National Gallery when we helped you three days ago, but there was nothing I could do, everything was happening so fast."

Out of the corner of my eye I saw an emaciated-looking man approaching, one of his cronies helping him remove his black shirt. His eyes were huge and kind of haunted-looking, as if the dark-smudged lids had shrunk around them.

"The world, or what's left of it, has to find a system again," Muriel was blabbering, "and we can only find the right kind through leaders like him, don't you see that? Our lives are not as important as his."

"So offer him your blood," I suggested.

"There's no need when I can take yours," Hubble pointed out.

He shuffled aside to let the thin man through and I winced when I saw the ulcerations and bruises that covered the newcomer's naked arms and upper body. His companions placed a small black case like a doctor's bag (maybe it *was* a doctor's bag) on the carpet by my feet and opened it. As another Blackshirt spread a dingy tablecloth across the floor by the chair I was tied to, the one with the bag drew out a thin length of rubber tubing with what appeared to be flanged steel needles at either end, some metal clips, and what looked like half a syringe.

"Don't you understand?" I appealed to Hubble. "It's crazy. It won't work. You have to be matched with the same blood type for it to do any good. You'll just kill us both this way."

Hubble turned back to me, that mad shine still there in his dark eyes. "But I have nothing to lose, Mr. Hoke. If the transfusion fails, it only means a different sort of death." He might have chuckled then, or a small expulsion of blood might have gurgled in his throat, I couldn't tell. "Besides," he went on, pointing his stick, "we will try the procedure on this noble volunteer first."

The half-naked man, who was settling onto the tablecloth on the floor, gazed up at him like an acolyte at a god.

"He'll die," I promised.

"He's prepared to do so. But really, Mr. Hoke, aren't you aware that even centuries ago the South American Incas regularly carried out blood transfusions with far more primitive instruments than we have, and, so history informs us, most occasions proved successful. All we need to do is make two small punctures in the correct veins and allow gravitation to do the rest."

Wilhelm Stern was close enough to be easily heard. "But it was also outlawed in Europe in the seventeenth century because of the many deaths transfusions caused."

I was glad of his intervention, but wondered if it was for my sake, or because he didn't like the idea of being the next guinea pig.

"Nobody knew about blood types in those days. To them, blood was blood and there were no differences," he reasoned. "Transfusions were successful only between people who, by chance, belonged to the same grouping. *Mein Gott*, they even used the blood from pigs and sheep at that time. Muriel—Miss Drake—you must make this man understand, you must explain that what he is about to try is impossible."

"But I'm not a doctor. How can I tell him what I don't even know?"

Cissie's eyes were wide and pleading. "You saw for yourself what happened at the sanatorium, you know how their experiments failed each time."

"We didn't know anything at all! They wouldn't even discuss individual cases with us, they kept us in the dark about everything."

"If different blood types could be mixed, then the doctors would have saved themselves!" Cissie reasoned.

Hubble, irritated by the squabbling, smacked the side of my chair with his cane. He got our attention.

"There is one thing I'm sure they didn't try," he said in that creepy faraway voice. of his. "They did not take *all* of the donor's blood and transfer it into the recipient's *empty* system."

It was breathtaking in its flawed logic and now I knew he was completely insane. I wondered if his mental state had always been shaky, or if the disease itself was rotting his brain.

"That's ridiculous, you fucking lunatic!" Couldn't help it, had to make him aware of my considered opinion.

This time his cane bounced off the side of my skull. The blow was too weak to hurt much, and I had the satisfaction of seeing him stagger, only McGruder at his side preventing him going down all the way. A chair was quickly brought over, and when they'd settled him into it, facing me, about two yards away, I noticed every part of him—his hands, his legs, shoulders, head—was trembling. His chest was heaving as he tried to regain his breath.

"No, it is not ridiculous," he insisted between gasps, as if I were the lunatic. "The recipient's blood will be *slowly* drained as blood from the donor will be *slowly* used to fill the veins."

I laughed. Maybe it was hysteria, but I honestly appreciated the humor in his twisted reasoning. It was so outrageously and brilliantly simple.

"You will kill both persons."

For once I didn't mind the "*vill*'. After all, Stern was speaking up for my benefit as well as his own. They'd kill me anyway, whether they carried out the transfusion or not, but I preferred a fast bullet to a leisurely bleeding.

"Your man will have died from blood loss before his body will accept the new blood." Stern spoke quietly, authoritatively, a teacher explaining a difficult problem to a child. "Conflicting blood types will not even be the cause: you will kill this unfortunate man just as surely as if you had slit his throat with a knife."

"His blood will be replaced as quickly as it is lost!"

The shout set Hubble wheezing again and McGruder watched over him anxiously. The Blackshirt leader held a handkerchief to his mouth, his body doubled-up in the chair, his shoulders jerking as spasms ran through him. When he straightened and took the handkerchief away I could see it was specked with blood. He took in a long, deep breath and I heard a peculiar faint whistling sound from inside his chest. His eyes were blurred with dampness now, the luster in them dimmed.

"We're wasting time," he said weakly. "Let's get on with it."

Someone grabbed my shoulders from behind and the goon who'd been rummaging around in the bag on the floor held up both ends of the rubber tubing, a stupid grin on his face.

"Wait, wait a minute." I was out of laughter and getting more desperate by the moment. "Listen. There are only four of us with the right kind of blood to resist the disease, five counting the rink here." I nodded towards Muriel, but she wouldn't even look at me. "Don't you get it? Even if the transfusions did work, you could only save a handful of your people. The rest are gonna die."

"Ah, then you admit the transfusions could be successful?" The notion seemed to please Hubble.

I shook my head violently. "Not a chance in hell. I'm just applying common sense."

He smiled at me. Bared his yellowed teeth and smiled. "This first transfusion will be our test, and it will be successful. By our second or third attempt, the procedure will be perfected."

I understood now why Hubble was prepared to wait: let any

mistakes be made on the first couple of mugs, so that any problems would be ironed out by the time it got round to his turn. Maybe he wasn't so crazy after all.

"After that we will move out of the city into the suburbs and surrounding countryside where we will find others like you. Eventually every one of us will be saved." He barked the order, eager to proceed. "Attach the tube to him! Miss Drake, will you be so kind as to assist—I'm sure you must have learned something about transfusions during your stay at the sanatorium."

I wasn't sure of the expression I caught in her downcast eyes as she leaned over me. Was it fear, or plain old-fashioned misery? Was she beginning to regret double-crossing her friends already?

"Listen to me," I whispered as she turned my wrist beneath the rope, exposing the veins of my forearm. Our heads were close. "Tell them it isn't gonna work. Think of us, Muriel, think of Cissie. D'you want her to be killed?"

Her voice was low, too. "She's a Jew, isn't she?" she said.

My head straightened, knocking against the high back of the armchair. I don't know why, I should've expected it, but I was shocked. Under that sweet veil of English genteelness beat the heart of a viper. And in the three days I'd known her, telling her of my folks, the reason I'd joined in the bloody war long before my own country had been forced to come off the fence, making love to her, sleeping with her, I'd never once suspected the hatred she nurtured for her fellow man, the prejudices that had twisted her soul so that she believed her allegiance lay with a Fascist bigot who had been prepared to betray his own country. And I realized she hadn't concealed a thing. The plain truth was that none of our conversations had ever drawn close to the darker side of her nature. I hadn't asked—and presumably neither had Cissie in all the time she'd known Muriel—her opinion of Jews, niggers, gypsies, of Adolf Hitler and his Master Race ideology, Fascism, Nazism, hadn't even mentioned it. And nobody had asked her if she'd be prepared to turn in her friends to the people who meant to steal their blood. You see, she hadn't lied. She just hadn't been honest.

And then I wondered again about the look I'd caught in her eyes. It was fear, not regret, I was sure of that now. So what did she have to fear? I suddenly had the answer.

"You realize it's gonna be your turn sooner or later, don't you?"

I'd kept my voice low, find I took pleasure in seeing her hesitate for a split second. I watched her push the unacceptable truth away, her expression hardly changing, just that remoteness returning to her eyes, and I knew there was nothing more I could do. I raged inside as she stretched the skin of my lower left arm, pushing the muscles aside so she could locate a particular vein.

Tin buckets were being brought in by other Blackshirts; they placed them close to the man lying by my chair, while the bag-man drew out a scalpel.

"One more question, Muriel," I said to delay the inevitable. "How did you find these people? How did you know where to look? All the years playing cat-and-mouse with these creeps and I've never known where they came from. If I'd had any idea where their HQ was I might have taken the battle to them."

It was Hubble who answered for her and, despite his poor condition, he did it with some delight. "One man against a fortress? I hardly think so, my bumptious American friend. You see, while you had your palace, I had my castle." He wiped moisture from his lips with his blood-flecked handkerchief. "But Miss Drake merely used her common sense and returned to the place where she had first set eyes on us. The National Gallery is one of our control centers, you see—at least, it was in our efforts to capture you. Didn't you realize that some of my men had followed your mongrel dog to the Palace? How do you suppose we finally located you? Fully aware of just how elusive you could be, we had vehicles waiting at as many main road junctions as possible, all controlled from the great gallery at Trafalgar Square. Miss Drake found several of my soldiers still at that control point just ten minutes after leaving this hotel. After that it was only a matter of waiting for the right moment, when you were relaxed with a good meal and perhaps a little the worse for alcohol. The plan worked very well, wouldn't you agree?"

I felt a sharp pain as Muriel drove the hollow needle into a vein. She put a metal clip over the rubber tubing as blood began to flow. The man on the floor suddenly shrieked as the bag-man cut into his wrist and held it over one of the buckets. Muriel released the clip and blood quickly filled the tubing to emerge in a thin stream from the point of the needle at the opposite end;

confident no air bubbles would be carried into the recipient's veins, she pushed the needle into his arm.

"You're murdering me, Muriel," I said quietly, but she just turned away.

"You can't do this to him!" Cissie had struggled to her feet, but one of the guards caught her by the hair and pushed her down again. Old Albert Potter was outraged by that and lumbered up to defend her, shoving the Blackshirt away. Wilhelm Stern also decided it was time to do something about the situation and grabbed the nearest guard's rifle, using it to lever himself off the floor. Another goon quickly stepped in, smashing his club hard against the back of Stern's head; the German went down on one knee, his arms raised to ward off the next blow. Cissie wheeled round, despite the hold on her hair, and jammed her knee into her attacker's groin. He yowled with pain as he let her go

But it was over in seconds. The Blackshirts swarmed over them, clubbing them with sticks and guns, knocking them down and kicking them as they lay sprawled on the floor. And there was nothing I could do to help my friends. As much as I struggled, I couldn't break free from the ropes that bound my wrists. But I could use my feet.r Muriel swiftly stepped aside as I kicked out and the man behind me, who had held my shoulders all this time, fought hard to pin me down. I dug my heels into the carpet, rocking the chair, more Blackshirts rushing towards me, pushing past Muriel, the big guy, McGruder, among them. My right hand gripped the end of the chair's arm and as I jammed my heels into the carpet, I lifted, pushing backwards, the guard behind desperately trying to stop me. The armchair tilted, overbalanced, began to topple.

The guard did his best to hold it, but my legs were straightening, calves and thigh muscles straining. The first Blackshirt stumbled into me and his added weight sent the chair completely over, so that it fell backwards, tilting to one side because of the obstruction behind. We went down with a crash, landing on the half-naked man lying on the floor, and I felt something loosen with the jolt.

We lay there in an untidy heap, the man beneath the pile feebly trying to push us off. For a short while there was silence, as if everyone had been taken by surprise. My head was against bare flesh, my wrists still bound to the chair. I could see the tubing lying a few inches away, the steel needle missing, blood oozing from the open end. The Blackshirt on top of me was trying to disentangle himself, the reek of him and the one underneath me filling my nostrils.

I was almost ready to quit. Sick as these clowns were, their numbers were overwhelming. My body sagged, giving in to pain, giving in to despair. This time we really were sunk.

Then I heard a familiar noise. A kind of distant rumbling.

|16|

It didn't take long for the German bomber pilot to find his target for the night—hell, he must have seen those hotel lights from twenty miles away. I lifted my head to see everyone staring up at the high ceiling as though the noise was coming from the rooms above. The chandeliers began to vibrate.

Then there was a deafening blast as the windows of the next-door restaurant blew in, glass and stone shrapnel roaring through to the room we were in, bringing with it more glass from the dividing wall. The whole building seemed to rock to its very foundations, the chandeliers waving in the wind the explosion caused, the walls and pillars around us trembling, shaking off dust. The tall mirrors cracked and furniture was swept forward as if carried by some invisible tidal wave. Brittle cadavers disintegrated, their various parts tossed into the air, and saucers and cups, cake tiers and lamps, withered plants and rotting napkins all flew towards us, carried by the storm, pulverized by the broiling gust.

Some Blackshirts dropped to the floor, hands over their heads for protection, others cowered where they stood: they were the unlucky ones, the force of the blast knocking them off their feet, sending them crashing into the furniture or pillars, their screams faint under the thunderous row. I was lucky: I was shielded by the back of the chair I was tied to and the goon on top of me. Even so, chair, Blackshirt and I were pushed across the floor, pellets of glass and masonry tearing into the soft cushioning of material and flesh. The Blackshirt howled and rolled away from me, writhing as he tried to reach a glass shard embedded in the back of his neck.

One of my wrists was loose—it was the chair's arm I'd felt give a little when we took the tumble—and it didn't take much to tug it from its bindings. I was twisting round to work on the other one when another earth-shaking *boom* set the world spinning once more. The second bomb must've landed on the Savoy's roof, because the crashing, tearing noise continued as it dropped through the upper floors. The final explosion threatened to demolish the whole building. Great drifts of dust cascaded from the ceiling and lights, enveloping the lounge in a powdery mist.

Although dazed, the pain in my ears threatening to split my skull, I worked on the rope, blinking grit from my eyes and spitting more from my mouth. Frustrated, I got a foot against the chair's arm, then pushed against it, at the same time pulling the rope with both hands. The cushioned arm came away from the rest of the chair just as the third bomb hit another part of the building, this one falling on the other side, somewhere near the main foyer. The avenging angel of the night skies was making the most of this dazzling target and I knew he'd be banking already, turning sharply to get back over us again. I yanked my arm free as a section of ornate ceiling right above me began to crack. A chandelier crashed to the floor, followed by another, this second one demolishing a macabre tableau of mouldered corpses that had taken silent tea for the last three years in a discreet corner of the room. Two brown marble pillars in the same corner collapsed, bringing down a large section of ceiling with them, fire from the room above falling with the debris. There were shouts and screams from all around as Blackshirts tried to flee and I saw two disappear beneath a shower of rubble as another part of the ceiling broke away. A kneeling woman, her hair white with dust, her black uniform in tatters, was trying to pull a piece of glass, shaped like a long, curved scimitar, from her chest, and when it finally came free it released a cascade of blood that splattered onto the carpet. She fell backwards, her dark-fingered hands clawing the wound, and was drenched by her own blood.

A deep *whooshing* alerted me to more trouble to my right and as I turned my head a huge tidal wave of flame billowed through from the main entrance foyer, swallowing up everything in its path, burning carpet, walls and furniture. I fell back, drawing my legs up, head tucked in, arms folded over my hair, fearing the fire would not stop until it had swept through to the other side of the building. But I felt the heat instantly recede and when I looked up it was being sucked back into the foyer. I guessed incendiaries had been sent with the bomb, all exploding together, causing the firestorm. The fire still filled the top of the short stairway to the foyer, and it had left smaller blazes behind in its retreat. Shapes moved before it, figures rushing to and fro in panic, not knowing which way to go, which way to get out. As dark rolling clouds of smoke curled through, poisoning the air, stinging eyes and scorching throats, the lights began to flicker.

Only a few feet away from me, Hubble lay on his side, his chair on top of him, and just for a moment, one brief wink of time, and in all that confusion, our eyes met. Now tiny needles of fire glittered in those dark eyes of his and I felt as if I were looking into the burning hatred inside his soul. His mouth opened as he shouted something, but I couldn't hear what it was over the storm of screams, crashing masonry, and the crackle of fire.

I pushed myself to my feet and stood there, unsteady, half-crouched, my joints stiff and my head reeling, dust and smoke filling my eyes, a bedlam of sound filling my ears. As I raised my hands to wipe dirt and tears from my eyes I noticed the flanged needle was still sticking from my arm. I pulled it out and tossed it away, globules of blood oozing from the wound. There was no time to stem the flow—I had to make a break for it before the Blackshirts got over their panic and before the goddamn room collapsed in on itself. Instead I tore off the rest of my shirt and quickly dabbed at the blood before dropping the bloody rag to the floor. McGruder and another goon were on their feet and leaning over their leader, pulling away the chair that pinned him to the floor; Muriel was closer to me, on her knees, body crouched over, her silver dress torn, a flap hanging loose to expose her shoulder. I quickly searched the immediate area for a fallen weapon, figuring I'd kill all four before I took my leave, but suddenly an arm wrapped itself around my neck from behind.

In a reflex action, I fisted my left hand in the palm of my right, and shot my elbow back, as swift and hard as I could. Spittle dampened my cheek as my attacker huffed and doubled up. I spun round and kicked his legs from under him; he went down like a sack of bricks. Wasting no more time on him and forgetting about dealing with Hubble and his goons—but having to resist

178 / JAMES HERBERT

the urge to snap Muriel's neck as I rushed past her—I joined Cissie and Stern, who were struggling with their guards. The German was being held by one Blackshirt, while another was beating him with his fists, and Cissie was tussling with a black-garbed, crop-haired woman, who gripped both her wrists and was trying to force her back down onto the floor. Punching the Black-shirt in front of Stern in the kidney area so that his hands dropped to protect himself, I belted him hard in the side of the jaw. His head snapped round away from me and his knees buck-led. Without waiting to see if he was permanently out of harm's way, I wrenched the second goon away from Stern and drove my fist into his stomach first, then followed through with a punch to the bridge of his nose (the best place if you really mean business). His eyes crossed and Stern helped by chopping the underside of his hand against the man's neck, so that he fell without a murmur. I swiped the first man, who hadn't quite gone down yet, with the sharp point of my elbow and felt bone in his already damaged nose disintegrate. He might have screamed as he tottered back—his mouth opened and his neck stretched—but another explosion from a room somewhere close by drowned out all other sounds. The floor seemed to heave and cracks appeared in the mirrors and walls as they shuddered. It was like being in an earthquake as more of the ceiling collapsed and pillars shifted their positions.

Cissie and the woman fell to the floor, the Blackshirt on top and still clinging to Cissie's wrists. It took two steps to reach them and I dragged the woman off Cissie and threw her aside. She lay there screeching, but the fight had left her.

As I turned to help Cissie to her feet I noticed Stern stoop to pick up a discarded Sten gun, then aim it at someone rushing at him from out of the smoke. Just as the Blackshirt reached him, Stern jerked the weapon forward into his belly and pulled the trigger. The man did a little jog, his arms flapping, boots stamping carpet, as the bullets disassembled his innards.

A wave of heat engulfed me once more as the fire bloomed out from the broad staircase to the foyer and lobby area, gusts of air sucked in from the blitzed entrance exciting the flames. The grand old hotel was finished: it had survived the worst London air raids, wounded but always unbent, but now there was nobody to quench those flames and repair the damage; fires in other parts of the building would join with this one, making one huge conflagration that would only be extinguished when there was nothing left to burn. There was no more time to waste; we had to leave, and we had to leave now.

"*Look out, Hoke!*"

Cissie had screamed the warning almost into my face as a tall Blackshirt loomed up over my shoulder. When I wheeled round, his rifle was raised to smash down into my head. I started to duck, even in that split second aware there was no way I could avoid the blow, but gunfire rattled through the smoky air and the butt-end of the weapon wavered above me, only inches away. Then it just dropped away, the goon holding the rifle falling with it. Stern joined us, a wisp of smoke curling from the Sten gun's muzzle.

He leaned close to my ear and shouted, "*We must get out!*" and I was dumb enough to nod my head at the obvious.

"*Through that way!*" I pointed towards an opening at the side of the big room which led past the cloakrooms and into the corridor where all the private dining rooms, including the Pinafore, were located. Although I'd been unconscious at the time, I knew Hubble must have brought us that way into the lounge.

We started off in that direction, moving as one, Cissie clinging to my bare arm as if afraid to let go, Stern on the other side, Sten gun held hip-high, covering the ground before us. Once again, survival instinct had kicked in, helping me to operate despite a groggy head and some stiffness from the beating, and we dodged around figures who seemed oblivious to us as they rushed around in the swirling smoke, afraid the whole building was gonna tumble down on them. But if we had the idea that all of Hubble's Blackshirts had forgotten about us we were soon proved wrong: a whole bunch of them were suddenly standing between us and our intended escape route, pistols and rifles raised towards us, staves and short axes brandished by the few women amongst them. They wouldn't want to kill us, I knew that—we were useless to them dead—but they could wound us easily enough; besides, they had another reason for negotiation, a hostage.

In all the commotion and natural anxiety to get out of there fast, I'd forgotten about Albert Potter. He was on hands and knees, one of the Blackshirts crouched over him, holding a blade to his plump throat.

The three of us came to a halt, Cissie calling out the old warden's name, her fingers digging into the flesh of my arm. Stern brought the Sten gun up to his chest and aimed it at the group. I could only spit more dust from my mouth.

It was a stand-off, smoke swirling between us, the flames from the stairway and other parts of the room licking everything orange. The electric lights flickered again, dulled, came back, the generator in the hotel's basement beginning to run slow, then picking up; either the bombardment had caused problems, or three years of lying idle had upset the machinery. I didn't care which, I just prayed for a total blackout. Sure, the fires would still provide some kind of light, but it would be unsteady as well as poor, and any edge was better than none at all.

Hubble was among the group holding us up, his ever-faithful goon, McGruder, by his side, supporting him. Hubble took an unsteady step forward, McGruder careful to go with him, making sure his leader didn't fall.

"Don't make one more move!" Hubble shouted in that weak, high-pitched way of his. "If you do, this man will be killed instantly." He pointed a shaky, dark-stained finger at Potter. The blade at the warden's throat pressed into the soft flesh, not enough to draw blood, but enough to make a furrow. "His is old blood anyway and we'd prefer the younger, more healthy kind," Hubble said, as if we'd appreciate his reasoning. "Your kind, Mr. Hoke. And your companions'. Good, vibrant blood."

How long was it gonna take the mad bomber to make his turn and get back over target? He wouldn't let an opportunity like this go by without dropping every last bomb and incendiary on board. No, he'd douse those glowing lights with fires of his own making, and then he'd spit on the wreckage as he headed home to the Fatherland. C'mon, Fritz, knock this place out, gimme a chance.

I pulled Cissie behind me and scanned the immediate area for fallen weapons. Okay, the Blackshirts would go for non-fatal wounds, tricky for any marksmen. And they'd have to try for the kind that didn't bleed too much; off hand, I couldn't think of any. So: Dive for the nearest gun before they cut the legs from under you. Already tense, I tensed some more.

"Kill Hubble first," I told Stern.

"*No!*" Cissie tugged at my arm. "You can't do that, Hoke, they'll kill Albert."

"They'll kill us all anyway," I replied, still searching the floor. "Do it, Stern, do it now."

The German turned his head towards me, then looked back at Hubble. Something crashed in the foyer, beyond the wall of flame.

"Hoke, I cannot—"

"None of it matters!" I snapped, at last finding what I was searching for, a pistol lying close to an upturned chair on the littered floor. "Shoot him now and let's finish it."

"You're insane," said Cissie over my shoulder.

I felt myself grin. "Yeah," I agreed as I judged the distance between myself and the fallen weapon.

Stern leveled the Sten at the Blackshirt leader, who suddenly looked less sure of himself. But the German lowered the submachine gun, then dropped it onto the carpet.

"It is senseless," he whispered, as if to himself. It was as if not just his energy, but his spirit too, had drained from him. Then, to me: "There has been too much killing. We must reason with these—"

A number of things happened before he'd completed the sentence: Hubble nodded at the goon with the long knife, who nearly slit Potter's throat; the lights surged, then fell almost to nothing; I went down, rolled forward and came up with the German's discarded Sten gun, finger already tightening on the trigger.

| 17 |

I'D FIRED TOO WILD AND TOO SOON, BECAUSE McGRUDER PULLED
Hubble to the floor before I could take proper aim at him. The
bullets caught a couple of Blackshirts who weren't quick enough
to duck, while others in the group blocking our way scattered,
some diving for the floor, others just scooting off, heading for
cover. A mirror shattered on the far wall and splinters flew from a
marble column. The lights brightened again as the generator
below ground revived and I had the chance to pick out Hubble
with the Sten gun. He was crouched on the floor, his loyal hench-
man's beefy arm thrown over his shoulder for protection, and he
was watching me like a paralyzed rabbit. His time was up sooner
than he'd figured, and I was the gun-packing reaper, both counts
pretty hard for him to take.

I pulled the trigger and nothing happened.

Tried again, but it was useless. The gun was jammed or empty,
God knows which, but it was all the same to me. I threw it away
and went for the pistol I'd spotted earlier.

But even as I hit the deck it seemed to rise up beneath me,
slamming into my body so that I turned over from the shock. The
blast—heavy, thunderous, like nothing I'd heard before—overwhelmed all other sounds, and the shell of the building juddered
so violently I thought it must come tumbling down on us all. The
Bomber King had completed his turn and was back over target. I
guessed he'd dropped his whole bomb-load in his determination
to blot out the beacon below. A great wind from the foyer swept
through the lounge, carrying with it lethal shrapnel and fireballs,
and I hugged carpet, pressing my body into its softness, riding the

reverberations, sparks and burning cinders scorching my naked back and arms, pellets of masonry and splinters of wood raining down on me. My hands were over my head, but I heard more crashing sounds, then screams, shouts, and the floor beneath me continued to tremble. Although there were more close-set explosions, I decided it was time to be up and running again.

The broad stairway leading to the foyer and main entrance was totally engulfed in flames by now, and I knew everything beyond it—the reception area, reading lounge, and the staircase to Harry's Bar—would have been completely destroyed. Powdered glass and dust filled the air like thick smoke as other chandeliers broke loose from their fittings and hurtled to the floor, while whole ornamental mirrors fell from the walls and more pillars cracked as they shifted under the strain of the collapsing ceiling. But I was on my feet, looking round for Cissie and the German, swiping at the smoke with my hands as though it were concealing veils.

I soon found them both behind me. Stern was pulling bright red cinders from Cissie smoldering hair, his face covered in blood. Cissie's nose was bleeding and I saw her lips were moving; she was shouting at me and pointing, but I couldn't hear a thing—my ears, and probably theirs too, had been deafened by the explosions. As Stern flicked away the last cinder, smothering the smoldering strands with his other hand, Cissie touched my face. Her fingers came away stained with blood and she showed them to me. I wiped my face with my own hands and felt no wounds or embedded glass or shrapnel, so was sure all I was suffering was a nose-bleed from the blasts and from the look of her, that was Cissie's only problem too. Stern though, had a deep cut over his brow and blood was streaming down into his eyes; he kept clearing it with his sleeve so that he could see, but still it poured out, blinding him each time. His clothes were ripped and I wondered if he'd shielded Cissie from the worst of the blasts, because her dress was relatively untouched.

Taking them both by the arms, aware they couldn't hear a word even if I screamed at them, I pulled them towards the opening I'd intended to make for before. I took time out to kick over a Blackshirt who was just lumbering to his feet in our path and, although he went down fast enough, there were others all around, dark shapes looming up in the smoke mists like specters in a graveyard. Something brushed my cheek, a sharp arrow of air, and even though I hadn't heard the gunshot, I knew someone had recovered enough to take shots at us. Pushing the girl and Stern on ahead, I paused only long enough to lift an upturned coffee table from the floor and hurl it at the murky forms closing in on us. Then I was running again, quickly catching up to the other two, who had almost reached the passageway, and it was weird, unreal, rushing through that silent chaos, slow-moving figures around us, the fires bathing everything, even the smoke, orange, old corpses beginning to smoulder with the advancing heat. Then my ears suddenly popped and the full horror hit me with its sounds. Shots were being fired, people were yelling and screaming, and a terrifying low rumbling-grinding was coming from the building itself.

I couldn't see Hubble anywhere, but then I wasn't bothering to look for him. I only had one thought and that was to get through that archway into the passage before one of the bullets found a target. As if to still that intention, a hail of bullets ripped through a group of tables and chairs close by, shredding the husked corpses seated there, and sending fountains of splinters and broken crockery into the air. I ducked and swerved, managing to grab at Cissie as I went, bringing her down with me when I fell. I heard Stern cry out, saw him stagger as another wild volley was sent our way. He seemed to recover, stumbling on, and as he disappeared through the archway I was already pulling Cissie to her feet and pushing her after him.

We made it. We rushed into the wide passageway, the smoke thinner inside, the air more breathable, and we kept going, catching up with Stern, who was holding his shoulder as he ran. The three of us almost made it to the turn in the passageway too, the point where it continued past the private dining rooms where a couple of hours ago we'd been enjoying a fine meal with rare wines and excellent brandies; almost, but not quite, because some of the goons—it may have been only one; I didn't take time to look back—had reached the entrance to the passageway and had fired after us. Stern staggered again, this time into the closed door directly ahead of us, and I caught him as he bounced off it and started to fall. I dragged him round the corner and out of sight of the Blackshirts just as wood splintered and holes appeared in the same door the German had crashed into (the door to the Gondoliers Room, I noticed when reaction made me glance at it). Stern sagged in my arms, but I wouldn't let him go down; I kept him moving, even though he was crying out at the pain. I could hear footsteps pounding the floor-tiles behind us.

"Hoke, there's a stairway!" Cissie shouted.

The lights stuttered again, almost fading to complete darkness. They came back, too soon for my liking—some darkness would've been an advantage to us at that moment—but not to the same glory; I prayed for the generator to help us out a little by giving up entirely.

"Help me with him," I said to Cissie, pulling Stern's arm over my shoulder.

She took the other side and we went down the stairs, moving as swiftly as we could, but taking care not to stumble. We heard shouts and more running footsteps from above and we tried to keep our descent as quiet as possible, shushing Stern when he started to groan. The further we went, the gloomier it became; not because the generator was failing, but because there were fewer lights in use down there when the machinery controlling them had originally shut down. That suited me line: the more shadows to bide in the better. There were husks on the stairs, all dressed in faded Savoy livery, and it was over one of these uniformed corpses that I tripped, bringing both Cissie and Stern down with me. The German shrieked at the sudden aggravation to his wounds and as I clamped my hand over his mouth we heard more shouts, then footsteps on the stairs. I was up again as quickly as I'd fallen, bringing Stern with me, then bending his body with my shoulder, hoisting him in a fireman's lift. He was goddamn heavy, but I clenched my teeth and kept going, whispering to Cissie to go on ahead and clear the steps of other obstacles. Down and round we went, the sounds of our pursuers growing louder, closer. At the bottom of the stair-case we found a narrow corridor and we hurried along it, the light in this basement area almost non-existent. My load was growing heavier and my limp decided to make a comeback after a day's absence. Another corridor, this one broader, rooms off it leading to boiler rooms, machine rooms and store rooms; there were thick pipes running along the ceiling, smaller ones running alongside them. The walls were of white brick tiles covered in dust and grime, and long cobwebs hung from the pipes; our own footsteps seemed even louder in this place, but still we could hear the Black-shirts drawing closer. We came to a heavy door and Cissie pushed it open: we were in a smart hallway, doorways on both sides, a stair-way not far away leading up. I recognized where we were: the stairs led to the riverside entrance and behind the doors were the hotel's grand function rooms and banqueting halls. Tempting though those stairs were, I knew I'd never get up them fast enough carry-ing the injured man—I could hear our pursuers behind the door we'd just emerged from and they'd be bursting through after us at any second—so I grabbed Cissie's hand and pulled her into the open doorway on our right.

She realized where we were the moment we were over the threshold and in the gloom I felt her go rigid in my grip. She began to back away, shaking her head.

"We gotta hide," I hissed at her. "Just long enough to shake 'em off."

"Not here," she whispered back.

But it was already too late to change our minds. We heard the door to the hallway open.

"Quick." I pushed her ahead of me towards one of the cur-tained bunk-beds. Pulling the curtain aside, I unloaded the semi-conscious German onto the narrow bed, then ordered Cissie to climb in after him.

At first I thought she was going to resist, but voices outside the door took the choice away from her. She slid in after Stern and I climbed in after her, drawing the curtain closed behind us. Some-thing softly broke beneath our bodies and in the darkness a pow-dery dust smelling of fossilized mushrooms rose up around us. Stern gave a feeble moan and I groped for his face, finding his mouth and covering it with both hands. He tried to twist his head away, but he was too weak to succeed; I held him there, hands clamped tight, and soon his body went limp. Afraid of suffocating him, I immediately lifted my hands an inch or two away from his mouth, ready to bring them down should the need arise. Beside me, Cissie was trying to control her own breathing—I could feel the slow rise and fall of her chest within the close confines of the veiled bunk. Her fingers clasped my bare shoulder.

The sour odor of decay became almost overwhelming, giving us another reason to restrain our breathing: it was difficult to shake off the notion that the foul dust floating around inside that enclosed refuge would poison our lungs. That smell and more soft crumblings beneath us confirmed what I already suspected and what I really did not want to know: we were lying on top of the crusted body of someone who'd crawled inside this darkened space a long time ago to escape the invisible killer thing that was in the air itself. Cissie must have realized at the same time, because she made a sudden lunge across my shoulders, and only by twisting my body and pinning her to the wall with my back did I prevent her from tearing open the curtain and tumbling out. Her breasts heaved against my shoulder blades and for an uncomfortable few moments I thought she was gonna throw up all over me. She held on though, her panic giving way to a more controlled fear, her breathing slowing down; and soon I felt her tears on my back. Beneath me, Stern began to moan and I quickly eased my weight off him again and held a hand to his lips. Despite the pain he was in, I think maybe he was aware of our situation—or at least, that we were in danger—because he became quiet and lay still once more. In inky blackness we waited, and I wondered how many other rotted corpses lay about us in this reinforced tomb. Cissie had sensed them when I'd first brought her here, and I admired her willpower now; me, I was used to the decayed remains of the dead—I even collected them—but she was still learning to accept it all.

Voices tensed us.

"They're not in here," someone said.

"How d'you know?" came a hushed reply. "It's too dark to see."

"They'd have gone up the stairs. There's a way out up there."

"They didn't have time, we'd have seen 'em. They've ducked in here, or one of those doors opposite."

Another voice joined in, quiet and out of breath like the others, as if afraid of disturbing the dead. "What's behind all them curtains?" it said.

"Looks like some kind of bunker in there. Probably the hotel's own shelter when the Blitz was on."

Shuffling footsteps as they entered.

"Fucking hell, it's creepy."

So they felt it, too. Enough to make them change their minds

about searching the place? Somewhere far off there was a muffled crash or explosion, I couldn't tell which.

"This whole place is gonna come down."

"Fucking Germans."

"Well let's get out before it does."

"No, we gotta check. If Hubble found out we hadn't, he'd have
our guts for garters."

"Shit, I had a better time in the army."

"He pulled us together, didn't he? Gave us all a chance. It'd be
every man for hisself without Sir Max."

"Okay, okay, let's get on with it."

I swore under my breath. They were moving further into the
room. I shifted my weight, got an elbow beneath me, and Stern
gave a soft moan.

"D'you hear that?"

"What?"

"There was a noise, sounded like someone moaning."

"I never heard it."

"It came from over there."

I parted the curtain at its center a fraction, just enough for me
to peek through. There were three of them, as the voices had
indicated, their figures vague and shadowy in the poor light from
the hallway. I was surprised, assuming more had chased us down
here; then I realized the main group had probably gone straight
past the stairway so they could search the private function rooms
along the upper hallway, while these three had broken off to
investigate the basement. I let go of the curtain and pulled back
as the three men drew near.

"It came from behind one of these."

Through the material of the curtains I could see the lights outside were fluttering again.

"Here, I don't want to be in this bleedin place if the lights go
again."

"All right, let's make it quick then."

The swish of curtains being drawn back came to us. They'd
started at the beginning of the row of bunks we were hiding
among and were working their way along.

"Why don't I just put a burst through the lot of 'em?" came
one of the voices.

"What, and kill the people we're looking for? We need 'em to survive, you bloody fool."

"So Hubble says."

"Yeah, well he's right. You saw the American and his friends— they all look healthy enough, none of 'em's touched by the disease. They've got the good blood and we need it. It don't take a genius to work that out."

Another curtain was drawn aside, this one over the next bunk down. I heard Cissie gasp in a sharp breath.

The material in front of me ruffled, then dim light accompanied by a long-bladed knife (the same one that had slit Albert Potter's throat?) came through the parting. There seemed no point in *waiting* to be discovered.

I pulled back the curtain so smartly that the man on the other side shrieked in surprise. My other hand gripped the fist around the knife and pushed it upwards and back so that its point sank into the startled Blackshirt's throat. His shriek became a choking gurgle and rising air forced splatters of blood from the throat wound and his mouth. I felt its warmness as it sprinkled my face and shoulder, and I leapt out of the bunk, shoving the choking man away from me into the Blackshirt behind him. This second one's pistol went off as he staggered backwards and I ducked instinctively. The bullet hit the ceiling and the man fell to the floor with the weight of his knife-struck pal on top of him.

The thing of it is, and as I keep saying, these poor saps were not the men they used to be. The Slow Death had weakened their muscles and slowed their reactions, otherwise they'd have cornered and captured me way back. I was no superman, no *Übermensch,* as Hitler had liked to call his elite, but I was still pretty fit—working on the allotments and lifting bodies on a near-daily basis had taken care of that—and living with constant danger had kept my wits sharp enough, so I had the edge on these characters. And knowing I was no good to them dead had always encouraged me to take risks, which was why I'd taken the fight to them at that moment and almost shocked them rigid.

The third man was still gawping at me as I started towards him. His weapon, a Thompson submachine gun, whose round magazine made him look like a hoodlum from one of those gangster movies that were all the rage before the war, was frozen in his hands. No Jimmy Cagney or Edward G. this guy, though, because I was already diving for his legs before he remembered to pull the trigger.

I was under the Thompson's stubby barrel so the bullets only ruined the floor as I struck his knees, unbalancing him and bringing him down on top of me. I kept rolling and came up behind him. Reaching over his hunched shoulders, I grabbed the submachine gun's warm barrel with one hand and its butt with the other, jerking the weapon upwards so that it cracked against his lower jaw, knocking what little sense he had from him. He clung to the gun though, but his grip was slack. I pulled it back against his windpipe, squeezing hard and, I guess, crushing or breaking something inside, because he suddenly went limp, all life gone from him.

I heard a scuffle and looked up to see Cissie's shadowy figure hurl itself at the second Blackshirt, whose pistol was aimed in my direction as he sprawled on the floor. He dismissed her with a backward slap of his hand and pointed the gun at me again. But this time it was Stern he had to contend with.

The German aimed a kick at the gun-hand, but missed and struck the Blackshirt's wrist instead, spoiling the shot. I was already scrambling across the floor on all fours and before he got a second chance, I'd smashed my fist into his nose (never fails). The back of Iris head hit the floor with a sickening smash, but just to make sure he wouldn't be a nuisance any more, I snatched the pistol from his sluggish grip and brought the butt down hard on his forehead. His head slowly lolled to one side as Stern sank down beside him. Aware that the gunfire would have attracted the attention of other Blackshirts who were hunting us, I was on my feet in an instant.

"Stern, you okay? Can you get up?"

He swayed on his knees, head lowered, eyes downcast. "With your help," he managed to murmur.

A stain that could only have been blood was darkening his shirt collar and when I touched his shoulder I felt the slick wetness soaking through his jacket. Pistol in one hand, I reached beneath his arms and hauled him up, then held him there while I quickly looked towards the open doorway. Cissie pushed herself off the floor and skirted round the man with the knife in his throat, his hands still on the handle, his body quivering as his sick blood drained from him. She joined us and took Stern by one of his arms to help me support him.

"He's badly hurt, we've got to do something about his wound," she said urgently.

"No time," I told her as I ripped open his shirt collar, then pulled the fancy silk handkerchief from his suit's breast pocket. I tucked it under the shirt collar, feeling for the wound. "Okay, hold it there, try to stem the flow as best you can."

She pressed the already blood-soaked silk against his neck, aware that Stern's wound needed a proper dressing and that he shouldn't be moving about.

"Hoke." Stern had raised his head and was trying to see me in the gloom. "Leave me the other weapon, the Thompson. I can hold them off for you, or at least take up some of their time."

Don't think it wasn't tempting. But I said: "We're getting out together, Wilhelm." No V for the W, just a straight "Wilhelm." Despite his pain, he managed to clap a hand on my shoulder. In the light from the doorway I noticed he'd even managed a faint smile.

"I was a spy, you know," he said.

"Yeah, I know," I replied. "But it doesn't matter anymore. Now, let's get going before the rest of 'em find us."

Tucking the pistol into the waistband of my pants, I guided Stern towards the light, stooping to pick up the Thompson as we went. I took a quick peek out into the hallway while Cissie held the injured German steady.

"All clear," I told them. "The river entrance is up those stairs and it's the easiest and quickest way out."

One of Cissie's arms was stretched across Stern's chest as she kept the makeshift pad tight against the bullet wound, and her other hand was wrapped around his upper arm.

"Can we really make it, Hoke?" she asked, her wide eyes studying my face for the truth. "Won't they realize we'll try and get out that way?"

"Depends. I'm hoping those bombs have caused too much confusion for Hubble and his people to think straight. We got other choices—it's a warren of rooms and passages down here— but I don't think our friend would make it. The sooner we break out, the sooner we'll be able to fix him up."

If I'd been on my own, or even just with the girl, it would've been a cinch. I'd taken time during my stays at the Savoy to locate all the trade and staff exits, every outlet from the basement area, as well as the quickest way to them; but now I had an obligation. Stern had saved my life—twice—and I wasn't about to let him down. Sure, he'd riled me with his arrogance earlier that evening, but he'd just been hitting back, mocking my expectations of him as a German. And it was *Muriel* who'd joined up with the Blackshirts, not Stern; *he'd* help me fight them.

We were halfway up the stairs to the riverside entrance hall when we heard the trampling of many feet from somewhere over our heads. Stern was making a fair effort of getting himself up those stairs without entirely relying on me and the girl, but it was slow progress and I wondered how long his strength would hold out. Concentrating on each step, he seemed oblivious to the noise from above, but Cissie looked across him at me, her panic not far from the surface.

"Keep him coming," I said to her, letting go of Stern and racing up to the entrance hall above.

I'd just reached the top when I saw the first of the Blackshirts beginning to descend the stairway from the first-floor foyer and I lifted the Thompson just as they set eyes on me. With cries of alarm they backed up, a couple of them turning to run, and I sent a hail of bullets after them. The Thompson submachine gun never was an accurate weapon, but it had a good effect, enough to hold the goons off 'til Cissie and Stern were stumbling past me towards the glass exit by the side of the revolving door. Another burst to give the Blackshirts something more to think about, then I was rushing through the exit behind them.

Glass shattered around us as the goons returned fire, sprinkling our hair, peppering my naked skin, and I turned in one last effort to keep them back, the muzzle of the Thompson already spitting flames. One of the bolder Blackshirts was halfway down the stairs when my gunfire raked his chest, knocking him over, his arms outstretched, rifle flying into the air. He started to slither the rest of the way down, but I didn't stay to watch: I was out in the open, running along the alleyway created by the zigzag barrier, quickly catching up with Cissie and Stern. I kicked away the plank across the entrance to the alley and then we were out into the night.

But we stopped dead at what confronted us.

Lights still shone dimly from the Savoy's shattered windows, some of those lights a flickering orange, the glow of fires inside, and their reflections were thrown across the narrow roadway and park opposite. The moon lent its own illumination. All of it revealing the people gathered outside the hotel, their numbers scattered, some in small groups, others solitary.

They watched the burning building, upturned faces shimmering in its glow, and there was a strange emptiness in their staring eyes. Without counting, I guessed there were a couple of dozen of them, maybe a few more than that, some of them, obviously sick with the Slow Death, supported by healthier friends or relatives, most dressed in fine clothes, a few—mainly the single people—in tattered rags. There were children among them—a little girl, no more'n five or six, clinging to a woman I assumed was her mother (or maybe her adoptive mother); two boys, twins by the look of them, about seven years old, holding hands and standing close to a man and woman; a toddler, around two years, clutching a dolly and in the arms of a bearded man—and, unlike the adults, these children had a look of wonder on their faces as they gazed up at the lights and flames. Then they began to notice us, and soon all of them were looking in our direction.

Several backed away, as if in fear, but going only as far as the park railings. Others watched us with surprised curiosity, and maybe with hope.

"Hoke," Cissie said breathlessly, "who are these people?"

"Beats me," was all I could reply.

Stern, leaning heavily against Cissie, looked at us both. "Like moths attracted to a flame," he said, his voice strained. "In this case, to the lights, don't you see? Hoke, you must warn them."

A noise from behind, a scuffling of leather on concrete, made me wheel around before I could say any more. The Blackshirts were filing along the alleyway, trying to move quietly now that they saw we were no longer running. I fired from the hip, taking out the first two, sending the others scuttling back. But that last burst had used up all that was left of the ammo and the Thompson was lifeless in my hands. I cursed as I threw it away—there should've been fifty rounds in the drum magazine, but much of

the ammo must have been used up earlier by the Blackshirt I'd
taken it from—and drew the pistol from my waistband.

"Hoke!"

I turned at Cissie's cry and saw more dark figures rounding the
corner from a side street further along, Blackshirts who'd found
other exits out of the blazing building. They came to an abrupt
halt when they saw the silent strangers standing in the roadway
and on the opposite pavement. A shout went up when they spotted us next.

"Oh God, we're trapped." Cissie had spoken to me as if I
didn't appreciate the seriousness of the situation.

"No we're not. We can get through the park." I pointed the
pistol in the other direction where there was a small gate in the
iron railings.

"But these people—we've got to help them."

I took Stern from her, pulling his arm over my shoulder once
more, keeping my gun hand free. "There's nothing we can do for
'em, they'll have to take care of themselves!'

I moved off, slowed down by Stern, using the brick barricade
as a screen between us and the Blackshirts who were outside the
riverside entrance.

"Keep up with us!" I yelled back at Cissie as she hesitated.

"Run!" I heard her shout at the waiting people. *"Don't stay
here! Don't let them take you!"*

When I looked over my shoulder they were still standing
there, confused, probably afraid, not knowing what the hell was
going on. I fired a couple of shots over their heads to put some
life into them, but although one or two started to run away, the
rest cowered or sank to the ground.

"Cissie, come on!"

Reluctantly she began to follow and when shots were fired
from the goons near the corner, she caught up fast. There were
more figures loitering in this stretch of road and we tried to
convince them that it was in their best interest to get away, but,
like the others, they seemed too bewildered to move. Maybe they
thought we were the villains, that those uniformed people were
the only law the city had left; or maybe they thought they'd be
shot if they did try to escape. I didn't know, and right then I
couldn't help 'em: I was too busy saving my own and Stern's skin,

and I guessed that Cissie was now of the same mind—she'd caught up with us and was taking some of the injured German's weight. We couldn't help them if they didn't want to be helped; we could only offer some hurried advice. And we did. Even with bullets whistling over our heads, we yelled and tugged at those closest to us as we made our way to the park gate; but it was no good, they just crouched low to the ground to avoid being hit. Of course, it was really the strangers who were helping us, because not only were the Blackshirts afraid of harming any part of this precious new consignment of healthy blood, but our rarity value had depreciated considerably.

Dodging through the space between two curbside cars, we were soon at the park's entrance and I took one last look at the scene behind us. Blackshirts were already rounding up the onlookers, with only three of them chasing after us. Still supporting Stern with one shoulder, I took careful aim and brought down two as they ran. They both screamed, the first dropping to his knees, clutching at his chest, the second spinning across the hood of a car and slowly sliding to the ground. It was enough to discourage the third. He skidded to a halt, the metal toecaps of his boots scraping sparks off the roadway, and shouted something after us. He remained where he was though, neither retreating nor advancing, just loitering there, shaking a fist and cursing. I took a bead on him, but Stern placed an unsteady hand on my arm.

"Better that we just leave," he said, his words tight, as if squeezed through a constricted throat.

I spat on the curb, knowing he was right, that there was nothing we could do for these other people. Reluctantly the three of us turned and I led the way through the thick shadows of the neglected park.

|18|

I TOOK THEM DOWN TO THE EMBANKMENT WHERE THE OLD RIVER ran pure silver under the uncloaked moon, its waters free of human detritus, driftwood and loose craft the only blight. A short flight of stone steps over the river wall led us to a wooden jetty where I kept a small motor launch, tanked up and regularly serviced like all my escape vehicles. Soon we were heading downstream, the quiet throbbing of the boat's engine and the distant, fading drone of the Dornier, one contented *Kraut* bomber on his way home, the only sounds. We'd heard more gunfire behind us as we'd made our way to the jetty, but now it'd ceased, leaving us to wonder about those poor souls we'd found waiting outside the Savoy. How many had been shot or beaten for resisting the Blackshirts? How many of those suffering the Slow Death had been killed where they stood, eliminated because their blood was useless to Hubble and his parasites? And how many more of those pilgrims had arrived at the front of the hotel, at the shattered main entrance, attracted by the lights blazing through the night sky? Had they been captured too?

While Cissie cradled Stern in her arms and did her best to stanch his bleeding, I steered the motor launch close to the riverbank, keeping us under the cover of buildings and walls, checking over my shoulder to see if we were being followed, watching the grand old hotel burn. Its electric lights, sirens to the survivors, a beacon to the Dornier's pilot, were finally doused, but by then the flames had taken over, more than compensating for their loss. It was nothing new to me, this kind of senseless vandalism, but still it was a tragic sight and a heaviness weighed on me. The Savoy had served as a resolute symbol of London's unbreakable spirit during the Blitz; by tomorrow it would be a gutted shell, maybe even reduced to rubble. It had survived the war almost intact and three years later it'd taken just one man, guided by a company of fools, to destroy it.

Cissie was quietly weeping, but there wasn't much I could do to comfort her. Nor could I help the wounded German—all my efforts had to go into getting us away from there. Rumpled barrage balloons drooped like small gray clouds over the blackened city, testimony to mankind's inventiveness and absurdity, and the river stretched ahead like a broad, metallic highway, taking us to a quieter part of the graveyard.

We journeyed into the concealing darkness of the river bends.

| 19 |

No. 26 Tyne Street was at the very end of a long and narrow cobbled turning that looked like a cul-de-sac, but wasn't, just off Whitechapel High Street—Jack the Ripper territory—and we approached it through a covered alleyway that had a thin, waist-high post at one end—an ancient cannon barrel rooted upright in concrete, an iron cannonball fixed firmly into its muzzle—and a tall gas lamppost outside the other. Less than twenty minutes earlier we'd left the motor launch moored to a set of mossy stone steps that climbed from the river to a wharfside passageway. Between us, we'd carried the wounded German to the roadway where I soon found an open-top Austin Touter in reasonable working condition and with enough juice left in its tank (gasoline had completely evaporated in many of these stranded vehicles) for the next phase of the journey. The three of us had crammed into it, Stern semi-conscious and moaning softly, Cissie through with weeping, but withdrawn and silent, and I'd driven past the old Billingsgate fish market—the worst of its foul stench had long since faded, but it was still bad enough to wrinkle your nose—and then carefully through the canyon streets of the City, once London's thriving financial sector, where the roads, sidewalks, and doorways were littered with dark shapes, unrecognizable bundles that had once been the life-pulse of this glittering square mile. A glance at Cissie told me she didn't like it here—her eyes shifted uneasily, her head kept jerking as if she'd seen something in the road ahead, or in one of the doorways—and I remembered her nervousness when I'd first shown her the Abe Lincoln Room at the Savoy. She was perceptive to ghostly things, I guess, and the events of the evening hadn't helped her nerves any. Hell, I had to grip the steering wheel tight to stop my own hands from trembling, and I was relieved when we were through the area. A few minutes later we'd reached our destination.

I'd parked the Austin outside a wash-house on Old Castle Street, a road that ran parallel to Tyne Street, then carried Stern over my shoulder through the little alleyway that connected the two streets. No. 26 was three doors away from the alley and tucked into a corner facing *up* the cobbled street. Like the turning it was in, the house itself was narrow, with three floors squeezed on top of one another and a cellar, and it was in a strategic position (a prime reason for choosing it as a refuge) because nobody could enter from the high street without being observed from one of its five front windows. The dwellings at the top end of Tyne Street were gutted shells, bomb-wrecked, but in the middle it opened out to a tiny square before continuing towards 26 with two-story houses on one side and bigger, three-story houses on the other, all of them terraced and with defunct gaslights mounted at intervals along their walls. The London Docks were not far away and the *Luftwaffe* might have done Tyne Street's residents a favor by demolishing the rest of the houses during one of their hit-and-miss raids on dockland (as long as those residents weren't inside), because these places were slums and had been for a long time.

Behind 26 and its neighbors were tiny, concrete backyards filled with mangles, bicycles, tin baths—all rusted now—piles of coal and outside lavatories, the yards themselves backing onto a bigger compound where some of the traders from the big bustling street market called Petticoat Lane kept their stalls and barrows. Sally had brought me here one Sunday morning, not ashamed of showing me a rougher part of her town, and I'd remembered Tyne Street and the usefully positioned No. 26 after my first run-in with the Blackshirts when I was looking for safe havens. Sure, I had my pick of thousands of such places, but all my eventual choices had something to do with Sally.

The back windows of No. 26—and oddly, there were only two, both over the house's creaky wooden staircase that twisted up from the end of the short, ground-floor corridor to the bedrooms at the top—overlooked the yards, the lower one providing a handy exit should the enemy come pounding on the front door.

Most of the family furniture was packed into the ground floor's only room, making it the parlor/kitchen/dining room and (because it had the only sink in the whole place) bathroom. It was about sixteen-feet square and its single window looked out onto the street. In one corner, close to the deep enamel sink with shelves overhead, cups, and pans hanging from them, stood a cast-iron gas stove and, instead of a fireplace, in the wall opposite the window there was a huge black range built into the chimney breast, with ovens at the sides and a fire grate in the middle; an oversized kettle, more saucepans, along with a small camp cooker I'd brought here myself, cluttered its flat surface. Next to it was a lumpy armchair with frayed armrests, a flower-patterned sofa, where I'd dumped some of my clothes, taking up most of the wall on that side of the room; sitting on a veneered hardboard side-board under the window was a Bush wireless set and a stoneware vase filled with shriveled flowers I'd never bothered to throw out. Just behind the door to the corridor was a plyboard kitchen cabinet, its pull-down work-top closed, and nestled between this and the gas stove stood a tall lampstand with a tasselled shade, an arrangement imposed by jumble rather than design.

The wall here was nothing more than a wooden floor-to-ceiling partition separating the room from the corridor, painted cream and brown like the door, window frame and sill, and the mantelshelf (these days loaded with cigarette cartons) over the range. Deep brown, patterned linoleum covered the floor, almost worn through in places, and at the room's center, with barely enough space between it and the surrounding furniture, was a steel Morrison shelter substituting for a table, the wooden chairs around it pushed tight against the wire mesh sides. All I'd found on it when I'd first entered No. 26 were a half-empty jar of furry lemon curd, a split packet of dried Weston Biscuits, a can of Keating's bug, beetle, and flea powder, and a yellowed copy of the *Daily Sketch* dated 24th March 1945, the very day the Blood Death rockets had fallen.

Mercifully, the house had been empty of corpses and it hadn't taken long to collect those on the cobblestones outside and transport them to the stadium; as Tyne Street was to become an

occasional home, I figured this was the least I could do for its
dead residents. After that I'd moved in with my own comforts
and weaponry (the bedroom above was stashed with canned food
and guns, as well as a few hand grenades I'd picked up from a
depot not too many miles from there, just south of the river). I
didn't mind that this place didn't have the comforts of my other
refuges; fact is, its shabbiness made it less of a target for the
Blackshirts—they'd never expect me to hole up in a shack like
this—and I'd always felt pretty secure here.

I kept the front-door key on the inside sill of the groundfloor
window; the window itself left open a couple of inches, so while
Cissie propped Stern up by the door I went and fetched it. She
didn't make a sound as I pushed the long key into the lock, but I
knew she was all in; even in the moonlight her face looked hag-
gard, her eyes full of skittish nervousness and concern for the
injured German.

Pushing open the heavy front door, I took Stern over my
shoulder again and carried him straight to the end of the short
corridor. The bare wooden stairs creaked and groaned under our
weight, the sounds exaggerated in the close confines of the tall
house. The bedroom door was open and moonlight streaming
through the two windows helped me work my way through the
boxes and stacked cans towards the bed. I laid him down carefully
and even before I'd drawn the curtains and lit the oil lamp on the
mantelpiece with matches lying next to it Cissie had removed
Stern's jacket and was unbuttoning his shirt.

"I'm gonna boil some water," I said to her. "Use something to
try and stop the bleeding."

She stopped me as I reached the bedroom door. "Hoke. The
bullet . . ."

I tried not to think about it. "Yeah. It'll have to come out.
That's why we need lots of hot water."

"You'll do it?"

That's what I hadn't wanted to think about. "Unless you want
to volunteer."

She didn't reply and I shrugged. "I'll do what I can."

I hurried downstairs and lit the camp cooker on top of the
range. I'd never risked lighting a fire here, nor anywhere else
unless out in the open, because chimney smoke could attract the

wrong kind of attention, and I wasn't going to light one tonight.
After adjusting the circle of flames, I worked my way round the
Morrison shelter and pulled the curtains tight together, then lit
the lantern on the makeshift tabletop. The room brightened, but
the shadows became more intense. I drew the pistol and laid it
next to the lantern.

Pipes clanked before water gushed in spurts from the tap over
the sink and I had to wait for a steady flow before filling a
saucepan; the pressure was weaker than the last time I was here
and it took a couple of minutes to fill the container to the brim.
Once the saucepan was on the burner I washed my hands with a
rock of carbolic soap from the sink's drainer, repeating the process when I was done, and shaking them rather than use the stiffened rag passing itself off as a kitchen towel on a hook nearby. I
needed a cigarette badly, but decided to wait.

Cissie's call came from over my head, followed by a loud
thump on the ceiling.

Holding my hands close to my chest to keep them clean, I
made my way back upstairs, glancing out the window opposite
the tiny landing as I went by. There wasn't much to see through
the weather-stained glass, save for shadows and the odd shapes of
stalls and trestles down in the bigger yard, but I was confident
that no one had followed us here. As I turned away I stumbled on
the last step to the landing and my shoulder bumped the opposite
wall; like the partition downstairs, it was made of wood and the
cracking sound that came from it was like a gunshot. Through the
open doorway I saw Cissie react sharply and I mumbled an apology as I approached the bed.

"Please help me with him," she pleaded, the lamplight catching the glistening of tears on her cheeks.

Stern was almost on the other side of the double bed, pushing
himself away as if to escape her caring hands. She knelt on the
mattress and tried to pull him onto his back, but her efforts were
too cautious, too gentle. The German shouted something in his
own language and his hand thrashed out, striking Cissie on the
shoulder. I quickly joined her and, forgetting about dirtying my
hands, grabbed his arm and turned him. I winced when I saw the
sheets were drenched with his blood.

"Take it easy," I told him uselessly as I pinned him to the bed with as little force as possible. But he twisted again and for the first time I clearly saw the blood bubbling from the wound in the back of his neck. It ran through puckered skin and livid burn scars that spread downwards from his hairline, across his shoulders and towards the halfway point of his spine. These were old markings though, and my attention returned to the fresh wound: I thought I noticed something imbedded there, a slight, blackish protrusion under the slick coat of discharging blood. I touched my hand to it to confirm my suspicion and felt a hard lump that I knew wasn't bone.

"The bullet's almost worked its way out," I said, more to myself than the girl. "At least it'll make things easier."

Next I examined the wound in his arm, close to the shoulder, and grunted when I realized there were two punctures, front and back. The bullet had passed clean through, taking tissue and muscle with it but, s'far as I could make out, without touching bone. Straightening up, I noticed the blood-soaked rag Cissie was holding in one hand.

"His shirt," she said.

"Christ. Okay, I'll find you something else." I remembered the mildewed towels and sheets in a cupboard across the room; they weren't ideal, but they'd have to do. "Keep him on his side, as he is. We'll deal with the arm wound first, try to stop the bleeding, then I'll get the bullet out of his neck."

"The pain's too much. Don't you have anything to give him?"

"Pills'd be no good, even if he could swallow them. Tomorrow I'll get to a hospital, find some morphine."

It was something I should have done a long while ago, in case of accidents to myself, but I guess I'd been afraid of having easy access to any powerful opiates; shit, booze was a big enough problem for me. There was something else, also: I hated those kind of places—hospitals and churches—because they were nothing more than huge burial vaults, crammed with the bodies of Blood Death victims who'd fled to them to be saved, either by medics or the Lord, Himself. No, I stayed clear of those kind of charnel houses.

"I'll get some proper dressings and bandages as well as the morphine, but tonight we'll have to use what we got."

"We need something to soak up the blood now, then something to keep pressed against the wound."

"Give me a minute. Just hold on to him, okay?"

I went to the cupboard set into the opposite wall and the musty smell was strong when I opened its creaking door (although the coppery reek of fresh blood coming from the direction of the bed was stronger). Reaching in, I pulled out all the linen and cloth towels I could find—not many, at that—then took a thin pile of bedsheets from a higher shelf. I carried them back to the bed.

"Do what you can with these while I get the water," I said, already heading for the door again.

The water was just beginning to come to the boil so I took time to rummage in the kitchen cabinet for a suitable instrument for some on-the-hoof surgery. The best I could find was a long, thin-bladed carving knife; it was a little big for the job, but the only one with a point strong and sharp enough to dig into flesh. Taking it over to the range, I lifted the saucepan and put the knife's blade into the small but fierce flames, slowly turning it over so that both sides and edges were sterilized without becoming blackened. I kept it in the heat for about two minutes, then replaced the saucepan with the knife's blade inside so that the water quickly came to the boil again.

I filled another saucepan and exchanged it for the one on the gas cooker and then, leaving the blade in the bubbling water, I carried the first saucepan upstairs.

Stern held out for some time before he started screaming. I'd had to probe deeper than I'd thought to get the knife's tip beneath the lump of lead, Cissie holding the lamp as close as she could while endeavoring to hold the German down with her other hand. Once, he rolled out of her grasp onto his back and I had to withdraw the blade quickly. When we got him on his side again, I went to work more ruthlessly, ignoring his screams and sliding the blade down through spurting blood and along hard metal while Cissie used her whole weight to pin him there. Twisting the knife and levering sharply and forcefully, I felt the bullet move. Stern's scream filled the room and probably echoed up the street as the bloodied lump fell out onto the stained bedsheet. I went limp thinking I'd killed him until I saw his chest still rising and falling. I saw there was blood on his lips.

Cissie finished up, cleaning and dressing both wounds while I went back downstairs to fetch more hot water. I brought it up and helped her change the bedsheets for new, if not fresh, ones, rolling the unconscious German to one side and covering the blood-sodden mattress with double layers of towels. I left her there to watch over him, wearily treading downstairs again to the jumbled front room, my bloody hands shaking so much it was impossible to light the cigarette I took from one of the cartons I kept on the mantelshelf; in the end I had to lean close to the camp cooker and light it from the blue flame. I sank into the armchair, rusted springs groaning under my weight, and rested my head back. I closed my eyes and filled my throat and lungs with smoke.

There was whisky in the kitchen cabinet, but I was too dog-tired to get it.

It was still dark when moans from over my head awoke me. I sat there and listened to Stern's agony, feeling pity, anger and helplessness. The pity was for Stern, something I never thought I'd feel for a German; the anger was against those bastards who'd done this to him; and the helplessness was because there was nothing more Cissie and I could do.

There were footsteps on the stairs—the whole house warned of any movement inside its walls with creaks and grumbles and even sighs—and then dread took a slow dive into the pit of my stomach when the shadowy form of Cissie appeared in the open doorway. I already knew what she was gonna ask me to do.

"Hoke, he needs medication now, something to kill the pain. Antiseptic, too, and fresh dressings and bandages to keep the wound clean. He won't last the night otherwise."

Oh shit, I thought. Goddamn bloody shit. I hauled myself out of the armchair.

�֍   ✖   ✖

The enormous, Gothic-grim hospital was a mile or so away, along Whitechapel, its edifice forbiddingly bleak in the moonlight. I'd taken time only to wash away some of the blood and to pull on a gray sweatshirt, its sleeves cut away at the elbows, to protect me from the slight chill that had come with the early hours. Taking the pistol—I noted for the first time it was a Browning .22—from the table, I tucked it back into the waistband of my pants and left the house. I ducked into the pitch-black alleyway, a hand running along the rough brick wall for guidance, and returned to the Austin open-top that had brought us here. The drive hadn't taken long, but I stayed in the car on the ramp outside the hospital's main entrance for a while, steeling myself to go inside. Only the thought that Wilhelm Stern had saved my life twice and the more I delayed the worse it was for him made me open the car door and mount the steps to the open entrance (those doors were open because old bones had jammed them that way).

Holding the lantern I'd brought with me shoulder high, I went inside.

I still hate thinking about those wards and corridors packed with human debris, some of the corpses piled on top of each other as if their last moments had been spent struggling, fighting for attention maybe; now they were locked together in eternal strife, or at least until their bones collapsed. There were smaller husks among them, the deteriorated bodies of children, but I refused to look at their little withered faces, treading through them carefully, my eyes averted, looking directly ahead. They were everywhere, those moldering things that were once living, breathing people, in every space, every corner, as I'd known they would be, and I shuddered each time my foot brushed against something brittle and crumbly. The sour smell was everywhere too and I clamped my hand over my mouth and nose to mask the worst of it.

It took almost an hour to find the room I was looking for and still I hadn't toughened myself against the carnage around me: I was scared to my boots, and nausea was only a heave away. Even as

I broke into locked glass cabinets and examined vials and jars, looked through cupboards for gauze and surgical dressings, then into drawers for pills and syringes, I kept looking over my shoulder, expecting to see something I really didn't want to see. I gathered up anything that might be useful, including sedatives, forcing myself to be calm, to take my time and collect essentials and maybe not-so essentials, loading scissors and safety pins, antiseptic creams and boxes of Elastoplast, anything that came to hand, into a laundry bag I'd taken from a storage closet. Only when I was sure I was done did I run from that place.

It was growing light behind the distant rooftops as I drove along the broad Whitechapel High Street and weariness was making my eyelids heavy and my hands like lumps of lead on the steering wheel. It didn't take long to find my way back to Old Castle Street, and I was soon hurrying through the alleyway, my legs hardly able to support me, then pushing open the door to No. 26.

Cissie was sitting on the stairs at the end of the short corridor, dawn light pressing itself through the begrimed window overhead to flush her hair and shoulders with its gray mantle. From her muffled sobs I knew I was too late. Stern was already dead.

|20|

WE LAY SIDE BY SIDE IN THE BEDROOM AT THE TOP OF THE HOUSE, both of us still fully clothed, Cissie watching me, one hand resting in the gap between us. I was on my back, looking out the window at the brightening sky, cigarette between my lips.

I'd led her to this room—next door was a much smaller, single-sized bedroom—and waited for her weeping to end, aware that those tears were not just over the death of Wilhelm Stern, whose body was covered by a single clean sheet on the bed in the room below us, but also over her friend's betrayal and everything that had followed in its aftermath: the botched attempt at blood transfusion, the slaying of poor old Albert Potter, the bombing of the Savoy, our flight down-river from the Blackshirts, leaving those other wretches, who'd been lured from their hideaways by the lights, to the mercies of a dying madman. Her bewilderment at Muriel's treachery only increased her distress, because they'd become true friends—or so Cissie had thought—during a period of massive upheaval when the world itself had been stripped of civilized guidelines and robbed of most of its inhabitants. Despite their different social backgrounds, they had formed an alliance, each one supporting the other in moments of despair, their companionship helping them keep their sanity. Until Muriel had discovered her own kind again in the form of Sir Max Hubble.

The guise she'd adopted in order to survive had fallen away like a cloak worn for warmth and not for taste, and that disloyalty—the choice Muriel had made—was something Cissie could not understand. The truth of it was—and I tried to make Cissie understand this—was that the bitch *had* been loyal, but it was to her own

208

class, to people of her own persuasion. Hell, Cissie had been there when Hubble had mentioned that Edward, England's abdicated king, demoted to dukedom, had aligned himself with the Nazi ideologies, along with certain others of the so-called British aristocracy. Before the war, their persuasions were no great secret, according to other pilots I'd spoken with, and only the formal outbreak of hostilities had hushed them. Breeding above principles, was their warped philosophy. Their own ideals were more important to them than their own countrymen. It was a decadent and self-serving system, one that flourished throughout England's history, and something my own mother had been glad to leave behind when she made her home in America, even though she loved her birthplace, and these "wrong-sorts," as she put it, were only a small minority. Muriel, I'd assured Cissie as I'd brushed her curls away from her grubby face, had only remained true to her own conditioning, and her double-cross amounted to little more than a natural alliance.

None of it seemed to help Cissie much, but maybe some of it eventually got through, because after a while she ceased her weeping, wiped her cheeks and nose with the back of her hand and started to talk . . .

"Wilhelm wanted you to know he was sorry."

There was a hollowness to her voice in this bleak room, its only furniture the bed we lay on and an armchair with wooden arms, a pile of boys' clothing—different sizes, so I knew they'd belonged to more than one—resting on its cushioned seat. I turned my head and her dirty face was not unlike a child's itself in the pale, morning light, only shadows beneath her eyes indicating the trouble she'd been through.

"He managed to talk?"

"Towards the end. I think the pain lessened, but because of that he knew he was dying."

"Why sorry?"

"Oh, not for what he'd done. He said he'd only been fighting for his country during the war, carrying out his duty, just like us."

"Yeah, his duty." I dragged on the cigarette, then took it from my lips, hanging it over the edge of the bed, smoke curling up between my fingers.

"He was apologizing for Germany's final action, not for his role as a soldier."

"He was a spy."

"Soldier, spy—it was all the same to him. But he was deeply ashamed of what Hitler did to his own country and the rest of the world. He said Germany's inevitable defeat should have been accepted with honor. He didn't want you—us—to judge his race by the mad dogs who ruled them. Only the High Command had known about the rockets and what they were capable of."

"What's it matter? Nothing can change what happened." My eyes closed. Yet, weary though my body was, my mind refused to close down: it was still buzzing with everything that had happened since yesterday.

"He just wanted you to know, Hoke, that was all."

"I figured him right and got him wrong. I didn't trust him, but he saved my life."

"Wilhelm understood that. He didn't blame you for your suspicions, Hoke."

" Did he manage to tell you what his mission was over here during the war?"

"He found it difficult to speak towards the end—he was choking on his own blood. But he tried . . . oh, he tried so hard . . ."

I thought the tears would start again as she cast her eyes downwards, but she straightened, her mouth set tight.

"He wanted to set the record straight between you and him, something about honor among enemies. I think he wanted to die with your respect, Hoke, not your hatred."

"He'd already earned my respect." I lifted the cigarette again and held it over my lips for a moment. "So what *was* he up to?"

"He told me his plane was shot down, but it wasn't over the East Coast, it wasn't in a Heinkel, and it wasn't in 1940. It happened one night in '44, a few weeks before D-Day, and the aeroplane was a . . . what was it? . . . a Junkers. Yes, he said it was a Ju 188. It was gunned down over the Solent and the seven others on board with him were all killed. He managed to bale out before the burning plane crashed."

Her gaze went past me towards the window and the oncoming day was reflected in her hazel-brown eyes.

"His clothes were alight when he jumped, and—absurdly, he said—he was more worried about the fire becoming a beacon in the night sky than burning to death. The rushing air put out the flames, though."

I thought of the scars on the German's back and neck and wondered at his courage. To parachute into enemy territory in the middle of the night, then to hide himself while search parties scoured the countryside for survivors, badly burnt and alone, well, that took a rare kind of guts. Another thought occurred to me.

"He told you there were seven others with him in the Junkers? That kind of bomber only carried a crew of four."

"It wasn't a normal crew. They all had official papers on them giving them Slavic names, not German. If they got caught their cover story was to be that they were Polish and Czech freedom fighters who'd stolen the plane to escape to England so they could carry on fighting with the Allied Forces."

I clicked my fingers. "Exbury Point."

"What?"

"I remember hearing something about a mysterious German bomber crashing at Exbury Point, near the Beaulieu River where hundreds of assault landing craft and barges were being made ready for the invasion on Europe. Rumors were that all kinds of secret activities were going on there—"

"Yes, that was it. He said German Intelligence had learned that pilotless rocket aircraft were being tested along the inlet from the Solent and it was his job to discover how far ahead the British scientists were with their experiments. Only three men on the Junkers were meant to parachute into the area—the rest were crew members, but with the same kind of papers as the spies in case the worst happened."

"And it did." The end of the cigarette glowed brightly as I drew on it. "But how the hell did Stern get by after he'd jumped?"

"He hid for two days, then was able to reach his contact in the New Forest when the commotion died down."

"But his burns . . ."

"He was a bit special, wasn't he?"

And some, I thought, guilt over my treatment of this war ace nagging at me. "What happened to him?" I asked.

"Well, he stayed in the area feeding back information to his bosses until the invasion took place. He said it was important for you to know that he did very little harm to the Allied Forces' efforts down there, because once the counter-invasion on Europe had started—which was very soon after he'd arrived—his intelligence reports had hardly any value. All he could do was try and survive himself."

I blew smoke and crushed the cigarette stub against the bare board floor, my fingers brushing against the pistol lying there. When I rolled back, Cissie was propped on one elbow, looking down at me. Her curls fell loose over her face again.

"Hoke?"

I didn't answer, just stared back into her eyes.

"We imagined they were all evil, didn't we? The enemy, the whole German race, I mean. We thought they were all the same."

"They started the whole goddamn thing."

"Hitler started it."

"And the German people went along with him. People like Stern."

"We bombed their city first."

"Your country only retaliated for their first raid on London."

"It was a mistake. The German bomber was off course. They hadn't meant to bomb civilians. And our own government knew that when they ordered the raid on Berlin. Hitler's answer was the Blitz on London."

"Stern told you this?"

"He was dying, he wouldn't have lied. I never believed all the propaganda our government put out anyway, just most of it. Like everybody else, I suppose."

My eyelids were beginning to feel heavy once more. Cissie had a point, but I didn't have the energy to agree or disagree. Either way would've meant more debate and I was just too beat for that.

"Hoke?" She thought I'd fallen asleep.

I murmured something, or maybe I groaned, I'm not sure which.

"The last thing Wilhelm wanted you to know was that he didn't mean any of those things he said at dinner. He was just tired of your goading, he wanted to strike back and he regretted it. He despised the Blackshirts too. He said they aligned themselves with the worst of his countrymen, the bigots, the Fascist bullyboys. That's why he didn't join them last night. In fact, he said if he could live he would help you in your fight against them."

"I'm not fighting the Blackshirts, Cissie. I've always run away from them."

"Then why d'you stay here, Hoke? Why didn't you leave the city years ago?"

My mind was drifting and I found it very pleasant. "Too much to do," I mumbled, giving in to the creeping lethargy. The mattress beneath us may have been musty and full of lumps, but I seemed to be sinking into an overwhelming softness. Something was shaking my shoulder and I turned away from it. The voice persisted though.

"What, Hoke? Tell me what you have to do? Tell me . . ."

I was gone and soon, so was the voice. Mercifully, my sleep was dreamless.

I think it was the warmth on my face, the blaze against my eyelids, that woke me. My eyes opened and I turned away from the sun's rays, disturbing Cissie, whose arm had been curled around my waist. Our faces close, she blinked at me for a few moments; she didn't move away.

Everything came at me in a rush and I was suddenly alert, leaning on one elbow to check the open bedroom door, then turning towards the dirt-smeared window, squinting my eyes against the sunlight forcing its way through.

"What is it?" My reaction had frightened her.

I listened for a full minute before replying. "It's okay. We're safe." I couldn't really be sure of that until I'd taken a look outside, back and front of the house, but I didn't sense any danger right then and my instinct had always been reliable. I lay back on the thin pillow and realized I was aching in a hundred different places and hurting in a few more.

There was dried blood on my arm where they'd tried to bleed me last night, and the incision still throbbed a little. My shoulder was stiff, the dressing that had covered the bullet graze now missing, and various cuts and bruises reminded me of the hell I'd been through these past few days; even breathing too deeply caused a dull pain, but I could tell my ribs were only bruised, not cracked, otherwise that pain would've been a whole lot sharper. My ankle felt okay, although a mite sore, and I rotated it one way, then the other, just to test it: it complained right enough—a sudden twinge, was all—but there was no swelling any more, so I knew I could get around okay. Anything else—cuts, gashes, sores, and contusions—didn't matter: there was nothing to cause me serious problems.

The back of Cissie's hand brushed against my cheek.

"What's the diagnosis? You going to live, Hoke?"

"I reckon."

Lifting my head from the pillow, I inspected the room, checking all was as I'd left it from my previous visit some months before. I hadn't had the chance before we'd fallen asleep in the early hours, and the room had been dim anyway; now I saw it was the same as always, the kids' clothes on the armchair, the fireplace full of cold ashes, the door to the corner cupboard that was stuffed with more clothes and only a few toys and comic books still slightly ajar.

"How're *you* feeling?" I asked when I was satisfied nothing had been disturbed.

"My legs feel like they've run a couple of hundred miles and my arm's still sore from the grip one of those Blackshirts had on me, but otherwise, 'cept for some bumps and bruises, I'm fine. I think."

As she followed me in scanning the room I studied her profile. Her jaw was good and firm, her nose neither dainty nor dominant, kind of just right, the thin scar across its bridge white against the dirt on her face. There was dust and glass in her hair and the evening dress was mussed up, torn in places, but like me, she'd suffered no serious damage.

"Who lived here before?" she asked, unaware I was watching her. "Were there bodies. . . ?"

I shook my head. "No, the place was empty when I moved in. But my guess is that a woman lived here with three young sons."

"No husband?"

"Mothballed suits in the wardrobe downstairs. And no shaving brush and mug by the sink."

"P'raps he had a beard."

"No men's underwear or socks either. The husband was either sewing in the Forces, or the woman was a widow. I think when the final rockets fell she took her kids to the Underground station round the corner at the top of the street. That's probably where they died."

Cissie gave a little shiver. Even after all this time and so much tragedy, the deaths of one poor woman and her deprived kids still caused her grief. How much more difficult then, when the victim was someone you knew and loved. Oh yeah, that could lead to your own disintegration.

"Look," I said, sitting up on the bed, "I'm gonna make coffee, tea if you'd prefer. You rest up and I'll bring it to you. Then we'll think about . . ." I shot a glance out the window, judging the sun's position ". . . we'll think about some lunch."

She rose too. "No, let me do it. You must still be all in."

I pushed her down again. "I know where everything is. And I'd rather be moving around than letting my muscles stiffen up. So what's it to be—tea or coffee?"

"Tea."

I swung my legs off the bed, but she caught my hand before I could move off.

"Hoke, those people outside the hotel last night . . . who were they, where did they come from? Were they part of Hubble's organization?"

"You saw the surprise on their faces, and you saw how the Blackshirts reacted when they ran into 'em."

"Then who . . . ?"

"Refugees, like us. Refugees from the Blood Death. At least nearly all of them were—they seemed to be taking care of the odd one or two who didn't look so good. I think they were a little whacky after so many years of hiding away and the Savoy being lit up like that, like some Christmas tree in a black limbo, well, I guess it drew them out, lured them away from their hiding-places all over the city. The lights probably gave 'em some hope, made 'em think a part of the old life was returning, and they had to see it for themselves. They made a bad mistake.

"What will Hubble do with them?"

"You already know."

She lowered her head and as I watched, a single tear dropped into her lap.

I touched her shoulder. "It takes some of the heat off us, Cissie."

I left her there on the bed, staring after me, my meaning slowly dawning on her. Maybe it was a selfish remark, but there was truth in it: Hubble had all the decent blood he needed for now, so he didn't have to come looking for us. Okay, I was thinking only of our own skin, but selfish as the notion might have been, it gave me some passing comfort. Unfortunately I'd underestimated Hubble's hatred of me—or was it his *obsession* with me—after all this time. Yeah, I'd underestimated it badly.

| 21 |

ON THE TINY LANDING OUTSIDE THE TOP BEDROOM, I TOOK TIME to stretch a leg across the winding staircase and rest my foot against the edge of the deep windowsill opposite. it was an easy maneuver—the gap was less than four feet—and by leaning forward I was able to pull open the curtainless window. It swung inwards towards the adjacent wall, displaying a fine view over east London's rooftops, the white spire of Spitalfields church rising into the bright sky in the distance, its clockface forever frozen to one moment in time. It said ten-to-four, and I wondered what day, what month, what year it had stopped and how meaningless that very second must have been with no one around to notice. I don't know why, but it felt to me that this day was a Sunday— maybe it was because Sally had always brought me to the market here on Sunday mornings—and, judging by the sun's position, it was around noon. The month was July or August, I wasn't sure which, and the year was '48. Yeah, so call it a Summer's Sunday, 1948. It had no significance, and I had no idea why the muse had come upon me; unless some kind of order was slowly filtering back into my life. Was Cissie's presence doing that, this awareness that she'd be depending on me? Was having another life to consider about to bring about some kind of pattern to my own?

I snapped out of it and scrutinized the yards directly below, making sure no one was creeping Up on us down there. A drop of maybe thirty feet below was No. 26's backyard, half of it roofed over by several sheets of corrugated iron that was meant to keep the rain off the coal heap and rinsing mangle underneath; in the open section I could see a tap fixed to the wall and the door to the outside lavatory. All was quiet down there, as I'd expected, and I pushed myself straight, using the banister post on the landing to haul myself back.

The wooden stairs creaked as usual as I descended to the next landing, and I paused outside the door of the bedroom where Wilhelm Stern's cold body lay. I decided not to look in—what was there to see? The shrouded shell of what was once a very brave man? No thanks, not today—and went down to the ground floor, my left hand sliding round the thick central beam that rose from the corridor below to the landing at the top of the house. When I filled the kettle I noticed the water was running brown, something I hadn't been able to discern the night before. I shrugged and put the kettle on the gas cooker—boiling heat would kill any germs and we'd just have to put up with the taste. It was as I was reaching for the matches to light the canned gas that I heard the noise.

A scratching sound, coming from the corridor outside.

Mice? Rats? Tiny animals who were survivors like me? Creatures lurking behind the walls or under the floorboards? As I struck the match, the noise came again. And this time I realized it was coming from the front door.

Blowing out the flame, I made my way round the Morrison shelter to the window. I leaned between the withered flowers and wireless set on the sideboard and peered through the parted curtains. The street outside was empty.

The quiet yelp I heard next had me scooting into the corridor and drawing the bolts of the front door I'd locked in the early hours of that morning. Turning the key and without thinking, I pulled the door open and there was Cagney sitting in front of the doorstep, his paw raised to scrape the painted wood again. he howled when he saw me, but it was a small, exhausted sound, and he tried to stand on all fours, his tail twitching in a feeble attempt at a wag. He almost toppled over with the effort and I saw that his haunches and back legs were covered in blood, the pavement underneath him sticky with the stuff. There were bloody stripes across his back and flanks, as if someone had taken a whip or thin stick to him.

"Oh Jesus, boy . . ." I dropped to one knee and Cagney tried to lick my face. "What have they done to you?"

Opening up my arms to him, I leaned forward and he shuffled towards me, desperate for my comfort, the drool that sank to the ground from his jaw flecked with red. Bad thoughts surged through my mind just then, a deepening rage welling inside me that was only contained by my pity for the half-dead mutt that was my friend and companion.

"Cagney—" I began to say, when the doorframe beside me erupted into a powdery flurry of splinters.

I fell back into the corridor, the machine gun's roar and wood shrapnel shocking me off-balance. The second burst of gunfire caught Cagney full-on and small explosions ripped open his back, lifted him into the air, his agonized shriek piercing the air over the sound of the bullets.

This time I screamed his name, knowing when the last bullet tore open his head he was already dead. His quivering body slumped across the threshold and I had no choice, self-preservation, as much an ally as Cagney had been, taking over and instinctively making me kick him out again. Nothing to jam the door now, I kicked it shut.

Bullets pierced the thick wood, showering me with splinters, thin rays of sunlight penetrating the tiny holes to shine through the dim, dust-filled air like a dozen narrow flashlight beams. I heard footsteps on the cobbles outside and something slammed against the door, shaking it so hard I feared it might fall inwards. Taking a chance, I reached up for the key, twisting it in the lock, then I scrambled away from those beams of light, rising to a crouch as someone began to prise open the door's vertical letter-box. From the room beyond the partition wall came the sound of breaking glass.

I fled up the stairs, taking them three at a time, cursing myself for stupidly leaving the pistol beside the bed, reaching the first landing as furniture crashed over in the room below and more bullets bit into the tough front door, probably around the lock itself. Something crashed and I knew they were inside.

On the first landing I ran into Cissie, who was barefoot and— beautiful, gutsy lady—was clutching the gun I'd left behind.

"*Back up!*" I yelled at her, no time for explanations. Besides, I think she'd figured it out for herself.

Running footsteps and shouts along the corridor below.

Snatching the gun from her, I pushed Cissie up, barely giving her the chance to turn. She tripped, but regained her balance instantly, using her hands on the stairs above to help herself climb.

"We'll be trapped up here!" she shouted back at me, but I shoved her onwards, speeding her on her way.

I paused only long enough to lean round the stout center post and shoot at the leading shadow below. The shadow's owner hesitated, reluctant to risk the next bullet, and it gave us time to gain the top landing.

"How did they find us?" Cissie cried, clutching at me. "I thought they didn't know this place."

"They followed Cagney," was all I could tell her as heavy boots pounded the stairs. I realized the Blackshirts must have caught Cagney back there at the hotel, trapped him in a room, as likely as not, just in case he might come in useful. They'd beaten the poor mutt, half-crippled him so's he couldn't move too fast, and then they'd let him go in the hope he'd head straight for one of my sanctuaries. And Cagney knew my routine, even if I wasn't properly aware of it myself. Y'see, I always came here after the Savoy, it was a rut I'd subconsciously fallen into over the years. The palace, the hotel, downgrading to Tyne Street, from there to an apartment near Holland Park, back to the palace to repeat the process. It could've been natural instinct that had brought Cagney after me, but I figured it was more likely to be the set agenda, one he'd gotten used to. And of course, he'd used the alleyway to get to the house as we always did, a route I believed would be invisible to the enemy, bringing his trackers with him. Hubble had gone with his hunch, and it'd paid off. What I couldn't understand was why he'd gone to so much trouble now that he bad a healthy blood supply.

Machine-gun fire sprayed the wall next to the landing window opposite us and Cissie screamed as she backed into the tiny bedroom with its single cot behind us. I caught her arm and hauled her back out onto the landing, firing three shots over the stout balustrade to give the Blackshirts something more to chew on. Their reply was another burst of machine-gun fire that smacked into the ceiling over our heads, dislodging plaster and fragments of timber.

It suddenly dawned on me. These lunatics weren't out to capture me—hell no, they didn't need my blood any more. This time they were out to kill me. Call it revenge, anger over the killing of some of their own by me and the dance I'd led them over the years, or maybe just plain envy because I had something they hadn't—good, wholesome, disease-free blood. These boys were out to nail me once and for all—and I guess that included anyone who was with me.

"Cissie," I said, more calmly than I felt, "we're gonna jump."

She looked at me as if I were crazy. Then her gaze went to the open window and panic took over. She tried to yank her arm away.

"There's a roof just below," I said quickly, holding her tight. "We'll be okay. Just trust me."

Bullets thudded into the plaster ceiling again and chipped wood off the edge of the landing. Gunsmoke rose from the stairwell, its cloud mingling with the floating white dust. There were more excited shouts down there and one or two banshee screeches. Heavy boots clumping on wood, single, wild shots. They were coming up.

"Now, Cissie, *now!*"

She came with me, no hesitation at all, hopping across the gap onto the window's deep ledge, our figures blocking the light for no more'n a fraction of a second as bullets shattered glass and frame beside us. We were gone, dropping like stones through the air, falling in an eternity of dread that took maybe three seconds, possibly less, the corrugated roof rushing up to meet us.

We both yowled in terror as the old, rotted iron gave way beneath us, a neat section breaking off like a trapdoor. Our fall continued, but was soon over as we landed on the piled coals in the yard below. Like the tin roof itself, it broke our fall, saved our legs, maybe even our backs, from being broken. We rolled down the small hillock in an avalanche, then sprawled across the concrete floor of the back yard.

I sucked air, too numbed to feel pain just yet, my eyes unfocused, seeing only a spinning blue expanse of sky above. The weight on top of me was Cissie and I let her head rest on my heaving chest while the dizziness slowed down. The edge of the roof we'd fallen through came into view, then the brickwork of the house itself, rising impossibly high into the sky—or so it seemed lying there on my back with lumps of coal digging into me. The little landing window was about a mile away.

My senses, nudged by fear, returned fast: Any moment now there'd be gun barrels poking through that opening, aimed down at us. I pushed myself to a sitting position, bringing Cissie with me, my hands on her shoulders. She was blinking hard, trying to regain her own equilibrium, as I examined her face. But she got the question in first.

"Are you all right?" Her voice seemed distanced from the dazed uncertainty in her eyes.

Instead of replying I got a knee under me, then hauled us both to our feet. My gun was gone, lost when we'd crashed through the roof, and I swiftly scanned the yard. A stirrup pump stood in one dark corner and a two-handled zinc bath leaned against a wall; a dried heap of soiled clothing stood in a straw basket next to the rusted mangle; coal was scattered everywhere, making my search more difficult. But I found the Browning lying on the small drain covering beneath the yard's tap.

Grabbing the gun and quickly checking it for damage, I bundled Cissie towards the back wall as more noises came from inside the house, shouts and footsteps beating the stairs, growing louder as they descended. We had to be over the wall before they pulled the double bolts of the big back door and turned its stiff key. And before those weapons appeared at the top window.

Without a word, I tucked the pistol into my waistband and folded my arms around Cissie's lower legs. As I lifted her she reached for the top of the seven-foot high wall and dragged herself up, a final push from me helping her on her way. Then I climbed after her, toe-cap digging into the rough brickwork, elbows levering myself upwards. All this had taken a matter of moments, from leap to climb, and by the time I'd straddled the wall, Cissie had dropped to the other side. I took a swift glance at the landing window before following her.

Sure enough, the first gun barrel had shown up, a strained face looming behind it; I realized the Blackshirt was being supported by his cronies on the stairs below, because they hadn't figured how else to reach the window. It gave us an advantage, gave us a chance to skip through the long stallholders' yard at the rear of the houses before they'd worked out a decent way to take aim at us. Something crashed against the back door.

I knew it was dark at the end of the corridor inside No. 26, even during the day, a small set of steps leading down to the yard door, another flight descending from there to the cellar, and because of the lack of light the Blackshirts were now scrabbling around for the door key and bolts and banging at the wood in frustration, all of which was allowing me and Cissie extra time. I decided to use it.

My left hand cupping the fingers of my gun hand, I took careful aim at the wrinkled-up face at the window above and gently squeezed the trigger with the pad of my index finger. The Blackshirt saw me though and his head plunged from view—now you see it, now you don't—as the gun spat flame.

I heard faint cries as he fell onto the men supporting him and hoped they'd all taken a tumble. Wasting no more time, I dropped from the wall, grabbed Cissie by the waist, and started running through the debris of rotting stalls and barrows, weaving around wooden packing cases and lumps of metal, old wheels and mouldering cardboard boxes, making towards the big gates at the end of the yard.

We were halfway there when Cissie tripped over wire sprung loose from a busted orange crate. She stumbled into another box and went down, with me sprawling over her. That fall probably saved our lives, because at that moment a round of bullets whined over our heads, breaking up a trestle and snapping a stall's wooden upright a few yards in front of us. Still on the ground, I aimed the pistol over my shoulder.

There were now two faces up at that top window, the Blackshirts' shoulders crammed together, elbows on the sill supporting their bodies. One was pointing a machine gun, the other a rifle, and it was the machine gun that was spitting fire. Below them, arms and hands were appearing on the wall as the goons who'd managed to open the back door tried to follow us. I fired at the window first, four or five rapid shots in desperation, praying my ammo wouldn't run out.

Even from that distance, the two holes that appeared on the forehead of one of those faces were neatly precise, but it was the shot man's buddy who screamed and disappeared from view;

the dead guy just slunk away, slipping out of sight like someone sinking into quicksand. My next shots were at the head appearing over the wall, the bullets chipping brickwork; luckily it was enough to make our pursuers duck down again. The hammer clicked on empty with my next attempt to warn them off and I knew that was it—the gun wasn't jammed, it was empty. I tossed the useless piece of iron away.

Cissie and I rose together and we both realized we'd never make it to the end of the yard—once the enemy regained its nerve we'd be like targets in a shooting gallery. There was only one hope for us and there was no time for words: I pushed Cissie towards a nearby stall that backed up against a back-yard wall to our left. Leaping onto the stall's flat bed, I reached down and hoisted Cissie up after me just as the Blackshirts began clambering over the far wall again. We scrambled over and dropped down into another enclosed backyard. I almost whooped with relief when I saw the back door to the house was wide open. We rushed straight into the welcoming shadows and, once inside, I wheeled around and slammed the door shut behind us, praying the Blackshirts hadn't had time to witness our change of direction.

Cissie had sunk to her knees in the dim hallway we found ourselves in, but I didn't allow her to stay there. Just a tug did it, and she was in my arms, leaning against me, her breasts brushing my chest as she gasped for breath.

"We can't stay here," I told her between my own harsh breaths. "We gotta find someplace else to hide before they start searching all the houses along here."

She drew away a couple of inches so I could see her nod in agreement. There was blood on her shaded face, a cut in her forehead probably caused by our fall through the iron roof, or by the stumble in the big yard. She opened her mouth, about to ask a question, but I pressed my fingers to her lips. For a long moment we looked into each other's eyes, hers wide and frightened, the whites gray in the gloom, my own probably the same, even though I was more used to the chase than her. I hoped she couldn't see how scared I was.

Without another word I led her along the hallway to the front door. Controlling my breath as if the wrong ears might pick up the sound, I undid the latch and peeked out. To the left, further down the road, was the lamppost that stood near the entrance to the alleyway leading into Tyne Street, beyond this and on the other side of the road, the Austin Tourer outside the wash-house. To try and reach it would be too risky—it would mean going past the alley—so I decided the opposite direction was the only way. We'd have to move fast though. Beckoning Cissie to follow, I slid out into the sunshine.

We heard more shouting and an occasional burst of gunfire— the goons shooting at shadows among the rubbish or just in frustration?—beyond the row of terraced houses as we stole along the street, keeping close to the windows and walls, Cissie limping worse than me. At the corner I brought her to a halt

The side street here could be crossed in four long strides it was so narrow; but it led directly to the yard gates fifty yards or so along, and so it was a vulnerable point. Even though I knew those gates were locked, I was also aware that a hefty kick would open them easily enough. More voices, pretty damn close—near the other side of the gates, I guessed. They sounded kind of angry.

I had no idea how many Blackshirts had come after us, but their noise told me there was quite a crowd; soon they'd be spilling out into that little side street.

"You got enough juice left to go full lick?" I whispered to Cissie.

She set her jaw and nodded. "Just watch me."

"Okay. No clatter." We both looked down at her bare, bleeding feet and I shrugged.

Then we sprinted.

We'd lost ourselves in the maze of market streets once known as Petticoat Lane, stopping to catch our breath only when we were sure we weren't being followed, or could hear no distant calls and crack of gunfire, moving on as soon as we'd got our wind back, searching for a safe haven. There were plenty to choose from, but only when we'd passed through an archway and found ourselves inside a courtyard overlooked by ornamental iron balconies did we pick a flat at random on the second floor. Its flaky door was unlocked and once inside we'd bolted it, only then collapsing onto its hallway floor.

After a while Cissie had roused herself and, without a word, crawled into my arms. I'd held her there, my back against the wall, legs spread across the hallway and touching the opposite side, my chin nestled into the curls of her matted hair. And she'd felt good to hold on to, good to keep close, and when eventually her hand reached up to my neck, her fingers curling round to caress me, well, that felt good too.

But, as time wore on and my strength returned, my anger began to burn.

|22|

CISSIE HAD PLEADED WITH ME LONG INTO THE NIGHT, INSISTED IT was insane. But I hadn't listened. I knew what I was going to do.

"You're only one man," she'd argued.

"Yeah, but *they're* dying. Nothing slows you down more'n that."

"Hoke, please . . . let's just get away from here, out of the city, me and you . . ."

"I've done enough running. It's time to quit, time to bring it to an end."

I'd struck a match and lit the Woodbine I'd taken from a pack lying on the kitchen table.

"Besides, others are involved now. Maybe I can save 'em if it's not too late."

"But where will you find them? They could be anywhere in the city."

"He told us, don't you remember?"

She'd looked at me curiously, slowly shaking her head.

"When they had us in the Savoy, me trussed up like a turkey, ready for some bloodletting. Hubble said something like, while I had my palace, he had his castle."

I'd exhaled smoke, creating a cloud between us.

"S'far as I know," I'd gone on, "there's only one castle in London, right?"

I'd watched her steadily.

"Right?" I'd said again.

|23|

I TOOK A FINAL DRAG ON THE LAST WOODBINE AND DROPPED THE butt onto the ground, for some reason—old habits?—grinding it into the concrete with the heel of my boot. It'd been a long morning. And it was only just beginning.

From where I stood near the top of the hill, I could take in the whole north-west spread of the ancient fort and the great towered bridge looming beyond it. Wrinkled blimps, some lower than others, hung listlessly over the dockland wharves along the river's edges, while the jagged ironwork of tall cranes reached into the pale skyline like broken church spires. The bridge was raised, each side vertical, so that they almost scraped the two high walkways joining the twin towers: the tall ship they'd once opened for (it must have been something spectacular for the bridge to be fully raised like that) had long since drifted onwards to berth alongside some distant wharfside, its crew and passengers all dead, its cargo no longer needed, leaving the guardian of this stretch of the river frozen open behind it, the hands that had worked the bridge's machinery by now shriveled to bone and gristle. A lone gull flew between the towers, then wheeled around in a swooping arc as if changing its mind, sensing this necropolis was no place to be; it headed back downstream, its white wings catching the early sun.

Squinting my eyes, I studied the castle, searching for signs of life. There were none.

Its center keep—the White Tower, it was called—rose over the ramparts, a disheveled flag drooping from the flagpole on its roof, its walls and corner turrets washed gray by centuries of city dirt and weather grime, as were the bastions of its outer walls. Even so, speckles of white showed through like chalk on a cliff face as if to reveal the real glory beneath the dulled façade; and buttresses, relieving arches and tops of battlements were like bleached bones, as if someone had scrubbed them clean; but it was no more than the nature of the stone itself, this effect, and had nothing to do with care and attention. Part of the northern bastion had been demolished by a lucky strike from a *Luftwaffe* raiding party, and the surrounding walls and railings were nicked and scarred by near misses. Otherwise, the Tower of London stood proud and impregnable as it had throughout centuries of English history. On this summer's day though, in the year 1948, it had only a single invader, one who wasn't expected. And that would make all the difference.

I crouched to look inside the canvas bag at my feet, checking its contents, pulling its strap over my neck and shoulder as I straightened up again. Flipping open the button holster at my waist, I drew the Browning P35 high power automatic, pulling its slide to load a cartridge into the chamber. The double click as the slide came back, then returned, was a good sound, a satisfying sound. I'd chosen the GP-35 because it was one of the best 9mm automatics around, if not *the* best, accurate and carrying thirteen rounds in its magazine (I had an extra mag in my left pocket and another in the bag). When the *Krauts* had occupied Belgium, they'd taken over the factory that manufactured these guns, which soon became a substitute service firearm for them; but what they soon discovered was that many were being sabotaged in production and were as likely to blow their hand off as stop an enemy. Fortunately, the one I had came from Canada, so I knew it was okay. I slipped it back into the holster. Leaning against the low parapet wall in front of me were three more weapons. I'd left it 'til now to make my final decision on which one I'd be using that day.

My first choice would've been the Bren gun, one of the best light machine guns of all time: reliable, pretty fair accuracy, steadiness in firing, and with a reasonably low rate of fire, which allowed a better aim without too much ammunition wastage. Also, it had only three kinds of stoppage factors (certain similar weapons had twenty-three, for Chrissake!) and I knew how to fix all three, and smartly at that. But now I nixed it, because even with its bipod folded forward, the gun was awkward to carry if you intended to be moving fast—and before the hour was out I intended to be moving *very* fast.

So I turned to the Thompson, nicknamed the Tommy gun, lifting it and feeling its weight. It handled well and could be switched to single-shot if required; but this one, the military version, carried a twenty-round box that took only two seconds of automatic fire to empty (with the fifty-round magazine cartridges would rattle around like nuts and bolts in a tin box, which could be a mite embarrassing if you were sneaking up on an enemy position). It also had a "spray" effect, which was fine for trench warfare, but not so hot if the good guys were mixed up with the bad guys. I needed more control.

Laying down the Thompson, I picked up the Sten gun that had been standing next to it. This would have to be the one. Its main advantages were that it was easy to carry, especially using a fitted sling, and it was simply built, so there were fewer things to go wrong. Another advantage was that the magazine fitted into the gun's left side so that it could lie across my forearm for additional stability and wouldn't interfere if I had to hit dirt and fire from the ground. It also had a thirty-round capacity which, with two spare mags inside the bag, should be more than enough for my purposes. Before I'd brought this particular model along I'd been faced with another choice. During the war, commandos and raiding parties understandably had favored silenced weapons, so a variation Sten gun had been produced with its own inbuilt silencer and canvas heat-resistant cover, and these particular versions were among the collection I was able to pick from. After a few seconds' deliberation, I'd elected the unsilenced MKY, a quality 1944 model with wooden stock, pistol grip, and rifle foresight, deciding that today I'd want *plenty* of noise.

Removing the magazine, I shook it against my ear just to hear the slight but reassuring shift of cartridges, then slapped it back in. It entered smoothly, no fuss at all.

Satisfied with the "artillery," I reached under the back of my sweatshirt and slid out the double-edged commando knife from the sheath attached to my belt. The thin, ridged handle was wrapped in leather and the tapering blade with its wickedly sharp point was coated in non-reflective black. It looked vicious and I hoped to God I wouldn't have to use it—I didn't want to be that close to the enemy. I put the knife away again, but left the handle protruding outside the sweatshirt for easy access.

I'd been lucky that in the early hours of the morning I hadn't needed to travel too far to find other items I'd be using that day, because when the *Luftwaffe* had turned its attention towards the Soviet Union back in '41, giving London's East End a breather from their bombing raids, quite a number of factories and firms in these parts had converted to war production, manufacturing anything from demolition charges to safety fuses, from dynamite to shells fitted with explosives; just across the river at Woolwich was one of the country's biggest armories. For the hand weapons I'd paid a visit to a deep shelter transit depot I knew of only a couple of miles from where I now stood, a place where troops waiting to be shipped overseas had been billeted, equipment and all, until time to go. Unfortunately, the last lot hadn't gone any-where—the Blood Death had seen to that—leaving the depot well stocked with all kinds of weaponry and tackle. It wasn't pleasant searching the stores down there, and only a deep seething rage that overwhelmed all else got me through it.

Oddly, I was no longer trembling. It'd been a bad night, I'd hardly slept thinking of what I had to do, and laying there in the dark, my hands had started to shake and my throat had tightened up so that it was difficult to breathe. My mouth had dried too, and there was a dread in my gut that felt like a physical lump. It was a relief to leave the bed while it was still black outside and set things rolling. And now, after a lot of hard work and some travel-ling, my hands were steady and my mouth wasn't at all dry. There was a grim determination in me, a kind of dark coldness that had taken over from the rage to stifle any other emotion. Sure, I was scared, but for the first time in three years I felt I was in control.

With one last sweeping inspection of the old castle and its bat-tlements, I moved out.

|24|

As I WALKED DOWN THE COBBLED HILL TOWARDS THE CASTLE'S main gates, I remembered the first time I'd visited the Tower of London. It was in '43 and, because this tourist attraction was closed to the public for the duration, I went along without Sally. The British government encouraged US and other allied forces to visit its country's historic places and monuments—it was a great exercise in public relations—and I was just one of thousands of American servicemen stationed over here to drop in on the Tower. I was among a small group of flyers, about half-a-dozen if I remember right, two of 'em English, and we had a guide—one of those scarlet-tunicked Beefeater guys—all to ourselves. He was thorough, enjoying his own country's history and traditions, but I'd forgotten most of what he told us, although I still retained a fair idea of the layout of the place and had a vague notion of its past glories (and infamies). Last night I'd been puzzled as to why Hubble and his not-so-merry band of blood thieves should choose the castle as headquarters when they had the choice, like me, of London's finest mansions or hotels—those still left undamaged by the Blitz and unchecked fires, leakages and gas explosions, that is—but I eventually came to the conclusion that the Tower of London, with all its historical associations and grandeur, suited Hubble's own vision of himself. His crazed mind considered himself the new overlord of civilization, the baron of rebirth, if you like, military master of the New Order—why else the martial uniforms and his sham, jackbooted army?—so what better center of command than the fortress of England's most famous conqueror, William? Hubble had an acute sense of destiny. Besides, there were comfortable enough living quarters within the walls and I was willing to bet old Sir Max had claimed the best for himself. And that was where I hoped to find him this morning.

Carcasses and a few abandoned vehicles, some of them military, littered the road and broad pavements of Tower Hill, and halfway down I passed the remains of a carthorse still attached to its waggon's shafts, the body almost picked clean, the bones yellowed by the sun. The cart, laden with boxes, had its rear against one of the many short iron posts (small French cannon captured in the Napoleonic Wars, like the one at the end of the alleyway in Tyne Street, set upright in concrete and painted black) and I remembered being informed by that fancy-decked guide on my previous visit how the carters from Billingsgate fish market (just down the road and not far from where I'd moored the motor launch two nights ago) would back their waggon's tailboard against a post whenever their horse got too weary hauling its load up the hill. Of the driver there was no sign—had he been one of the lucky ones, or just a Slow-Dier?—but the fish boxes on the cart had obviously been attacked for their contents at some time in the past—the marks and scratches on the wood were aged—although they remained unbroken. Still walking, my gaze went back to what was left of the horse and I suddenly understood what had happened here: unable to get at the fish packed inside the sealed boxes, the birds—had to be birds, judging by those marks on the wood—had eaten the horse. But what kind of bird could strip an animal that size of all its flesh? I thought of the lone seagull that had flown through the bridge minutes earlier and wondered, but it was a distraction that disappeared when I drew nearer to the tall, bomb-scarred gates at the bottom of the hill.

I waited a few seconds before entering, looking around first, listening, searching for the slightest sign of life. Ahead of me was the stunted, twin-towered gatehouse, the royal crest cut in stone above its archway: this was the entrance to the Tower itself and I almost expected to find a sentry on guard there, ready to challenge me. I heard and saw no one. But then, who would Hubble expect to invade his fortress?

The Sten gun had been hanging by its sling over my shoulder, and now I took it off, holding it before me, muzzle pointing directly ahead. I went on, feeling exposed, vulnerable, passing through the gatehouse and wondering if anyone had a weapon trained on me behind those arrow slits in its walls.

The air was cooler inside the archway, but it scarcely chilled the sweat on my brow as I studied the stone causeway over the moat. The sturdy Wooden gates of the larger, inner gateway towers across the causeway were wide open, but there was nothing inviting about them. I took a look over the low side wall at the dried-out moat below and frowned. During the war, this wide, grassed-over defense ditch had been full of allotments, Tower staff and soldiers digging for victory and supplementing their plain rations with their own fresh vegetables; those same vegetable patches were now unkempt and overgrown, parched by the hot summer. It occurred to me that if the Blackshirts really had taken up residence here, then why hadn't they maintained the allotments? They might be sick, but they still needed to eat. Suddenly I was doubting my own assumption. Had I got it wrong? When Hubble had referred to his "castle" had he meant something else, using the word as some kind of metaphor for his own grandiose view of himself? So far there'd been no sign of life, no sounds to interrupt that awesome, dead-city silence, so had I made a big mistake?

And then I spotted something down there that made me think again, a splash of red amongst the green and brown vegetation. Another, and still more. Different colors now, some of them easily camouflaged by the shrubbery around them. Most of those tones were faded, but the red was easily recognizable: they were the uniforms worn by the castle's keepers, the warders, the scarlet tunics of the Beefeaters. I understood instantly what had taken place here.

The inner wards of the Tower had been cleared of corpses by the new squatters, the Blackshirts themselves, those bodies dumped out of sight into the surrounding moat and left there to rot. The less visible carcasses were in khaki, the uniforms of regular soldiers, and the rest, I figured, were the forms of wives, kids and visitors on that fateful day, all dressed in wartime drab. The Blackshirts didn't give a cuss about the allotments and fresh vegetables, not when other food was so readily and easily available, so the vegetation was left to cover the mass grave.

So okay, the game was still on.

I stole from the cover of the archway and dashed across the causeway. Now I was inside the fortress itself.

Once through the next dim passageway, I grew even more cautious, sure I was drawing closer to the hub of things. To my left was a little road called Mint Street, where in the olden days the Tower had its own money-making operation going; there were quaint, tiny dwellings where the Yeoman Warders and their families lived, as I recalled. Part of the street was in ruins, another lucky bomb-hit. In front of me was Water Lane, its uneven, cobblestone roadway dangerous if you were in a hurry; I made a mental note to watch my step when things heated up later on. At the corner where these streets met was another tower, this one with a bell house jutting from its top, and the windows in its thick walls set me feeling exposed again—it was too easy to imagine marksmen watching me from inside, waiting for the right moment to shoot. I moved across the intersection in a crouching run, coming to a halt only when I was around the tower and flat against the wall on the other side. From there I made my way along Water Lane, keeping close to the wall, alert for any sound, any movement, not stopping again 'til I'd reached another archway opposite a set of steps leading down to the water-filled entrance known as Traitors' Gate, where criminals, political criminals, and dignitaries alike had been brought to the Tower by boat. Sunlight shone through the iron bars of the massive gate and the grille-work above it to pattern the still waters below, this grim pit partially roofed by a wide sweeping archway carrying a timbered building, whose windows overlooked my position. Yet again, I felt too vulnerable, so I didn't linger.

I scurried into the shadows of the passage beneath the Bloody Tower (yeah, that name seemed about right), going down on one knee at the end of it to survey the wide, open area laid out before me, re-familiarizing myself with the lie of the land before advancing any further.

A broad walkway with a couple of sets of rising steps stretched out ahead of me, the long overhanging branches of untrimmed trees from untidy greens on either side creating welcome shadows, the great square edifice of the White Tower, *the* tower of legend, looming at least ninety feet on the right of the final set of steps, the ragged flag I'd spotted from outside suspended limply from its roof. To my left was a high gray wall, broken by a narrow opening where steps led up to the next level. I knew that up there, beyond the wall, were two adjoining rows of Tudor houses and cottages, all white plaster and wooden beams, among them the Queen's House, the official residence of the Tower's Governor, and there, I guessed, was where I'd find Hubble.

I was about to make my way towards it when movement caught my eye. Keeping perfectly still, I let my eyes search out the disturbance (you never try and duck out of sight if any motion on your part might give away your own position), and then I saw them, sinister black shapes moving about the tall grass in front of the White Tower, creeping, it seemed to me right then, like dark assassins closing in for the kill. I released my breath when one of the creatures fluttered its wings—the same one who'd caught my attention a couple of seconds before—and flew to a post at the top of the timber stairway to the tower's entrance. The big bird sat there on its perch, its long beak stabbing the air. Another appeared on the side wall to the steps ahead of me, then another hopped across open ground in the distance, and it was only then that I realized that these were the Tower of London's legendary ravens. At least six of them had been kept here through the centuries by clipping their wings so they couldn't fly, the superstition being that any fewer meant the monarchy would fall. Obviously these birds had bred unsupervised after the Blood Death and, although it was common for other ravens to devour new eggs and some males might even kill off their own young out of jealousy, quite a few here had managed to survive. I guessed that this new breed, with no one around to clip their wings, stayed in, or always returned to the castle grounds out of habit, or because of some kind of natural instinct passed from generation to generation.

Now I understood what had happened to the carthorse on Tower Hill, and was glad I hadn't examined any of the human corpses lying thereabouts. But with that thought, there came another, one that hit me so hard—like it always did—that my body sagged and my head lowered so that my chin was almost touching my chest. This thought was like a nightmare, one that was constant and came in waking hours as well as in dreams, an image I'd tried so hard to suppress, but one I could never forget. It visited me as fresh and horrific as its moment of reality, a harsh vision of Sally, my wife, outside the cheap basement flat we'd rented, lying in the stairwell, so still, so dead, her eyes gone, her . . .

The bitterness erupted and suddenly I could no longer see

clearly, everything before me had become blurred, watery . . . My
shoulders hunched over as I leaned forward on my knees, forehead inches away from the ground. But I fought it, I fought hard,
forcing myself up again, shaking my head as if to loosen the sight
trapped inside. The fingers of my free hand cleared my eyes and
slowly, deliberately, I made myself think of what lay ahead of me
that morning—after all, it was for Sally as much as Stern and
Cagney and all those other victims, and it was for myself, it was
especially for myself . . . And oddly, it was the thought of Cagney
among all those others that brought me back to the present. Not
because of what the Blackshirts had done to him, but because of
those sinister black birds maundering around the castle grounds.
What *they* had tried to do to him.

It hadn't been a couple of miles from this very location that
the dog and I had first set eyes on each other, the time I'd been
digging in the allotment to look up and discover Cagney watching
and sniffing my lunch from a safe distance. The day Cagney had
been attacked by ravens and together we'd fought them off.
Those ravens had come from this place, I knew it as sure as I
knew Hubble and his maniacs had set up camp here. My hands
tightened around the Sten gun. I wanted to blast those evil, stinking predators into oblivion, blow everyone of 'em into a puff of
black feathers and shredded flesh, because I associated them
with all the vermin that still roamed this world, human and animal alike. I thought of Cagney on the doorstep, his hind legs
bloodied and crippled, and I thought of every victim of the Blood
Death, not destroyed by some manufactured disease, but by the
wicked intent of the corrupt few we'd once shared this planet
with. And I thought of those malign bastards still left running
loose to kill and maim, to take what didn't belong to them . . . Oh
yeah, I wanted to kill those ravens and what they represented,
and I even took aim at the one on the post; but the cold calmness
came back to me before I could squeeze the trigger. Those creatures were not the real badness; they just looked like it to me at
that moment. I lowered the weapon.

I got to my feet and, swiftly and quietly, I entered the narrow
opening in the wall on my left and climbed the mossy steps.
Before reaching the top, I knelt down and peeked round the low
wall that overlooked another neglected lawn and the two terraced

rows of Tudor houses and cottages. There didn't appear to be any life inside those dwellings, but I noticed two rusted water trucks parked untidily in front of them, and they told me all I needed to know. The antiquated waterpipe system of the old castle and its quarters hadn't been able to cope with the severity of the previous two winters, the pipes probably cracking, the system flooding, everything breaking down, so the residents here had had to bring in their own supply. I waited a few minutes before making my next move, and when I did it was almost a mistake.

The dark-garbed figure emerged from a concealed set of steps at the far end of the smaller houses opposite just as I came out from the cover of the wall. Whoever it was over there had obviously come from a rampart tower, whose entrance was on a lower level to the cottages and green, so that first the head appeared followed by the shoulders. I'd already dodged back behind the wall, disobeying my own rule of remaining still because I'd have been noticed anyway. It was a chance I'd had to take, and it seemed I was in luck—there were no shouts of alarm, only the distant sculling of boots on concrete. The figure was *marching*—and I mean marching—across the courtyard, past the site of the Tower's notorious chopping block towards the castle keep, the White Tower itself. I stayed out of sight, peering over the wall only when I thought it was safe. But the marching figure was gone from view and I had to stand erect to catch a glimpse of it again. The dark-uniformed man was just disappearing behind the far corner of the White Tower.

Keeping low, I ran forward on the balls of my feet, making hardly any noise at all. In a clear area of the great yard I noticed a solitary machine gun on a tripod; it looked like a Vickers Mk 1 and I was relieved to see its fabric ammunition belt was empty. The gun had probably been left there by garrison soldiers and the Blackshirts had enjoyed themselves taking potshots at easy targets: a black sentry box near one of the cottages was a mess of bullet holes and splinters. Maybe Hubble took his military pretensions so seriously he insisted his followers keep up target practice. I wondered if he had them parade marching as well.

Leaving my cover, I crossed open ground to the corner of the White Tower, pausing there to scan the area. Across the yard to my left was a small chapel and directly opposite was a huge multi-windowed block house, complete with elaborate battlements and gargoyles, an octagonal tower on either side of its entrance. I thought I heard noise coming from somewhere in that direction, but although I listened hard nothing else came. Sneaking a hasty look around the turret I was leaning against, I caught a flash of black uniform entering a second raised doorway to the White Tower.

So, was this it? Was this where the Blackshirts and their hostages were gathered? The rest of the grounds seemed deserted and it made sense for Hubble to keep his captives in one location. So what better place than the White Tower itself? There were large display rooms inside, the exhibits anything from cannon to armor, with plenty of space to hold prisoners. And plenty of room to . . . I prayed to God they hadn't already begun the transfusions.

I knew I couldn't waste any more time. I slipped round the corner and raced towards the stone staircase leading up to the keep's doorway, at any moment expecting the Blackshirt to reappear; but it didn't happen, I had a clear run. Without breaking stride, I grabbed the iron stair-rail and climbed, taking the steps two at a time, holding the Sten gun in one hand by its pistol grip, muzzle aimed at the doorway above, my hand sliding along the top of the rail to steady myself. I reached the small landing without incident.

The double doors to the keep were wide open, but there were no sounds from inside. I snuck a quick look, then pulled back again, allowing the impression of what lay beyond the opening to sink in.

The room was below door level, a vast basement chamber with archways and flagstone floor, helmets and chestplates mounted around its dingy walls and cannon of various sizes arranged in neat rows inside alcoves along its length on either side of the central area. Iron chandeliers hung from the high, dusty ceiling, but much of the light came from lanterns placed around the room, the rest from the big doorway itself, revealing a scene so horrific I really didn't want to take a second look.

Leaning back against the outside wall, my eyes shut tight, I fought the nausea that threatened to force its way up my gullet and splatter the stone at my feet. But it wasn't only the sight of those half-naked bodies down there, corpses of men and women sprawled in their own gore, rubber tubes still attached to some of their arms; the smell of excrement, thick with the stench of blood, that caused the sickness in me; no, it was my own sense of failure that helped. I'd let them down, left it too late. The

Blackshirts had already carried out their stupid, desperate plan to purge their veins and replenish them with new blood, and those first volunteers had paid the price along with their victims, because they lay dead too in that terrible crimson flood. I prayed to God Hubble was down there among them.

I forced myself to take another look, hoping there might be some that were still alive, a few I could help before they bled to death. And I was curious to discover if Hubble really had been destroyed by his own lunacy. I guess I was curious to know about Muriel, too.

Some of the Blackshirts were still slumped in wooden chairs, their "donors" lying beside them; others lay curled up on the soaking floor, their hands curled into claws, mouths open as if in silent screams, as if the infusion of alien blood had sent their bodies into paroxysms of agony. I wanted to scream at them for their reckless stupidity, for the useless barbarity of it all. Why hadn't they at least waited, tried the transfusions one at a time so that when the first or second failed, they'd give it up? I guess I was underestimating their desperation—what the hell did they have to lose anyway?—as well as the damage already done to their brains and their unfailing belief in their leader. But the only pity I felt was for the victims; I felt nothing at all for the parasites.

I stepped inside and stood on the small platform overlooking the charnel house, ignoring its stink as I searched among the contorted shapes; unfortunately, several were face down, or on their sides with their backs to me, and others were half-hidden in the alcoves. To be sure that Hubble and Muriel were with them I had to go down for a closer inspection.

As I went into that nasty hell-hole I began to realize there were not enough corpses here to account for all the Blackshirts and the people outside the Savoy, and that puzzled me. And the women and children—where were they? S'far as I could tell, there were no women here, and definitely no kids, yet two nights ago there'd been a whole bunch of them. I figured there were about twenty bodies that I could see, and Hubble's army alone must've amounted to triple that number, despite their losses in the air raid on the hotel and those I'd killed personally. I reached the bottom of the stairs and stepped over outstretched limbs, avoiding the worst of the blood lake, working my way along the alcoves, peering past the battered cannons into the dark corners, looking for more bodies, hoping to find some live ones.

I must've been concentrating too damned hard, because he was almost on me before I heard the first sound.

I hadn't forgotten about the man I'd followed into this place, my mind had just been distracted, is all. It was the splashing of his boots through the blood that caused me to wheel around in his direction. He must've been waiting inside an opening at the far end of the chamber, watching me all the time and now he was coming at me in a rush, a medieval pike held out before him, its nasty-looking metal point aimed at my gut. In that instant I realized it wasn't a Blackshirt uniform he was wearing, but the navy blue day-duty tunic of a Yeoman Warder. His long coat was dusty, torn in places, the red braiding frayed, even missing in places, and his unkempt hair hung in loose tangles over his crazy-man eyes, spittle glistening in his long, matted beard. Close as this, I could see two things about those wild eyes: they were leaking blood, and they were filled with a malevolent hatred that was just for me. Jesus, they almost rooted me to the spot, but my reflexes kicked in.

I stepped towards him instead of backing away, turning my body to lessen the target area. There was no time to shoot him (besides, I didn't want to alert any others who might be lurking in this place) so I looped the Sten gun's sling over the pike's metal tip as it skimmed past me, just inches from my stomach. The sling caught on the red and gold silk tassel between the point and wooden staff and I yanked the weapon towards me, twisting away from the demented warden, using the pole as a lever to knock him off balance. He fell to his knees as I completed the turn and he yelped like the crazy he was as I drove my left fist into the back of his neck. He went down hard, his face smacking against the wet floor. It'd been a smart maneuvre on my part, but it worked chiefly because of the man's own sluggishness; he had the sickness in him, same as the Blackshirts.

I pounced on him, my knee against his spine, the pikestaff still caught up in the gun's sling. I dug the fingers of my free hand into his matted hair and jerked his head up, then smashed it back down against the flagstone. He gave a small gurgling kind of scream, then lay motionless. He wasn't out though; a low moaning came from him. I was about to repeat the process, send him on his way for good—sure, I knew it wasn't his fault, his brain was as diseased as his blood, but I'd spent too long at war with his kind and there was no sympathy left—but I thought of the victims around us, innocents who'd been murdered because they were different, had something the bad guys wanted for themselves. And I remembered there might be others still alive, but waiting to die. I lifted his head again.

"*Where are they?*" I hissed close to his ear.

He wasn't so mad that he didn't know I'd crack his blood-drenched face against the floor again if I didn't get an answer. Through bruised lips and cracked teeth he managed to say: "They . . . they took them."

"*Took them where?*" I deliberately pushed my anger, allowing it to overcome my own revulsion at what I was doing. Tightening my grip in his hair, I tugged his head up another couple of inches. He got the message and mumbled something so fast and incoherent I couldn't catch it.

I pulled his head back even further so that I could look into those terrible eyes. I winced at the leaking blood and the burst veins in his cheeks. The fingers of his hands spread out before him were blackened and swollen, smelling of gangrene. I wanted to choke.

"*Where?*" I spat out through clenched teeth.

I guess he didn't like the wildness in my own eyes, because his diction suddenly improved. "They . . . they needed . . . God's help."

I stared at him.

"Sir Max . . . Sir Max said God . . ."

His words trailed off in a whining moan, the saliva that drooled from his cracked lips turning pinkish as it flowed, becoming a deeper red by the time it reached the floor. His body began to convulse beneath me, gently at first, a trembling that became a shaking, and then a violent thrashing. He began to cry out, then to scream, and I had no choice, I had to stifle the sounds, stop him arousing others who could be anywhere inside the keep.

This time I put all my strength into smashing his head against the bloodied flagstone and the sickening thud it made was a hundred times worse than the soft groan that came from him. His body went limp and his head lolled sideways; on his bloody face was an expression of contentment, as if he were glad to be off somewhere else. At least, that's what I told myself to ease my conscience. I didn't know if he was dead—his body wasn't even twitching—but I guess I hoped so. Better for him, that way.

I untangled the Sten's sling from the pikestaff as I got to my feet. And it was then that I heard the strains drifting through the open doorway above my head. It was organ music.

I remembered the chapel across the great courtyard.

|25|

IT WAS A WEIRD, TORMENTED SOUND THAT WAFTED THROUGH THE warm morning air across the wide, open space between the keep and surrounding buildings, muted and agonized organ music that had more in common with Lon Chaney than religious adoration. It came from the little church tucked away in a far corner of the yard, an overgrown, weed-ridden green with untidy trees spread before it, a bell tower rising over its rough-stoned walls and slanted roof, the bell inside its open turret visible from where I stood at the top of the White Tower's steps. I took a deep breath, dreading what I might find over there, before descending those stairs and scooting across the courtyard, the soles of my boots sticky with blood, heading for the nearest cover, which was the grand neo-gothic building opposite, expecting to be challenged at any moment.

Nothing happened though, no sudden challenge interrupted my flight across open ground, and as soon as I reached the opposite wall, I went down on my haunches, facing out, the submachine gun weaving left and right, ready for the slightest disturbance. Apart from the faint, creaky organ music from the chapel, all was quiet and still.

I caught my breath and moved on, keeping close to the wall like always, using all the cover I could get, and before long I was crossing the passageway between the blockhouse tower and the chapel itself. Standing on tiptoe beneath the first of the five tall leaded windows, I peeped in, but the glass was too thick and too filthy for me to see anything clearly. All I caught was movement inside, although I heard other sounds over the organ music, voices shouting, others pleading.

Afraid my shadow might be seen, I ducked again and made my way along the row of windows, skirting round two big, lichen-covered tombs set on plinths along the path, searching for the chapel's entrance. I found the door around the corner, between the west wall and bell tower, a cart for carrying small boxes or sacks standing close by. The door was open a few inches and the droning music was bad enough to make me want to block my ears. I thought I heard a child's wailing as I crept closer.

Back against the door, I used an elbow to widen the gap, the Sten upright, close to my chest. I lowered the barrel as the door swung slowly inwards, turning my body at the same time towards the chapel's interior.

The aisle before me, a few feet wide, led straight to a small, plain altar, a gold crucifix at its center, a decorative leaded-glass window overlooking it. Light from all the high windows was dulled by the dirty glass, and the ceiling beams of dark wood cast their own oppressive gloom. To my left was a set of high arches, inside the first an alabaster tomb-chest, a stone knight and his lady laid out on its surface; further along the covered area was a massive wood-carved organ with tarnished pipes; beyond that, at the end wall, another door.

Dust motes floated in the subdued rays of light that played on the heads and shoulders of the congregation and there was movement everywhere, bodies shifting on the benches, distraught children waving their arms in the air, Blackshirts patroling the center aisle, weapons at the ready. Some of these people were moaning, others could only cower in fear, but all were looking at the diminutive figure standing before the altar.

Hubble had his back to them, and the tall Blackshirt, the one called McGruder, was helping him remove his shirt, exposing a thin, bruised arm and a hand that was now darkened almost to the wrist. Hubble's bare shoulder was hunched and covered with nasty blemishes, the blood beneath the skin visibly thickened. It was an ugly sight, which stirred up the nausea I could still taste in my mouth.

He began to turn in my direction and I stepped behind the half-opened door in case he saw me.

With some effort, Hubble straightened himself. His chin jutted as he stood with one hand on his cane in a pose that he probably imagined made him look strong, invincible, a leader of men. But his sunken cheeks and the dark bruising around his eyes, the blueness of those tight-drawn lips, the sickly pallor of his skin, almost translucent now, so that the network of tiny broken veins beneath was clearly visible, his thin hair—once immaculately groomed, now straggly and brittle, falling forward over his waxen forehead—and the stubborn stoop of his shoulders, not to mention the palsied quivering of his limbs—all this only mocked the old image, reduced him to a hideous parody of the man who'd enthralled thousands of similar bigots with his Fascist oratory before the outbreak of the second—and last—world war, a man who'd marched at the head of a neo-Nazi army, subordinate only to Sir Oswald Mosley. Yet those bloodshot eyes still burned with a zealot's fervor and I realized he was more dangerous than ever: Hubble didn't have long for this decimated world but his dementia was driving him on, giving him the strength and the will to inflict even more misery.

I remained hidden behind the angled door, figuring out my next move.

The tuneless organ music finally droned to a wheezing halt when the Blackshirt leader raised a trembling hand towards the player, an obese, bespectacled woman with shorn hair, who wore the same black garments of terror as the men of Hubble's army. She twisted her bulk to face the altar, the effort difficult for her, and even from where I stood peering round the door at the far end of the chapel, I could see the marks of death on her loose-fleshed face. A couple of guards shouted for quiet, another striking out at hostages close to him, as Hubble began to speak.

"Almighty God, forgive our blindness in not seeking Your blessing and guidance . . ."

His voice was frail, almost quavery, yet it filled the small church, quietening the crowd more successfully than any threats from the guards.

". . . and look down with favor on our poor mortal bodies and everlasting souls. We thank You for our deliverance and ask that You bless those here among us . . ."

His shoulders shuddered and hunched even more, and he coughed into a hastily drawn handkerchief, holding it to his mouth 'til the spasm passed. It was already bloodstained and when he took it away there were fresh, deeper blotches. His voice still had that peculiar distance to it, yet it was clear and I wondered what this man's power had been like in the old days, when he was fit and able.

"Those among us . . ." he went on, as if nothing had occurred ". . . for their selfless sacrifice to the greater cause. Let their pure blood spill into our veins and replenish our sick bodies."

There were cries of protest from the people packed into those benches and the Blackshirts sitting among them hit out, one of the patrolling guards even poking his rifle into the head of a skinny youth on an end seat. Their objections were quickly subdued.

"This we ask of You, dear Lord . . ."

Hubble's deranged eyes were appealing heavenwards, a martyr suffering for his God. My finger twitched restlessly on the Sten's trigger.

". . . in the knowledge that we are Your chosen few."

And there you had it. This crazy man sincerely believed—as had his all-time hero, Adolf Hitler—that God was on his side, that he and his followers were the natural inheritors of the Earth by God's command. The fact that Hubble's blood was the wrong kind for survival barely made a dent in Iris twisted logic; that was just part of the hardship the righteous had to endure and finally overcome, all part of the great test. Hubble had gotten it a little wrong before, but now he'd seen the true way, so was seeking help from the Divine Saviour—something he'd foolishly omitted to do before—to make the transfusions successful so that his and his Blackshirts' reign would continue. He was too far gone to realize it wasn't simply goodwill he was asking of his Maker—it was a miracle! I was too disgusted even to smile. I edged the door open further.

It seemed Hubble had completed his devotions or supplications, whatever he considered them to be, and he made a sign with his hand. A Blackshirt on the front bench rose, dragging someone up with him. McGruder, standing protectively close to his leader as usual, beckoned the Blackshirt forward and I saw whose arm he clenched.

Muriel was no longer wearing the long, silver evening dress I'd last seen her in: she'd found, or been given, a man's black shirt a couple of sizes too big for her, which she wore outside gray slacks. (I caught this when she moved into the center of the aisle just in front of the altar.) She seemed reluctant to accompany the goon—she kept trying to pull her arm away—and I soon began to understand why.

There was a chair by the altar, which McGruder helped Hubble into (it was odd the way the big man fussed over his leader and I wondered what Hubble had done for him in the past to earn such slavish loyalty) while the other Blackshirt pushed Muriel forward. Y'know, Hubble managed to give her a twisted kind of smile as he settled himself, like she was offering herself willingly and he appreciated the gesture. I noticed her back stiffen.

Something else I noticed right then: beneath the cross on the altar was a tangle of rubber tubing, sunlight glinting off the attached steel needles and clips.

So that was the plan, and Muriel was to be the first. After all, to Hubble's unhinged way of thinking, she had the purest blood of all. She was healthy, beautiful, with a fine brain that was in tune with his own (what a bonus!)—and most of all, this kid had the *breeding*. A lord's daughter, no less, a member of the aristocracy, the ruling class. Oh yeah, her blood would do fine. And Hubble knew he didn't have much time—Christ, I could see even from that distance how much he'd deteriorated since a couple of nights ago. The transfusions in the White Tower had failed, but now they had atoned to God, asking for His forgiveness and guidance, and naturally Hubble (what did I say about his kind of people?) had chosen the best for himself. Hallelujah!

McGruder ripped open the front of Muriel's shirt, tugging one side over her shoulder and pulling her arm out of its sleeve.

"No, don't!" I heard her plead. "You can't do this to me, Max. I helped you. We believe in the same things."

He only continued smiling up at her like some old, benevolent uncle—a mad-as-a-skunk, depraved old uncle with lechery in mind. He didn't utter a word though, didn't even nod his head; McGruder knew what to do and was already making himself busy. Unlike most of his companions, and certainly his leader, the Blood Death seemed some ways off for the big man: his movement was a little slow, but he still appeared powerful enough as he held Muriel with one hand while he reached behind for a length of transfusion tubing with the other. Several more pieces fell to the floor as he pulled one free and there was a cry from the side of the chapel. The fat, bespectacled organist was stumbling towards the altar, a wail of anguish coming from her open, blue-lipped mouth. On the way she pounced on someone sitting on the front bench, and when she held her thick arms aloft, she was holding a child, a small girl. (You see the lunacy of these people? How much blood did the fat lady expect to get out of this kid? Enough to fill an arm?) She tried to carry the girl to the altar, but somebody screamed and a woman jumped up—the little girl's mother or guardian, I figured—and tried to snatch her back. Uproar followed as other hostages leapt to their feet and began struggling with the nearest Blackshirts. Women screamed, kids bawled, and the few men among the "donors" started punching, all of them only too aware of what was in store for them even if they hadn't themselves witnessed the deaths of those others of the same blood. McGruder let go of Muriel and rushed towards the overweight organist, who was struggling with the hysterical woman, the child between them; but by now, other Blackshirts suddenly had the same idea as the organist. There were only a cer-tain number of "donors" left, much fewer than the number of Blackshirts present, and none of those goons wanted to be left out. Other guards began dragging victims towards the altar.

I saw one Blackshirt, a skinny guy who looked as if he hardly had the strength to carry his submachine gun, grab a female by the hair and attempt to pull her off a bench, but she fought back, giving him a shove that sent him toppling into the opposite row of benches. She turned and ran, making for the exit.

She was halfway down the aisle before she saw me in the open doorway, the door pushed wide now, the Sten gun chest-high, pointing straight at her.

Behind her I could see Hubble, on his feet again, his wizened face screwed up in a blaze of fury, his lips moving, mouth open wide, as if he were trying to bring some order to the party. McGruder was punching the fat lady to the floor, the mother had hold of her screaming kid again, and other goons were hauling resisting victims into the aisles, clubbing them with their fists and weapons, just sane enough not to shoot any of 'em. And maybe that fact had finally dawned on those hostages, that they were no good to the Blackshirts dead, because they were suddenly putting up one hell of a fight.

It was bedlam inside that chapel, a madhouse of shrieks and shouts, and warring factions, and through it all, through that pandemonium, Hubble finally clapped eyes on me. His anger turned to blank surprise. And then his pale, shrivelled face arranged itself into a trick-or-treat mask of sheer venom. Something more though, in fact a whole lot more, was in that expression: loathing, sure, but a kind of abhorrence too, as though the devil had arrived on his doorstep. I was the oddity, you see, I was the *abnormal.* Just like the AB-neg types fighting his own men. The disease had rendered us the freaks of society (whatever society he imagined was left) and I was his No. 1 freak. The problem was that no matter how loathsome I was to him, I had what he needed. And that made him hate me even more.

Yeah, well, I could live with it. I tucked the Sten into my shoulder and squeezed the trigger.

I'd aimed high for fear of hitting my own kind and the window above the altar shattered, the noise of breaking glass and gunfire suspending the action for a second or two. Heads looked my way, eyes were startled, and then the screaming started all over again. The pandemonium was worse than before when I fired off another burst. People ducked for cover as bullets spat into granite, dug into wood and smashed glass; I eased up so they could hear me yell:

"Get outta here, just run, get away, go!"

Muriel was one of the first to get the idea, even though my words hadn't been intended for her. Our eyes locked briefly and I saw the uncertainty in hers—she didn't know if my next bullets might be for her. But she must've decided I was a better bet than Hubble, because next moment she was breaking free of the brawl and heading my way. McGruder made a lunge at her, but I fired off another burst (I would've taken his head off if there'd been no danger of hitting innocent people), and he took a dive, disappearing behind a wall of bodies. Sustained fire caused the nose of the Sten gun to rise and I let it, shooting high into the walls, swinging round almost leisurely towards the windows on my fight. They exploded one by one, creating the fresh panic that I wanted.

The woman who'd been the first to spot me in the doorway began crawling forward along the aisle, moving fast, her head down as if afraid to look at me again. Muriel wasn't far behind, but more people were tumbling into the aisle, blocking her path. She had pulled the shin back over her shoulder and was clutching the material together over her breasts even as she struggled to reach me.

"Come on!" I yelled again. *"Time to go! Move it!"*

I only meant the hostages, but some of the Blackshirts had taken to the notion: they started running for the small door at the other end of the chapel. Hubble had had enough of all this. He stood on the step before the altar and jabbed a darkened finger at me, and even over the uproar I could hear his high-pitched voice shrieking orders. McGruder's head and shoulders appeared over the crowd and he grabbed two nearby Blackshirts, pulling them close around Hubble, forming a protective shield against any gunfire I might send his leader's way. I took aim anyway, but as I did I realized Hubble wasn't pointing at me at all; his finger was waving at Muriel as she fought her way down the aisle towards me. McGruder and one of the bodyguards started after her, knocking people aside as they went.

And that set me to revising my plan. Hubble wanted the girl as much as he'd wanted me when he thought I was the only healthy blood type left in the city—let's face it, her bloodline was a few grades up from mine (if you believed in that kind of thing, that is, and Hubble, just like his demagogue, Hitler, clearly did) and that thought gave me a second option. The original plan had been to snatch Hubble; now I realized Muriel might be an even better hostage, because she'd come willingly.

That first woman crawled past my legs and then was gone, out the door, making—I hoped—for pastures new. An older woman, grey-haired, wrinkled face, was climbing over benches towards me, a boy of about sixteen helping her. Then came the two boy twins I'd noticed outside the Savoy, hustled by a middle-aged woman. A young girl, no more'n fifteen, leapt from the benches and scooted in my direction, bumping my elbow as she went by. They'd all caught the drift, they'd seen their chance to escape. But I couldn't leave with them, not 'til Muriel was by my side. And not 'til Hubble had time to organize his men for the chase.

Bullets thudded into the wall beside the door, causing me to crouch, then return fire. More shouts, more screams—more gunfire. But the crowd before me was thinning, everybody scattering for cover. A man—a fleeing hostage—fell into me, knocking me back against the open door, and when he slumped to the floor, clawing at my clothes as he went, I saw the blood spurting from the holes in his back. A great crush of people surged towards me and I knew if I didn't get out the way I'd be trampled underfoot, gun or no gun. Muriel was close to the front, but somebody tripped in front of her and she and others behind her went down in a tangle of arms and legs.

Another burst of gunfire just to keep things hot and I stepped forward, reaching into the jumble for her, my fingers managing to close around her wrist. I pulled hard and she came up fast, crashing into my chest, her hands resting on my shoulder. I thought I heard her say my name, but there was too much clamor, too many screams and moans, to be sure. I took her with me, backing towards the doorway, watching the advancing Blackshirts among the crowd as we went.

One particular goon was too close for comfort and I knew I had to stop him. Couldn't chance the Sten—too inaccurate with so many women and kids around—so, shoving Muriel behind me I tossed the submachine gun into my left hand and reached for the P-35 with the other. I shot almost from the hip—no time for anything else—and the goon screamed as he clutched at his belly and staggered. He fell to his knees, then went down as bodies piled on top of him. Others behind the heap hesitated, watching me warily.

I stepped away from the exit and waved at it with the pistol. *"Come on, get going!"* I shouted. *"I'm with you!"* The bolder ones among them believed me and ran outside.

By now Hubble's army had worked themselves into a frenzy and those with guns started blazing away at the ceiling, frustrated because they still didn't have a clear line on me. Blue smoke curled in the air and the uproar was deafening; I figured it was time to make my exit. At any moment those Blackshirts would be up on the benches to get a better shot at me, so I re-holstered the pistol and bundled Muriel out the door, breaking into a run as soon as we hit open air. I gripped her wrist to keep her with me and carried the Sten by its body. Those who'd already fled the church were scattering across the courtyard and I silently wished them the best of luck, hoping they wouldn't quit running 'til they were on the other side of London. Muriel and me, we cut across the overgrown lawn, our steps high through the long grass, heading diagonally towards the broad stone steps and path that led to the passageway beneath the Bloody Tower. The lane beyond it led to a wooden bridge, which crossed the moat to the wharf road, and if the Blackshirts didn't cut us down before we reached it we had a chance. We were running on a prayer, but that was nothing new for me.

We passed the empty Vickers machine gun, so far, so good, and kept going; if we could get to the path below the steps we'd be out of sight for a stretch, maybe even long enough to get under cover of the passageway before they opened fire on us. But wouldn't you know it, it was at that point that Muriel decided to take a tumble. I tried to hold her, but her shoe just slipped from under her and she went sprawling, squawking as she rolled over.

Instead of minding her I whirled around, pulled out the used-up magazine and inserted a fresh one from the bag I carried, my hand slipping into the Sten's pistol grip as I faced them. What was left of the black army was pouting round the corner of the chapel, still a few hostages among them, the Blackshirts too interested in us to bother with them. No doubt Hubble's orders were to get Muriel and me, the others could be rounded up later, and that was fine, that's exactly what I wanted. I gave them a short burst of fire, just enough to slow 'em down but not to lose interest. A peculiar sight then, one that would've had me screaming with laughter at any other time: that two-wheeled cart I'd noticed outside the chapel door came into view, McGruder pushing it, Hubble crouched inside like a big kid being taken for a ride. I shook my head, assuring myself this was really happening, it wasn't just another stupid nightmare after an evening hitting the booze. Nope, I wasn't dreaming, the bullets chipping concrete in front of me told me so.

I sent a spray of bullets of my own back and had the satisfaction of seeing the cart swerving and Blackshirts hitting the deck. I heard a groan from Muriel and threw a quick glance her way. She was half-sitting, nursing a bleeding elbow that peeked through a hole in her shirt.

"*Are you hit?*" I yelled.

She gave a quick shake of her head and regarded me with some fear. She was scared all right, and not just of the Blackshirts: I guess she thought I might turn my weapon on her.

"Okay, get up. You know what your new pals want from you, so start running again. I'll cover you."

"We'll never get away." She spoke breathlessly, her small exposed breasts heaving, her frightened gaze sweeping past me towards the mob. "There are too many of them, we can't outrun them all."

Yeah, I thought. Too many of them. Too many to kill with only bullets. And I wanted every damn one of 'em accounted for. I scuttled over to her and leaned close. "Just get on your feet and scoot." I hauled her up with one hand and pushed her towards the steps. She was unsteady at first, fastening a couple of shirt buttons as she went, then she broke into a run that started the Blackshirts surging forward again.

I followed close behind, but backstepping, gun trained on our pursuers just to keep 'em at bay. Timing was everything, y'see; I had to get this exactly right. Luckily they were smart enough to slow down, 'though they kept coming, watching my every move, playing me out. I took a swift head count and figured there were around forty or so of them left and that surprised me. Even if there were some still inside the chapel, the Slow Death had claimed a whole mob of 'em since the Blackshirts and I had first become acquainted. Well, it didn't cause me any grief—the less I had to deal with today, the more chance I had of coming through in one piece.

Hearing Muriel's shoes clattering down the steps, I did a turnabout and made a dash for them myself. A roar went up from the crowd as I disappeared from view and I knew we had only a few seconds to get into the passageway. Quickly catching up with Muriel, I took her arm again to help hurry her down a second set of steps and she cried out in protest, afraid we were both gonna break our necks. Ravens on the green in front of the White Tower flew into the air in alarm, their shrieks—that harsh, croaky kind of *kaa*—sounded like cursing to me, as if they were warning us off, intruders unwelcome, and I was of a mind to blow one or two of 'em out of the air just for the hell of it. But I kept going, landing on the path with Muriel, dragging her onwards, the short, dark tunnel opening up ahead.

More shouts, more gunfire. Bullets splattered the ancient wall of the Bloody Tower, warning shots telling us we'd better stop running or else . . . We plunged into the cool shade of the archway as more bullets ricocheted off the cobbled path, their sound growing louder as they beat a line towards us. I pushed Muriel against the wall and the bullets pounded on past us, their impact thunderous in the confined space. I held her there, waiting for the row to stop, the echoes to fade, my face pressed into her hair and our bodies tight together as chips of stone spat up at us. I caught the faint whiff of faded perfume, felt her softness against me and, stupid though it was under the circumstances, remembered her nakedness beneath me, her arms curled around my waist, pulling me into her. I remembered how afraid, how vulnerable, she'd been that night at the hotel. And then I remembered how she'd betrayed her friends.

I pushed myself away from her then, and with an almost contemptuous side-swipe of my arm sent her reeling towards the other end of the short tunnel. As the Blackshirts spilled down the steps I went back to the entrance, showing myself to them. They hesitated yet again, some cowering on the steps, others trying to run back up them, as I raised the submachine gun. I took careful aim and pretended to squeeze the trigger.

When nothing happened they raised their heads or stopped where they were and looked at me. Surprise turned to glee as I tossed the weapon away and disappeared back into the shadows. One of 'em even laughed aloud, thinking the Sten had jammed.

They came after us then like hounds after a wounded fox, baying for our blood—yeah, literally.

Out in the open on the other side of the archway, the sun stinging my eyes for a moment, I held Muriel by the wrist again and we fled, sweet Jesus, how we fled, the uneven roadway doing its best to trip us, the howling mob behind us giving us all the encouragement we needed. The bridge over the dry moat wasn't far, but my chest was beginning to burn and my breath was scorching my throat. As wild gunshots whined through the air I could feel Muriel starting to slow down, dragging on me, her pace becoming awkward.

"You gotta keep going!" I yelled at her.

"We can't make it!" she croaked back.

"We can. They're slow, don't you see? We've just gotta keep ahead of 'em!"

We reached the archway exit and pounded across the wooden bridge, and now that we were outside the old fortress, Muriel's energy seemed renewed: she picked up speed and her movement became more controlled. Before us was the River Thames, ancient cannon set in a row all along its edge, pointing south across the water as if fearing an invasion from London's other hall A wartime concrete pillbox stood among them, solidly square but useless against the enemy's last invisible weapon. To our left, Tower Bridge rose high and proud, its bridge frozen open for all time, the river beneath flowing clear and pure in the sunlight.

Me in the lead, we headed towards it.

|26|

SHE DIDN'T UNDERSTAND WHEN I PULLED HER ROUND TO THE stairway.

"The docks," she gasped as she tried to break away. She drew in quick, sharp breaths. "We can lose them easily in the docks."

She had a point. The road under the northern span of the bridge led straight into dockland—or what was left of it after the fire-bombs had done their worst—where there were plenty of side streets, alleyways and ruined buildings to get lost in. Sure, it would've been easy to shake off the Blackshirts in that labyrinth, 'cept that wasn't any part of my plan.

"We're going onto the bridge," I told her, trying to catch my own breath. Sweat trickled down my back and my throat felt burned dry.

"You're insane. The bridge is raised—we can't get across!"

"We can use one of the walkways at the top."

She looked at me as if I really was crazy, but there was no time for argument, so without another word I pushed her into the covered stairway. The lead Blackshirts were about forty yards away, and for now they'd given up shooting, no doubt confident they'd soon catch us. Coming up the rear was Hubble, pushed by McGruder in that ridiculous perambulator, waving his arms and bitching orders as he bumped over the cobblestones. With one last look, Muriel scuttled up those steps.

At the top of them, a short tunnel led back under the bridge's roadway, and another flight of stairs went up to the bridge approach itself. Our footsteps echoed around the clamp walls together with the sound of our own labored breathing and even

2 5 7

before we'd reached the second flight of stairs I heard pounding feet and shouts coming up after us. By now we were running on adrenaline—my old ally—and I could only pray it'd sustain us for a little while longer.

Up the stairs we scrambled, both of us using the iron rail set in the brick wall to pull ourselves forward, my other arm clamping the canvas bag against my side to stop it bouncing around. We burst into bright sunlight again and the bridge's north tower loomed over us, battleship-gray suspension girder-chains on either side of the roadway rising away from us in great, swooping slopes towards the upper reaches. With its stone cladding, arched windows, moldings and niches, turrets at each corner, the tower resembled some sinister Gothic castle straight from a creepy Grimm's fairy tale. Fairy tale? Hell, with its shallow balcony near the top and spires and finials around the roof, it felt as if we were making straight for Bela Lugosi's town house. Bloodsuckers on our tails, a virtual mountain to climb ahead of us, I closed my mind and kept going.

Through the great archway at the base of the tower where traffic once flowed onto the bridge itself we could see a huge concrete wall plugging the gap. Rusted buses, trucks, and automobiles still queued before it as though waiting for the bascule (that concrete wall was the raised bridge section itself) to lower so they could continue their journey into the city's southern sprawl. On the other side of the bascule was a sheer drop to the river below and directly opposite was the underneath of its sister bascule, this one also raised and standing erect against the south tower.

Beside the archway was a narrow flight of stone steps leading up to an inset doorway, and this was the entrance into the tower, which I wanted to be inside before the mob got too close. Once there, it meant a long haul to the fourth level where the high walkway that spanned the river, joining both towers, would take us across. Although it would be a tough climb for us, I knew it would be even tougher for those unhealthy freaks on our tails.

Along the approach we raced, traffic that would never move again on our left, a thick, ornamental iron rail to our right, howling Blackshirts hard on our heels, and blue skies and dead city all around. Somehow it felt as though I were taking it all in for the last time: the battered, broken rooftops across the city, those wrinkled balloons sagging in the sky, buildings that used to be thriving warehouses now empty shells along the river's edge, bent and crumpled cranes, boats and barges still moored to quaysides, stirring in the drift. Three years I'd remained in this open mausoleum when survivors with more sense had fled, three years of tidying the streets and getting nowhere. D'you still remember the point of it all? the familiar sneaky little voice inside my head jeered. And if you did, was it still worth the effort? Forever hunted by sick people turned to vampirism, hiding away like an animal, killing just to stay alive, always vigilant, always afraid, carrying on the war when it should have finished with the Blood Death genocide. Did it make any sense at all? No, 'course it didn't, none whatsoever. Sally was gone, she knew nothing of this even though your obsession was because of her. Her and . . . well, you know. You're crazy, Hoke, crazy like the human leeches chasing you now. Have been since you lost the world. And you know it. But at least it's coming to an end, this madness. Yeah, another end, and this time you'll probably be included. You should've listened to Cissie, Hoke. *She* told you you were crazy, too . . .

Bullets whistled over our heads again, interrupting that sly, taunting voice inside my head, a voice that was my own good sense, snapping me back to the here and now. Fact was, I had no choice anyways: my idea had progressed too far to call it off. Those Blackshirts were still trying to frighten us into stopping, but their shots only encouraged us to make a final spurt onto the pier that ran around the base of the tower. The bridge's control cabin, protected by sheaths of steel plating and sandbags, nestled beneath the tower itself, and I noticed its green signal was still raised to allow nonexistent ships through. Out of sight underneath the pier were the cogwheels and accumulator tanks that helped operate the bascule on this side of the river.

"Up the stairs!" I ordered Muriel as I wheeled around to check on the hounds. Shit, the first goon, who was just about one of the healthiest-looking specimens in a black uniform I'd seen for a couple of years now—healthier even than McGruder, I'd say—was only ten yards away. I could've dropped him easily with the Browning, but I didn't want to discourage the crowd from following us into the tower, so instead I turned my back on him and scooted up the steps after Muriel. She'd already pushed open the door at the top and we went through almost together.

"Keep going," I said to her, pointing to the rising stairs inside, and without even glancing at me she did as she was told. Her shoes clacked on the iron treads and her breaths were now emerging in short, sharp cries. I waited in the shadows behind the door, listening to the approaching footsteps outside. They grew louder, broke as the Blackshirt leapt the first few steps, then resumed, coming closer.

Waiting 'til the last moment, I slammed the door in the goon's face and heard a muffled shout, then a series of yelps as he bounced back down those steps again. I'd busted the door's lock in the early hours of that morning, so I couldn't shut the Black-shirts out and give myself a chance to get a good head start on them up those stairs before they broke in. I raced after Muriel, taking the steps three at a time and soon catching her up.

Like I said, a long haul to the top, two hundred and six steps in all (I'd counted them some hours ago), the hydraulic lifts naturally out of action, bullying Muriel all the way. Pounding footsteps followed us up, the occasional, useless shot ringing out (we were well protected by the solid staircase as long as we kept two flights ahead of the pack), our hearts thudding faster, our legs growing heavier, and our lungs heaving painfully with each step. Oh Jesus, we were never gonna make it, we didn't have the strength. But still we went on, every turn an inducement to reach the next. Although there were plenty of windows, the glass was filthy, so seeing our way was another problem. Quite a few times one of us tripped, but when it was Muriel I just lifted her again and pushed her onwards, and when it was me I cussed and used the thick wooden handrail to pull myself up. The higher we went, the more exhausted we became; and it was getting harder for both of us to draw breath. To make matters worse, the commotion below seemed to be growing louder, the pack drawing closer and closer. Impossible, I kept telling myself, those people were in worse condition than us, we were still way ahead of them. If only I could've believed myself.

Some of the Blackshirts, I began to realize by sound alone, had taken the other staircase—there were two inside the tower—and they seemed to be making better progress than those behind us. We caught a glimpse of this bunch as they poured onto one of the spacious landings below, and a roar went up when they spotted us, too. Muriel almost collapsed in front of me.

"They . . . they've got us, Hoke," she stammered, her chest and shoulders heaving. "We can't make it."

So much for the Bulldog Breed. "We're nearly there. One more flight, that's all. We'll be okay up there, I promise you."

I stepped alongside her and grabbed her by the wrist. Her whole body was shaking and she seemed to spasm with every breath she drew, but I half-carried her with me, using whatever strength I had left to keep her moving. At first, she weighed on me, but when she saw the staircase opening out onto the top landing, some of her strength—and her spirit—returned and she began to climb by herself. The gloom brightened too and, I guess, in some foolish way that gave her more hope. She stumbled on ahead of me.

We virtually dragged ourselves up those last few steps, using our hands on the higher treads, our knees on the lower ones. And then we arrived at a wide area with windows overlooking the river and city on three sides, the sun piercing the grime and lightening the room with broad dust-swirling shafts. There was no time to rest and though Muriel's legs were giving way and dry retching noises came from her throat as she sucked in air, I forced her on, taking her to the half-glass double doors across the room from us. There were other doors here, cupboards or doors to private offices, as well as tables and chairs, cleaning equipment and all kinds of clutter, but the important thing for us was those wide double doors—we had to get through them before the mob reached this level.

And we managed to, staggering onto the long walkway that stretched across the River Thames, running parallel with its sister footbridge a short distance away to join the north tower with the south. We were a hundred and forty feet above the water here and a coolish breeze drifted through the open iron latticework of its side walls, ruffling our hair, brushing our skin, helping to revive us. We drew in deep gasps of clean air, filling our labored lungs with its sweetness, our eyes closing at the sheer pleasure. Yet still I wouldn't let Muriel linger.

"Down to the other end," I told her wearily, heading that way myself. The noise of the approaching Blackshirts was muffled by the double doors that had swung closed behind us, but it was growing louder by the moment.

"Yes," she said meekly, breaking into a stumbling run. Her face was racked with exhaustion, but there might have been a smile there, a faint glimmer of relief showing through. There was a chance now, she was thinking, a chance if we can just get through those other doors at the end of the long span. Most of those people following were in poor condition and they'd be in even worse shape than us after the climb. Once on the other side of those doors it would be easy to descend, we'd easily get away from them, and then out into the south side of the city, losing ourselves in the streets there. Oh yeah, I could see her thinking all that and, although she was dog-weary, she was already beginning to pick up speed as she avoided debris and piled boxes along the pedestrian bridge, hurrying past equipment covered by tarpaulin that protected it from the elements, stuff that might have been stored there since the walkways had been closed to the general public at the outbreak of the war. Shadows were already falling on the glass section of the double doors as I followed her, the room beyond becoming crowded.

The walkway was wide enough to allow at least five pedestrians to walk comfortably side by side along its length and enjoy the spectacular views of London through the intersecting iron girders; those girders sloped inwards so that the ceiling was narrower than the floor below, and rising above the opposite footbridge I could see the slate roof and spires of the south tower. Across the gap, inside the sister walkway, an anti-aircraft battery had been installed and I remembered thinking more than once about coming up here one night and waiting for the stubborn German bomber pilot to fly his Dornier along the river—like the *Luftwaffe* before him he always used the Thames as a guide into London and the docks—then blasting him out of the sky as he went by. Nice idea, 'cept I knew as much about heavy artillery as I did about knitting cardigans, so I abandoned the idea. But the thought, inspired by my first privileged tourist visit here, had always kept Tower Bridge in my mind and last night, knowing Hubble and his black army were garrisoned in the nearby castle, a different notion had come to me.

I passed a corpse wearing the dusty blue uniform of a custodian or maintenance man precariously perched on a straight-backed wooden chair halfway along the footbridge and I had to skirt around the covered boxes it seemed to be watching over. The jacket was loose over slumped skeletal shoulders and the dead man's shrivelled eyes were cast down at the concrete floor; strands of white hair on the naked scalp were too brittle to be stirred by the breeze. Avoiding more boxes, I went after Muriel, who was almost at the end of the walkway by now.

We both heard the double doors behind us burst open and the yattering rabble surge through, but neither of us bothered to look. I began to slow clown though, popping the flap button of my holster as I did so.

Muriel made it to the doors, almost crashing into them in her eagerness to get through. She was sobbing as she grabbed the vertical handles on each side and pulled. I heard her cry out in dismay when nothing happened. She tried again, yanking the double doors with all her might, rattling them in their frame. Still they held tight.

She looked over her shoulder at me as I drew near. *"They're locked, Hoke!"* she almost screamed. *"Oh my God, they're locked!"*

I came to a halt and turned to face the advancing mob, drawing the pistol from its holster in a smooth, easy movement.

"Yeah," I said to her. "I know."

|27|

SHE STARED AT ME AS THOUGH I'D FINALLY FLIPPED AND I GUESS my grim smile confirmed her suspicions.

"We're trapped," she said incredulously between hard-fought breaths.

"So are they," I remarked, nodding towards the small army of Blackshirts, which was now beginning to slow down to a stroll as they realized our predicament.

S'far as I could tell, most of them were on the walkway now—a few were probably still climbing, but they'd be here soon—and their unhealthy faces were filled with weary triumph. Some were unsteady on their feet, others were being helped along by their buddies; one or two were holding on to the iron girders for support and sucking in great lungfuls of the high fresh air. They filled the footbridge, a shabby band of sick bigots and hopeful (and hopeless) parasites, stealing forward, coming to a halt when they saw the gun in my hand. Weapons were raised towards me.

I waved the Browning in the direction of Muriel and said, "She'll be no good to you dead. And neither will I."

Even the dullest of them got the message. They stopped shuffling forward.

"Don't shoot."

I recognized the feeble, high-pitched voice easily enough, but wondered if Hubble was talking to me or his rabble army.

"We have them now, they can't escape."

The crowd moved aside as he was helped through from the back, McGruder and another Blackshirt supporting him by the elbows. That pleased me a whole lot. Hubble had made it, and that had been my main concern.

Muriel had come away from the locked doors to stand closer to me and Hubble frowned at her.

"Keep away from him, Miss Drake," he warned, fixing her with those fanatical eyes of his, the dark tints around them making him look like the villain in one of those old silent movies. He tried to straighten his body, an effort that was only partially successful, as if to assert his former power. "This man is a savage, but he won't harm you. That's right, isn't it, Mr. Hoke? You wouldn't shoot such a fine young lady."

"I guess not," I replied, and pointed the gun at his forehead.

His unwholesome smile withered and he lost his grand pose: his body sagged to its old lines. He glared at me.

"You can't kill us all, fool," he hissed through his grimace. "One shot and my men will tear you to pieces." His eyes sought Muriel again. "Step away from him. Join us again, your friends, your true kind. I was desperate before, otherwise I would never . . ." he left it unsaid, still smart enough not to spell it out for Muriel. "We have this one now, we . . . I . . . can use his blood . . ."

Unbelievably, Muriel took a step towards this degenerate. But she looked around at me before going any further, confused and uncertain.

"Go ahead," I said, weary of the game. "Join them if that's what you want to do. But he'll bleed you, Muriel, he'll steal your blood and leave you dry."

"But what else can I do, Hoke? How else can I survive?" She looked beaten, her strength gone, her breathing still unsteady. "They'll kill us right here if we don't go with them."

"My dear Muriel, of course we wouldn't do that." Hubble had dropped the "Miss Drake" in favor of a more paternal address, and there was something obscene in the wheedling tone he mistook for charm. "We're the same, you and I, and your father was a valued friend. Whatever your decision, I promise you'll not be harmed in any way."

And if you believe that, Muriel, I thought to myself, you deserve all the hell you'll get from him. But this banter was okay, all this talk was giving the stragglers time to reach the walkway.

Raising my head, I looked past those in front and saw two Black-shirts stumbling through the doors at the far end. They had to be the last of the pack judging by the numbers here. Okay. Time for the finale.

I lifted the canvas bag from my neck and flipped it open. Four steps took me to the girders on the inner side of the footbridge and, using a diagonal strut for support, I pulled myself up onto the handrail that ran along its length. Over their heads I could see a shadowy figure beyond the glass half of the distant doors. Good. Cissie had left her hiding place and was sliding an iron bar through the handles on the other side of the double doors, lock-ing them good and tight. She wouldn't have done it unless the stairs were empty, so I silently wished her God speed on her jour-ney down.

The Blackshirts were watching me uneasily, unsure of what I was up to and waiting for their chance to rush me; I kept the pis-tol bevelled at Hubble, hoping that would hold them back.

"You got a choice, Muriel," I said, much calmer than I felt and keeping an eye on the crowd rather than looking at her. "Come with me, or stay with this vermin and die."

That confused her even more, but there was no time for expla-nations. McGruder let go of Hubble to take a couple of steps towards me; the gun redirected at his head gave him second thoughts.

"It'd give me great pleasure," I let him know, and his agitation settled. He was still too close for comfort though, and I decided it was now or never. But it was my turn to be surprised when Hub-ble began to make odd gagging noises, as though something was stuck in his throat.

He clutched at his neck, his black fingers shivering, pulling open his shirt, his body starting to convulse. His eyes looked as though they were about to pop from their sockets, and they were bleeding from the corners; blood was pouring from his ears also, and then from his open mouth. He stooped even more as McGruder reached for him, and then began to squeal, an awful drawn-out sound that was more animal than human. His hands grabbed at his chest, then his stomach, then a shoulder, his body contorting as he tried to touch the pain. His black pants were drenched as liquid poured from his lower orifices, and I knew it was blood that was soaking them; that blocked arteries inside him were bursting, discharging their dammed-up load; soon other, smaller veins were breaking, discharging their flow and we could see the darkness spreading beneath his sallow skin. His muscles cramped, major organs began to falter, then fail. The moment he had dreaded and had known was approaching fast was finally here. It was time for Hubble to die.

His squealing became a high, keening scream that ended when a fierce gusher of blood exploded from his mouth to splatter the floor and those close to him. His dying was violent and it was horrific, and we watched as if mesmerized. That is, we watched until I decided that no person, no matter how twisted, how evil, deserved such an agonizing death. I shot him between those leaking eyes and he dropped without another murmur.

Everything happened fast then, and I moved like a jackrabbit to keep ahead of it all. A howl went up from the crowd and McGruder went down on his knees beside Hubble's blood-oozing body. Others hurled themselves at me and by the gleam in their eyes I could tell they wanted to haul me down and tear me to pieces with their bare hands. I lashed out with my foot, kicking one in the jaw—that same, healthy-looking guy whose face I'd slammed the door against downstairs—sending him reeling back into the mob and giving me time to pull something from the canvas bag hanging loose from my shoulder. Holding it in my left hand, I took careful aim along the walkway with my right, my elbow looped around the iron strut, the extra height on the rail giving me the angle I needed. I pumped three rapid shots into the blue-uniformed corpse on the chair surrounded by covered boxes.

Those shots did two things at once: the noise stunned the Blackshirts enough to paralyze them momentarily, and the corpse tumbled over sideways onto the floor, releasing the lever of the hand-grenade it had been sitting on—I'd carefully pulled the pin earlier that morning, y'see. I had a few seconds to get off the walkway before the grenade exploded and set off the dynamite inside those covered boxes.

One more thing to do before I left the scene: I dropped the pistol, shrugged off the bag on my shoulder, drew the pin of the grenade in my left hand and tossed it into the crowd, close to the disguised explosives on the other side of the walkway. Then I was gone.

Dizziness hit me as soon as I'd squeezed through those struts and was on the outside of the footbridge. The river and south pier below seemed to leap up at me, the sudden vast *emptiness* around me nearly making me lose balance. But I fought against it and quickly slipped down through the gap between the walkway floor and outer ornamental rail, my foot finding the top edge of the raised bridge just below. Those few seconds I'd needed to escape had passed and I wondered if the grenades were going to blow—there was no way of knowing what those years in storage had done to their mechanisms—and I had time to look up and see Muriel's white, frightened face peering down at me through the girders, then someone scrambling past her before I ducked under the footbridge.

The explosions came and the world around me erupted, the first one mingling almost instantaneously with the second. I clung to the great bascule as it shuddered beneath me, and the air thundered with the blasts, the roof above my head juddering wildly, threatening to collapse on top of me, now another blast joining the first two, the sound alone almost sending me reeling into the waters so far below. Flames shot out from the footbridge, only the thick concrete a few feet above my head protecting me, and huge balls of fire rolled into the sky. I screamed against the noise and my own horror, aware that Muriel's body had been carried ahead of those flames, narrowly missing the opposite walkway to fall away through the air, only one arm outstretched, the other one missing, her clothes torn from her but her skin burning. It was a fleeting glimpse, but one that was fused into my brain, a sight I knew even then would never fade—*if* I lived through this. I shut my eyes, but the image was even stronger.

I began to slip, the trembling of iron and concrete beneath me increasing, so that I had to open my eyes again to find ridges, projections, anything I could cling to. Debris of all sorts—bits of wood, fragments of iron, pieces of bodies, whole bodies—was flying outwards, tumbling almost leisurely to the river below, and smoke, flames, fire, and dust billowed into the air. The top of the bascule was wide enough for me to lay on, and metal ridges and holes containing bolts that locked both sides together when the bridge was lowered helped me cling there while the entire structure shook and groaned. I was afraid the whole bloody thing would come down because when I'd hidden the dynamite along the walkway in the twilight hours of dawn, Cissie helping me haul it all up those tower stairs, I'd no idea how powerful it was or how unstable. Like the grenades, it'd been in storage a long time, so it was unpredictable. Well, now I was finding out, and I didn't like it one bit.

Massive black smoke-clouds darkened the sky and the bascule continued to vibrate like a vast tuning fork. I began to pull myself towards the other side of the span, only too aware of the long drop on either side and soon I was at the rail that ran by the road-side, the thick, ornamental balustrade that would serve me as a ladder to the pier below. And as I lowered myself over the edge, biting into my lip, scared I was gonna lose my grip and fall at any moment, I looked up to see McGruder, his face black and scorched, hair burned off his blistered scalp, crawling towards me along the top of the bascule. I just had time to remember the figure I'd seen climbing past Muriel through the girders, when the world lurched away from me once more.

Both of us slipped, McGruder managing to fling an arm over the wall that was the vertical roadway, me linking an arm through the decorative end of the rail as I slid down. We held on to the bridge as it began its rumbling downward journey. But it abruptly juddered to a halt and I was almost thrown off again. My legs swung free and I clawed desperately with my other hand as the arm through the hole was nearly wrenched from its socket. I grabbed another part of the patterned rail and my feet found a hold further down. Still deafened by the noise of the explosions, the world a strangely silent place around me, I hung on for my life, happy to stay where I was 'til my nerve came back.

But there was a further movement. A trembling ran through the ironwork, and I realized the bridge hadn't stopped at all, that it was slowly, ponderously, continuing its descent. The machinery controlling its operation had been disturbed by the blasts, cog-wheels and pressure points released so that the bascule's own weight was bringing it down. A quick glance across the river to the opposite bascule told me only this side seemed to be affected—the other bridge didn't appear to be moving at all. I wasn't sure how it was possible—the big engine room that con-trolled Tower Bridge was on the Thames's south side, far away from the explosions—but guessed it was the levers or braking system inside the control cabin on the south pier that had been disturbed, along with the bascule itself, the balance shifted, with nothing to hold it in check. The cogwheels could only control the fall.

I pulled myself tight against the rail, prepared to ride it all the way, hoping the bridge wouldn't level out with too much of a jolt. I might even have enjoyed the trip, knowing my game plan had panned out, I'd fought the battle and won, if a black-stained, raw-scalped, red-eyed head hadn't appeared above me. McGruder hadn't been thrown off when the bascule had shifted—hell no, he'd hung on and then crawled along the apex to get to me. And now he was a spit away, gaping down at me with hate in his eyes and murder in his heart.

His clenched fist struck my forehead, almost dislodging me. He tried again, reaching over as far as he could, but this time I dodged. With his next lunge, he'd grabbed my hair and was hauling me up. Tears blurring my vision, I gripped his wrist and forced his hand away, some of my hair going with it. My feet slid from their holes in the rail and I was hanging by one hand, my legs kicking empty space while he took full advantage, clambering down the other side of the rail, using its openings and decorative swirls as a crude ladder as I had. Then he was leaning round, trying to break my grip on the rail, pushing at my shoulder, tugging at my other arm, all the while the bridge continuing its sluggish, lumbering descent. My ears suddenly cleared and I could hear the straining of metal against metal, the groaning of rusted machinery forced into motion after years of suspension. And I could hear McGruder's frustrated grunts, too, as he tried to tear me loose.

I swung out over the river, the bascule at least a third of the way down by now, and dizziness nearly overcame me again as the river spun beneath my feet. From that height, I knew hitting the water would be like striking concrete.

A searing pain shot up my arm, the one poking through the rail's fancy ironwork, and I yelled hard and loud, my neck stretched as I tried to see the cause. On the other side of the rail McGruder had his teeth sunk into my bare flesh.

I swung my leg, managing to get a toehold on a metal lip above a line of rivets, then, with the added support, I began to hoist myself back up. Ignoring the pain, I made sure I was secure before pulling the arm that was under attack from McGruder's teeth out of the hole. Blood—that precious AB-neg stuff those parasites cared so much about—streamed from the deep wound and somehow the sight of it renewed that old rage. I guess I'd spent so long protecting my own life's liquid that the thought of this bloodsucker gorging himself on it—yeah, I know, he was only trying to make me lose my grip, but I wasn't exactly rational by then—while I was busy doing other things sent me a little crazy myself. Scarcely realizing my own actions, I was suddenly hauling myself over the rail, that anger stirring up whatever last reserves of strength I had (yeah, more *last* reserves). I jumped down onto the steep road on the other side and pounded McGruder's upturned face with my fist.

Keeping an arm linked around the top of the thick rail, my feet braced against the slope, I slugged him again and again, showing no mercy, giving him no chance to strike back. His body slid under me, only one of his hands maintaining a hold on the ironwork, his back against the stone slabs of the tilted curbside and for a moment—just one fleeting moment—I thought I had him licked. But he came up with all the power I'd known he had, sickness or no sickness, almost defying gravity for a split second by lifting his back from the stone and shoving me away from him with both hands. I swiveled round, my spine striking the rail with a jarring thud, almost losing my grip, and as he began to slip down the incline, he wrapped his arms around my lower legs, checking his descent, his weight weakening my own grip. And he was chuckling, he was holding on and twisting and tugging to make me let go of the rail, and goddamn chuckling while he did it. I brought my free fist down on his head and neck, but it seemed to have no effect on him, none at all. He only laughed all the more, grinning up at me so that I could witness the full extent of his madness. And then he did something even more peculiar: he twisted his neck and deliberately looked down the slope, the movement so exaggerated I knew he wanted me to follow his gaze.

I did. And I understood his intention.

At the bottom of the ever-decreasing hill, where the bascule joined the tower's approach span, was a long dark trench stretching across the road. Inside there, inside the pier itself, were the cog-wheels—the quadrants, I think they were called—that helped raise and lower the bridge on this side of the river. I had no idea what other machinery was inside the black hole, but knew McGruder wanted to take us both sliding down into it. What the hell, he didn't mind a quick death, so much better than a slow one. I hit him harder, turning my own body to shake him off, but it was no good, it was as if he didn't feel the blows. Without warning, one of his hands shot up and grasped my wrist, the one holding on to the rail, and he started to tug at it, trying to pull it away. My fingers began to open, the strain on them too great; soon only the tips were around the ironwork.

My other hand found his throat and I squeezed, my thumb pressing into his windpipe. His grin only broadened as my boots began to slip on the concrete. My hold on the rail was almost broken, my fingers almost straightened.

And then I remembered the knife.

Letting go of his throat, I reached round to my back and drew the dark blade from its sheath. It slid out smooth and easy, and I plunged it down hard between McGruder's shoulder blades, just beside his spine.

His eyes bugged in shock, their tiny veins almost embossed on the whites. Whether it was because of the sudden pain, or it was intentional, his arm clamped even more tightly around my legs, causing me to jerk upright, my hand releasing the knife. But he lost his grip on my other wrist and his grin vanished, his eyes took on a distant look. The pressure on my legs slowly lessened, and then he was slipping away from me, his fingers clawing their way down my leg.

But when his hand had almost reached my feet, the fingers suddenly wrapped themselves around my ankle, jerking it from under me, so that I fell flat on my back. Sheer reaction made me grab a lower part of the rail again as I started to slide, but it took all the strength I had left—and there wasn't much—to hold myself there as my body stretched, dragged down my McGruder's weight.

My arm trembling with the strain, my back flat against the stone, my spine feeling the vibrations rumbling through the groaning bridge, I raised my head to look down at McGruder. He was on his stomach, the knife angled into his back, and both of his hands were now clenched round my ankle as he tried to drag himself back up the incline. There was no expression on that blackened face now, even though his eyes still stared into mine.

He pulled himself upwards, using my leg as a rope, his shoulders quivering with the effort. And as his head drew level with my knee, that sick, lunatic's grin returned. Oh the eyes were still distant, kind of glazed over as if his mind was off in some faraway place, but those blistered and cracked lips were spread wide, the blood-smeared teeth bared in a grin that was just for me. I raised my other foot and smashed the heel of my boot into his nose.

Blood—bad blood, diseased, coagulated blood—burst from his nostrils like lanced poison, and his hold on me relaxed. Then he was falling away from me, slithering towards that long black narrowing gap at the bottom of the slope, his last gaze fixed on me all the way. I turned over and scrambled upwards, reaching for the top edge of the bascule, dragging myself up onto the apex. I slumped there, riding the summit, one leg and arm roadside, the other half of me over the edge, and I watched McGruder as his fingers raked the roadway and his legs slid into the thinning gap.

His chest rose from the concrete and I realized the bottom of the bascule was angled to join the underside slope of the roadway itself when the bridge was level. The rest of his body was too bulky to go through.

It was terrible, but I couldn't turn away, I couldn't close my eyes to the horror. McGruder screamed and screamed as hundreds of tons of concrete, iron, and lead crushed his hips and legs, the sound abruptly cut off by the thick explosion of blood that squeezed through his body to erupt from every opening in his head.

The gap closed completely and the bridge was down. And I was falling, shaken off my perch by the sudden fierce bump as the roadway leveled, tumbling over and over 'til I hit the cool waters thirty feet below.

|28|

CISSIE WAS YELLING AT ME AND PUMPING MY CHEST AT THE SAME time, and I'm not sure if it was the pain or her shouts that brought me out of my stupor. I retched river water and tried to turn onto my side. She helped me and began thumping my back. I started to protest, but more water belched from me. I could only moan and gulp in air between heaves, my head jerking off the soaked concrete with every spasm.

"Why?" she was yelling at me, her voice ringing off dank cavern walls around us. "Why didn't you listen to me? Why did there have to be more killing! You bloody, bloody fool! You nearly got yourself blown to pieces, just like I said you would!" She began to sob, her blows becoming more feeble. "You never listen and you never talk. I still don't even know why you stayed in this bloody awful city, living with corpses, always on the run, killing just to stay alive!"

She babbled on, weeping and cursing, pounding water from my lungs and generally giving me hell 'til I started to laugh. My chest and shoulders lurched as though I were having some kind of fit, but the laughter expelled the last drops of water I'd swallowed in my swim across the Thames to this tiny quayside underneath the bridge's northern span. Luckily for me, the shock of falling into the river had helped put some life back into my exhausted body, just enough to get me fighting again, kicking water, keeping myself afloat on the currents. I knew I'd drown if I didn't make the effort, and that seemed pretty silly after all I'd been through, so I struck out for the shore (the currents had already carried me close to the north tower), swimming through debris and human flotsam thrown from the high walkway by the explosions. I clung to the pier for a while, fingers digging into the cracks between its stone blocks, getting my breath back and working up some strength for the rest of the journey, then worked my way round, every so often my numbed hands slipping off the concrete's slimy surface and my whole body shivering from cold or shock, probably both. On the other side I could see the stone steps leading up to the covert landing stage tucked beneath the first span, and where once they probably dragged suicidal bridge jumpers from the river; it didn't seem so far and, goddamn it, I was gonna try for it. What choice did I have? I kicked off my boots, unbuckled the gun holster, and headed for shore.

I think I went under two or three times—it's hard to recall just how many—but on each occasion I'd pop up again, thrashing out with more vigor for a few strokes before settling into a weary but steady rhythm. When I thought the game was up, only yards from that little hideaway dock, and began to sink, my feet touched something solid underneath me, something I could push against to get me back to the surface. Another couple of strokes and I was able to stand; I could walk—I could stagger—up the long, sloping ramp towards the two sets of steps leading to the landing stage and, when the water was only waist-high, there was Cissie running down those steps, calling my name. She'd jumped into the river and waded out to meet me, tucking herself under my shoulder, and helping me reach safe ground, weeping and babbling on about how she'd watched me fall from the bridge, knowing it was me even from that distance because I wasn't wearing black, and how, when she'd searched for a boat, she'd found the tunnel leading to the concealed landing under the approach road. She had to drag me up those slippery steps and that's when I'd buckled and she'd begun pounding my chest, afraid I was going to drown on dry land.

She didn't understand I was laughing—she thought I was choking—and she beat my back even more, shouting at me not to give in, that I was going to pull through, and please, please, *please,* don't die, Hoke, don't *die.* I lifted an arm to ward her off, but I was too weak.

"Cut . . . cut it out," I managed to gasp, and she quit immediately.

"You're all right." She seemed stunned.

"I guess," was the best I could do. I didn't have the energy to laugh again, but I stoked up a grin.

She just wailed. She just threw herself on top of me and blubbered. Pretty soon I was blubbering with her.

And eventually, when our tears had dried and we both sat shivering in that gloomy, damp, brick cave, my arm around her shoulders, holding her close, I told her why I'd never left the city.

|29|

THERE WAS NOTHING LEFT FOR ME HERE ANY MORE. NOTHING LEFT for me to do.

I eased the military truck through the paralyzed traffic as the huge column of smoke and fire rose up over the rooftops far behind me, the funeral pyre only a gesture, a symbolic mark of respect for the passing of so many, those thousands of burning corpses representing the millions that perished in this city. I'd never had the chance to visit Wembley Stadium in wartime, but now and again, when I'd been unloading all those carcasses I'd collected from the streets, I'd heard—I was *sure* I'd heard—the ghost-echoes of cheering masses, voices raised in praise of human skill and endurance. They'd never frightened me, those spectral ovations; no, they'd only deepened the sadness, made me even more aware of my own isolation, my own loneliness.

Some miles back, I'd stopped the truck and leaned out the side window to watch the fire, maybe just to make sure it was effective. The blaze was awesome. Giant black clouds, edged with gold and crimson, curled up to the heavens, the flames that drove them violently beautiful as they consumed the heaped legions of fuel-soaked corpses below. I could do no more for the deceased citizens of that once-great place and Cissie had been right when she'd said that the rest would turn to dust in their own time.

But she *had* finally understood why I'd never left the city.

Under the bridge, huddled together, my strength slowly returning, I'd told her of my love for Sally, how we'd met at Rainbow Corner, a club for US servicemen in Piccadilly, she with girlfriends from her office, me with a couple of pilot buddies from another squadron, how one hello, one dance and one light kiss had meant instant love. We were married less than six months later, both of us sure of our feelings, realizing the risk that came with the war, but that same risk making us see there was no time to waste . . .

I hadn't even known she'd been pregnant when I came searching for her three weeks after the Blood Death rockets had fallen; she hadn't told me, I guess, because she hadn't wanted to burden me with another worry, at least not 'til there was no way of disguising her condition. I wasn't allowed to leave the airbase when the country's population started dropping dead, because all pilots still breathing were kept under guard in case the enemy launched a grand attack now that they'd knocked out our defenses. Hah! It was all so laughable, so insane, none of us knowing what had really happened, communications with the outside world kept tight by our surviving commanding officer, who was carrying out his last orders to the letter. And before long, everyone on the base had gone down with the disease, everyone 'cept me. I was alone and scared out of my wits, but I was finally the only one left alive. That's when I'd fled to London and the real nightmare had begun.

I was already traumatized by the time I found Sally lying outside on the steps leading down to our basement fiat, and the sight of her nearly finished me. Her eyes were missing, her flesh torn open. The rats had eaten into her belly and ripped the fetus of our unborn child from her womb. They'd left it on the step, close to her outstretched hand, half-eaten, almost unrecognizable. I'd known what it was though and I'd given in to the hysteria right there beside them both, my wife and our baby, given in to the madness that had sustained me for at least a year afterwards. Maybe not all that madness had left me yet.

All I could do—all I could *think* of doing—was burn what remained of their poor bodies. There was nothing there to honor, you see, nothing recognizable to pray over. That wasn't Sally lying on those steps, and it wasn't our baby next to her. They were just pieces of discarded meat. Leavings. Waste. Not my family.

I took them inside the house and set fire to the curtains. Within an hour, the whole row of houses on that side of the small street was ablaze.

And the madness drove me to gathering up other exposed and vulnerable dead ones, hundreds, *thousands,* of them, and taking them to a suitable burial ground so that they would not just be fodder for the surviving vermin that now openly roamed the streets, to an enclosed place where eventually I could lend some dignity to their passing. Even when the craziness wore off—the bitterness never did—I couldn't give up. It gave my life some small purpose, I'd told Cissie, it gave me a reason, no matter how senseless, how hopeless, to carry on.

Like I say, Cissie had understood.

But now it was over, burned from me. I think I even smiled at the thought.

She was waiting for me with the others at the corner of Westminster Bridge, just under the statue of Boadicea. I could see them up ahead as I turned the corner from Whitehall, smaller figures among them, the kids and adults I'd set free in the old castle. We'd rounded up fewer than a dozen women and children when we'd returned to the castle grounds, only two men among them, one middle-aged and in poor condition, the other hardly more than a kid himself. Oh yeah, and we'd caught sight of two Blackshirts scurrying away, trying to hide from us; but that didn't worry me—how long did they have left anyway?

One of the kids saw me approaching and began jumping up and down, tugging at the skirt of the women closest to him and pointing in my direction. They all started waving, the two boy twins and some others even running forward to meet me. Cissie stayed where she was though. She was unmistakable in her new blue frock, one hand raised in greeting, the other on her hip. Even from the truck I could see she was smiling.

I passed the battered Houses of Parliament, Big Ben tall and looming, and carefully drew the vehicle to a halt, wary of the kids rushing forward in their excitement.

"You ready?" I called from the open window, returning Cissie's smile.

"It's done?" she said in reply.

"Can't you see?" My thumb indicated the huge cloud of smoke darkening the horizon behind me.

She nodded. "I hope it burns the whole city. We don't need London any more."

The women, helped by the two men, were already lifting the children into the back of the truck.

"Sit up front?" I asked Cissie.

She strolled over and opened the passenger door. The sun was behind her, shadowing her face as she leaned in, but I could still see the whiteness of her smile, the fine little scar running across her nose. She climbed up, hopping purposely into the seat beside me.

"You needed to ask?" she said.

"Guess not," I replied. "Ready to roll?"

She banged on the screen behind us. "Everybody set?" she called.

A chorus of yeses came back, followed by a few muffled giggles.

"We're ready," Cissie declared. She looked ahead through the dusty windshield. "I always fancied the Surrey hills."

"I always liked the sea."

"Does it matter?"

"Not one bit. There's plenty out there just like us."

I pushed the stiff lever into gear and pulled the truck away from the curbside—funny how they'd all been waiting safely out of the road—and we rolled onto the bridge. As ever, the river beneath us was silver with specks of dazzling gold.

For no particular reason—old habits again?—I glanced into my wing mirror and my foot almost slipped off the accelerator. Without saying anything to Cissie, I stuck my head out the window, looking back. I wasn't sure what I was searching for at first, it seemed so, well, so out of place. Then I grinned. It was, it really was.

The zebra—yeah, four legs and a whole lot of black and white stripes—was ambling across the broad road some distance behind us, heading, I figured, for the overgrown green in Parliament Square. I ducked back inside the cab again, just in time to swerve round a Ford parked in the very middle of the bridge.

"What are you grinning at, Hoke?" Cissie was still smiling herself.

"Nothing," I told her. "Nothing at all."

And maybe that zebra was nothing. It set me thinking though. And hoping, too. Although I had no idea what I was hoping for.

Author's Note

'48 REQUIRED A HUGE AMOUNT OF RESEARCH INTO WORLD
War II and conditions in London around that time.
Where possible, I've stuck to the facts, but in instances
such as the escape along the Tube line between Holborn
and the Aldwych, which was in truth closed down during
the war years, I've allowed the story to stretch the actual-
ity. There also appears to be some confusion between the
experts as to whether trams were allowed to run through
the tunnel beneath Kingsway during those dangerous
years, so again I've opted for artistic license (or not, which-
ever the case may be). Most other details should be accurate, but please forgive any mistakes I'm bound to have
made and certain elaborations used for the sake of
dramatization.

—James Herbert
Sussex, 1996

JAMES HERBERT is firmly established not just as Britain's best-selling writer of horror fiction—a position he has held ever since the publication of his first novel— but as one of its greatest popular novelists. His sixteen previous novels—which include *The Magic Cottage, Haunted,* and *Portent*—have been hugely influential and widely imitated, and have sold more than thirty-two milion copies worldwide. Major films have been made of his novels, *Fluke* and *Haunted*.